THE GREEN PROGRESSION

Tor books by L. E. Modesitt, Jr.

The Green Progression (with Bruce Scott Levinson)
The Magic of Recluce

THE ECOLITAN MATTER

The Ecologic Envoy
The Ecolitan Operation
The Ecologic Secession

THE FOREVER HERO

Dawn for a Distant Earth
Silent Warrior
In Endless Twilight

THE GREEN

PROGRESSION

L. E. Modesitt, Jr.
and
Bruce Scott Levinson

A TOM DOHERTY ASSOCIATES BOOK
NEW YORK

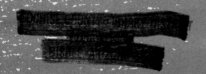

THE GREEN PROGRESSION

Copyright © 1992 by L. E. Modesitt, Jr., and Bruce Scott Levinson

This book has been printed on acid-free paper.

A Tor Book
Published by Tom Doherty Associates, Inc.
175 Fifth Avenue
New York, N.Y. 10010

Library of Congress Cataloging-in-Publication Data

Modesitt, L. E.
    The Green progression / L.E. Modesitt, Jr.
        p.   cm.
    "A Tom Doherty Associates book."
    ISBN 0-312-85212-6
    I. Title.
PS3563.0264G74   1992
813'.54—dc20   91-32253
                                                         CIP

First Edition: January 1992

Printed in the United States of America

0 9 8 7 6 5 4 3 2 1

In appreciation,
for Jules and Priscilla,
and to Nancy,
and all those who made this possible.

1

A CAPTAIN WEARING A SIDEARM in a well-worn leather holster came to attention as General Voloninov entered the anteroom.

As he stepped forward, the General's eyes took in the decorations on the Captain's dress browns. Virtually all were from the Afghanistan campaign. Those and the limp he displayed were the sole indications as to why a battle-seasoned officer had received such easy duty so young.

"Heroism has not been forgotten," Voloninov said to himself. Too often the choicest assignments were reserved for the children of party officials who served their motherland under far less trying circumstances. The sons of peasants and politicians rarely bore equal burdens.

The Captain gave a brief, crisp knock. After waiting ten seconds, he opened the massive wooden door with his right hand and, standing aside, gave a flick of his left wrist to motion Voloninov inside.

"General Voloninov, a pleasure." A heavyset man with dark blue eyes peering out from under dense gray eyebrows rose from a chair on the far side of the polished conference table. Besides the heavy amber ashtray, the stacked papers were the only other items on the smooth wood surface.

Voloninov briskly stepped forward, shook an uncallused hand, and walked to the other side of the dark rectangular table. In the ashtray was an unlit pipe. The table could easily have accommodated twenty men, and would again later in the day. The white walls were bare, containing none of the socialist hero portraits obligatory in earlier times. The General evaluated the cut and cloth of the other man's suit. Obviously foreign and probably Finnish.

1

"General, before the others arrive and we venture on to our regular business, I would talk to you about Colonel Kaprushkin." The foreign-suited man sat back down and edged the papers to one side, waiting as Voloninov pulled out a chair.

"Kaprushkin? Why?" Voloninov raised his eyebrows.

"You proposed terminating his program. Or, more accurately, you have reorganized one of your bureaus so that program will not be funded in the next year."

"So?" Voloninov shrugged. "I thought you and your friends were pleased to see the old swept away. We live in a new era. Besides, Kaprushkin's program has always been my responsibility. Do you propose changing that?"

The bushy-eyebrowed man leaned forward and picked up the pipe. Producing a small gold metal lighter from his pocket, he tamped down the tobacco with the flat bottom before turning it over and lighting the contents of the bowl. The sharp spicy smell of Latakia filled the air, reminding Voloninov of the incense used in a temple he had visited while on duty in New Delhi. A gift from Syrian friends, no doubt, the General thought.

"Vasily Ivanovitch, this is no longer just a question of your responsibility or my responsibility. Kaprushkin's program has the support of some very senior people."

"I would have hoped that our 'senior' people would have something more important to worry about than American gardening regulations. If they were more familiar with the actual workings of the American system, they would be less impressed with the officials Kaprushkin claims work for him. Imagine if the Americans controlled some of our bureaucrats—it would serve them right." Voloninov laughed, a quiet bitter sound.

"You and I know Kaprushkin has done far more than that."

"I hope you appreciate the irony of the situation. For several years now, even before the coup, you and the others have urged me to move away from operations which directly attack the West and toward more passive intelligence-gathering activities. We need American knowledge. We need export credits. That is what I have heard. Now that I propose to do just that, you and your superiors become distressed." The General shook his head, then cleared his throat, waiting.

"You and I both know that our economic weakness is the real reason for all the talk of peace and cooperation. We still have real differences with the West. More than ever, we must strengthen our position. If we do not, my friend, if all continues the way it has, we will see enough tears to convince even you that there is a war. Let us work to lessen those tears from our own people."

"Tears? War? You and Kaprushkin and all this talk of war without armies." You are the one who tells every television camera and reporter in sight about the new peace. Not that such changes have been bad for you." The general coughed into his fist and cleared his throat. "One day, you are just another party functionary. The next day the tanks roll, and suddenly you are one of Russia's leading experts on democracy and capitalism. You certainly made the most of that little . . . surprise. Just how did you move around all the others—with peaceful phrases?"

The man in the suit shrugged. "I am a patriot, not an idea-logue. Our policies are to meet new needs, fight new threats, and, of course, serve our new country." A smile appeaed within the smoke.

"I realize our new policy is accommodating the West, but I did not know that even our most 'forward' thinkers favored making the capitalists' workers safer and their farmers richer. So . . . perhaps they cannot build as many weapons. Even after their words of peace, they still manage to build more than enough. And would you have me believe that they will not use them, after their Gulf adventures?" Voloninov's measured tone did little to disguise his mounting anger.

"I have a greater belief in weapons, of all kinds, than you. But remember, Vasily, a weapon that is not built cannot be used. And technology progresses. With the information from their com-puter industry, we are profiting immediately. As for weapons— so the Americans have a surplus of current weapons? But what about the next generation?"

"Gardening regulations will take care of that?"

"There is an irony to that. But I think you are the one who has missed it." Another puff of the fragrant smoke punctuated the comment.

"Missed what? That you want to spend what little hard cur-rency we have on gardening reports and inane tinkering with regulations instead of serious intelligence activities? We have enough bureaucratic problems ourselves without learning new ones from the Americans."

The busy-eyebrowed man exhaled, a smoky sigh. "You talk about regulations as if they were nothing more than bureaucratic excrement. Do you know the impact of those regulations? What occurs if the Americans no longer produce machine tools because the rules they have adopted make buying from Japan easier? Do you recall how we obtained the silent propeller technology?"

Voloninov remained impassive.

"You say the Colonel makes the American farmers richer. Do you know just how he does this? Do you know how any of the American grain price support programs work?"

"I am familiar with the details of my operations." Voloninov's frosty words cut through the smoky haze.

"Their government guarantees a minimum price for grain," the man continued as if Voloninov had not spoken. "The government lends the farmer money—hard currency—equal to a set value for each crop. If prices go higher the farmer repays the loan and keeps the surplus. Otherwise he lets the government keep his crop and he keeps the money based on an inflated price of grain. Some of Kaprushkin's people work to raise that guarantee price a little bit. The higher the price paid, the more their farmers produce."

"I know how enchanted you are with capitalist theory."

"No. I do not deal in theories. That is what happens. The American farmers produce so much that they have other programs to curb food production. Even so, they produce far more than our own hybrid systems. But their system fails completely in distribution. If they were paid enough, the American farmers could feed the world . . . and they would still have people starving in the streets of their cities.

"You know how much difficulty we have producing enough to feed all our people. Programs like Kaprushkin's help us obtain the extra food we need. After the American government's warehouses are filled with surplus grain, they must sell it. And they sell it to us cheaply as a way of getting rid of it. They would never think of feeding their own people. Then the Europeans and the Canadians sell us their surplus food even more cheaply to get rid of it and to compete with the Americans for sales.

"That is a triumph of Leninism, the way of making capitalism serve socialism."

"I'm sorry. I never realized what a devout Leninist you still are. It must have been all those speeches about market forces that confused me."

"Look, Vasily Ivanovitch, we can argue about the direction our economy should follow. But if we do not obtain food from the West—a lot more of it this year—we won't have anything to argue over. Do you want to see another round of food riots?" The pipe cracked down against the heavy ashtray. "Until our own people perform something resembling real labor during the workday, the way they do in Japan, Germany, and even America, instead of lying around drunk and fighting each other, we will need foreign resources. I suggest we do our best at managing the situation." He retrieved the pipe from the ashtray.

Voloninov nodded slightly. "I will take your advice under consideration. However, if Kaprushkin's program is as important as you say, I'm sure you will have no trouble convincing your superiors to support some additional funding for my department . . ."

The man in the suit exhaled again, another wreath of smoke.

Voloninov smiled and waited.

2

"LARRY WANTS TO SEE US." Jonnie Black had eased inside the half-open office door. The silver rimless glasses, thin face, black hair, and prematurely graying beard combined with faultless British tailoring and a soft voice to provide an impression of inadvertent culture.

"Now?" McDarvid cupped his hand over the telephone. "I'm holding for Killorin." He added, "Standards and Regs. DEP."

The younger consultant shook his head. "Always talking to your old greenie buddies. Which case?"

"Amalgamated Electric . . ."

"Hello?" The words were scratchy, typical of the connections throughout the entire Department of Environmental Protection.

"Jerry? Jack McDarvid here."

"How are you? Haven't talked to you in a while. What can I do for you?"

"Mostly just touching base. I was talking to Ellie the other day. She said that Hank was planning another reorganization."

"You've been here, Jack. Nothing changes. What can I do for you?"

McDarvid repressed a sigh. Jerry Killorin was having a bad day, but bad days were all too common at the DEP. "You know the revised PCB implementing provisions? I know you can't tell me where you're coming out yet, but I was curious about the timetable. Is it through Red Border yet?"

"Still at it, Jack? Well, the lawyers had some problems. There's a draft legal memo floating somewhere. The intra-agency review won't be complete for another week or so at best . . ."

McDarvid let Killorin spell out the timetable he had already gotten from Ellie.

"Anything else?"

"You guys ever resolve the conflict over the dredging? Last time I heard, Reid was insisting that the Water Act language mandated scooping out a hundred miles of the Mohawk Valley. I suppose it was his memo."

"Who else? Nothing changes. You can guess what it says. The same arguments he used in the proposed rule last time."

"He's got to have added something," mock-protested McDarvid.

Jonnie stood in the doorway of the small office—pointing up the hallway toward the office of J. Laurance Partello.

"Get there when I can," mouthed McDarvid.

Jonnie acknowledged the message with a nod and eased back out of McDarvid's office, large enough only for the desk and chair, the computer, a credenza, one neatly packed bookcase, and a single narrow armchair for visitors.

"Not much," continued Jerry Killorin. "He does say that incineration techniques have advanced enough that they meet best available demonstrated technology standards."

"But BADT doesn't apply to an existing problem."

"Since when has that stopped Reid?"

They both laughed.

"Well . . ." added McDarvid, "that's really it. I needed an update. Do you mind if I call in a week or so?"

"No problem. If I'm not in—I'm going out to the National Enforcement Investigations Center in Denver—you can talk to Greg or Ellie."

"Thanks, Jerry." As he hung up, he wondered why the Standards and Regs chief was going to NEIC, but, then, according to Ellie, Killorin seemed to visit everywhere. McDarvid jotted down fragmentary notes on the yellow pad—letter size, not legal. He hated the oversized pads that all the lawyers carried as professional props. As he stood up and passed his computer, he cleared the screen.

That was another thing. Why was it that most lawyers had to dictate or scribble incomprehensible notes? Why couldn't they master the directness of a computer? Or did they like the image of the secretaries and paralegals and junior associates hanging on their every word?

He shook his head, brushing back blond strands that were getting too long. Too long and too filled with gray.

"Oops . . ." He swerved to avoid crashing into Juanita, Larry's secretary, although the collision would have been most pleasant—physically. Staying around for Juanita's precisely placed comments wouldn't have been.

The circular table in Larry's office stood in front of the floor-to-ceiling windows and was empty except for Jonnie and Larry. The matching and even larger desk at the far end of the thirty-foot office glistened, vacant except for the datebook and the pen set presented to Larry upon his departure from the Department of Justice.

". . . should be right along. He was talking to DEP."

J. Laurance Partello, Esquire, one of the founding partners of Ames, Heidlinger, and Partello, P.C., environmental attorneys par excellence, looked up. "Close the door."

McDarvid always forgot to close the door, and Larry always wanted it closed, even if he were talking about football scores. McDarvid hated football, and especially the Washington Redskins.

"Reid is going to push for incineration. He'll claim that it's necessary to meet the ARARS."

"Thanks. We'll take that from here. George thought so, and he'll do the brief. Bill the hours to Amalgamated." Larry looked at the closed door, then back to McDarvid, then to Jonnie. "That's not why I wanted to talk to you. I need some background work done."

Larry looked toward the door again. McDarvid wondered why all the secrecy. He and Jonnie had been hired by Larry for environmental regulatory consulting and problem-solving, not for espionage. The information that they had was client-sensitive, but not classified. That was just Larry's way, though, as if everything were top secret.

"Chlorohydrobenzilate—the people who make it, that is."

"Chlorohydro . . . what?"

"Chlorohydrobenzilate," growled the lawyer. "It's the active ingredient in a pesticide used to stop fruit flies. Not used much in the U.S. because it's most effective on the Mediterranean fruit fly . . . never been registered under FIFRA . . . still under the original submission . . . manufactured in Texas by a subsidiary of JAFFE, the French metals and chemical combine . . . patent's expired."

"Let me guess," interrupted McDarvid. "Some other manufacturer wants to register it, but DEP is going to propose an RPAR—excuse me, a special review—that will lock up the market for two years."

"How—"

"It's an old trick to extend a pesticide patent."

"That's not the problem, Jack," growled Larry.

"Sorry."

"The problem is that we don't have a client. But we might." Partello unwrapped a long crimson and green cinnamon stick—his substitute for the cigars he had relinquished all too regretfully. He held up his right hand, the one without the candy. "JAFFE may be looking for U.S. environmental counsel. I need to know what their problems will be."

McDarvid pursed his lips. "It won't stop at pesticides. More likely that they'll have bigger problems with something they haven't thought about. What sort of operation do they have in Texas? Manufacturing or just formulation?"

Larry broke off the end of the cinnamon stick and popped it in his mouth. "I don't really know. That's why you're here. They didn't say. But it's not all done in Texas. They have facilities in Georgia and California, plus a few other places. You probably need to make a list."

"What sort of interests do they have beyond chemicals?" interjected Jonnie.

Partello smiled and crunched off another chunk of the cinnamon stick, chewing noisily. "Now that you mention it, they're involved with some specialty metals—chromium and beryllium, maybe cadmium and gallium."

"Just nice clean high-tech metals," added Jonnie, the deadpan sarcasm evident only to those who knew him.

McDarvid snorted. "Right. Except you need the stuff for virtually every high-tech defense application known to the military."

Larry looked from one to the other.

"Larry, do you want to handle someone like that? That stuff is dirty."

The senior partner grinned. "They'll pay. Besides, specialty metals are necessary. Even I know that the next generation of high-speed computer chips will use gallium."

"Money now? We're actually going to consider making some money?" Jonnie's voice remained soft.

"I didn't say that," corrected Larry. "I said I needed to know what their problems are. Bill the hours directly to me. The sooner you two can find out, the better. Try to keep it under forty for the two of you. Hours, not days. We're not moving in geologic time here."

"That's it?" asked McDarvid.

"For now." Larry mumbled as he ground down the cinnamon candy and stood up, grabbing the heavy gray coffee mug with the monogrammed JLP on it. The gray stripe on his wide red suspenders matched the light gray wool of his hand-tailored suit.

The two regulatory specialists exchanged glances as the senior partner headed for the kitchen to refill the empty cup—the usual Partello dismissal. They walked back along the corridor, past the larger offices of the partners, and into McDarvid's office.

"I don't get it," McDarvid said. "Larry did water stuff at

Natural Resources. That and pesticides are his big things. He wouldn't know a specialty metal if it bit him."

"He knows money."

"Yeah. He does know money." The older consultant glanced through the narrow window out into the gray afternoon that threatened rain, then back at the three desk boxes filled with papers. "What do you want to handle?"

"The usual. I'll check the regulatory calendars, talk to Commerce . . . pick up some background and financials on JAFFE."

"Have Sallie check the dockets on all four of those—shit."

"What?"

"You'd better have her check the dockets at OSHA as well. Just for any comments by JAFFE."

"By the way, Jack, what are we looking for?"

"Money, Jonnie. Money. Regulatory problems that the esteemed firm of Ames, Heidlinger, and Partello can resolve in the most effective way possible."

"You didn't mention expensive."

"Sorry." McDarvid looked at the piles of paper on his desk. "I shouldn't have forgotten expensive."

"I'll let you know."

"Leave the door open."

McDarvid looked out the window again. He was going to be late again, and he ought to call Mrs. Hughes, but he didn't. Instead, he punched out another number at DEP, settling into the battered desk chair and turning the yellow tablet to a fresh sheet.

3

"WHAT MAKES YOU THINK WE WANT ANY PART OF SUCH A CRAZY SCHEME?" The squat, black-haired man crushed his cigarette stub in the ashtray and looked at the strolling shoppers outside the mall eatery.

"C'mon, Boris. I can't believe that you wouldn't kill for a chance to monkey-wrench our nuclear industry."

"You live in the past." The dark-eyed man laughed. "First, I am a diplomat and engage in no activities incompatible with that status. Second, I do not kill. I do not even know anyone that does. However, in your case it is possible that I will make an exception." The squat man gave an oily grin and continued in an accented voice, "Amateurs think they have all the answers. The problem with amateurs is they so often believe in violence. That leads to accidents, nasty accidents."

"Are you threatening me?" The younger man half rose from the plastic seat, his greasy hair bobbing as he moved.

"Your question says much about you. Let me make this very clear. We will not take any action to damage or discredit the American nuclear industry. We are only interested in peaceful cooperation with your country."

"So all you want is to suck up to Uncle Sam. More interested in trade credits than stopping the military threat to your own country. You still might want to reconsider your position. The problem with amateurs is that if we screw up, we blame other people . . . and other countries."

"I advise against such a course of action. Given the new relationship between our two nations, any such accusation may be met by . . . more . . . anger from your own countrymen than from mine. We are used to libel. If you are genuinely concerned about nuclear power, then you do not have to worry. Your industry is more than capable of discrediting itself without outside interference. After all, we had nothing to do with Three Mile Island."

"You really ought to think this over, Ivan," warned the man in the dirty rawhide jacket.

"I have. We also remember Chernobyl. We do not operate like your spy books say. (We never did.)." The squat man gave one last smile, stood up, and disappeared into the throng of late afternoon shoppers. The coffee he purchased remained untouched.

The remaining man tugged on his scraggly beard before finishing his soda and leaving.

4

AS HE TURNED OFF RENO ROAD and onto Fessenden, shifting from second into third, McDarvid wondered if he shouldn't have bought a car with more power.

"Washington deserves more . . ." The radio volume jumped with the commercial, and he thumbed the AM button for the all-news station.

". . . news briefs of the day . . . Intelligence Committee reveals new deficiencies in U.S. cold war intelligence operations . . . Housing protest marchers descend upon the Capital . . . Drug enforcement agents make major bust . . . A new round of antinuclear protests in the making . . . The Mayor unveils a new snow removal plan . . . And another drug-related killing, this time almost at the Capitol . . . But first this message—"

He flicked off the radio. He was almost home. "Commercials . . ." It had been a long day, especially with Larry's latest project on top of the Amalgamated Electric case. Best available demonstrated technology, for Christ's sake. Next, Reid would start denying there was a G.E. precedent on the PCBs. Sure, just dredge up all the contaminated sediments and stir up all those PCBs so they contaminated every drinking water source along the Hudson. McDarvid shook his head. The damned PCBs were safely locked in the clay and sediment, where nothing short of an atomic blast—or a DEP dredge—could dislodge them. Why ask for trouble? As he pulled into the driveway, McDarvid realized that Allyson's car wasn't there. More trouble, since he was forty-five minutes late. Had Allyson already gone to the PTA? Or was that tomorrow? He didn't lock the car, figuring that anyone who wanted to steal one of the cheapest imports ever made deserved it. He should have bought a Japanese car, at least, instead of the cutting edge of Korean technology.

Thenkk. Even the car door sounded tinny. Briefcase in hand, he hurried toward the front door.

"Ohhh . . ." After catching his balance, McDarvid looked

down at the object protruding from the bushes—the handlebars of Elizabeth's bicycle. His ankle throbbed. "Damn. Why does she always leave it where . . ."

The front door was locked, as usual. After rummaging through his coat pockets and extracting the keys, the door opened away from him.

"Good evening, Mr. McDarvid." Mrs. Hughes already had her brown coat on, handbag in hand.

Thoreau the cuckoo clock completed belting out seven o'clock as McDarvid looked tiredly at the sitter. She smiled placidly back at him.

McDarvid didn't even try to bluff Mrs. Hughes. He just handed her the extra five. Overtime was always in cash. Allyson paid the flat rate by check weekly.

"Thank you, Mr. McDarvid. I will see you tomorrow."

He stepped aside to let her leave.

"Oh. By the way, Dr. Newsome said that she would also be late."

"Thank you."

"Daddy! Elizabeth said a bad word! A real bad word!" screamed Kirsten.

"I said she was an immature imbecile. She is," affirmed Elizabeth, looking over the top of *A Summer Love*.

"Dad! What's for dinner? Do we have to eat that stuff in the 'frigerator?" David's sneaker laces were untied, and a large blot of chocolate decorated the brand-new green and white University of Miami sweatshirt. He had received it the day before as a belated birthday present from McDarvid's youngest sister.

"Mother had another emergency," announced Elizabeth, still slouched sideways on the family room couch.

McDarvid walked to the enclosed side porch that served as a study for Allyson and him, set the briefcase on the floor. Off came his coat, which he laid over the chair before he trudged into the kitchen. Kirsten was sitting on the other side of the counter in the far right-hand stool. David jumped into the one next to her.

"That's for Elizabeth!"

"I can sit where I want!"

"Kirsten! David! Knock it off!"

Silence descended.

"Did your mother say when she would be home?" He looked at David.

David shook his head. Kirsten shook her head.

"Elizabeth?"

More silence.

"Elizabeth!"

"Yes, Father?" Elizabeth's voice came from the family room, as though nothing had happened.

McDarvid stopped clenching his teeth long enough to repeat the question.

"Mrs. Hughes said, 'Tell your father that Dr. Newsome will be rather late.' "

"Thank you, Elizabeth. Please put down the book and join us." By then, he had the casserole into the microwave and had begun to pour the children's drinks.

"Elizabeth!"

"You oughtn't yell, Father." She took the chair on the end. Since Allyson was going to be late, dinner would be at the kitchen counter.

"That's mine!"

"You weren't sitting there, David." McDarvid set the four water glasses out. Then he took out the salad and retrieved the light Italian dressing from the refrigerator.

"Super tuna gloop and salad, right?" David put both elbows on the counter tile, with his head in his hands.

"Right, old man. Be glad you've got something."

Elizabeth's eyes rolled, and McDarvid caught himself before he launched into a short statement on world hunger. Local hunger was the real problem he faced.

"Super tuna gloop coming up!" While the casserole steam dissipated, McDarvid finished tossing and serving the salad.

Dinner was silent, or almost silent, except for David's slurping, and McDarvid only had to motion to his elder daughter once to get her to stop chewing with her mouth open.

"Dishes," he announced.

"It's Elizabeth's turn," bellowed David.

"I accommodated you last night so that you could watch the football game."

"Mondays are your turn. It says so on the calendar."

"David."

"Yes, Dad." The redhead picked up the sponge. "It's not fair. Tuna gloop is messy."

"You should have considered that yesterday. We always have tuna on Mondays," announced Elizabeth.

Brinnngg . . .

He grabbed the wall phone right behind Elizabeth's back, before she could answer it in the calm superior tone that was so charming the first dozen times someone heard it. "Hello."

"Jack. This is Jonnie. I'm sorry to bother you at home . . ."

"What's the matter?" asked McDarvid. Jonnie almost never called him at home.

"Larry. He was killed in a drug gang cross fire about an hour ago."

"What? He was going to see the Chairman. Up on the Hill. The Rayburn Building, not southeast. They don't have drug wars on Capitol Hill."

"They do now."

"Larry?" McDarvid mumbled. "The bastard gave up cigars and chewed cinnamon sticks. He installed air bags on the Seville."

"Daddy! Elizabeth's using nasty big words again!"

McDarvid motioned Kirsten away. "What do we do now?"

"I don't know. I just thought you ought to know."

"Daddy!"

McDarvid glared at Kirsten. She didn't look at him, just pulled at his sleeve.

"Jonnie . . . I'm a little frazzled right now . . ."

"Your wife working late?"

"Yeah."

"All right. I'll see you in the morning."

"Jonnie?"

"Yes."

"Thanks."

"No problem. Just thought you ought to know before it hit the papers."

McDarvid hung up the phone. *Elizabeth!*

"Coming, Father. Is the little informer misinforming you?"

He took a deep breath. "Elizabeth Anne McDarvid! Intelligence is no excuse for insolence. You're still not too big to consider a soap mouthwash. And don't bother with the stock comment about violence being the last resort of the incompetent."

His dark-haired daughter looked up at him, almost demurely.

"You can help David by wiping off the counters. You—Kirsten Lenore McDarvid—can empty all the trash in the house, starting with your bathroom." McDarvid wiped his forehead, ignoring Kirsten's muttered "See!" Walking out of the kitchen, he picked up the littlest redhead's backpack, and two jackets from the dining room. Four library books were strewn across one end of the family room couch, with *A Summer Love* spread open and upside down across the pile.

"Elizabeth? Have you finished your homework?"

"Father, it is ineffably boring."

"I take that as a no. If you don't get on it now, all your books go back to the library, and I'll ground you to your room *without* them."

He could feel the sigh that signified reluctant agreement.

"David, you haven't even opened your backpack. What about that science report?"

"Yes, Dad . . . I'll get to it."

"I hate trash," announced Kirsten, dragging a green plastic sack partly filled with refuse down the stairs, one step and one bump at a time.

"Did you separate the metal and glass?"

"There wasn't any. Mommy took that out this morning."

McDarvid retrieved the trash bag. "You start your tub."

"David's first."

"You. David hasn't finished his homework."

"But . . ."

"You. Now."

"Yes, Daddy." Kirsten trudged back up the stairs.

McDarvid let her trudge as he carried the trash through the kitchen and out into the garage. He shook his head. Larry, for Christ's sake. How would Larry have gotten involved in a drug shoot-out? Larry didn't even know what drugs looked like.

And what did that mean for him and Jonnie? The idea of using regulatory consultants as direct support for the law firm had been Larry's idea. Allyson wouldn't say anything. She had never wanted him to leave EPA—as if he'd had any choice.

He tied up the garbage and headed back into the house.

5

FORMER JUSTICE OFFICIAL
KILLED IN CROSS FIRE

A FORMER ASSISTANT ATTORNEY GENERAL WAS KILLED on Monday night as he stepped out of his car within two blocks of the Capitol, the apparent victim of a cross fire between drug dealers.

In this most recent drug-related slaying, a volley of shots brought police less than a half block from the Library of Congress where they found a body lying on the sidewalk.

The victim, J. Laurance Partello, a partner in the law firm of Ames, Heidlinger, and Partello, was Assistant Attorney General for the Lands and Natural Resources Division of the Department of Justice from 1981 until 1986. More recently, as one of the name partners of the environmentally oriented law firm, he represented such clients as General Electric, Consolidated Waste Disposal, and Western Power Systems.

Partello died on the spot, according to sources at George Washington University Hospital. Police said they knew of no motive for the killing, which occurred about 7:10 P.M.

Fragmentary evidence at the scene indicated that Partello may have unwittingly interrupted a drug transaction, but police sources declined to comment pending an investigation.

6

MCDARVID SET THE BRIEFCASE ON THE DESK, opened it, and began pulling out the folders he hadn't even looked at the night before. Had it just been the night before? Allyson had been sympathetic but preoccupied. He couldn't blame her, not after hearing about the little girl whose mother had brought her in claiming that the child had fallen—a medical impossibility for the placement of the deep bruises. Child abuse was even uglier than drug murders.

McDarvid flicked on the computer, then closed the briefcase.

Buzzz . . .

"Mr. McDarvid, you're scheduled to meet with Detective Ngruma at ten-thirty."

"Detective—?" He didn't recognize the voice. "Who's this?"

"This is Alice."

McDarvid didn't know an Alice, but then, the law firm turned over receptionists like short-order cooks turned hamburgers. He looked at the clock—nine-fifteen. "Thank you. In my office?"

"That's what he requested."

"Fine."

McDarvid wondered whether he should finish up the JAFFE backgrounder. Then he smiled. Larry had asked for it, and McDarvid needed the billable hours. Ames was a jerk, but an honest jerk, and the firm would pay. Besides, JAFFE might be Heidlinger's potential client. He and Larry worked on some larger projects together. That might explain the metals angle.

He tucked the briefcase under the desk and tapped out a number.

"RCRA Policy Office."

"Is Angela Siskin there? This is Jack McDarvid."

"I'll check. Would you hold?"

Not having much choice, he agreed.

"Jack! Sorry to keep you. What's up?" Angela Siskin had a quick, almost chirpy voice and a set of mannerisms that left the impression of a scatterbrained blonde. As McDarvid could attest to his regret, she was definitely not dizzy.

"Not much." Not unless you consider an accidental murder and the fact that I might not have a job. "I was doing some background work for my boss. What can you tell me about beryllium, cadmium, gallium, and chromium? I mean, from a regulatory point of view."

"I don't know that much about gallium. The other three are part of the metals initiative that the Secretary is considering. Both cadmium and beryllium are real problems, especially airborne particles. NIOSH thinks there might be some carcinogenicity with cadmium."

"NIOSH? Is OSHA doing anything on the workplace standards?"

"I really don't know. The metals strategy isn't even in draft, and, of course, those aren't the only metals we'll be considering . . ."

Wondering why DEP was revisiting standards for metals already tightly regulated, McDarvid took notes as Angela talked.

". . . some really bad actors here. At high levels especially, cadmium is a definite cause of kidney disease. Beryllium causes something like asbestosis, except worse. You remember the big debate about hexavalent chromium—didn't you do a briefing paper for OMB on that?"

"Yeah," admitted McDarvid. He hadn't been particularly proud of that one. The risk assessments indicated chromium wasn't exactly the workers' best friend. On the other hand, it was needed for too many steel alloys, and the only places you could get it were South Africa and Russia. But the Administrator of the U.S. Environmental Protection Agency had wanted—that was before it became a Cabinet department . . . He shook his head. He needed new information, not past memories.

"Nothing's changed there. We're going to have a conference with OSHA next month. Develop a joint strategy. Handle both the environmental and the worker protection aspects of the metals questions all at once."

"Whose idea was the conference?"

"I don't know, really. It came out of the Secretary's staff meetings a couple of months ago. Might have been Carson Newell. You remember . . ."

"I remember. Is he still up on the twelfth floor?"

"He's still there."

"I think that's what I needed to know."

"Anytime, Jack. Stop by if you get a moment."

"I will." And he would. In fact, he had been a little lax in touching bases at DEP, falling into the lawyers' habits of shuttling between the paperwork, the client, and the bigger-name government policymakers, forgetting those who did the real work . . . and who knew what was going on. It was time to do more of what Larry had liked to call streetwalking.

He checked his watch, then looked outside. Nine-thirty and threatening to rain. His fingers tapped out another number.

"The Secretary's office."

"Jack McDarvid for Carson Newell."

After five rings, McDarvid was about to hang up.

"Mr. Newell's office."

"I take it that Carson's not in? This is Jack McDarvid."

"No, Mr. McDougall, he's at a meeting. Can I take a number?"

"Yes . . . and it's McDarvid. M-C-D-A-R-V-I-D." He left his number. Outside, on Nineteenth Street, the rain was beginning to turn the dark gray asphalt black, and the umbrellas were popping out like spring flowers—except it was fall now.

He ducked out into the corridor to find Sallie, to see if she had managed to run down docket lists on the metals. A metals initiative, for Christ's sake! That might be a big case.

He frowned as he thought about it. A big case, but how many deaths from excessive exposures? That was the trouble with working on the industry cases. Some of them were fighting regulatory overkill, and others just wanted a license to kill, and you never could tell which it was until you got into it. Even then it was your judgment versus theirs.

Sallie's cubicle—comprised of portable dividers carpeted in lawyer's gray—was empty.

"She's at OSHA, Mr. McDarvid."

"Thanks, Betsy." Betsy Enchor was Norm Casteel's secretary. Casteel was the senior partner who wasn't on the letterhead. He didn't know much law, despite the degree from Yale, but he seemed to know everyone, and no one complained that he didn't do much besides bring in business. What he brought in was good business. That, and his pleasant mannerisms, excused a lot of drinking.

McDarvid headed for the kitchen and his morning cup of tea—another trait that separated him from the lawyers and their endless cups of coffee. The kitchen was empty, but he stopped and looked at the bulletin board, noting that the office flag football team was scheduled to play Beveridge and Diamond in a battle of the environmental titans on Thursday afternoon.

Cup in hand, he headed back to his office, where the computer and the report on the status of PCBs and Amalgamated Electric awaited him.

He closed the door. Sitting down before the screen, he called up the file as he took a sip from the too-hot tea. Amalgamated was another of the in-between cases. When they'd discharged the PCBs years earlier, no one had realized the dangers, and the oil had been used in transformers across the country. Now NRDC, Ecology Now! and every other environmental organization wanted them removed—except that dredging would probably cause more damage than leaving the PCBs buried in the sediment and linked to solid clay.

The door edged open.

"Mr. McDarvid? I'm Detective Ngruma, Metropolitan Police." The black detective with the neat pencil mustache and short dark hair wore a brown suit and carried a thin notebook.

McDarvid motioned to the single chair. "Have a seat."

"If you could fill in a few details . . ."

The consultant nodded, resettling himself in the chair.

"How long did you know . . ."

"About what time . . ."

"Were you aware if Mr. Partello ever used drugs . . ."

"Did he always drive himself to Capitol Hill . . ."

McDarvid answered the questions as well as he could. The police were hardly likely to find Larry's killer, not with drug-inspired killings averaging more than one a day in Washington. The only reason the detective was in the office at all was that the murder of a white lawyer, particularly a former Assistant Attorney General, required some inquiry.

Both he and Ngruma understood the ritual and conducted it as quickly and painlessly as possible.

"Thank you, Mr. McDarvid. If you recall anything else, please let me know." Ngruma extended a card.

After the detective had left, McDarvid looked out the window, not really seeing much of anything. What was going to happen next? The other lawyers had let Larry run his operations as he pleased, but George Ames had always opposed the use of consultants as law firm employees. Ames wasn't even fond of paralegals.

Should he have left Environment? He really hadn't had much choice. The new Administrator had wanted his own people in political slots, and Policy Analysis was definitely a political slot.

Thrap . . .

He swiveled the chair. "Come on in."

Jonnie stepped inside and closed the door. "You've talked to Ngruma?"

"Yes. Answered all his questions."

"Did you ask him any?"

"No. I read the story in the *Post*. Poor Larry just parked his car in the wrong spot." McDarvid gestured to the chair. "You know, poor Larry hated that Seville. He always wanted a big car, like a Lincoln Town Car or a Fleetwood. He could have bought either. Ames and Heidlinger didn't even like the Seville. Environmental lawyers don't drive big, long expensive cars, especially environmental lawyers who need to use their Hill connections. Now he's dead in a freak shooting, and he never even got to drive the car he wanted. Stupid. Not even a reason behind it."

"There was some reason." Jonnie's voice was mild. "It could have been a drug dealer mistaking Larry for someone else. Then, maybe, Larry was into something else. In this town, no one really knows anyone."

"I suppose so. It still seems odd."

Jonnie shrugged. "It's an odd town. Last month's *Washingtonian* had another article on the continuing coke abuse by professionals."

McDarvid sat up. "You think some drug dealer shot Larry on purpose? No way, José. You remember that story that Henry told on poor Larry, when they were in law school together, about the guy that offered Larry some white powder, and Larry said, 'What's that?'

"The guy says, 'It'll make you feel good,' and Larry says, 'If

I want to feel good, I'll get laid.' That's Larry. He's always been that way, and that's why he and Jeannie split. One wasn't enough." McDarvid looked out the window again.

"That's exactly right." Jonnie's voice was low, as usual. "I asked the detective about the shooting. He didn't say much. So I called the reporter who wrote the story. They found a pair of plastic bags under the hedge next to Larry's body. Cocaine, probably. But his wallet wasn't touched, cash and credit cards still there. He died from a single shot straight through the heart. Like you said, Jack, it does seem odd. How likely is it that only one person is going to be shot in a drug dealers' shoot-out? Or that they're going to be hit just once?"

McDarvid shrugged. "They're killing more people every day now. Too many of them are bystanders."

"Who said it was drug dealers?"

McDarvid stood up. "Who else? All Larry lives for . . . lived for . . . was politics and environmental law. And sex, probably," McDarvid added as an afterthought.

Jonnie shook his head. "He was going to see the Chairman. The time was blocked off on his calendar, but he never told anyone why. Even Juanita doesn't know. I'll bet the Chairman's office doesn't, either."

"Of course not. They sat in Sam's office and drank too damned much Italian wine. You don't write that on a calendar."

"Maybe. Maybe not. I want to check on a few other things." Jonnie stood up.

McDarvid stood by the computer. Jonnie didn't usually see conspiracies—he was too damned cynical.

"Yeah . . . sure . . ." Except . . . except Larry had seemed nervous about the JAFFE possibility. And it wasn't in his normal expertise. Metals . . .

McDarvid glanced at the computer, the screen reminding him of the unfinished Amalgamated update. The metals angle probably didn't amount to anything, but it wouldn't hurt to look a little deeper. Besides, if he and Jonnie could still land the JAFFE account . . .

"One step at a time, McDarvid." He pulled out the chair and eased back before the computer.

Buzzz . . .

McDarvid looked at the telephone.

"McDarvid."

"A Mr. Llewellyn for you, Mr. McDarvid."

"I'll take it." McDarvid frowned. Llewellyn? The name was familiar. "Jack McDarvid."

"Jack, this is Ned Llewellyn. I'm over at Treasury. Office of Policy. We met at the federal environmental policy conference when you were at Environment."

"What can I do for you, Ned?" McDarvid knew what was coming. Poor bastard, he'd been there before. Too many times.

"Well . . . Chris Bierbeck had actually suggested your name. The Secretary's been here for almost the two years he promised the President, and it struck me that it was time to think about leaving myself. I wanted to explore the options. Chris suggested that since I'm not a lawyer, you might be able to provide some insight."

"Be happy to, but free advice is worth about that." McDarvid covered the phone and coughed, then continued. "The big question is what your objectives are . . ."

As he talked, McDarvid wanted to shake his head. Llewellyn was one of the bright ones, who understood that you were dead if you waited for the hard evidence. His call also confirmed that the Secretary would be leaving, probably soon after the first of the year. Assistant Secretaries of the Treasury, exploring options or not, do not call mere consultants, even respected ones, until they have explored more profitable opportunities.

". . . unless you're a lawyer or at the Deputy Secretary level, you'll probably end up taking a pay cut—unless you can land the top spot at a trade association."

"That's what Chris had said."

McDarvid glanced at the computer screen. Washington was hard on the technicians and outsiders. They never understood how thoroughly the city operated on vague hints, half-glimpsed patterns, and intuition. Only a handful of people had real power, whatever that was. The rest operated in the shadows, and sometimes power was just one of the shadows. The outsiders kept thinking that their jobs were secure as long as they performed, never fully understanding that they could be gone in a minute, never understanding that a carefully cultivated paranoia was essential to survival.

"If you want to send over a résumé, I'll be happy to look at it and see what I can do—not that I can promise anything . . ."

"Thanks. That's all I'm asking, Jack . . . Appreciate it."

After hanging up the telephone, McDarvid stared blankly at the computer screen for several seconds, reflecting that, unlike Llewellyn, he no longer had to rely totally on the whims and moods of others. If Heidlinger didn't want to keep him, independent consulting would cover most of the bills—at least as long as he showed some results.

He turned back to the computer.

7

"WHO'S GOT THE FACILITY PLAN?"

"Lay it out over here, where we can overlay the map with the topography. We'll need to know how much lead time before they can bring up the troops."

"Oh, Peter, they won't use troops. They might have a few reserves, but that's it. They're expecting signs and peaceful protests."

"That's what we'll give them." The bearded and black-haired man smiled crookedly.

"I thought—"

"We'll talk about that later. Where's the plan?" Peter raised his voice. "Where's the fucking plan?"

"Here . . ."

Peter's finger jabbed at the map. "The protesters will be picketing from here to here."

"Doesn't that crowd the highway?"

"Of course it does, you fuckhead. That's the point. How are you going to make the evening news if you don't cause a traffic jam? What business does a nuclear processing facility have that close to a metropolitan area, anyway?"

"Won't the—"

"The media loves this kind of stuff. Another six and eleven o'clock news special on the poor citizens protesting the building of nuclear weapons in their backyard. And the dust will ensure that everyone gets the point."

"It's not the same stuff."

"Who cares? You think the media will know the difference when the Geiger counters go off the scale? Radioactive is radioactive." His voice rose another half-octave. "You mean that they're using other radioactive materials there that no one knows about?" His voice dropped to its normal baritone. "Believe me, baby. That's the last thing they're going to want to discuss. After all, we're just peacefully opposing the use and building of nuclear weapons."

"This isn't real peaceful." The auburn-haired woman frowned. "Even scattering a little dust along the fence line could eventually hurt someone."

"You're thinking like a real greenie, Veronica. They never do anything."

8

THE ENVIRONMENTAL ATTORNEY, his bushy red beard scarcely trimmed and showing white streaks that made him seem older than his age, stood by the reception table. He glanced at the two men at the end of the buffet, then back to the entrance of the committee hearing room. His name tag bore the words "Ray Thomas, Counsel, Ecology Now!"

"What's your problem, Ray?" asked the woman behind the linen-covered table on which were arrayed the name tags for the VIP guests, most of whom had yet to appear. The lights on the large wall clock showed why—a roll call vote in the House.

"Why's Cal talking to Richards?"

"Congressman Richards? He invited him, that's why."

"He invited Bang-Bang Richards? What on earth for?"

"I suggest you ask him yourself." She turned to the woman who had appeared at the table. "Congresswoman Sperlen. Would you like a name tag?"

"No, thank you . . . I was looking for . . . There he is, thank you." The rangy Representative from Oregon eased past the table and headed toward the silver-haired and well-tanned Congressman and the founder of Ecology Now!—both still immersed in their conversation.

As Congresswoman Sperlen neared, the two men turned.

"Gladys!" Richards' voice boomed across the still-muted voices around the buffet tables. "My favorite debating partner!"

Cal Griffen smiled at the Congresswoman, said a few words lost in the rising hubbub, and stepped back, still smiling, turning toward a sandy-haired man in a three-button charcoal pin-striped suit. "Andy! I'm glad you could come."

"You know my personal concerns, Cal . . ."

Thomas shook his head, turning away from the two men. Both fists clenched at his sides for a moment, and his jaw tightened before he took a long deep breath, then another.

"Easy, Ray."

"Right. Right. Politics makes me puke." Thomas watched as the balding ecologist talked for a few moments more with the sandy-haired businessman before excusing himself and heading toward the reception greeting table.

"Cal?"

"Just a minute, Ray." The ecologist leaned over toward the dark-haired woman who had tried to calm Thomas. "Has the Chairman arrived yet, Martha?"

"Chairman Sloan? No, but he was leading the floor debate on the tariff bill. Bill said he'd make an appearance at least."

"If he comes in and I miss him, get me. Same if Mort Hancock should show up."

"We'll take care of it."

"Thanks, Martha." Griffen turned toward his staff attorney. "Ray, you look like . . . Loosen up a little."

"You invited Bang-Bang Richards?"

"Congressman Richards? Sure," Griffen answered.

"Why? He sees commies under every bed, and he'd nuke them all, even if his own mother was sleeping there."

"He's kind of conservative on defense, but you couldn't ask

for a better voting record on most environmental issues." Griffen looked past the attorney at the Hill staffers—primarily junior legislative assistants and interns—edging toward the food.

"Kind of conservative?" Thomas' voice was harsh. "That man never met an atom bomb he didn't like. He thinks the NRA are a bunch of weenies for stopping with just supporting the right to carry assault weapons. He feels they should have demanded the right to keep and bear MX missiles."

"You're exaggerating. In case you don't remember, he was the one who persuaded the Chairman to force DOD facilities into compliance with DEP cleanup schedules for Superfund sites. He also blocked oil exploration off the Carolina and the Delaware coasts last year."

"That's only because he didn't want to see oil towers when he went marlin fishing in that fancy boat of his. Anyway, his constituents would have handed him his head if he hadn't."

"Still, no one without his seniority and position could have faced down both the defense contractors and the oil industry. Besides, he's a nice guy." Griffen's voice dropped into weariness.

"How can you deal with someone like that? When you started Ecology Now! the idea was to avoid wheeling and dealing." Thomas waved at the tables still loaded with food and the waiters removing empty plates and glasses.

"I guess that all depends on whether you're interested in accomplishing something worthwhile or mouthing self-righteous slogans. Richards is someone to talk to if you want to accomplish something. Now, if you'll excuse me . . . We happen to need some support on the joint DEP/OSHA initiative."

Griffen turned and eased toward a heavyset man heading toward Richards, timing his approach to coincide with the younger Representative's.

Thomas headed for the bar, his jaw set and his head shaking.

9

PYOTR KAPRUSHKIN STARED OUT HIS WINDOW at the gray slush, gray concrete, gray sky. Was he in the same country—or even on the same planet—as his old home in Slyudyanka on the southern tip of Lake Baikal? The air, the water, even the vegetables all had had a fresh taste, like spring water. That had been then.

Now the great lake smelled of dirt, on good days, and so did the food. Looking at the gray outside, he shook his head. Then he wiped his damp forehead. His fingers moved to loosen the heavy woolen uniform jacket.

"The heat . . ." The Colonel did not finish the sentence as he studied the sealed window of the modern Western-style building. "At least in the old offices, the windows opened." He shook his head again slowly. "This city living. It softens people. With the first chill in the cities, everyone hurries into an oven to bake. They can't breathe. Yet they want to come here. They beg and bribe for the chance to live in Moscow. How will we survive if farmers want to leave the land—their life—to live in a concrete hovel?" The Colonel struck his fist lightly against the unbreakable glass.

Tap . . . tap . . .

"Yes?"

"General Voloninov is here, Colonel."

The Colonel nodded and stepped around the desk toward the burly General.

"Greetings, Pyotr Alexandrovich." Voloninov's voice rasped through the warm air. His forehead was also damp under the short and heavy silver hair.

"Greetings, General Voloninov." The Colonel gestured toward the leather armchair he had obtained just for Voloninov.

The General had not waited for the invitation, but gestured from the red leather chair toward the wooden armchair across from it. "Sit down."

The Colonel sat.

"So . . . Pyotr, you have a new agent in place. Will he give me the plans for the American space laser or stop them from building their new bomber?" General Voloninov's voice, almost soft, rumbled toward the Colonel. "Or will he at least support technical aid for our industry?"

"The new agent is a woman."

"Ah, yes." The General looked past the Colonel toward the gray reflected in the window. "You spend our money—hard currency—on recruiting 'special' agents in the American government. Will this one ever supply anything more than pesticide control plans, Pyotr Alexandrovich?" The General's deep-set eyes fixed on the Colonel, and his voice dropped almost to a rumbling whisper. "Information—or results. Those are what I need."

The Colonel knew to keep silent.

"So . . . Colonel, how did you recruit this new person? As you did the others?"

"Yes, General. With the same strategy." The Colonel let his voice reflect the role of the correct senior officer. "We found someone who bent a few rules to accomplish what she thought was right. She needed money. Her son is in a private hospital—a drug problem. One of our people thanked her by paying the back bill before the boy was thrown out on the street. She was shown the record of the payment and told that future bills would be taken care of. She doesn't even know who she's working for." The Colonel shrugged his shoulders.

"Now she is ours. But what will she do for us?"

"She determines the safe level of exposures to workplace chemicals. She will be encouraged to make those levels as low and as safe as possible."

"And will that stop the Americans from building their advanced tactical fighter?" pursued Voloninov.

The Colonel shrugged. "It will increase the cost of any materials fabrications, General. And since cost drives the military procurement system, it will reduce the number of weapons built."

"They still build too many."

"But less each year," observed the Colonel.

"For all the good that will do us." Voloninov shrugged, then stood. "Make your reports as usual."

The Colonel had risen with the General.

"Do not trouble yourself to see me out, Colonel."

The heavy door closed.

The Colonel looked at the door, then turned and looked at the gray outside. His steps took him to the window.

The meeting had gone like all the others. Explaining his work to Voloninov was like describing Copernican astronomy to a medieval pope. The General listened, but he never seemed to hear. The plan wasn't too complicated or advanced to understand. If the Americans were induced to develop environmental and health laws that made high-technology industry and weapons building more difficult, then war would become more difficult—and far more costly. The American war machine ran on money.

Voloninov wanted industrial secrets, yet the General did not appreciate what the program had already provided. Did he understand that the environmental disclosure rules—another coup—had revealed more technical details than the Americans had ever realized?

The rain, ice crystals in water, splashed against the glass. Pyotr wiped his forehead again, wondering who had protected his program for so long without ever stepping out from the shadows.

For years General Voloninov had interrogated him, and before him General Salnikov, yet his operations had remained funded, at a low level perhaps, but enough to continue with an ever-increasing number of agents.

Kaprushkin pursed his lips, then pulled out the desk chair. It should have been time to report success, but full knowledge of the extent of his success would be his undoing.

"And yet it moves," he muttered to himself. He began shifting papers from his desktop to the second drawer, the one in which he always placed them before leaving the office. "It moves."

10

JONNIE BLACK STRAIGHTENED HIS TIE one last time. The real reason he was going to the Ecology Now! reception on the Hill was boredom. Ever since Sandra had decided their relationship wasn't heading anywhere, his nights had been more than slightly lonely.

Not that he had been invited to the reception. Crashing Hill parties was a skill mastered during his days as a foreign-policy student at Georgetown. Really no trick to it at all. Dress well; shake a few strangers' hands; greet a passing acquaintance who was also crashing. Pretty soon you were accepted, even expected, at almost any of the meet-greet-lobby events which constituted the core of professional congressional social life. Only a handful actually required invitations. After all, no lobbyist wanted to admit there was someone he didn't know at first sight, and there were always one or two Congressmen who looked young enough to be interns.

At the first few parties, Jonnie had concentrated on guzzling free booze from the open bars—before he had realized that the food was the real treasure trove. The lanky figure in the well-cut suits who was thought to be some variety of congressional aide would methodically consume a balanced gourmet meal from the buffet tables. Crab-stuffed mushroom caps, caviar canapés, and jumbo shrimp became his nutritional mainstays.

During his low-budget student days, it had been more of a matter of survival. Now it was mainly nostalgia. Sometimes, if rarely, he picked up worthwhile information.

Besides sustenance, the receptions had provided Jonnie with a simultaneous introduction and advanced course in Washington politics—as well as a few lady friends. By listening and talking, especially listening, the young student learned how much real power resided in a mastery of details and controlling the process. Never mind the broad philosophical statements made in public. The committee reports and legislative subclauses told the true story—a lesson that more than a few old hands had failed to learn.

A veteran representative of the corn industry who had enjoyed corrupting young minds with facts had found a ready student in Jonnie. A long discussion at a well-endowed buffet in the Cannon Caucus Room years earlier had left him with an insight into the whys and wherefores of Washington, an abiding belief in the need for reasonable grain prices, and an ongoing interest in researching obscure legislative language, especially arcane numbers buried in committee reports and regulatory preambles.

Jonnie checked his watch. Six-ten. Not too late, although the shrimp would be gone before he arrived.

By the time he had walked the three blocks from his Potomac Place apartment building to the Rosslyn Metro station, it was close to six-thirty. The street was still slick from the day's on-and-off drizzle, but the air was pleasantly cool and damp, a trace chillier than normal for late September.

Despite the refreshing breeze off the river, Jonnie thought once again about whether he really wanted to attend the Ecology Now! reception. He needed to do something to take his mind off Larry's death. Besides, he might meet someone interesting and attractive.

The in-bound blue line train took him all the way to the Capitol South station. As he stepped off the escalator and walked to the corner between the Capitol Hill Club, the Cannon Building of Congress and the Library of Congress Annex, he glanced to his right, down past the library annex and the church—right where Larry had been gunned down. He turned toward Rayburn, his steps measured.

He marched up the walk beside the circular drive, ignoring the pair of black limousines, through the ubiquitous metal detectors, showing the contractor ID card he used in his free-lance work, and toward the main hearing room of the Energy and Commerce Committee. The Capitol policeman paid more attention to the young intern who followed him.

Jonnie did not share the young officer's enthusiasm, perhaps because the girl looked more like one of the increasing number of high school–age interns.

Once inside the committee room, out of habit, he found himself sidling up to the food. The shrimp were not gone. There had never been any—not with the question of overshrimping the Gulf waters. He contented himself with the mushrooms stuffed with crab, eyeing the crowd as he maneuvered toward the other end of the hearing dais, where he recognized the senior Representative from South Carolina.

The fresh veggies came last. They'd last all night. He worked his way through seafood, beef, and chicken and was just considering the crudités.

"Do you really want to eat them? Those are Mexican tomatoes. They still use DDT and 2,4,5T," announced a young woman with auburn hair down to her waist and lightly tanned arms extending from a short-sleeved and low-cut black dress fringed with red.

"What about the apples?" He eyed her long, shining, and well-combed hair.

"The growers say they're not using Alar, but all the tests show they are."

"I'm Jonnie Black," he offered, rather than comment on her statements about the food.

"I'm Veronica Lakas."

Jonnie nodded, realizing belatedly that the long hair had drifted across an Ecology Now! name tag bearing her name. "How long have you been with Ecology Now!?"

"I started as an intern a year ago. But I've been involved with the issues for a while."

"You find it interesting, I gather?"

"The politics are fascinating. We use pesticides to boost farm production, and then we guarantee that agribusiness gets taxpayer-financed price supports for all the extra grain. We also encourage them to use pesticides and chemical fertilizers by keeping oil prices low. Even after the Iraq mess. And the small farmers, and the ones who use organics, have to fight to keep their land. That doesn't even include the effect of the tax cuts on the environment."

"Tax cuts?" Jonnie asked politely, again looking to the end of the room and toward Congressman Richards, his silver hair and hawk nose visible between the woman and two men in the small group. "The environment is important," he added noncommittally, trying to figure out the balding man talking to Richards.

"It's not just the pesticides," added Veronica. "That's why I like working at Ecology Now! Cal is so good at showing how it all fits together. I mean, the real cause of the big Alaska oil spill wasn't a drunken captain, a single-hulled tanker, or a greedy corporation. It was caused by not enough mass transit and because too much natural gas is used to make synthetic fertilizers we don't even need."

Cal? Jonnie puzzled, then nodded. The balding man was Cal Griffen, the founder of Ecology Now! But what did Griffen have in common with the defense-minded ranking Republican on the House Armed Services Committee? "You really think fertilizers are that big a problem?" he asked absently, his eyes focusing on the low vee neckline of the black dress.

"They're just one part of the problem . . . What sort of environmental work do you do?" She looked at his nearly empty plate.

"I work with environmental regulations, mainly solid waste and water issues, but from the financial side. Very boring, I'm afraid. And you?"

"Agriculture, mostly." She smiled, but her eyes did not lighten as the corners of her mouth turned up. "I'd like to do more, but there's so much to learn . . ."

Jonnie nodded sympathetically. "Everything in Washington is deeper than you think, even when you've lived here for a while. It just takes time . . ." He grinned. "Then you realize you'll never learn it all."

This time, her smile was a little more genuine.

"Let's not talk shop," he suggested. "What do you think of Washington so far?"

"It's a beautiful city."

"Have you ever seen the Jefferson Memorial at night?" asked Jonnie. "Or the Lincoln Memorial at night from across the river?" Like from my balcony, he thought.

"No."

"I know where you can get one of the best views . . ."

11

MCDARVID BRUSHED PAST THE USHER and made his way down the side aisle and out of the church. Above the whisper of soles and voices, the organ continued playing. Bach or something equally baroque, McDarvid decided. Funeral or not, the ordered and sterile melody conflicted with the modern decor of the church and even more violently with the life of the thoroughly modern Joseph Laurance Partello—he of the gunmetal gray Seville that should have been a Lincoln Town Car, or the red suspenders, or . . . yet Larry had been dated in his own ways, preferring sex and good wine over drugs and wall-screen televisions.

Saint Mark's emptied quickly, despite the hundreds of people who had come to pay last respects to a man whose obituary had taken nearly a quarter page of *The Washington Post*—but, like Larry himself, on the inside of the paper. Then again, Saint Mark's was a suburban church, chosen because Larry's older daughter belonged, and because Larry had belonged to no church, at least not one that wasn't of his own making.

As McDarvid stepped into early October sunlight, he looked to his right toward the black limousine parked directly in front of the modernistic amber glass panels that framed the center doors. Two young women, not much past college age, and dressed in tailored black, stood there, accompanied by a young man. No one else joined them for several moments, until an older woman, wearing a dark purple woolen suit, paused for a few words.

Then another woman stopped, and a man.

Behind the pair stood Bill Heidlinger, accompanied by George Ames. With Ames was a white-haired lady who looked as though she could only belong to the fussy accountant who posed as a lawyer.

McDarvid shook his head, recognizing only a handful of others from the crowded church—Steve Greene, Norm Casteel, Carole Sturteval, Aaron Greenberg . . .

"Jack?"

McDarvid turned to see Steve Greene approaching. He waited until the young attorney halted before speaking. "Looks like the firm's out in force."

"Yeah. I saw Carole and Norm." Greene ran his hand through wispy brown hair that would disappear before he turned forty. "Here they come."

"Jack, Steve . . ." Norm Casteel nodded toward the two. "Carole and I were discussing how many people respected Larry." A vague gesture encompassed the still-crowded parking lot.

Beside him, Carole Sturteval, her short, red-blond hair kept in place by two dark blue barrettes that matched her coat, nodded. "He was an amazing man."

McDarvid remembered how Casteel had avoided speaking to Larry whenever possible. "I wonder how many of them really knew him."

"Larry was a household word in the legal community," Casteel mentioned amiably.

Obscenities were also household words, McDarvid reflected, looking over Casteel's shoulder at those hurrying toward the parking lots. He looked again at the small throng that had paused by Larry's daughters to say a word or two. McDarvid had thought about joining that group, but he had never met either girl, only recognizing them from the pictures on Larry's credenza. Everyone at the funeral had been predictable, except for the dark-haired nymphlike woman in the third row. McDarvid had noticed her because there had been a pronounced space on either side. One of Larry's women? He looked past Larry's daughters and shook his head.

"Yeah," added Steve Greene, "getting murdered by accident. It just shows how strange life is."

"Tragic is more like it," observed Casteel. "George drafted a complaint to the Mayor, suggesting more action and less talk about improved police protection."

Greene shook his head.

McDarvid agreed.

"You're going to be handling the pesticides clients, aren't you?" The older attorney turned to Greene.

Greene shifted his weight from one foot to the other. "Well

. . . I think so. Carole will do more on the RCRA stuff that Larry brought in."

McDarvid wanted to ease backward, out of the conversation. Somehow, showing up and saying how sorry you were when the main reason for the sorrow was the fact that you might lose your job was almost more than McDarvid could handle, and having Larry's clients divided before he was buried wasn't helping.

"I'll do what I can," murmured Carole.

"You'll all do fine," rumbled Casteel. "I need to say a word to Nancy and Linda." He turned and lumbered toward the group surrounding Larry's daughters.

Carole and Steve looked at each other, then at McDarvid.

"Funerals . . ." mumbled the thin-haired attorney.

"Social and political rituals," observed Carole. "Very necessary."

"I suppose so," temporized McDarvid. "Well . . . I need to get on the road . . ."

"See you later, Jack . . ."

McDarvid turned, glancing back toward the church. He looked again, feeling eyes upon him, and caught sight of a tall and muscular younger man dressed in a plain gray suit, his eyes shielded by dark sunglasses. The man's brown hair was longer than a Secret Service agent's and well styled, but he had the same air. McDarvid didn't see the omnipresent earplug, but the man's carriage and his scanning of the thinning crowd were obvious. So was his age. Outside of the man in the gray suit, Steve and Carole, and Larry Partello's daughters, McDarvid was one of the youngest people at the memorial service.

McDarvid shrugged and crossed the drive, then a small strip of grass, and turned right, walking past two Saabs, a pair of Mercedes, and an older Lincoln. His car—off-red, cheap, and very out of place—was parked between a royal-blue Volvo 760 and a black BMW 635 CSI with a leather shield over the front hood.

Was it only his imagination, or had the other mourners parked their vehicles a touch farther from his than from the cars on the other side?

He opened the door, creaking after less than a year, and edged behind the wheel. The door creaked again as he shut it behind him. The dealership had assured him the week before that the creaking had been repaired. The assurance, and the silence of the door, had lasted three days.

Another forty minutes to get back to the office—why had he gone at all? Jonnie hadn't. Maybe he was more worried about the office politics than Jonnie was. Or did he just have a stronger stomach?

Outside of the attorneys from the firm, the only other person he had known was Larry, and he was dead. And he hadn't even really known Larry. He'd never been to his house, and only eaten with him when they were entertaining clients. But that was Washington, he supposed. It really hadn't been any different when he'd been doing economics for the Agency or running Sam's congressional office.

He pulled the seat belt tight, a habit that had lasted from his years in the cockpit, then turned the key. With the tiny engine whining, he flicked on the radio, turning up the country music. At least, it had some emotion.

Then he pulled out of the parking lot and onto Vale Road, back toward Vienna. Hoping he wouldn't get lost in the winding roads of northern Virginia, he edged up the volume on "Dusty Dixie Road." Everyone left something or someone behind. Even Larry.

12

BILL HEIDLINGER'S THIN LIPS SMILED from a round face. His eyes remained china blue above his bulging pin-striped vest. "JAFFE has expressed an interest in retaining us on the chlorohydrobenzilate problem."

"It's more than a problem. Because it's an animal carcinogen, the Office of Pesticide Programs is thinking about a cancellation." McDarvid frowned, although Jonnie's face was calm.

"JAFFE would agree to voluntarily suspend all sales in the U.S. for the duration of a special review. That way Environment wouldn't need a cancellation."

"I don't know if that's possible."

"That's what Larry promised Devenant." Heidlinger shrugged. "If you can see any way to do it, draft up a strategy, the way you did for Larry, and I'll be happy to run it by them. They aren't interested in a legal retainer for the metals issue unless we tackle the pesticide problem as well. It's a package deal."

"We'll work up a proposal this afternoon." McDarvid looked at Jonnie, but the younger man's face remained politely attentive.

"Monday or Tuesday would be fine. Take the extra time and make it good. Mr. Devenant won't even be back from Montreal until next Thursday."

"Tuesday," McDarvid confirmed.

The two consultants stood as Heidlinger picked up a folder and began to study it, pointedly ignoring them.

McDarvid walked out into the corridor.

"I need to take a walk." McDarvid turned into his office.

"I'll meet you at the elevators," said Jonnie.

"Right." McDarvid rubbed his forehead, then took his gray suit coat off the hanger on the back of the door, stuffing his arms into the sleeves. He scanned the desktop, fingering the message slip. Carson Newell had finally returned his call while he had been in with Heidlinger. That was always the way it was. You could wait forever, but the minute you were tied up, the bureaucrat you needed to talk to invariably called.

McDarvid stopped at the front desk. Was it Alice? "Alice?"

"Yes?"

"Jack McDarvid. I'll be out for about an hour."

The thin woman looked at the plastic board. She kept looking. Finally, McDarvid reached over and pointed to his name. Then he pushed through the double glass doors, turning to see Jonnie repeating the same procedure.

"Christ," McDarvid muttered as the other came out, "Larry's not even cold in the ground, and no one even remembers who we are."

"They didn't know who we were before he died."

"Just who are we, anyway?"

Cling. The elevator arrived, empty except for the Federal Express deliveryman and an empty dolly.

"I've often wondered that myself."

They rode the elevator down silently. Outside the building, the wind whipped leaves along the gutters as the two men walked up Nineteenth toward Dupont Circle. High puffy clouds cast occasional shadows, making the wind feel even colder.

"JAFFE might want to set up a deal like that," McDarvid began. "Larry wouldn't have let them. Not good old cash-on-the-barrelhead Larry."

"You're right. Larry would have insisted on a full year's retainer."

McDarvid laughed softly. "Yeah. But somehow Heidlinger gets to me. Maybe it's his backdoor way of saying, 'Play my way, and I'll take care of you.' At least, Larry was up front."

"Very up front," said Jonnie. "Wasn't his favorite expression, 'Just do it, fuckhead!'?"

"Thanks for reminding me. Maybe I'm just getting too old for this game." He stopped at the edge of Nineteenth and Dupont Circle, ignoring the traffic lights. Then he dashed across both lanes. "You know," he continued, brushing his hair off his forehead, "I haven't had a job since I graduated from Amherst where I couldn't be killed or fired at a moment's notice."

McDarvid walked toward the now-empty marble fountain in the center of the circular park. At the far side of the circle, across from the newer brown brick building that fronted the Dupont Plaza Hotel, he could see three chess games proceeding on the concrete tables in the shade of the yellowing oaks.

"Oh . . . ?" asked Jonnie, hurrying to catch up. "You don't talk about it much."

"Not much to talk about. Flying wasn't exactly the safest thing invented, not off a bird farm, not in Southeast Asia. Of course, the Navy wasn't selling safety. Glamour, maybe, but I wasn't near good enough to be a Blue Angel. After that, selling real estate didn't exactly work out. Nor did the other things. Then there was the time on the Hill. If the Congressman didn't like what you wore to the office, he could fire you. Sam was pretty good, but the threat was still there. But that wasn't even the worst part."

Jonnie made no comment.

"It was the unreality. Every Congressman sends more than fifty thousand personal letters every year, composed on computer, signed with an autopen wielded by an intern. He gets one-page summaries of issues that affect millions written by research aides who never heard of the problem before they write it up."

"So . . . isn't that what we do?"

"Point taken." McDarvid laughed. "Anyway, EPA wasn't much better, not with the White House insisting on environmental body counts before acting and the Congress insisting that the world had to be made safe for asthmatic pigeons."

"I know about EPA," observed Jonnie.

McDarvid slowed to avoid being hit by a young black man on a bicycle. "I guess I'm just getting tired."

On the grass on the north side of the statue, two bearded men in fatigues stood beside a low platform. A dozen posters fluttering from poles stabbed into the turf proclaimed, "Free Elections Now!"

"I still don't understand what's so bad about the JAFFE proposal," commented Jonnie. "We do what we can on this pesticide, and that will get us the access and the resources to find out what's really going on with the metals. It will also keep us employed."

"You don't have to remind me. But if the guys at Environment are right, chlorohydrobenzilate is one of the worst pesticide carcinogens left unregulated. It's not really even used much here. That's why it wasn't a high priority."

"So why is that a problem?"

McDarvid sighed. "I keep forgetting. No one outside the industry understands the technicalities. Even if DEP restricts a pesticide's use or even cancels its registration, it can be manufactured here. Even under a special review."

"Heidlinger said they would stop U.S. sales."

"U.S. sales. What about sales to Mexico, Latin America, the Philippines, and half the third world?"

"Oh . . ."

"Yeah. That's where the money is. Their plant is here. So they ask for a special review, which can drag out two or three years. They obligingly stop the U.S. sales they probably don't even make, and they manufacture and ship like hell for the next couple of years. And, with a special review going on, no one else who isn't already manufacturing the stuff can. It gives them a guaranteed profit for at least a couple of years."

They turned and started back along the concrete walk toward Nineteenth Street.

". . . Freedom . . . now . . . Freedom . . . now . . . Freedom . . . now . . ."

McDarvid looked to his left, toward the police car with the flashing lights and the banners behind. Another noontime protest march upon Dupont Circle. Just who wanted freedom from whom? And who cared?

"What do you want to do?" asked Jonnie, ignoring the protesters.

"Do I have any choice? I don't have another job."

"What's your interest in metals?"

McDarvid shrugged. "Call it a long-standing involvement. I keep wondering why there's been such a push for regs that cripple high technology . . . and who's really behind it. Now someone wants to pay us to look into it."

"You don't need JAFFE for that."

"Are you ready to start an independent consulting service this afternoon?" McDarvid stopped at the curb. To his right, across the divided lanes of the circle and in front of the drugstore, two homeless men sat, placards before them proclaiming their hunger and need for donations.

"Sure. Are you?"

The light changed, and they walked across the two sets of lanes that represented traffic largely from Massachusetts Avenue.

"No. Six months from now, maybe, but not at this minute."

"But what about chlorohydrobenzilate?"

"I promised to present a work plan. I never promised I could implement it successfully."

"You do like to live dangerously." Jonnie glanced down Nineteenth Street.

"No different than the lawyers who appeal losing cases all the way to the Supreme Court."

Jonnie laughed. "That's different."

"Not really. We'll make a good-faith effort. Heidlinger didn't say we had to succeed. We'll draft a cover letter indicating that both projects have to proceed simultaneously if the metals issue is to be successful. That way, we're not tied to success on the pesticide thing."

"Can we go to Devenant directly?"

"With what? We're not lawyers."

"We have a very dead boss."

McDarvid shrugged. "So Heidlinger's our boss—for now. I doubt that JAFFE could care, except for the momentary inconvenience. Remember, we're talking about a foreign company."

"They still have a couple of big problems," reminded Jonnie.

"So do we. So do we."

13

OVERSTRAINED EYES LIFTED FROM THE PAPERS. Large pale green ledger sheets divided by brown lines into innumerable boxes filled the center of the desk. To the left was an almost forgotten mug of a once-hot beverage. To the right was a stack of identical thin green file folders.

Each folder summarized the key items about an agent in three sections. The first consisted of the name, agency, job title and description, and other personal information about each agent recruited in the American government. The second section contained summaries of the key accomplishments of each compromised official and a list of goals for that person in the upcoming year.

Kaprushkin's more detailed weekly reports on each American were stored somewhere in a central records warehouse.

The final section, the focus of the Colonel's attention, contained expense accounting—the amounts spent, the reason, and the authorizing authority.

Kaprushkin paused and took a swallow of lukewarm black tea before continuing with transferring the summary numbers from each folder to the ledger sheets. Compiling his year-end hard-currency operational expense report was just the first step in preparing his preliminary budget request for the next year. The budget request, in turn, was but the starting point of initial departmental budget negotiations.

The Colonel laid aside one folder and opened the next.

Although the details differed from folder to folder, the similarity of the operations presented the ever-present danger of blurring together actual agents with those identities which served as accounting devices necessary to support his real mission.

Kaprushkin tried not to think about the consequences of discovery of the identity behind those accounting devices. Even if such a discovery occurred, perhaps they would believe he had only been corrupt. He paused, then shook his head before making another set of entries on the ledger sheets. Then he reached for another folder.

14

MCDARVID FOLDED THE DISH TOWEL and looped it over the oven handle, glancing around the kitchen to ensure that everything was either in the dishwasher or put back into the cupboards. The napkin holder was empty, and he rummaged through the bottom of the small pantry closet until he wrestled the oversized former cookie tin from behind the plastic shopping bag filled with paper grocery bags. He levered off the top and riffled out a handful of napkins. They went in the holder, which he replaced at the end of the table next to the bay window that overlooked the backyard.

Even in the fading light, he could tell that the grass was more than ankle deep. In another year or two, maybe by the next summer, Elizabeth might be mature enough to be trusted with a lawn mower. Maybe.

After reclaiming his coat from the study, he looked from the front hall. David remained slouched in front of the television. Elizabeth was—what else—reading on the living room sofa.

"Let's go, Elizabeth," McDarvid called. "David, turn off the television." He took two steps backward and yelled up the stairs. *"Kirsten!"*

Nothing happened. Elizabeth remained on the couch. David's eyes remained glued to the television, and only silence returned his call from the second floor.

"Let's go!" He waited. Nothing. "One, two, three . . ." He hated the counting routine, almost as much as Allyson, but it worked. Sometimes, with clients and children, you had to go with what worked, or nothing happened. ". . . four . . .*five!"*

"All right, all right, I'm coming," grumbled David.

"Stop, Daddy. Here I am!" Kirsten bounced down the stairs.

"Father, I will be there when—"

"Seven . . . eight . . ." McDarvid continued implacably.

"Father!" Elizabeth scrambled off the dark brown couch and dropped the book on the battered coffee table that Allyson kept threatening to replace.

McDarvid opened the door. "Elizabeth," he added, turning to his older daughter, "you're the one who needs the dress. You could be ready to go."

"I am indeed prepared, Father."

McDarvid pinched his lips together, considering that someday Elizabeth would have children. Had he been that much of a little prig? Spankings hadn't helped, even when she had been little, and the therapist had insisted that only firm, considered, and insistent follow-through would be effective. It had helped—some.

"I get the front!"

"It's my turn!" insisted Kirsten.

"Father? Would you resolve this dispute?"

"David, you're in back on the way. Kirsten, on the way back."

"It's not fair."

"It doesn't matter. For less than eight blocks, we're not arguing." McDarvid opened the driver's-side front door.

Creaaaak.

"Father, you really should—"

"—have it fixed," completed McDarvid. "I know. But they fixed it two weeks ago. It didn't stay fixed. Do you want to take it back to the dealer for the third time?"

"Where are we going, Dad?"

"Woodies, first." And last, I hope.

"Can I go over to the record store?" asked David.

"Not unless we actually go into Mazza."

Parking at Woodies wasn't too bad. McDarvid found a spot in the next-to-last row of the covered parking. With the darkening clouds and the possibility of a cold winter rain, the decision to drive looked better.

"How long is this going to take?"

"As long as it takes to get Elizabeth a dress."

"Why don't *I* get a dress?"

"Because your mother got you yours last week when Elizabeth was sick." McDarvid pushed open the store door.

"Can I wait here?" asked David, standing by the appliance section.

McDarvid really didn't like leaving David that far away.

"Please, Dad. I don't want to hang around dresses."

"All right. But you stay here."

"Thanks."

"Can I stay?"

"No."

"Why not? You're letting David stay here."

"No."

Kirsten's shoulders slumped.

"Come on, girls . . ."

The juniors' department was on the far side of Woodward and Lothrop.

McDarvid eyed the dresses on the front rack. The shiny silver against the black looked cheap. Lifting the sleeve, he checked the price tag. Sixty-four ninety-nine—hardly cheap for a dress for an eleven-year-old.

"Elizabeth?"

"Yes, Father? That dress is not suitable."

"I know, I know. It's also too expensive." He saw a green and black dress. The skirt section was black, gathered to a wide drop waist. The bodice and sleeves bore alternating black and green bands, too wide to be called stripes. The material was heavy enough, almost a flannel, for winter wear, at least in Washington.

"That's ugly," offered Kirsten. "Elizabeth should get something bright and pretty."

McDarvid studied the dress, then passed it by. They'd come

back to that one because the colors would look good on Elizabeth, as would the drop waist. The next rack held a set of dresses
that combined red-and-black-striped leggings with a red over-
skirt. The neck was scooped, and the sleeves were tight and
tapered. His gangly daughter would look like a combination of
pipe stems in it.

"I like this one!" Kirsten looked at her older sister.

"Elizabeth can try on several." McDarvid sighed. "Elizabeth,
have you found anything?"

Elizabeth held up a shiny green dress, short-sleeved, with a
long row of tiny white buttons up the back.

"How will you button those?"

"Father, they're not real buttons. There's a zipper underneath."

McDarvid looked beyond his daughter toward the main aisle,
then back toward Kirsten. A man in khaki trousers and a gray
windbreaker looked back at him, meeting his eyes.

McDarvid felt his guts chill as he recognized the pseudo–
Secret Service type he had seen earlier at Larry's funeral. The
same bold look, the same midlength hair. McDarvid forced himself to stare back at the other until the younger man dropped his
glance and turned toward the jewelry.

"Elizabeth, Kirsten. We have to get David. We'll come right
back."

"But—"

"Father . . ."

"No. I shouldn't have left David."

Both girls looked at each other, then at their father. It took all
McDarvid's will not to sprint for the escalator as he dragged the
girls with him.

"He won't be happy," piped up Kirsten.

I just hope he's there, thought McDarvid. I shouldn't have left
him.

"Father . . . you're hurting my arm . . ."

"Sorry. Please hurry."

McDarvid's eyes ranged across the housewares section toward
appliances once they cleared the escalator.

He took a deep breath as he saw David, standing next to an
older boy in front of the wide-screen television.

"David?"

"You guys done already?"

"No. I need you to come with me."

"Dad . . . you promised . . ."

"David . . ." McDarvid's voice was ice.

His son looked from his father to his sisters. "All right, all right. It was getting boring, anyway."

"I told you he wouldn't like it," observed Kirsten cheerfully.

"Father, can we get back to selecting a dress without further confusion?"

McDarvid took another slow deep breath. "Yes. Just remember. Sometimes fathers make mistakes."

"We know that," noted Elizabeth coldly.

"Look, Miss Perfect, I am the one buying your dress."

Elizabeth was silent as they took the escalator back upstairs. McDarvid squeezed her shoulder, then David's.

The man in the gray windbreaker was gone, and, thankfully, none of the red-legging outfits came in Elizabeth's size.

McDarvid wiped his forehead as he and Elizabeth looked in the three-way mirror. She had on the black and green.

"What do you think, swanlet?"

"I prefer this one."

"I like the bright green better," said Kirsten.

"When are we going?" asked David.

"As soon as Elizabeth changes, and as soon as I pay for her dress."

"Can we have a fire?" asked David. "Will you play checkers with me?"

"We'll see. We'll see." He thought about the man in gray. "Yeah. I'd like that."

"Then, you have to play Old Maid with me," insisted Kirsten.

"I'll do that, too."

"I'd like the fire," added Elizabeth, "if I can read in your chair."

McDarvid smiled. "Just while I'm playing games with them. Now, get that dress off so I can pay for it." He still felt cold, thinking about the man who had been at the funeral showing up at Woodies. Who was he? Could it just have been coincidence? His eyes flicked from David to Kirsten and then to the dressing room doorway, as he waited for Elizabeth.

The fire would feel good, even if it weren't that cold outside.

15

"MR. CORELLIAN IS HERE," the intercom on the battered wood desk announced. The scratchy metallic tone all but disguised the gentle Caribbean lilt of the secretary's voice.

"Send him in." Esther Saliers rose slowly from the battered brown executive chair. She stood to one side of the desk, waiting.

"Ms. Saliers? I'm Andrew Corellian." The visitor extended his hand. Wearing a dark gray suit, starched white shirt, and burgundy, silver, and navy rep stripe tie, Corellian looked both dignified and completely unremarkable, almost, to Esther Saliers, as she imagined a Mercedes salesman—mature, thoughtful, confident, and wanting something.

"Sit down, please." The gray woman with the plump pleasant face and strained impatient expression seated herself.

"Thank you," responded Corellian smoothly as he took the straight-backed gray plastic government visitor's chair closest to the desk.

"Why did you insist on seeing me? We already have your computers, and they're not what you claimed. God knows why we bought them." Esther's thumb, in a hitchhiker motion, pointed to the machine in the corner.

"First of all, although I'm with Lao Systems, I'm not a salesman. I didn't come here to talk about computers. If you have any suggestions, I can certainly relay them to the sales and manufacturing offices. I'm actually head of our Corporate Responsibility Office. That includes our gifted students' outreach and endowment effort."

Esther blinked. "What does that have to do with pesticide exposure and effects? This is the Health Effects Division, you know."

Corellian cleared his throat. "I'm trying to explain. The outreach and gifted student programs are designed . . . well . . . frankly . . . for what our founder called the disenfranchised middle class—for the young man or woman who has grades and the ability to succeed at a first-class university, but who is neither poor nor necessarily a minority. Like your daughter, Keri."

"But . . . why . . . how?"

Corellian shrugged. "We can't find them all, nor, frankly, could we fund all those who fill the qualifications, but we do the best we can with what we learn. You may have seen the application cards . . . but we also go on recommendations. The stories about your husband's illness . . . they all mentioned her talent. So we contacted the school to determine if she was eligible. Her scores and grades are outstanding."

Esther put out a hand and steadied herself against the desk. Her husband's battle with cancer was no secret at Environment. Even the local papers had mentioned it—ecologist loses long fight with cancer.

As for Keri, many people knew about her problems, but so what? They had their own kids they couldn't afford to put through college. After she finished her senior year, Keri would have to work, and in a year or so, once they were back on their feet, would go to college somewhere.

"I'm not quite sure I understand . . ."

Corellian beamed. "The Lao Foundation outreach program has authorized me to present a scholarship grant to your daughter." The tanned, sandy-haired executive produced a piece of paper and handed it across the desk with a single fluid gesture. "That's a copy of the certificate we'll send to the school for presentation to her officially."

"I can't accept this. It's against all the rules." Esther's voice mixed both sadness and confusion.

"Nonsense. It's for Keri, not for you. The outreach program is sponsored by a chartered charitable corporation. That is only a certificate, showing that her room, board, and tuition, up to the amount on the certificate, will be paid to whatever accredited four-year college your daughter attends. In addition, each semester, she will personally receive a small check of one thousand dollars for books, fees, and the other incidentals necessary for a college student.

"The terms are pretty much standard for such grants. She has to finish her senior year with the same level of achievement she has thus far shown, although," and Corellian smiled briefly, "we do anticipate a bit of a senior slump after an award like this.

Once in college, she must maintain a three point average and remain a student in good standing. If she graduates with some sort of distinction, she may also be eligible for graduate assistance."

"But . . . I mean, the rules . . . Why are you telling me?"

"Because we are not a well-publicized foundation. What would you have said if the school or your daughter called up and told you that she had received this? Besides, the parents have worked the hardest. I'm a little selfish. I'm a parent, too, and I wanted to tell you first."

"I'm still not sure—"

"It's no problem," interrupted Corellian cheerfully. "Even the strictest rules don't prohibit scholarship grants to children. Besides, you're not at all involved with procurement or contracting, are you?"

"No, not at all. I work with pesticides, not procurement." Esther leaned back in her squeaky brown chair and took a slow deep breath.

"Even if you looked into the spirit of the ethics rules, how could a grant such as this be unethical? You don't deal with procurement or contracts, and my company's not involved with pesticides. The thing to remember is that your daughter won't be penalized because of your husband's medical bills or because you've chosen to work, rather than be poor. She can go to almost any college of her choice."

Esther looked blankly from the first stack of papers on her desk to the second, then to those piled in her "in" basket.

Corellian waited a few moments before continuing. "I must admit I was pleased to be able to meet you. I've always been interested in environmental issues. I suppose that's why I ended up in Corporate Responsibility." He paused again. "I know that the title of your office is Health Effects, but"—the sandy-haired man shrugged—"exactly what does that mean? I mean, what sort of work do you do with pesticides?"

"I'm responsible for determining the health and environmental effects of the active ingredients in pesticides."

"So you decide which pesticides can be used?"

"Oh, no. That comes much later. The division basically determines how much exposure to what chemicals is dangerous. Or exactly how dangerous. Then the regulatory types use our models to determine whether a pesticide should be registered and under what conditions. That's an oversimplification, but roughly how it works."

"I have kids myself. I worry about their health, and their education," Corellian said amiably. "If you have a chance someday, I'd like to hear about how your work contributes to keeping unsafe products off the market."

"I don't know about that," Esther responded. "Even around here, people's eyes glaze over when I talk about dose-response curves. I try my best, particularly since Derik . . ." Her voice caught momentarily, and she swallowed, then retrieved a tissue from the top left-hand drawer, quickly wiping her eyes. "I'm sorry. I just don't know . . ."

"No . . . I really mean it. Sometime, when you have a little time, I'd like to know more about how you establish . . . is it the health effects?"

"Well . . . they're actually modeled health effects, based on animal studies and human epidemiology. It involves applying the appropriate risk assessment models . . ." She broke off. "You see? I'll have your eyes glazing over, and that's not even why you came." She paused. "I still don't believe this . . ."

"Why not? We at Lao have enjoyed some considerable providence over the years and feel fortunate that we can pass some of it on. In particular, by helping those children who will become the custodians of tomorrow." Corellian rose to leave and extended his hand. "I won't keep you any longer. You might want to act surprised when Keri tells you her good news, in a week or so, when the paperwork gets to the school. If you want to tell her before then, that's your choice. But I know how you feel and wanted to let you know first."

Esther quickly rose and stepped around the desk. "Please do feel free to call me. Anytime after next week. With the ethics rules . . ." She laughed nervously. "Perhaps you wouldn't mind brown-bagging it, and I could bring in a special dessert. I do bake a decent and real French cheesecake."

"I'll give you a call, and I'll count on the cheesecake."

As soon as the sandy-haired man had left the office, Esther looked at her watch, then at the stacks of paper on her desk. For the first time in months, she actually felt like looking at them. Not telling Keri about the scholarship was going to be hard, but not nearly so hard as it would have been telling her daughter that college was impossible. She shook her head, thinking absently how fortunate Keri was, and how, strangely, she looked forward to a simple brown-bag lunch with the amiable Andrew Corellian, the first corporate type since she couldn't remember when who hadn't bullied or patronized her.

She checked her watch again. Still a good hour before the car pool left, and time enough to dig into the latest McCorvey mouse studies.

With a faint smile, she picked up the top file from the "pending" box.

16

THE LIGHT BLUE WALLS OF THE SMALL CONFERENCE ROOM, the one Larry had always used for his client meetings, held cool and tasteful pastel watercolors of Washington—the Supreme Court building, the old Library of Congress building, and, strangely, one of the Taft Carillon near the Senate Office Buildings. An overhead projector sat on a cart in the far inside corner.

Both the men sitting at the circular table were heavyset. Bill Heidlinger overflowed his once-tailored gray pinstripe, and the yellow power tie merely reinforced his bulk and his pale face. The other man—dark-complected—wore a double-breasted dark blue chalk stripe with wide lapels. Both men rose from the table as the two consultants entered.

"I'd like you to meet Jack McDarvid," began Heidlinger, "and Jonathon Black."

"Pierre Devenant. I am pleased to meet you."

"Jack McDarvid."

"Jonnie Black."

McDarvid offered his card, ignoring the senior partner's frown. Jonnie offered his card as well. Devenant did not return the favor. McDarvid sat down across the circular blond-oak pedestal table from Devenant's chair.

"I am the Washington representative of JAFFE International," began Devenant. "That is the parent company of JAFFE USA." His voice bore but the slightest tinge of an accent, and not one that McDarvid would have pegged as French. "As I have told the late Mr. Partello, and now Mr. Heidlinger, we have always regarded United States environmental laws as a cost of doing business." He paused, then added, "In the United States. We see a new problem, and that is the example of these laws in other countries."

McDarvid frowned. Foreign environmental laws were beyond his expertise.

"The problem is not what you might call . . . shall we say . . . reasonable environmental protection. Politically, it becomes . . . difficult . . ."

"If those capitalistic, anarchistic Americans have adopted a set of health and safety standards, they cannot be that hard to meet?" asked Jonnie.

"Precisely."

"Do you have a particular standard in mind?" inquired McDarvid.

"We have already discussed two standards with Mr. Partello, and, more recently, with Mr. Heidlinger. I believe you prepared"—he lifted two sheets of paper from the table—"this work plan." Devenant smiled. "Mr. Partello had praised your . . . creativity. I would agree. If you are successful, then we will see about a more long-term arrangement."

"What sort of profile?" asked Jonnie.

"Profile?"

"The extent to which you wish to be identified," inserted Heidlinger.

"Very little. Our relationship would not be a secret. But . . ." Devenant shrugged, using his hands as well as his shoulders.

"The lower the profile, the better?" asked McDarvid.

"I would say so. Excessive secrecy is just as bad, I . . . we . . . have found. So do not go to great lengths . . ."

McDarvid nodded. "We'll need to work on both issues simultaneously. I'd also like to know if you have low-level-exposure data on chlorohydrobenzilate."

"Low-level-exposure data?"

"The data in the docket is all on animal exposures at high

levels, extrapolated to derive a probable human risk for low-level chronic exposure. We can search for lower exposure studies, but it would save time . . ."

"And money, doubtless, if we have such. Our science chief should know." Devenant jotted something on a thin notebook that fit within his left palm.

"You realize that we have more to work with on the metals?" McDarvid pursued. "We may need a facility visit for that."

"Ah, yes. I understand. But both are important. Even some delay . . . for the pesticide . . ."

Heidlinger's lips were pursed tightly.

"We understand," McDarvid affirmed. "I wanted to make sure you knew about the relative difficulties."

Devenant smiled, and his eyes seemed to twinkle. "The metals—they may not be so easy, either."

"Somehow, we never get the easy ones," McDarvid parried.

"That is so, we have heard. So . . ." Devenant shrugged again.

McDarvid didn't like the Gallic shrug. All big outfits were the same. Rape 'em and leave 'em.

Heidlinger stood. "Thanks for dropping in, Jack, Jonnie."

Devenant stood as well. "A pleasure to meet you both. We look forward to working with you." Suddenly, cards were in his hand. "If you need anything, please call me. Do not hesitate."

A look of quick confusion flitted across Heidlinger's florid face, a look that disappeared behind the professional exterior.

"I hope we don't have to, Monsieur Devenant," responded McDarvid, "but in this business, anything is possible."

"Thank you." Jonnie nodded as he took the card.

McDarvid held the door for Jonnie, looking back at Devenant and Heidlinger. Both consultants continued onward to McDarvid's office.

Jonnie closed the door. "Did that strike you as a little strange?"

McDarvid nodded. "More than a little strange. Heidlinger wasn't expecting Devenant to give us his card. He cut Heidlinger right out, except as our boss."

"He's not French."

"Canadian, you think?"

Jonnie shook his head. "He's not Quebecois. He could be anything. JAFFE was a multinational conglomerate before this country's biggies ever realized there were customers in the rest of the world." He settled into McDarvid's single client chair.

McDarvid dropped into his desk chair, looked at Jonnie, then at the pictures on his credenza. For some reason, he thought about the man in the gray suit.

"What is it?"

McDarvid's eyes flicked to the photos again. Should he mention the man in gray? "Just . . . thinking."

"What do we do now?"

"Standard drill—two at once. Since chlorohydrobenzilate is a pesticide, we can at least use risk-balancing. A policy paper—just a couple pages—outlining what it's good for. I'll do the first draft on that. You need to start on a benefits quantification."

"Value of crops saved, international citrus trade—that sort of thing?"

McDarvid nodded.

"After that?"

"By then, if he doesn't call, I'll call Devenant about the low-level studies. If they show what I think, we can do another paper demonstrating that the Pesticides Programs Office screwed up the risk assessment."

"Did they?"

"They always do. Usually, nobody calls them on it."

"So why are we?"

"We're getting paid to."

Jonnie stood up. "Are we on the right side on this one?"

McDarvid shook his head. "The Pesticides Office probably did screw up the risk assessment on this one."

"That's not what I meant."

"Yeah. I know. I just won't know whether we get to wear gray hats on this one or black hats. Not until after I finish reading through the rest of the docket and all the reports. Then we still have to finish our own policy papers."

"I don't like being a black hat."

"I don't either."

"And papers won't solve Devenant's problems."

"Don't quote Larry at me. I know that, but I need paper to press flesh, to create doubt and confusion. We also have to do the same thing on the metals. There's something there." McDarvid turned in the chair. "Cadmium and gallium especially."

"They'll use gallium arsenide for the next generation of computer chips," reminded Jonnie, "but why that would affect a French multinational, unless they're moving more into computers, isn't clear. Offhand, the metals rules seem more likely to affect U.S. companies and the Japanese."

"Let's not get this any more complicated." McDarvid shook his head. "I may have to talk to Devenant or their scientists, after I go back over that contractor report. That's why I mentioned the need for a plant visit."

Jonnie eased himself out of the client chair that was never used for clients. "I'll start on the quant stuff."

McDarvid nodded. As Jonnie left, his eyes drifted to the window, taking in the near-noon congestion on Nineteenth Street. Should he have told Jonnie about the business at Woodies?

He turned the chair toward the telephone, picking up the two message slips on the spindle—Ned Llewellyn at Treasury and Fredricka Salonge in the pesticides registration office.

First, he needed to call Angela Siskin. Maybe she would give him some more background information on cadmium, or at least let him have some of the background documents. He could get a messenger over to DEP within the hour.

If she were in the office. If she returned his call before he had to go pick up the car from the third attempt to fix the creaky door. If . . .

McDarvid reached for the telephone.

17

JONNIE HELD THE RECEIVER in his right hand and listened to the ringing.

"Hello."

"Veronica? It's Jonnie." He glanced out into the darkness, through the sliding glass door and over the railing at the lights of the Lincoln Memorial.

"Jonnie?"

Jonnie frowned. Had he made that insignificant an impression? "Jonnie Black. At the Ecology Now! reception?"

"Oh . . . Jonnie! I thought you were someone else."

Someone else? "How have you been?" he asked, ensuring his voice sounded cheerful and unworried.

"Not bad. Yourself?" Veronica sounded professional.

"Fine personally." *But I'd be better if you sounded more interested.*

"That implies you're less than satisfied with all that fancy consulting."

"Work? Yeah. You're right. SSDD."

"SSDD—is that another government acronym or just consulting jargon?"

"Same shit, different day." When there was no response, he added, "Listen, since you're fairly new to the area, I was wondering if you would like to go sight-seeing this weekend? I know all kinds of interesting places."

"Besides your balcony?"

"Yes. Besides my balcony."

"What did you have in mind?" asked the cool voice.

"It all depends. We can do the standard touristy-type things, the museums and Mount Vernon, or I can take you on Jonnie's patented tour."

"I think I've seen enough of Washington—either museums or patented tours. It's been a long couple of weeks."

Jonnie frowned. "Well, if you're tired, how about a picnic on Saturday? Ever been to Roosevelt Island?"

"No . . . except looking at it from the bridge. What about the weather? It is October, you know."

"It doesn't get that cold here. If it rains, we'll work out something."

"Okay."

"Great. I'll pick you up at eleven. On one condition, of course."

"Oh?"

"You tell me where you live."

"Out in Maryland—way out. You know where the Merriweather Post Pavilion is? I live behind it."

"Pretty well. At least, you get to listen to a lot of music. You're right off Broken Land Parkway?"

"Oh, you do know the area. Do you know anyone else up here?"

"No, no . . . I've just been to a lot of concerts. Now," he added quickly, "what do I do after I get on Broken Land? I do turn there, don't I?"

"You make a left. Then take the next left. The street curves to the right. My building is the second driveway on the right. The number is 112."

"No problem. I'll see you then."

"Saturday at eleven, then." There was a pause. "Since you're providing the transportation and scenery, I'll bring the food."

"Are you sure?"

"I'm sure. I'll see you on Saturday."

Jonnie looked at the receiver. Strange—very strange. Almost as if she were treating a picnic date as an appointment. Just like too many other Washington women. She hadn't lived in Washington long enough to claim that prerogative.

18

MCDARVID SCANNED THE POLITE PHRASES OF THE MEMO for the critical points.

From: WLH
To: J. McDarvid & J. Black
As a result of the partners' meeting yesterday . . . your special expertise . . . and the interest of JAFFE International . . .
. . . continue on current accounts until resolved . . .
. . . trial period for the next 4–6 months to determine the probable future needs of your services . . .
. . . responsible to me . . . work product copies to Norm Casteel . . .

"In short," muttered McDarvid, "within six months, you and Jonnie will be on your own unless you bring in all sorts of hours that the attorneys can bill at their usual three-to-one exorbitant markup."

Leaning back in his chair, he glanced from the picture of Allyson to the framed certificate certifying that he had indeed been Director of the Office of Policy Analysis at the United States Environmental Protection Agency. Now the old EPA was the new DEP, and nothing had changed except the name.

He frowned as he recalled Pierre Devenant, apparently as little thrilled with Heidlinger as he and Jonnie were. The whole JAFFE approach bothered him. The metals issue still seemed somehow linked to Larry's death. But he had nothing but a gut feeling.

So far, all the research and all his conversations showed the same pattern. Everyone seemed willing to talk, and no one knew anything. Yes, there was a metals initiative, but it was barely under way, and any details were premature. Yes, feel free to keep in touch. Yes, everyone would be interested in any analytical or policy documents McDarvid could provide.

Since the data package from the chief of research for JAFFE USA hadn't arrived, he couldn't finish the first paper.

He looked at the computer, then at the half-open file drawer in his desk. Besides solving JAFFE's problems, he and Jonnie still had a few other projects on the other issues—like the question of statistical testing methods for groundwater, ambient exposure levels for benzene, and whether use of a toxic waste as an on-site fuel qualified for a waiver of the disposal permitting requirements under the recycling exemption of RCRA. There was no end to the fascinating and thrilling projects.

He glanced at the desk clock—part of the pen set he had received at his EPA going-away party. Still enough time for a long afternoon before he headed home to the kids. Another late Thursday—had it only been two weeks since they had done the work plan for JAFFE?

Which attorney had picked up the fuel waiver for Moreland Reclamation and Recovery? He fumbled for the other memo— the one from George Ames. Carole Sturteval had the waiver, which made sense. Carole had come from the DEP Office of General Counsel, lured in earlier in the year by Larry.

McDarvid laid out the waiver folder. Then he dug out the benzene file. Nothing he could do with that until the latest data sets arrived from the consulting engineers. He hoped the data would show that the indoor air levels of benzene were so much higher that further hazardous air-pollutant requirements were meaningless. What sense did it make to regulate outdoor air pollutants to levels safe for asthmatic chipmunks living right on the smokestack when people filled their homes with far higher levels voluntarily? But people never thought about the residues from gas stoves or self-cleaning ovens, from their dry cleaning, household cleaners, and polishes, let alone the gasoline stored in so many suburban garages.

Not that the Clean Air Act hazardous air-pollutant requirements had ever made sense. Even the ultra-greenies at Environment understood that. And they had avoided dealing with such absurdities—until the environmentalists had gotten the Supreme Court decision on vinyl chloride.

Now the Chairman of the House Public Works Committee was pushing his good buddy Norm Dennis—Chairman of the Energy and Commerce Subcommittee on Health—to hold oversight hearings to pressure DEP to act. Sloan's control of the water grants, his knowledge about every member, and his PAC money sources just about ensured that Dennis would hold those oversight hearings. Hell, Sloan's personal staff had done all the drafting for the present statute and handed it to Dennis on the proverbial silver platter—held, of course, in the velvet-covered fist of Sam "the Hammer" Sloan. Those amendments already required DEP to issue more stringent standards—standards that even some of the old-line bureaucrats were balking at because they were unworkable.

McDarvid looked at the half-drafted status report on the computer screen. He snorted. "Where do you start, McDarvid?"

Finally, he reached for the fuel waiver folder. He still had to pay his share of the mortgage.

19

"WHO ARE YOU SEEING TODAY?" asked the guard in the pale blue blazer.

"George Rendhaas," McDarvid said. "Congressional. That's 260-5200," he added as the guard picked up the telephone.

"A Mr. McDarvid to see George Rendhaas. A badge number, please . . . 358240. Thank you." She handed McDarvid his pass.

"Thank you." McDarvid nodded and stepped past the guard desk and to the elevators. Two maintenance men poked at the nearest one. Nothing changed. The elevators hadn't worked when he had worked at EPA, and they still didn't.

As the right elevator door opened, a courier in a black Lycra cycling outfit and a worn camouflage jacket stepped out, mumbling into a hand-held telephone, ". . . leaving DEP, Fourth and M, for Dupont Circle . . ."

McDarvid stepped into the empty elevator and tapped the "8" button, approving of the refurbished interiors, the light wooden paneling and new carpeting. At the fourth floor, two women and a man joined him.

"Jack! How are you? Still in the consulting business?" asked the man.

McDarvid racked his mind for the other's name. "Just fine . . . it's the same old thing. Not much different than here, same type of crisis—" He recalled the name—Sam, Sam Jensen, Office of General Counsel, Pesticides Section. "Still worrying about pesticides, Sam?"

"No. I'm going to be the associate general counsel for drinking water."

"When does that start?"

"Next Tuesday."

The elevator lurched to a halt one floor up.

"I've got to run, Jack, but stop by."

"I will," promised McDarvid.

The taller woman—the one with the short blond hair, the

hawkish nose, and the rumpled tan wool dress—refused to look at the consultant. The black woman in the neatly tailored blue suit and cream blouse smiled softly.

McDarvid returned the smile before he got off the elevator on the eighth floor and walked to the south end and the reception area for Congressional Affairs. George's modular cubicle adjoined the Assistant Director's.

"He'll be right with you, Mr. McDarvid. He's on the phone."

"Thank you." McDarvid sat on the saggy couch that had been in the office since before he had joined EPA. "Pretty busy these days?"

The secretary nodded as she reached for the telephone. "Congressional Affairs . . . No, Ms. Mertz is on the Hill right now. May I take a message?"

The telephone buzzed again, and the secretary shrugged.

"Jack, come on in." George Rendhaas stood well over six feet, rail thin. What hair he had left was ginger red and short above his ears.

McDarvid settled himself into the chair across the narrow modular government-issue desk.

"What can I do for you?"

"I'm just touching base. Usual end-of-session rush?"

"I wish it were. Congress may stay in session until Christmas."

"You think you'll get a new clean-air bill?"

"Who knows? It hasn't been that long since the last one. The Administration has its amendments. Energy and Commerce has its amendments, and Chairman Sloan has his amendments."

McDarvid shook his head sympathetically. The Air Act wasn't even under the jurisdiction of the Public Works Committee Chairman, but Sloan maintained an ongoing interest in the Act, especially in air toxics, and his ideas somehow ended up in the final Energy and Commerce markups. "Sam can make life difficult. Some things just don't change."

"Not since you left, at any rate."

"Has Chairman Dennis decided to push on the benzene regulations? You know, the fact that consumer exposures are greater than industrial exposures?"

"Hannigan claims that the studies are window dressing. The new Assistant Secretary for Air is scheduled to testify on the twenty-third. They hope to send the draft rule to OMB before then."

"Back to zero involuntary exposure levels, then?"

George laughed. "You said that. I didn't."

McDarvid had his answer, not that the client would like it. The idea that no emission at all would be allowed would close more than a few plants—since zero emissions levels weren't technically possible without building an entirely new facility. Another industry headed offshore, and another opportunity for the Japanese and everyone else in Asia.

"What about the question of the California standards?" The previous Energy and Commerce Chairman had blocked tougher California state standards outside of the worst air pollution areas. Sloan wanted them nationwide, but it wasn't his committee, and he had to use Norm Dennis, who needed ever-larger contributions to defend a seat in an increasingly Republican district.

"Dennis wants them in all states with nonattainment areas."

"You mean . . . if any state has any monitoring station that fails to meet the ambient air quality standards . . ." McDarvid pushed the leading question.

"Not quite that bad. They'd get two violations for two years before the tougher standards and the new construction ban took effect."

"Wonderful. What do they want to do? Shut down all U.S. manufacturing? Close every dry cleaner in America?" McDarvid kept his tone sardonic.

George laughed. "Of course not. They want electric cars powered by biomass and solar power, bean sprouts in every kitchen, polyester produced without chemistry, and everyone to use mass transit without the subsidies necessary to make it work."

McDarvid laughed briefly. "Nothing's changed."

"You know that." George paused. "Did you hear about Bill Windreck?"

"Windreck? The Assistant Secretary for OSWER? No."

"Ended up in the hospital last week. Chest pains. Thought it was a heart attack, but apparently just an overdose of stress."

"That's a tough job."

"He's resigning—effective at the end of the year. They wanted him to stay through the Appropriations hearings, but Bill said enough was enough."

"Was Norm Dennis after him?"

"Do bears live in the woods?"

McDarvid shook his head slowly. "Any thoughts on his successor?"

"Leading candidate is Paula Nishimoto—Environmental Commissioner in Oregon . . ."

By one-thirty, McDarvid was walking into an office on the tenth floor.

"Hi there," he called, nosing his head around the open door.

"Hi, Jack. Come on in," returned the heavy woman in the maroon dress.

McDarvid lounged in the scruffy white armchair in the windowless inside office. How Ellie had managed to get an armchair, he had always wondered, but he often wondered how she knew everyone and everything, and liked them all.

Her desk was always spotless, except for the single stack of papers she was working on. Despite her weight, Ellie DiForio was attractive and well groomed. She was also soft-spoken and intelligent. Having her work for him had been a pleasure, even though she had insisted on remaining an analyst.

"What are you snooping around for this time, Jack?"

He grinned. Ellie had never beaten around the bush, either. "Two things. A pesticide called chlorohydrobenzilate, and the metals initiative everyone seems to be whispering about. Chromium, cadmium, beryllium, and gallium."

"Hmmm . . . chlorohydrobenzilate. That's Hassad's area . . ."

McDarvid said nothing.

". . . but I do know the Health Standards Division at OSHA requested NIOSH investigate its persistence and toxicity. Their report is being reviewed by Pesticide Programs. Very bad actor, according to OPP. The Health Effects people, Esther Saliers especially, are worried about it. High benefit level for specialized citrus, but limited uses. That's why nothing's been done yet. The Secretary has a decision memo recommending cancellation, but . . ."

"He's either not convinced, or he's swamped, and that's at the bottom of the pile," suggested McDarvid.

"Try the last one. This Secretary will do anything for the

environment, particularly when it looks easy. He still thinks he can do it by posturing, just like his predecessor."

"What about the metals?"

"After you asked about that one, I looked into it a little deeper. But that got a little sticky. Jerry's handling that himself."

"He's not an analyst."

"No. He's got Eileen doing the analysis."

"Oh . . . Why did Jerry get involved?"

"That's the funny part. Eileen found an old report about metals and showed it to him. He went to the Federal Facilities semiannual conference and talked about it. The DOE and DOD delegation ignored him, I guess. They didn't contradict him. They didn't dispute him. They just ignored him."

McDarvid shook his head. "So now he's out to prove it?"

"It's not that simple. Cadmium has always been a real problem, and everyone has tried to compromise on it. Beryllium's the same way, and you worked on the hexavalent chrome issue."

"What about gallium?"

"No one seems to know anything about it, and it's part of the initiative more because of its compounds. The arsenic side in particular is cause for concern. Jerry keeps asking about the manufacture of new computer chips and the possibilities for arsenic in the home, workplace and waste stream. What the concentration would be, how many tons annually? We don't have the answers. That was the way this started, more as an inquiry. But now, OSHA's grabbed it, and they're talking about restrictive worker exposure limits. That got the cross-media office involved, and they're asking why our standards for exposure are so much looser than those in the proposal OSHA is developing."

"It sort of growed, like Topsy?" asked McDarvid.

"That's as good a way as any of describing it."

"But what levels are we talking about?" he pressed.

"How about zero?"

McDarvid swallowed. "That's impossible."

"You're right, and they know that. So they're talking about a half microgram per cubic meter of air for particles."

"That's still effectively zero. No industry can afford to meet that."

"Jerry and Eileen say that's what industry always claims, but they manage to meet the standards."

"Yeah, those facilities that remain. How many copper and lead smelters do we have left? How come we haven't built a new U.S. oil refinery in more than twenty years, and why are all the new oil refineries being built offshore? How come most of our raw steel comes from places like Korea and India?"

"Jack . . . you asked those questions when you ran Policy Analysis. Look where it got you. They don't get asked now."

McDarvid accepted the correction. "Is there any evidence that these wonderfully tight standards will improve health benefits?"

Ellie laughed. "Of course. How can there not be? If you eliminate pollutants, there *must* be some positive impact."

McDarvid nodded. More cleanup was always better. Still, he couldn't resist a last argument. "Are they factoring in the heart attacks from closed plants, the suicides, the spouse and child abuse?"

"Jack . . . that's a cheap shot."

"Yeah. Cheap . . . but accurate."

Ellie frowned. "Do you think consulting has really been good for you?"

McDarvid straightened in the shabby armchair. "Probably not. Seeing the other side of the coin has strengthened my cynicism. I'm not sure I trust anyone's motivations." He forced a grin. "Not even my own."

"How is Elizabeth?" Ellie had only met his precocious daughter once, but always asked about her.

"As intellectually oblivious as ever. 'Yes, Father, I would be pleased to accommodate you,' or 'Oughtn't you turn in presently?' or . . ." McDarvid shook his head. "She's just Elizabeth. Sometimes I want to string her up; the rest of the time I want to keep the world from crashing in on her."

"She's a lot like you, Jack."

"Thanks." McDarvid returned Ellie's grin with a smile of his own.

20

KAPRUSHKIN SET THE MUG ON THE SCARRED DESK next to the recent photograph of an attractive black-haired woman, then glanced at the documents—the statistical abstract of U.S. pollution sent by pouch every three months.

"These people are killing themselves . . . and their children." Kaprushkin ran his hand through the still-thick gray hair. "Here we justify pollution by saying that the people's needs must be met before controls can be adopted. The rich Americans have the same pathetic excuses: 'We can't afford it. Our factories will close. People will lose their jobs.' " He snorted as he returned the topmost report to the file.

"Isn't it interesting that the only time the capitalists care about their workers is when their own wealth is at stake?" The woman in the photograph kept smiling. "An automobile is a necessity, but breathable air is an abstract goal. And we kill ourselves in order to imitate the Americans. They believe they have the right to lead disposable lives. That is their real ideology. Yet we spent so much time spying on the Americans, so sure that they had some great secret." Kaprushkin glanced at the latest U.S. landfill statistics. "We have discarded our ideology for theirs, and we still don't understand that there is no capitalism, no communism, only industrialism and its suicidal destiny."

At the knock on the door, the Colonel straightened the papers. "Yes?"

A young Corporal appeared. "I thought you might be calling for me."

"Really, Corporal?"

"No, sir." The Corporal disappeared more quickly than he had arrived.

Kaprushkin would study the papers tomorrow. They held no surprises. Besides, Irenia was waiting for him. He never regretted the stars she had undoubtedly cost him. The girl he had rescued from some of Moscow's seedier streets thirty years ago had not been an ideal match for the promising young intelligence officer, not even close. Friends had warned him that she would ruin his career. The intelligence community was as conservative as any monarchy in approving the mates of its heirs. And why not? thought Kaprushkin. They rule as imperially as any king. And often as foolishly.

Through all the upheavals, someone protected me, and my plan to help the Americans to rip their own economy to shreds. To make weapons production impossible, or impossibly expensive. He smiled, amused at how his superiors focused on the military aspects, how they failed to see the environmental impacts—all of them.

He put the empty mug in the center of the desk where the Corporal would have it clean and in the exact same spot in the morning, then opened the safe near his desk and placed the green folder inside.

The Corporal certainly had the combination, but nothing in the safe itself revealed the information that would damn him.

As Kaprushkin walked down the stairs and into the ice-slickened streets, he wondered yet again about the shadow man—men?—who had protected him for so many years.

Would that protector learn his real plans? Already, there were anonymous fliers and papers appearing in Moscow and St. Petersburg protesting the radioactive waste and filthy air. He shivered in midstep, but continued walking to the metro station, disdaining the car and driver to which his rank entitled him.

21

MCDARVID TOOK THE STAIRS DOWN to the ninth floor and the Air Office.

Tina Lederman's cubicle was empty. So was the entire bay. He glanced at the cards on the secretary's desk. On top was one he hadn't seen. He vaguely recognized the name, Andrew Corellian, but not the company—Lao Systems. Andy Corellian—where had he met the man? At some reception? The second card was that of an attorney—Ron Estermann—a former enforcement counsel who now specialized in representing Japanese firms.

"They're at a staff meeting," volunteered a young black man McDarvid had not seen before. McDarvid tried not to jump back from his snooping.

"How long . . . ?"

"It just started about five minutes ago."

"Well—tell Tina I stopped by." He handed the intern his card and made his way back to the elevator and down to the fourth floor. After passing the snack bar, he turned toward the mall, looking at the employee bulletin board.

A plain black-and-white notice caught his eye.

THE LAO FOUNDATION
Helping Provide the Best for the Best

McDarvid skimmed the text. ". . . 501 C(3) Foundation . . . dedicated to providing merit scholarships to outstanding students of middle-class backgrounds . . . allowing them a collegiate freedom of choice . . ."

He nodded. Elizabeth could certainly benefit from something like the Lao Foundation. He wondered how he and Allyson would ever afford college for three children.

The attached card holder was empty. It would be a few years before Elizabeth would be eligible for something like that, anyway. Still, it was nice that someone was looking out for the forgotten middle class.

Cocking his head, he wondered if the foundation were connected to the same outfit as Andy Corellian. He studied the fine print in the corner, but nothing indicated whether the Lao Foundation was linked to Lao Systems.

From the entrance to the mall area, he wound his way through the upper level of the Waterside Mall until he reached the area above the Safeway.

Angela was out as well. So he left his card and went down the corner stairs to the Waste Fuels Section. Although the doors were propped open, one of the cardboard arrows usually providing guidance dangled loosely on the wall. McDarvid looked for a clip or some tape, then shrugged and turned right, heading toward Roger Weinberg's section.

"Jack McDarvid. It really must be slow for you to get down here." Roger resembled the stereotyped environmental professional—thin, bearded, with gold-rimmed thick glasses. He wore a faded flannel shirt over equally shapeless khaki trousers.

McDarvid leaned against the worktable, the part that wasn't overflowing with charts, printouts, and reports. "What's new?"

"Nothing's new. We have the same old polluters, and they have the same old excuses . . ."

Glancing down, McDarvid saw the report title on the second pile—"Practical Limits of Analytical Measurement Technologies." He picked up the thick spiral-bound volume published by the DEP laboratory in Cincinnati. "This new?"

"I got that last week. It's nothing special—just what we all know about noise levels and statistics when you get to measurements in the parts-per-billion range."

"I thought we had a problem below ten parts per million."

"Oh . . . that's true for some organics, but that's because of the volatilization problems, not the analytics."

"They tell me that the new metals initiative is a half part per million."

Roger laughed, an open cheerful laugh. "That's what happens when you get policy ahead of science."

"You think five hundred parts per billion might be a little hard to measure accurately?" McDarvid lifted the book. "Does Carpenzio think so?"

"Hell, we all think so. Oh, with gas chromatography and good quality assurance . . . you can do it under laboratory conditions. But in the field, in a sampling well, or even in handling our stuff—especially waste oils—you've got a consistency problem."

"Could I borrow this?"

"Just take it. It doesn't say anything we don't already know."

"Thanks, Roger. It'll be useful."

Roger grinned. "If it's not, you'll find a way. What else is on your mind?"

"Definitions of on-site fuels."

"That wouldn't be the Moreland Reclamation issue?"

"Same one."

"Jack, that's nothing more than a sham recycling operation."

McDarvid nodded. "Let me ask a question, Roger. Now, of course, you're absolutely right that some of Moreland's operations have been . . . creative in their interpretation of the recycling exemption . . ."

"Creative is a polite way . . ."

"I understand. But in the fuel case, we're talking something else. None of this stuff leaves the site. That's not like the aggregate. This is burned in the cement kiln. What if Moreland installed a full set of stack monitors?"

"That's not our problem. It's the toxicity of the still bottoms, and they're not an on-site process waste."

McDarvid nodded. "What about . . ."

"That's not exactly what the exemption report language had in mind . . ."

"Did you consider the kiln's destruction removal efficiency . . ."

Back and forth, with McDarvid quietly presenting, Roger responding, the discussion continued for well over an hour.

"It is an interesting idea," Roger admitted.

"Let me write it up and send it over." McDarvid shrugged. "I think that Moreland might consider an expansion of the storage permit."

"I can't promise anything except to look at it."

"That's all I'm asking." McDarvid straightened, glancing at the clock. Nearly four. Not much else that he could do, not when three quarters of the agency would be gone within the hour.

"Anyway, thanks for stopping by. We might look at that other idea, too."

Other idea? What other idea had he given them?

"The one in your last paper—about sampling frequencies."

"I didn't realize I sent that to you."

"You didn't, but Joyce and I trade your stuff back and forth. Even the graphs are interesting, especially the creative way in which you use the scales."

"All the numbers are there."

"They always are. You're an artist, Jack. Too bad you couldn't stay."

McDarvid shrugged. "You know it wasn't my choice. I try to stay honest, even if I am on the other side of the fence sometimes."

"Well . . . there are a few of you in industry that we actually enjoy talking to—maybe two or three. You, the computer guy, and Maurice."

"Maurice?"

"You know, the former Deputy Administrator who founded Datron?"

"Oh, that Maurice. What's he doing besides getting all sorts of testing contracts for Superfund sites?"

"Jack . . . that's a little cynical."

"What else has changed?"

Roger looked at the clock. "I need to do a few things before I catch the car pool."

"All right. Thanks again for your time. I'll have that paper over in the next few days."

22

"JACK?"

McDarvid looked up.

Steve Greene, wispy hair drifting across his forehead, stood in the doorway.

"Come on in."

The attorney shut the door behind him and slumped into the client chair. "It's still like a whole new language. Or dialect, anyway."

"Pesticides, you mean?"

Greene nodded, then straightened up and leaned toward McDarvid. "Do they really believe this shit?" He lifted the copy of the letter in his hand.

"What shit?"

"This business about having to register a fucking alcohol as a pesticide before you can use it in a hospital sterilizer?"

"Yeah . . . unfortunately. It's a little more complicated than that. If you check the exact words in the CFR, you'll find that they could sell it without a registration, but only if the label gives its straight description as alcohol. If they use the words 'disinfectant' or 'sterilant' or any words that imply antimicrobial action, then they have to register the product."

"Common alcohol?"

McDarvid gave Greene a wry smile. "Even the twelve-year-old stuff."

The attorney shook his head. "The Water Act at least is technology-based, with some commonsense checkpoints."

"On the other hand," mused McDarvid, "you can do risk-balancing with pesticides. That's why Larry liked FIFRA. Claimed it wasn't all one-sided."

"I suppose," Greene said slowly. "Any word on the police investigation?"

"No. Detective called the other day with a few other questions. They don't have any real leads, other than the drug angle."

"I wish he were still handling FIFRA."

McDarvid grinned. "It's not that bad. You've been here, what? Eight years?"

"Going on nine." Greene looked across the desk. "Jack, sometimes I just don't know. When I started clerking for Justice Diener, I told myself that after that and a few years busting my ass to make partner, everything would be fine. But things haven't changed. Suzanne and I got married, and Cyndy and Malcolm came along, and it's ten years later, and I still put in a lot of seventy-plus-hour weeks.

"I'm up for partner next summer, and Heidlinger keeps hinting that someone who's partner quality doesn't mind spending the time—or billing the clients for every last second. He even claimed he bills for the time he reads opposition briefs on the john."

McDarvid smiled. "But the money's good."

"Yeah."

"You don't sound convinced."

Greene shrugged. "Where else could someone who's thirty-four make what I do? But if I don't keep working like this, I'll be one of the ones who end up out the door on July fourth. Or a permanent senior associate, making the same salary for the rest of my life."

"Perils of the fast track."

"You pay one way or the other." Greene gave McDarvid a lopsided grin as he stood up. "Sorry to keep you, Jack. But I couldn't believe the business about needing a registration for plain old alcohol."

"It threw me the first time, too."

After the thin attorney had left, McDarvid glanced at the computer, wondering whether Greene would be selected for partner. He shook his head. Steve didn't have the proper reverence. And the fact that Heidlinger had been so direct wasn't a good sign. When things became obvious in Washington, you were in trouble. Nothing was obvious until it was too late.

That was why there was rarely a good Washington book. How would you really write about life in the fogbank that was the nation's capital? No one would believe how things happened. Like Bill Windreck. Poor bastard probably spent every other minute worrying about either congressional hearings or the White House reactions to congressional concerns. But if you didn't see the subtleties or the rumors, you had no warning at all. And sometimes, when you saw the warnings, no one else did, or there was nothing you could do.

Like Ned Llewellyn . . . or like Steve.

23

THE BLACK CONVERTIBLE RUMBLED into the parking lot. At the sound of incompletely muffled exhaust, a thin woman pushing a blue denim baby carriage looked at the less than pristine bodywork of the not quite classic vehicle.

Jonnie grinned at the woman, who looked away quickly. "Maybe it's the beard."

From the space next to a rust-streaked blue Dodge van, he walked toward the nearest wing of the apartment complex. Apartment 112 was at the other end from where he had parked, but on the ground-floor level.

Overhead, a few puffy white clouds dotted the sky. The air was warmer than even the typical Washington Indian summer, but untypical of Washington weekends, when it usually rained. Jonnie rang the bell.

Veronica opened the door. "I'm ready," she announced, hoisting a bag from Sutton Place Gourmet.

"Wow. Looks great." Jonnie took a long look at the flannel shirt and the trim and faded jeans. The loose-fitting red-and-white-checked flannel shirt couldn't completely hide the shapely form underneath.

"You don't even know what I got for lunch."

"That's okay. I wasn't referring to lunch."

"Are you . . . Never mind." Veronica suppressed a half-smile and set down the bag beside the doorway. "Well, come on in. You might as well see my digs before we leave. Do you want a drink or anything?"

"Actually, a glass of water would be nice." Jonnie stepped through the doorway and past the closet and turned left into the living/everything room.

Veronica went the other way, into the small kitchen.

Once past the squared archway, Jonnie stopped, looking at the picture hanging over the battered tan couch. The image was of a younger Marx, but the look that would become famous in his later years was already obvious.

Behind his back, Jonnie could hear the sound of running water, followed by the sounds of a refrigerator opening and the clink of ice into a tumbler.

Besides the picture, he noted the battered desk in one corner and, strangely incongruous, the computer, complete with a large black plastic box filled with floppies. The external modem's red lights were dark.

"Here's your water."

Jonnie turned and accepted the glass. "Thank you." He took a deep swallow. Riding with the top down usually left him thirsty.

"This is home, at least for now."

He looked toward the kitchen.

"I'll take it. You don't even know where it goes." She took the glass, opened the dishwasher, placed it on the upper rack, and closed the door with a muted thump.

"I thought environmentalists didn't use dishwashers," he teased.

"They use less water than washing by hand, especially if you wait until it's full. That's what industry always says. And they're right about that."

Gesturing toward the portrait above the couch, Jonnie asked, "I take it this means you're a Marxist?"

"Of course. You know what leftists we greenies are. I even have a matching sweatshirt."

"I like it." Jonnie was going to enjoy this picnic.

As they reached the front door, Veronica picked up a plain blue windbreaker along with the lunch provisions.

Jonnie looked back toward the living room where Groucho, flanked by duck and cigar, leered down from the wall.

As they left the apartment, Jonnie stepped onto the still-green grass to avoid the same woman with the baby carriage. She did not even look at Jonnie, instead glaring at Veronica.

Veronica stepped up beside Jonnie.

"Which car?"

"The black one down there. I parked at the wrong end."

"The van?"

"No, it's behind the van."

"That one?" she asked at the sight of the 1967 GTO, black top down.

"It's just good basic transit. Besides, it's fun."

"Basic transit? Then why are there flames on the hood scoop?"

"Oh, a friend put those on. He said if I was going to have this car I might as well do it right."

"Is it environmentally sound? I mean, a car like that must get terrible mileage."

"Environmentally sound? Hell, it's not even very safe." He opened the door for her.

"Just a minute." Veronica paused and pulled on the windbreaker. Then she slipped into the passenger seat, looking for the seat belts. "You don't have shoulder belts." She finally fished out the buckle end of the belt from deep within the seat.

"Lucky to have seat belts. They were an option on this car." Jonnie shut the door.

"Oh . . ."

Looking back over his shoulder, Jonnie turned the key. The

lady with the baby carriage was nowhere in sight as he backed out of the parking space and eased the GTO out through the narrow apartment lane.

"Why do you live all the way up here?" Jonnie asked as he swung the GTO south onto Route 29 from South Entrance Drive. "Somehow, I imagined that you lived in town. Georgetown or Adams-Morgan."

"It's pleasant." Veronica raised her voice as the GTO rumbled. "I can catch most of the concerts at Merriweather without buying a ticket. The first part, at least. They turn down the volume at ten. I'll have some friends over, set up some lawn chairs or a blanket in the field by the parking lot, and enjoy the show until the volume drops. Besides, it's affordable. For what I pay here, including my car payments, I'd be watching the roach races in a tiny apartment in Adams-Morgan or Capitol Hill. And taking bets on how many times I got broken into each week."

Veronica shifted in the cracked vinyl seat as the wind blew back her hair. "How did you end up working where you do? I mean, you seem concerned about the environment."

Jonnie shrugged as he cut the car around a slow-moving Cadillac in the left lane. "Maybe because I am concerned. Sometimes, I think that the work I do does more to shape good environmental policy than all the yammering interest groups put together."

"You think that Ecology Now! is composed of yammering idiots?"

"It's not the individuals. It's the group process. Business or environmental group, they're all the same. Facts don't have much to do with beliefs." He paused, then tried to explain. "Look, I actually try to apply some analysis to show the consequences of proposed rules. Very little real analysis goes into policy proposals, whether by government, interest groups, or corporations. Hell, I think I fight more battles with my clients trying to get them to do the smart thing than I do with anybody else."

"You sound like it's a single-handed battle."

"Almost. I work with another fellow. We do the analyses and education work for the firm, the detailed practical analysis that lawyers avoid."

Jonnie eased the car around the circle at the District line and headed down Sixteenth Street. "As to how I ended up here, your guess is as good as mine. Just chance, I suppose. After I graduated from Georgetown, I spent a year at OMB before I went to grad school and got a finance degree from Chicago. After that, I went to General Brands and ran the pudding business."

Veronica's face crinkled with laughter. "The pudding business?"

"Sure. I was the pudding czar. I ran the financial side of their pudding business until I came to a stunning realization."

"What was that?"

"I hated pudding."

Veronica grabbed the dashboard as she broke into laughter.

"There was actually only one benefit to having worked there."

"What was that?"

"It's good for making cute girls laugh."

The car squealed to a halt, a little too sharply, at a light.

"That place was divorced from reality. You know they sell those frozen pudding bars? The kind that celebrities advertise?"

"Yeah."

"Well, they used to refer to those products as frozen novelties. They were marketed to kids. Then someone got the bright idea of selling a dietetic version of frozen desserts for grown-ups."

"So?"

"The company formally referred to them as adult novelties."

Veronica began convulsing with laughter. "Adult novelties? Was that because of the shape?"

"Nah. No one even thought of that, even though the shape is . . . suggestive. As far as they were concerned, it was just frozen fruit drink in the regular shape. But no one saw anything funny in the idea of selling frozen adult novelties. It just never occurred to them. I had to get out of there."

"Did you take any samples?" Veronica grinned lasciviously.

"I don't know. I guess we'll have to check my freezer." Jonnie grinned back as he floored the GTO to cut in front of a furniture delivery van. "Anyway, I saw a small want ad in the *Washington Post* asking for a regulatory economist. I'd already learned something about regulatory issues during an internship on the Hill, and that led to a year at OMB. Besides, I had a decent economics background coming out of Chicago."

From N Street, Jonnie turned south on Twenty-third. "So what's a nice girl like you doing in a town like this?"

"It's my turn?"

Jonnie did not answer as he ran the yellow light and began to merge the heavy car into the circle traffic.

"Well, somehow, and nobody in my family can quite explain it, I came down with political fever early. Even as a little kid I stayed up late on election nights to watch the returns come in. Once, in school, when I was running for class president, I promised a boy that I'd kiss him if he voted for me."

"Did you?"

"No. He was cute enough, but somehow I just never went through with it."

"Did he vote for you?"

"Of course." She grinned.

"You're right. You did learn politics at an early age."

Jonnie took the right-hand turn off the bridge that would lead him to the George Washington Parkway.

"Anyway, for politics, this is the place to go. Columbus just wasn't the spot for what I wanted. Somehow, between working, student loans, and help from my folks, I managed the tuition at George Washington. I could have gone to a better school than G.W. for less money, but I wanted to be in Washington.

"G.W. is expensive. Did you like it?" Jonnie asked as he hit the brake, then the accelerator. "Damned parkway . . ."

"It was okay. I went more for the access than the education. Some of the professors had the experience I was interested in learning about. Being in Washington also allowed me to get the internships I wanted. Like I said, it met my needs."

Jonnie repressed the urge to let out a whistle. Instead, he tapped the brake several times to warn the tailgating Volvo and flicked the turn signal before pulling into the island's parking lot. Veronica was showing more than met the eyes, and there was plenty to meet the eyes.

A spot large enough to accommodate his car was his immediate priority, but apparently the breeze had kept both tourists and locals away, or at least enough away that he had no problem in wheeling the big convertible into a parking slot between two diminutive imports.

"Here we are!" he announced, opening the door. He looked at Veronica, then continued past the trunk to her door, which he opened, wondering whether she appreciated the gesture. Not that disapproval would have stopped him.

She inclined her head, wreathed in windblown hair.

"I need to . . ." he mumbled as he headed back, keys in hand, to open the trunk and extract the old army blanket.

Thunk! The entire GTO shuddered as the trunk came down.

Veronica did not even look up as she reached down behind the seat to recover the shopping bag with the picnic inside.

Jonnie sauntered up, closing the door for her. "Ready for a short walk?"

"Of course." Sometime between his opening the door and returning from the trunk, she had brushed or combed the long hair back into place.

"This way . . ." Once clear of the parking area, Jonnie led Veronica up the gentle slope and through a stand of trees to a small clearing on the other side of the narrow island—on the shore downstream and across the river from the Georgetown campus. With the cool breeze off the water keeping both tourists and locals away, Jonnie knew they wouldn't be disturbed, especially as they were well away from the trails and picnic facilities.

The only people who had a chance to see them were the university rowers engaged in a practice session and a lone sculler making his way downriver.

"I never thought a place like this existed so close."

Jonnie spread the blanket on the ground. "You just have to look . . . like a lot of things." Then he sat down.

Veronica kneeled on the other corner, taking wrapped objects from the bag and setting them on a small tray she had included. Even a bottle of chardonnay appeared, complete with corkscrew and two glass goblets.

"You did bring everything."

"Why have a picnic if you're not prepared?"

He shrugged. There was no answer to that.

She continued to lay out the meal on the plates—actual crockery. "Why did you pick Theodore Roosevelt Island?"

"Why not? You can see Georgetown, the memorials, and in the fall not that many people come here. Besides," he added practically, "I don't know the area where you live that well."

"How many other girls have you brought here?" Her voice was, again, almost intellectually curious.

"Two."

Veronica made no comment, unwrapping another package.

"They both said they liked it, but I don't think either one really did."

"So why did you ask *me?*"

"I keep hoping to enjoy it with someone who also appreciates it."

"Would you open the wine?"

Jonnie obliged, even to offering her the first sip.

She took the sip in the same gravity as he offered it, and the wisp of a smile did not escape until after she had nodded.

"You approve?"

"Of course."

Jonnie poured both goblets half full, then set the still-cool bottle aside and took a small sip. "This is excellent!"

Veronica smiled softly. "Childhood legacy. My father's an oenophile. Wine tasting was part of growing up. He believed that was the best defense against secret drinking and an uncultivated palate. In high school some friends were passing around a bottle of Boone's Farm Strawberry Hill, in a paper bag, no less. I took a slug. My only reaction was 'My God, it's domestic!' "

Jonnie broke into laughter. "Are you as expert with food? This looks terrific."

"I hope so. It strained my frugal budget." She handed him a set of stainless-steel utensils.

"Real utensils to go with real food." He took another sip of wine.

"We greenies believe in the real things."

Jonnie almost choked at the deadpan tone as he saw another glimmer of a smile when she brushed back the long hair over her shoulder.

Threeeep. A sea gull wheeled overhead. "Noisy buggers."

"They fill a necessary ecological niche."

"Don't we all?" He set down the glass. "It's just wondering where our position is in the food chain that concerns me." He picked up the plate, starting first on the chicken jardiniere, then followed with the wild rice. Although Veronica had purchased rather than prepared everything, with the exception of the salad, she had put some thought into selecting the meal.

"Do all consultants eat like they're starving?"

Jonnie shook his head. "Just those who are—except Jack. Jack would use a knife and fork on fried chicken at a fast-food joint."

"Who's Jack?"

"The guy I work with. He probably knows more obscure environmental information than any three other lawyers or consultants in Washington. He's also a very proper sort who married a doctor and worries whether he holds up his end."

"He sounds insecure."

"He should have been a lawyer, except that he knew that he couldn't stand himself if he did. So he's a consultant." Jonnie took another sip of the chardonnay. "Enough of Jack. What about you? You're from Columbus?"

Veronica nodded. "That's true. I am . . . or was."

Jonnie took another bite of the chicken.

"I was born and raised in Columbus, Ohio, salt of the earth, and a very down-to-earth town. It is also a very *small* big town where everyone believes in home, family, job, and the importance of Ohio State football teams."

Jonnie listened as he polished off the rest of his chicken.

"I still don't understand how you ended up with Ecology Now!" Jonnie finished the last sip of the chardonnay in his goblet and shifted his weight on the old army blanket.

"I told you that protecting the environment was my main concern. There's no point in making the world a better place to live if it gets too poisoned to live on in the first place. There's no point in having political freedom if people don't have food and shelter. And there's no point in having jobs, or food and shelter today, if the air and water are going to kill you tomorrow."

Jonnie didn't try to argue with her logic. But what was the real value of clean air to a hungry child or pure water to a man trying to support his family after he had lost his job?

"In addition to the government internships, I wanted some experience in the real world. After my sophomore year, I worked as a gofer for a trade association—forest products. That was something else. Before my senior year I took an internship with Ecology Now! I wanted to work there because they hadn't become part of the bureaucratic environmental establishment. They also had a solid program that fits in with eventual postgrad work."

"You really planned things out, didn't you?"

"Sure. If you're going to accomplish something, you need a plan. You also need to decide what price you're willing to pay—and what price you're not willing to pay."

"What price have you paid?" Jonnie asked, looking Veronica in the eyes, somewhat taken aback by her unexpectedly somber tone.

"Besides my career as a Roller Derby star?" Veronica replied, the gleam returning to her eyes. "Anyway, I liked working with the group and took them up on their offer of full-time employment when I graduated. They gave me more of a hands-on operating role than anyone else would straight out of school. There's also enough flexibility and informality so that I'm not working a rigid schedule and have time for other activities on the side."

Nodding, Jonnie fished out a wrapped package from the picnic bag and began to unwrap the slices of ultra-chocolate cake. "Do you have a special field in mind?"

"Not exactly, and I know it's mostly baloney, but you need a doctorate to really get people to listen to you. And I still like time to myself." She glanced at the half-opened cake package. "You do like unwrapping things, don't you?" A smile accompanied the remark.

Jonnie looked up and slid the larger slice of the cake onto the other dessert plate, offering it to Veronica without answering her question.

"I bet as a kid you couldn't wait to unwrap all your birthday presents."

"What do you mean—as a kid? I still can't."

Veronica giggled as the rowers headed back upstream from completing another lap on the river.

"Is everyone in the organization as committed as you are?" Jonnie's tongue flicked chocolate crumbs off his lips.

"Oh, we get all kinds," Veronica replied as she picked up her slice of cake. "We get some good people, and we get some real flakes. Most people are amazed at the collection of zanies that have showed up."

"I bet you get some extremists."

"Like you wouldn't believe. Some of these people think that Edward Abbey was a moderate. They don't realize or just don't care that they're hurting the environment more than helping it."

"It's tough when ideals clash with reality."

"Some of these folks aren't even idealists. They're motivated by hatred, not environmental concern. They just happened to pick up on the environmental theme. There's one group that advocates burning down the forests so they won't be logged. They say that a good environmentalist should never be without rags and gasoline. I mean, what kind of sense does that make?"

"You don't allow people like that in, do you?"

"We can't keep them from coming to public meetings. But Cal keeps them away from everything else. We still get some real oddballs."

"Like who?"

"We had one guy last year who was a T.M.'er. He was a pleasant sort, kind of quiet, but did his work well. One day we were discussing the best way to introduce some legislation controlling pesticide runoff. I don't remember what triggered it, but all of a sudden he announced in a solemn, far-off voice that the Maharishi was the wisest man in the world."

"What did you say?"

"I told him that was okay, that I felt the same way about Jerry Garcia. He didn't talk to me much after that."

Jonnie began laughing.

"Hey, at least Jerry's trying to save the rain forests," Veronica said before joining in the laughter and moving closer to Jonnie. Her arm went around his waist.

Jonnie extended his arm around her, leaned closer to her, and licked a stray crumb from her cheek, almost from her lips.

"I thought you already had your dessert."

"I haven't begun to have dessert," Jonnie whispered in her ear.

"Neither have I."

24

"I'LL SEE IF HE'S IN, Mr. McDarvid," said the nameless woman on the other end of the telephone.

"Thank you." According to the EPA briefing papers, the rat studies, and the risk assessments, chlorohydrobenzilate was a probable human carcinogen. The health arguments were against JAFFE, but—

"Jack?"

"It's me. Just like a bad penny. I had a question for you. Nothing hush-hush, but it's hard to keep on top of everything."

"Will this cost me my wallet or my integrity?"

"Neither . . . I think." McDarvid cleared his throat softly. "Outside of North America, who are the big citrus producers? Besides Israel, I mean."

"Brazil's a great deal bigger than Israel. But, from our point of view, the Israelis are the ones that count."

"Would you be concerned if someone were proposing a regulation that would hit the Israelis pretty hard?"

"Hard to tell. We can't come down very hard on the economic stuff. Technology and financial flows are usually as far as we go. You know that. Who cares if the California citrus growers can't get all they want into Japan? Or if the Israelis have trouble competing with the Brazilians?"

"What about OMB? Backdoor?"

"Send me a package. One of your specials, with all the arguments laid out. Then we'll see."

"Look. I'd like the help, but this has to be on the merits. You don't see it that way, then let it drop. All right?" McDarvid waited.

"You got something bigger on the way?"

"Maybe. That one—well, I need a little more information, but . . . say a couple of weeks?"

"Let me know. Let me know." The line clicked dead.

McDarvid took a deep breath as he put the phone down. He turned in the chair, and his fingers touched the computer keyboard as he studied the graph displayed on the screen.

After he and Jonnie finished the pesticide paper . . . He shook his head. He wasn't looking forward to the trip to Savannah. But you never got a feel for the processes and the real scope of the problem without seeing the plants, and Jonnie understood numbers, not technologies.

Numbers were never enough, especially in Washington. By the time all the official numbers were clear, you'd either won or lost.

25

"MR. CORELLIAN IS HERE."

"My God, is it lunchtime already?"

"It is twelve-fourteen." The lilting laugh carried through the speaker.

"I'll be right there." Esther Saliers finished the seventh page of "A Cross-Correlated Cohort Study of Chlorohydrobenzilate Exposures in Formulation Facilities." With the oversized yellow plastic clip lifted from the ashtray whose only use was to store assorted paper fasteners, she marked her place in the thick study and shoved it to the right side of the blotter.

As she stood, her eyes darted to the picture on the credenza—also of a brown synthetic veneer that had once resembled dark oak. The smile on the teenager's face cast a light of its own into the small office with the single window. Esther smiled back. Keri had not yet received her scholarship notice from the Lao Foundation, but all that counted was that Keri could go to Emory, after all—the first step toward being the doctor she wanted to be.

Esther opened the door and stepped into the common area.

Andrew Corellian, brown paper bag in one hand, briefcase by his feet, sat talking to Renee. Seeing Esther, he stood. "Esther."

"It's good to see you." She nodded toward the door from which she had emerged. "Just go into the office. I have to recover my lunch."

The division chief did not wait to see if the sandy-haired man had followed her directions as she crossed the hallway into the staff bay. She retrieved her salad, contained within a plastic bowl, and the cheesecake. Carrying one in each hand, she nudged the refrigerator door shut with her hip.

He stood by her doorway, still looking like the luxury-car salesman.

"Go on. The office won't bite you."

His grin was almost sheepish, but he stepped inside. After

setting the briefcase on the floor and the brown bag on the corner of the desk, he took the plastic chair closest to the window.

Esther set the whole untouched cheesecake on the desk blotter, and then, rather than sit behind the desk, took the other plastic chair. "I'm glad you could make it."

"So am I. Things worked out fairly well, actually. I looked up an old acquaintance on the way." The executive lifted a sandwich from the bag, followed by the plastic container. "Wish they didn't pack these in plastic, but fruit salad in paper just doesn't make it."

Esther smiled. "You worry about disposable plastic salad bowls?"

Corellian set the bottle of natural lime soda on the desk. "I worry about anything that doesn't degrade in five hundred years." He looked at her bowl. "What's that?"

"A combination of cottage cheese, lettuce, cucumbers, tomatoes, and mild salsa. It's tangy enough that I don't miss the calories I shouldn't have, and allows me peace of mind when I eat things like cheesecake."

He took a bite of the roast beef sandwich, then looked at the picture on the credenza. "She's pretty."

Esther swallowed a forkful of salad. "She's also very determined. I took your advice, by the way. I haven't said a word. It ought to be her news."

"That makes it more exciting," agreed the sandy-haired man. He took another measured bite from the roast beef and rye before continuing. "But you promised to explain exactly what you do. The division deals with health effects . . ."

"It's more complex . . ." Esther stopped. "Why am I apologizing? It's important, and you asked. It's just that outside of EPA . . . I mean, DEP . . ."

"I understand."

"There are trace elements in everything, and knowing what levels are necessary, what levels are harmful, and the pathways of contamination all factor into health effects. With pesticides it can get even more complicated. Take Alar, for example. Well, that's a bad example because we never should have registered it. Chlorohydrobenzilate is a better example. It's an insecticide—"

"Chlorohydro—what?" Corellian looked blank.

"It's used against fruit flies—generally on oranges. But that's the point. Do you measure the residue level in pulp or in the rind?"

"Well, people eat the pulp, but what about oranges used for juice?"

"Even more farfetched"—Esther bobbed her head—"do you measure residue traces in the rind for those few uses—like candied orange rinds or the people who grate it up and put it in cake frostings or desserts or muffins?"

"Oh . . ."

"Exactly! Which residue level is more accurate? We can't exactly publish a finding which says that the risk is ten to the minus fourth if you eat the rind, but only ten to the minus seventh if you drink orange juice. Which number do you recommend for the risk assessment?"

"Hmmmm . . ." Corellian sipped the unnaturally carbonated natural lime soda, still holding the sandwich in his right hand.

"With fruits, it's even worse. Children eat a higher proportion of fruit, and they have a lower body weight and higher metabolism. Do you calculate the risk assessment and projected health impacts on children? At what age? If you pick the most sensitive segment of the population for each food, it's likely to be different in differing classes. I mean, how many children eat artichokes or eggplant? And some pesticides are used on a range of plants." Esther stopped and took a sip from her glass of water.

Corellian shook his head. "I knew it was complex, but I hadn't really thought the details. You want to protect people's health. Where do you start?"

"If I don't eat a few more bites of this salad, I'll get so wound up that I won't eat, and then my blood sugar will crash at three, and I'll end up looking for sweets or heading home like a grouch. After . . . Anyway, neither Keri nor I need that." She lifted a forkful of cottage cheese.

"It would seem that you'd want to set a safe level, one with a solid margin for error. That's what our quality-control engineers are always talking about, engineering to avoid failures. Can't you do that here?" Corellian held up a hand. "Sorry. Don't answer that until you finish at least three full bites of salad." He folded the paper that had held his sandwich into a small package and replaced it in the sack, then pried open the plastic fruit salad container and prodded the contents with his plastic spoon. "After all you said, can I eat this?"

Esther managed to swallow another bite of salad despite the half-cough, half-choke. "For you and me, it's not a problem. The ones we have to worry about are the hyperallergenics and children. Even the worst industry apologists are right when they push for looser standards based on average people. Looser standards won't affect most people—just a few hundred or a few thousand children out of two hundred fifty million Americans. Just a little more risk of cancer for less than two tenths of one percent of the population. Put that way, it doesn't sound so bad. But what if it's your child?"

"I wouldn't like it. In fact, when you put it that way, I don't like it at all."

Esther put the top back on the salad bowl and set it on the corner of the desk. "In a way, that's what we try to deal with. What are the health effects on which parts of the exposed population and how do we set tolerances and allowable residue levels to provide adequate protection?"

Corellian forced the plastic top back on the disposable plastic salad bowl. His eyes strayed toward the covered dish on the desk blotter. "The cheesecake looks better and better."

"I'll cut you a piece before I start to make your eyes glaze over with descriptions of dose-response curves."

Corellian nodded amiably, folding his brown bag and easing it quietly into the industrial gray trash container beside the desk.

"Turned out almost perfect this time. I did promise Keri I'd bring her home at least a piece, and Renee deserves one for putting up with a very cranky boss these past months."

26

"PLEASE REMAIN IN YOUR SEATS until the aircraft has come to a complete halt at the gate."

From his aisle seat McDarvid could see the lights of National Airport through the window to his right, across an empty seat and past the thin black man in the leather jacket who had snored most of the way from Savannah. The 737 turned off the taxiway and onto the apron in front of the north terminal.

"Please remain in your seats," repeated the flight attendant.

The consultant looked at his battered brown leather attaché case, bulging with the materials from JAFFE's Georgia metals plant, then checked his watch. Six forty-three. With luck, he might be home within an hour. He'd have to take the Metro—no way would a cab get him home more quickly in rush-hour traffic. He would have preferred to drive to the airport, but with the endless reconstruction, there was never anywhere to park.

Not likely he would get home in time for the PTA meeting. Not at all, but then, all they ever did was talk about how the teachers had to be more accountable. That meant more paperwork for the teachers, not more or better teaching. Sometimes he wondered if the whole country had lost its mind.

As the plane eased to a stop, McDarvid flicked off the seat belt. His head ached, and his mouth tasted like aircraft fuel.

"So why do you travel?" he muttered to himself. But there wasn't a good answer. Even the few trips that he took were too much. It played hell with Allyson's schedule, Mrs. Hughes, and with the kids.

Mrs. Hughes would glare at him, and David would ignore him until tomorrow. Elizabeth . . . well, Elizabeth was Elizabeth.

"The Captain has turned off the signs, and you may move about the cabin." Most of the passengers were already unbelted and rummaging for assorted cases, coats, and luggage.

McDarvid had the attaché case and the overnight bag sitting on the seat, ready for the shuffle that would lead him through the jetway and out into a too-warm October night.

The thin black man in the dark leather jacket yawned and stretched, revealing a series of heavy gold chains around his neck.

McDarvid nodded. Probably drug money. Was his immediate conclusion that prejudiced? Somehow he doubted it. He swung his overnight bag and briefcase into the aisle and walked toward the front of the plane.

"Good night, sir."

"Good night," he replied automatically, shifting his grip on the overnight bag as he crossed onto the jetway. Damp warm air, mixed with jet fuel, seeped into his nostrils.

As always, the terminal was crowded, mostly with returning business types, although he dodged around a woman with a stroller and two toddlers hanging on to her raincoat. One wore a harness linked to her wrist.

McDarvid smiled. They could have used a harness for David on more than one occasion.

Outside the north terminal, he glanced upward through the lights. Although it was cloudy and damp, no rain was falling. He turned south, heading toward the Metro.

His forehead was damp by the time he was ready to cross the exit road to the station, and he paused, waiting for the crossing light. He stood alone in the twilight.

"Guess everyone else is taking cabs."

The light changed, and McDarvid stepped forward.

Whhhssss . . .

With a lurch, he staggered back, nearly tumbling to the pavement in his escape from the dark car that had not bothered to heed the light.

"Damned diplomats," he mumbled, straightening up. He hadn't seen all the plate as the vehicle had rushed past, just the red and white and blue, and the initials—something like FC-021. Or had it been FC-012?

He shook his head and looked again, then stumbled across the road just before the light changed.

At least, a yellow line train was waiting as he marched onto the platform. The blue line train would have taken at least another ten minutes. The trip to Gallery Place was easy enough, the car nearly empty, and he only waited four minutes for the red line train to Friendship Heights.

The hard part was the walk home. While his legs were fine, his forehead was dripping by the time he reached the front steps. He still sweated like a pig with any exercise.

"Good evening, Mr. McDarvid. You had a long trip?" Mrs. Hughes had on the brown coat, handbag in hand, by the time he opened the door and struggled through.

"Too long, Mrs. Hughes. Any trip is too long." He dropped the hanging bag, set down the case, and fumbled for his wallet.

He handed her the extra five dollars for the overtime. "Any problems?"

"No, Mr. McDarvid. I will see you on Thursday."

"Father, is that you?"

"Yeah, the one and only. Come and give me a hug. It's been a long couple of days."

"Father . . ."

"Elizabeth . . ."

But she still gave him the hug.

27

"HOW WAS THE BATTERY PLANT?" asked Jonnie.

"It was a battery plant." McDarvid put the attaché case on his desk and thumbed one lock, then the other, stacking the materials, including the monitoring data, in piles.

"Find anything new?"

"You always find out something new when you visit a plant." McDarvid slid the empty case into the space between the desk and the wall, then nudged the wastebasket back into place. He looked over the stacks of papers he had left. "Never goes away."

"You look beat."

"I am. I don't like traveling. When I got home, Allyson had already left for the PTA meeting—and wasn't real thrilled about my not being there. We both hate it. Don't ask me why we go. I took the Metro home because there's no parking at National, and I have trouble justifying twenty-dollar cab rides to myself. Nearly got plowed by some damned diplomat—"

"Local hazard. You okay?"

"Fine. Just a pain after a long day. You know where you cross the exit road to get to the Metro station? When the light changed, I started to cross, but this idiot doesn't even stop."

"What country was he from?"

"How the hell would I know? The tags said FC something or other."

"Russia."

McDarvid glanced up from the stack of papers he was rearranging. "How do you know?"

Jonnie chuckled. "It's a standing joke. The State Department assigned the letter codes for each country. The idea was to assist FBI surveillance, but the codes were supposed to be a secret so that the local nuts didn't slash the tires of their favorite targets. The 'FC' is Russian because some wit in the State Department basement who assigned the codes decided that the Russians were 'fuckin' communists.' So . . . FC."

"You're shitting me."

Jonnie shook his head. "Nah. Whether the story's true or not, FC does mean Soviet or Russian or whatever they're calling themselves this week."

McDarvid sighed. "Anyway, after escaping that, and riding the Metro, it was so hot I was sweating like a pig by the time I walked from Friendship Heights home. It was a long night . . . What about you?"

"We bachelors don't have such logistical problems. I finished the quant stuff on chlorohydrobenzilate. You were right. DEP did screw up all the numbers—by about four orders of magnitude on the risk extrapolations."

"Assumptions?"

Jonnie nodded.

"That won't help much. They'll just explain that they're using the most conservative assumptions to protect public health. What about benefits?"

"It's all there." Jonnie pointed to the folder on the corner of the desk. "I also drafted a rough piece for the pesticide policy paper. It's in your pesticide subdirectory on the network."

"At least we can get that out." McDarvid dropped into his chair. "Then we can start on the metals papers." He gestured at Jonnie. "You know, the whole metals initiative doesn't make any sense."

"What do you mean—no sense?"

"They rebuilt the whole plant five years ago. Automated it, built separate clean rooms for the cadmium coating, trimming. They use positive pressure systems everywhere. It's a damned

modern facility. It cost almost a hundred million to rebuild."
McDarvid waited.

Jonnie frowned.

"Yeah. A hundred million for a facility that nets maybe five
million. When the twenty-microgram standard for cadmium
came down six, seven years ago, they had to rebuild. They
thought that a really automated facility would take on the Japanese plants in Mexico and Korea and avoid import tariffs and
quotas. So they gambled. The control systems let them comply
with the OSHA regs and stay in the business. But the Japanese
put even more capital into plants that were newer than JAFFE's
to begin with. And they put most of their money into process
engineering, not environmental controls. They didn't have to
meet the twenty standard. So JAFFE's barely hanging in after
spending a hundred million. Now there's a second round of
worker protection regulations, and they don't want to spend
another hundred million. Of course, the Japanese are sitting
pretty.

"Hell, the JAFFE engineers sweated blood to design for
twenty micrograms, and we're talking something forty times
lower."

"Do you think OSHA really wants that?"

"No. But even if they'll settle for just one microgram, that's
still a twentyfold reduction for a plant that took nearly a hundred million to get to twenty. And the offshore competition is at
forty, or higher."

"So unless we get a pretty big change, they shut down," Jonnie
concluded.

"I'd say so. Devenant didn't quite say that, but his treasurer's
books say so. The figures are here." He touched one of the piles
of paper.

"What about the other U.S. companies?"

"They're in worse shape, from what I can figure."

"Aren't they complaining?"

"Sure. To the trade associations and to Congress, and they've
all hired lawyers—none of which will do them any good."

"You're always so positive."

"Right, just good old cheerful Jack." He turned in the chair,
neither looking at Jonnie nor out the window. "Well, all we can

do is what we can." He paused. "And does that sound stupid." Then he stood, picking up a sheaf of paper. "Here are the cost numbers on cadmium. The beryllium numbers are coming from California. Do what you can."

"How soon?"

McDarvid shrugged. "As soon as you can without killing yourself."

28

"WHAT IS THAT?" asked Allyson, standing behind McDarvid's shoulder.

"What?"

"That cover. It looks like a satellite with an X through it."

"Good. That's what it's supposed to look like." McDarvid could tell she was frowning, perhaps because she had breezed through three years of calculus and two years of physics, plus biology, physiology, and everything else required for medical school. All McDarvid had managed had been Amherst's distributional requirements—two semesters of astronomy and two semesters of college calculus—and flight school, courtesy of the U.S. Navy.

"How much are you stretching things this time? What does a satellite have to do with environmental regulations?"

McDarvid turned. Usually regulatory work bored the hell out of his wife, the good Dr. Newsome. "A whole lot, in this case. It's all about power. Real power, not the political kind. Satellites need power, and half of their power systems are comprised of batteries."

"Jack, they use solar cells to get power."

"And where do they store that power? For when they're in the earth's shadow? Or for other uses."

"Other uses?"

"Burst communications and SDI," mumbled McDarvid.

"The space lasers . . . oh."

"Right. Lasers work on bursts of power."

"Now you've sold out to the weapons lobby?"

McDarvid flushed. "Do you know how many lives the weather satellites have saved? Or why transatlantic telephone calls no longer cost ten bucks a minute?"

"What do satellites have to do with your work?" Allyson's voice remained calm, nearly clinical.

"The metals involved. Most commercial satellites use nickel-cadmium rechargeable batteries. Chrome and beryllium are also used in key fabricated elements. This metals initiative by OSHA and DEP would close down most U.S. battery facilities and shift most beryllium fabrication offshore. Chrome's bad enough already, since you can only get it from the Russians or about three places in Africa, one of which is South Africa."

"What about the health side?"

McDarvid shrugged. "That's the strange thing. They want to set the level at a half microgram per cubic meter or a half part per million."

"Oh . . ."

"Yeah. It doesn't make sense. The current cadmium standard is around twenty micrograms. That's roughly the same as—"

"Jack, I was using micrograms before you—"

"Sorry. I sometimes forget. I have to explain to so many people."

"That's all right." Her long strong fingers squeezed his shoulder.

He just wanted to lean back and enjoy the sensation.

"If it's not the defense contractors, who's the client?" she asked after a moment, her fingers leaving his shoulders.

He could tell she was losing interest. "No one you've probably ever heard of. A French outfit called JAFFE."

"JAFFE? The big pharmaceutical and chemicals firm?"

"You've heard of them?"

"Be careful, Jack."

"What do you mean?"

"Just be careful. They're the biggest in the world, or close to it. They didn't like some research one of my professors at Harvard published. So they made his research life cease to exist for a decade." She half turned from him and looked into the darkness outside the study windows. "At least they hired you."

McDarvid bit his tongue. Allyson had said what she was going to say. He reached down and turned off the desk light, then stepped up behind her, letting his arms go around her waist, letting his head rest beside hers.

They stood in the dimness for a long time.

29

HE STUDIED THE HORIZON, squinting even through the darkness of the helmet visor. Far beneath his wings glittered the patchwork of white, broken only by an occasional highway and rail line. Always the winter—the ever-present winter. He let his fingers ease back on the throttle and edge the nose down.

Even through the helmet and the tightly fitting ear pads, the engines whined deep into his skull.

His eyes flicked from outside the cockpit to the gauges, part of the long-established scan. He checked the single small radar screen, then swallowed as a blip appeared at two o'clock—a red dot that pulsed intermittently. He squinted again toward the setting sun, trying to make out the bogey. Nothing. He flicked across the U.S. tactical frequencies.

"Klondike, interrogative lock-on. Interrogative lock-on."

"Negative. That's negative."

Behind the face shield, the pilot frowned, his fingers straying toward the burner light-offs.

"Satcom link down. Link down," the words scratched into the pilot's earphones. Even the reflections off the bare metal and the heavy rivets on the swept wings seemed directed at him, as though designed to blind him.

"Bogey bearing two-ten. Negative lock-on."

At the bearing information, his eyes flicked back to the instruments as the light above the screen flickered. He ignored the transmission, pulling the gees so hard that his vision flashed red in the turn, the stick now nearly into his gut. But the blinking of the light above the screen increased as the other pilot neared missile lock-on.

Still . . . he could see nothing to the west, nothing at all. No dark points against the sun, nor against the winter white below. Nothing except the radar beam from the unseen aircraft that indicated he could be dead.

The fuel needle showed the afterburners' thirst—less than half an hour left.

The red-tinged sun hung on the horizon, and a black dot that resolved into two dots appeared at the edge of the corona.

The red dot pulsed even brighter on the screen, and a host of red sparks showered from it.

"Shit . . ."

He jammed the stick forward, then into the turn, sucking his guts in at the gee force.

Into the turn back toward the field, he glanced at the radar screen, confirming two bogeys on his tail.

The lock-on light flashed a last time, before blaring red across the panel. The afterburners roared in his ears, but the red sparks on the screen grew larger, larger . . .

Red . . . red . . . *red!*

McDarvid bolted upright in his bed, feeling the pounding of his heart. Quietly, he eased the covers aside and swung his feet onto the carpet, trying to breathe easily. His forehead was coated in sweat.

He took a deep breath, then another.

The nightmare had been so damned real, just as though he had been back at the controls, as though no time had passed.

After a moment, he stood up and walked to the end of the bed, looking at his wife. The faint illumination from the streetlight showed her eyes were closed and her breathing regular.

With a last glance over his shoulder, he tiptoed out the bedroom door and down the dark stairs to the kitchen, his barefoot steps as soft as he could make them.

Inside the freezer was a box of Popsicles. He took out one and bit off the tip, chewing the lime ice into fragments. The cool air from the open freezer brushed his arm. After several more bites, he pulled the paper back over the uneaten portion and tucked the half-consumed Popsicle behind the ground beef.

Then he edged the freezer door shut and eased his steps back upstairs.

He stopped and peered into Kirsten's room. The littlest redhead lay there almost in a heap on top of her white bear, red hair spilling across bear and pillow, both illuminated by the nightlight next to her bedside table. McDarvid watched her breathe for a while, swallowed, and took the carpeted stairs up to the third floor.

He grinned at the pool of light seeping from under Elizabeth's door. Opening the door as silently as he could, he crossed the narrow room to the canopied bed, where he eased the book from under her cheek, slipped a marker in it, and set it next to the three others on her desk. He kissed her cheek.

"Mmmm . . ."

"It's all right," he whispered, patting her back. He left the light on.

In the other third-floor room, nearly pitch-dark except for the glow from the streetlight, David lay on his side.

McDarvid patted his shoulder. "Hang tough, old man."

Back in his own room, he slipped into his side of the queen-sized bed.

Allyson's breathing was regular, with the faint hint of a snore from her partly open mouth, he supposed.

He took another deep breath as he pulled the covers up, hoping the nightmare didn't recur too soon.

30

JONNIE WAITED WHILE THE TELEPHONE RANG, hoping McDarvid was home.

"I got a private label 386 for around two thousand. The whole package came to twenty-six."

"Great. Can you bring it—not yet, Elizabeth. Not yet."

"What was that?" Jonnie asked.

"I was telling Elizabeth that we don't have a computer yet."

"You will shortly. You going to be home?"

"Hell, yes. Allyson's at a professional seminar this weekend. In Boston. I'm into home repairs, like recementing the banister that David used as a vaulting bar. I'll be here for a while."

"I'll bring a couple of disks with games, too."

"You're all heart."

Jonnie shook his head. He wondered what it was like having children, having to plan every activity for weeks in advance, having to get baby-sitters, or always cleaning or fixing things. Then again, maybe McDarvid had a nanny or an *au pair*. Jack almost never talked about his family, except for how Elizabeth drove him nuts.

With a quick headshake, Jonnie carried the software case and tool kit to the elevator. On the way down to the garage, he stopped to check the mail. Nothing but bills, not even a Thanksgiving card, not that he would ever have sent one, not unless Hallmark put him on the payroll. He stepped back from his box and turned.

A man wearing a plain gray suit stood on the other side of the lobby. He looked back at Jonnie, meeting his eyes. Jonnie did not frown, but wanted to. With an earplug and slightly shorter hair, the man could have passed for Secret Service. Who else wore gray suits on Saturdays? Except maybe Jack, and, well, Jack was . . . Jack.

Ignoring the man in the gray suit, Jonnie turned his steps toward the doorway to the garage stairs. The GTO started on the second attempt and didn't even stall in the loading zone outside CompUtopia, the computer store that occupied the space that had once been a topless bar.

Everything was stacked on the counter, actually waiting. The salesman loaded the box and monitor on a dolly. Jonnie carried the color card, after checking the box to make sure it was the right card.

"The black . . . car? It runs?"

"Most of the time," Jonnie admitted as he opened the large trunk.

Thirty minutes later, he was unloading boxes in Jack's driveway.

McDarvid already had a computer stand waiting. Jonnie nodded. Somehow, that fit, too. The hardware was the easy part, easier than installing the software.

"Thanks again, Jonnie," McDarvid said as he followed the installation instructions for the spreadsheet program. "Do I really need this?"

"Probably not, but the firm bought it. So use it." Jonnie glanced around the room. Wide, nearly floor-length windows on the south side, with built-in bookcases on one of the short side walls and on each side of the back-wall doorway. The desk was on the other short wall, under another window. Two books, side by side at eye level and almost within reaching distance of the desk, caught Jonnie's eye.

"I hope this wasn't too much trouble."

Jonnie stepped over to the bookcase. "No trouble at all, especially if we need to free-lance . . . or set up our own office."

"Yeah . . ." McDarvid paused.

"Jack, what are these?"

"What?"

"These look like Russian, Cyrillic characters."

"Those? Oh . . . Russian dictionaries."

"Didn't know you spoke Russian."

"I don't. Had to use them when I did some projects back a while using Russian economic data." McDarvid entered another set of commands before continuing. "Have any trouble getting this together?"

"No. Except there was this guy in a cheap gray suit. He was hanging around the apartment lobby. I swear he was waiting for me, but then he disappeared."

McDarvid frowned. "Old guy or a young guy?"

"Looked like a shaggy-haired Secret Service agent. You know what I mean? Like he could have one of those plugs in his ears, and a dinky gold crest on his lapel?" Jonnie pulled another set of disks from his case. "Here's the rest of what we have to put on your system."

"Did you ever see the guy before?"

"Nah . . . just seemed odd."

McDarvid nodded thoughtfully. "Sometimes we imagine too much."

"You don't sound convinced."

"I'm not. A guy who looked like your man in gray was at Larry's funeral. Then I saw him again at Woodies—looked like he was following me and the kids. Scared the hell out of me. Haven't seen him since then."

"Father? Is this the new computer?"

Jonnie looked at McDarvid. McDarvid looked at his daughter. "Yes, but it's not ready yet."

"Will you have the latest version of WordPerfect?"

"Yes."

"Good." Elizabeth looked at the screen, then picked a book off the shelf to McDarvid's left. "Would you let me know when the computer is available for my use?"

"Never," muttered McDarvid.

"You said?" Jonnie grinned.

McDarvid shook his head. "It's hell when they're smarter than you are, or think they are." He paused, rubbing his chin with his thumb. "I still wonder about the guy in gray."

"So do I. But what can we do about it?"

"Damned if I know—except keep watching. We'll both end up paranoid."

"We'll also be here all night if you don't keep pushing disks," reminded Jonnie.

31

OUTSIDE, THE NOVEMBER RAIN PELTED AGAINST THE WINDOW, blurring into the twilight. McDarvid touched the buttons on the telephone.

"You have reached a nonworking federal number."

He touched three digits.

"Hello."

"Jack McDarvid for Eric."

"Would you wait a moment, Mr. McDarvid?"

McDarvid leaned back in the chair, glancing at the lights of the building across Nineteenth Street, glittering through the downpour.

"Hello. Jack?"

"None other."

"We thought you might call after your packages arrived."

"Why didn't you call me?"

"Your presentation was largely self-explanatory."

"How can I talk to someone about the first package?" McDarvid asked.

"You can't."

"Why not?"

"Because they don't want to talk to you. Citrus isn't a problem. It won't hurt the Israelis that much, and as for the Brazilians . . ." The silence indicated his opinion of the Brazilians. "Besides, on this one, JAFFE can take care of itself."

"I never mentioned the client."

The voice was silent.

"What about the economic impacts?"

"They're not insurmountable. Not on the first package."

"Thanks."

"You're as brazen as ever, Jack. Good thing you found your calling elsewhere. We do miss your intuition."

McDarvid smiled wryly. "I appreciate the flattery."

"We recognize talent."

"What about the second one?"

"We just got that one yesterday."

"You knew everything about the first one, apparently before you got it."

"That was different. Strictly economic and trade-related."

McDarvid nodded to himself. "I'll check back later on the second package. There's more there. You just might consider some follow-up."

"I'll look forward to your call. Give us a week. You might be onto something—even if you are a hopeless paranoid."

"Just because I'm paranoid doesn't mean that there's not someone out to get me."

"Violence isn't professional, Jack. It's also messy. And usually it doesn't work."

"People die."

"And the ideas and structures hum along just the same as before."

"Yeah. I know. Just like law firms. You've told me."

"But did you listen?" The voice paused. "Talk to you later."

McDarvid hung up the phone. He wondered why they'd never changed the number or the codes. Probably more than a dozen outsiders knew it by now, if not more. Then again, why bother? All the in calls were screened and traced, which might prove useful.

He shook his head. Why they acted the way they did still remained a mystery to him.

Through the pelting rain that was not quite ice, the lights glittered from across Nineteenth Street.

32

THE PLASTIC COVERS OF THE TWO BOUND POLICY PAPERS flashed in the sunlight from the window behind McDarvid. Two stacks of fifty copies each sat on the credenza. He picked up the thicker policy paper.

"The Metals Initiative—What Price for Illusory Environmental Protection?" Under the title were two black-and-white illustrations. On the left was a satellite slashed in half by an X. On the right was a bar graph illustrating plant closures.

"Looks nice," McDarvid mused. "We were right to do this one just in black and white. Looks more serious this way."

"Who'll pay any attention?" Jonnie Black sat in the single client chair. "You know OSHA and DEP don't care about price."

McDarvid smiled softly. "OSHA and DEP don't make the final decision—not if that decision impacts national security."

"You really think we can sell the idea that one health and environmental regulation will lead to the fall of the great American democracy?"

"Hell, no. All we're selling is that one environmental and health regulation—which won't improve worker health—will destroy U.S. production of all satellite power systems, will probably require the fabrication of critical parts of space lasers in France or Japan, and will require that all military communications and aircraft batteries be produced in third-world countries.

"And if they tighten the lead standard further . . ."

"Jack, I know all that. I did the financial analysis. We know all that could happen. But does anybody care? Anybody who can do something useful?"

"Who knows? The OSHA analysis is so bad, they don't even have the right number of affected employees. The subcontractor they hired to do the analysis—Jackass, Incorporated, or whatever they're called—did a criminally bad job. Half the numbers in their cost model are listed as 'To Be Determined.' And that's in the so-called final report. That's the point of our papers." McDarvid shook his head. "Yeah. I know. No one's going to read the papers unless . . ."

"Unless what?"

"We do our usual magic show and persuade them to." McDarvid set the economic paper back on the desk and picked up the health analysis: "The Metals Initiative—No Real Health Benefits?"

The second paper's cover also showed two black-and-white illustrations, on the left a series of worker figures and on the right a bar graph.

"What's the first trick in the magic show?" asked Jonnie.

"We distribute the papers and try for congressional and media attention. The space angle might work for Science, Space, and Technology Committee—"

"But will they do anything?"

McDarvid pondered. Would Renni Fowler really look into the issue? Especially if it might impact her boyfriend's engineering firm? Mike Alroy was one bright engineer. Finally, he looked up. "I don't know. They haven't so far, but it's too good an angle not to try . . . one way or another."

"Standard distribution?" asked Jonnie.

"Not quite. First, we have to get copies into both the DEP and OSHA official dockets. Then, this time, we'll send cover letters and the reports to the heads of the policy offices, noting that the reports have been submitted to the docket."

"You don't trust the docket office?"

"I don't trust anyone. Sometimes, I don't even trust me." McDarvid did not look at Jonnie, instead set the paper down. "Besides the Office of Management and Budget and that crew at Energy . . ."

"I assume you're targeting Defense." Jonnie's face was blank.

"Ohhhh, you can do better than that." McDarvid grimaced at the pun. "Anyway, you put together the list for DOD, NASA, and the President's Space Council."

"What about the black side? They certainly wouldn't want to depend on offshore supplies for their satellites' power systems."

"I might know someone," McDarvid said slowly. "Whether they would do anything is another question."

"You can only try."

"That's true." McDarvid looked out into the late afternoon glare, squinted, and stood, letting down the blinds to cut the glare. "I only have to persuade half the agencies in Washington to read them."

"What about OMB?"

"That's the easy one. They've been looking for a good procedural reason to zap both DEP and OSHA for a long time." He nodded toward the economic analysis. "This shows they ignored the Executive Order on costs. There's not one word on the economic impacts there. Not one."

"So . . . their numbers are always low. When they even have numbers."

McDarvid grinned. "The Executive Order is written funny. 12291 says that they have to estimate costs. They can be wrong. And they usually are. Each year they've gotten sloppier, but this time it looks like the contractor ran out of money or fell asleep halfway through. So the cost-analysis chapter doesn't have any costs in it—just formulas for calculating them. OMB can roast them without taking a hit."

Jonnie grinned back. "How do you know?"

"Because . . ."

"You already talked to someone?"

McDarvid nodded. Then he looked down at the desk. "That was the easy part." He glanced back at Jonnie. "Especially compared to the simple things—like having a job next year."

"That is a problem."

"So we need to start our education efforts." He paused. "Let's not forget to send some copies to the environmental groups."

"Why? Won't that just get them mad earlier?"

"They'll just call them industry apologies. Besides, if they yell too much, they'll upset the science fiction and space supporters in their own membership," McDarvid speculated. "Send them to the head of each outfit. Cal what's-his-name with the ecology bunch. Dick over at—"

"I get the picture." Jonnie shook his head. "You're the boss."

"I'm not the boss. Heidlinger is. At least, that's what he tells us."

33

AFTER HANDING A HEAVY ENVELOPE TO THE RECEPTIONIST, the messenger pulled out his radio and mumbled something into it, listened for a moment, then left.

The red-haired attorney, stroking his full beard, did not wait until the messenger was even out the door before moving toward the front desk. He cleared his throat as he crossed the room.

"What is it?" he asked the receptionist as he reached for the package.

"It's for Cal." She kept the thick nine-by-twelve manila envelope.

The attorney twisted his head to view the label. "Hmmmm . . . From Ames, Heidlinger, and Partello. They do a lot of environmental work."

"Stop hanging around as if you want me to open it on the spot, Ray. If it's legal, you'll get it, anyway."

Ray Thomas did not move.

Finally, the receptionist picked up a letter opener and carefully slit the end of the heavy envelope. From the envelope she extracted two plastic-covered bound documents and a letter with two attachments.

Thomas looked over her shoulder as she laid the papers down. The letter was addressed to the Assistant Secretary for Policy, Planning, and Evaluation at the U.S. Department of Environmental Protection. He glanced to the bottom of the page. "J. B. McDarvid, III" was typed below a scrawled signature.

"Do you mind, Ray?"

"Apologies for industry pollution . . ."

"After Cal sees them." The receptionist's voice was firm.

"Let me just skim the cover letter here. That way, I can look into the background . . ."

"I'll be happy to make you a copy after Cal sees it."

The attorney finished skimming the one-page cover letter over her shoulder before responding. "I'd like a copy."

"Fine. After Cal sees it."

"How about now?"

"Ray, you're not the only one who works here."

The attorney turned and walked back toward his desk. Why were such obviously industry-biased studies being sent to Cal? What he had glimpsed of the cover letter was bad enough— implying that environmental cleanup would destroy the space effort, including cleaner space manufacturing.

Thomas shook his head. Space! As if there weren't too much to do already on earth. Still, the letters were being sent to the Policy Office, and some of the political types worried about economics and future technology.

He picked up the telephone and punched in a number.

"Standards and Regulations."

"This is Ray Thomas. I'd like to speak to Jerry."

"I'm sorry, Mr. Thomas. Mr. Killorin is at a meeting. Can he call you back?"

"Yes, please. The number is . . ." Thomas hoped that Jerry wouldn't be too long getting back to him. The industry types were getting sneakier and sneakier.

34

SITTING ON THE EDGE OF THE BED, wearing just the black bottoms of his shorty pajamas, McDarvid looked toward the closet, wondering idly whether he should wear the gray or the blue pinstripe the next day. Probably the blue.

"Jack?" Allyson came out of the bathroom, wearing the sheer green nightgown.

He smiled in spite of his preoccupation.

"Do you want to talk about it?"

"Huh?"

"You've been worried about something for months. You won't talk about it, and it's not just Larry Partello's death. And you're having nightmares again, like when you were flying."

He eyed the still-lush figure under the sheer green. "I'm not thinking about that right now."

The redhead who was his wife smiled softly. "I am." She sat down cross-legged at the end of the bed.

McDarvid failed to raise his eyes to her face at first. "You sure?"

She nodded.

Brrrinngg . . .

He grabbed the telephone.

"No one there?" Allyson asked.

"Yeah. The phantom again. Benefits of divestiture and computerized telephone switching systems." He replaced the phone.

"Jack, don't change the subject."

"I don't know if I'm paranoid, or if I'm right, or both, or neither." His eyes met hers, then looked away. "Jonnie pointed it out first. How likely was it that Larry would be shot a block from the Capitol? Through the heart with a single shot? When it was nearly dark? He was nervous about the JAFFE account. The more I look into it, the more strange things there are."

"Tell me some of these strange occurrences." Allyson's voice was neutral, the tone of the physician reserving judgment.

McDarvid, giving up on any quick change of subject, swung his feet onto the bed and leaned back against the headboard. "That's the hard thing. It's all so nebulous. I see a man in a gray suit who looks like a Secret Service agent at Larry's funeral. Then I see him again at Woodies when I'm shopping with the kids. The account that Larry was nervous about is this metals initiative pushed by Environment and OSHA—but all the metals are already heavily regulated. Someone wants to regulate all of them a whole lot more than necessary. And all of them have defense implications. But no one at Defense wants to talk about it. No one at Environment wants to explain it. The Congress doesn't want to look into it. Hell, the affected subcommittees have ignored basic industry strangulation for nearly two decades." He shook his head. "I feel stupid even talking about it."

He looked at Allyson. She wasn't smiling, exactly, but she nodded for him to go on.

"It just doesn't feel right. I mean, as a country, we couldn't build battleships anymore even if we wanted to. We can't mass-produce combat electronics in a hurry—no matter what the DOD contractors say." He pursed his lips. "Then I worry about the job. Heidlinger keeps sermonizing about how it's not a con-sulting firm, but a law firm. Then that weekend while you were at the seminar, Jonnie comes over with the computer—"

"Elizabeth loves it."

"Yeah, I know. She requested that I inform her when the system was available for her use." McDarvid shook his head. "Anyway, Jonnie mentions in passing how this guy in a gray suit watched him leave his apartment. A cheap gray suit—on a Satur-day, for Christ's sake. And I didn't tell him about the guy in gray beforehand."

"Are you sure?"

He nodded. "I just thought it was my imagination. So I didn't tell anyone, either you or Jonnie. I mean, how many men wear plain gray suits in Washington? And to think one of them was following me? That's a sign of paranoia." He looked toward her before continuing. "Do I just feel this way because I don't want to be out of a job? Or because I don't want to throw the burden on you?" He shrugged. "It's so hard to sort it all out. And it all seems stupid, compared to your problems.

"So there's a regulation that's not right. Who does it affect, besides a big corporation? They'll pay, one way or another. So we can't produce as many weapons as quickly? Or some weapons at all? Are we really going to use them? But when you talk about dealing with battered children, or children getting leukemia, or even strep—that seems more important." He took a deep breath. "Sometimes, I even wonder . . . After all, some of the people I work for aren't good citizens. They don't always protect their employees or the environment. Guess that's what comes of marrying a doctor."

"I'm sorry you've been carrying all that around."

"Didn't want to bother you."

"We don't talk enough anymore," Allyson added, shifting her weight forward.

"Seems like we never have any time. If I'm not working late, you are. And Elizabeth never sleeps. To bed late and up early. 'Are you otherwise engaged, Father?'"

Allyson grinned at his mimicry. "Well . . . would you like to be otherwise engaged?"

McDarvid grinned back, sitting up and taking a deliberate leer at Allyson's chest.

"How about a kiss, Mr. McDarvid?"

"Yes, Doctor."

35

JONNIE TAPPED LIGHTLY on McDarvid's almost closed door. After a few seconds, McDarvid turned from the computer. Jonnie closed the door, set down his briefcase, an envelope of some sort on top of it, and sat down.

"You remember that, in addition to studying the regulatory dockets, I decided to do a little checking up on our friends?"

"Right. JAFFE."

"I was kind of curious about the folks who hired us. So for the past week I've been calling a few friends and acquaintances in New York and a couple of other places." A purple glow filled the small office as the end of the sunset cut through the fluorescent lighting.

"Other places?"

"London, Singapore . . ." Jonnie's voice trailed off. "I put it all, except for the domestic calls, on my own credit card. Our dear employer won't find out, and I won't notice a few extra calls. Anyway, I found out a few interesting things about our client." Jonnie rocked back on the chair's rear legs until the back of his head rested on the wall. "JAFFE's sort of a public company. They're traded on the Paris bourse, but a controlling—if minority—bloc of stock is still held by the company's founding family. The family's Corsican by the way, not French."

"Isn't that the same thing?" McDarvid saved the Moreland waiver update on the screen, and turned his chair to face Jonnie.

"Not to them, it isn't. Any suggestion that Corsican is French may significantly decrease your life expectancy. Anyhow, JAFFE was one of the largest companies to escape nationalization when Mitterrand took power. They release some financials, but most of them are worthless."

"Why? Financial statements are pretty standard, at least for public companies. JAFFE may be secretive, but they wouldn't lie on something that public—at least too much." McDarvid's chair creaked as he also leaned back.

"It's not a question of lying. It's a question of what they release and in what form. JAFFE's a conglomerate. Mostly chemicals, pharmaceuticals, and some other stuff. They only release consolidated financial statements. The statements give an idea of how big the total company is, but that's about it. Even the accuracy of those numbers depends on how they value assets, what they consider to be liabilities, and when they decide to declare a given revenue. There's no good way to tell how big a specific business is or how well they're doing. Sure, there are some glitzy photos and slick statements, but they don't provide any substance."

There was no noise from beyond the door. Most of the law firm's staff had already gone home. The general clatter and shouts of people who had never learned to use the intercom system had finally stopped.

Jonnie continued. "You know that JAFFE had its origin in the chemical stuff? And that they've been primarily a chemical house?"

"So?"

"They've sold off most of their basic chemical operations. Two months ago they sold off all their Latin American operations, which they have had for almost a century, for beaucoup francs."

"They're in trouble and need the money?" McDarvid's tone was skeptical.

"No, not as far as I can tell. It just seems as if they're cashing in. It does, however, explain their interest in chlorohydrobenzilate."

"To make sure that deal stays done?"

"Chlorohydrobenzilate was a big money earner for their Brazilian operation. The parent still holds the U.S. registration. By producing the stuff in the States, they can compete with their former subsidiary for the same customers."

"Nice guys, aren't they?" McDarvid turned to the computer, resaved the document he had been working on, and shut off the machine. "Just a second." He brought his briefcase up onto the desk and opened it.

"It's not a question of nice. They're businessmen. They have been for at least a couple of hundred years. What's most interesting is what they've done with the money."

"What?" McDarvid asked mechanically as he placed a pile of thin files in the briefcase.

"They've bought a major yttrium mine."

"Yttrium?"

"A rare earth."

"What's it good for?"

"I was never a chemistry major. Other than high-temperature superconductors, I have no idea what the stuff's good for."

McDarvid looked up from the briefcase, closing it with a snap.

"JAFFE also bought other mines, as well as other mineral stocks—including chromium, beryllium, and vanadium."

"The metals initiative . . ."

"Yep. So it would seem." Jonnie eyed the halo around the moon that was visible behind McDarvid and hoped it did not mean that snow was coming. Washington was not a city that could deal with snow, or even a rumor of snow.

"There's one other commodity that JAFFE has been actively purchasing."

"Atomic waste?" McDarvid's tone was sour. He stood up.

"Talent. An old professor of mine and a friend stationed in Singapore both said that JAFFE has been hiring some of the best people around—for substantial salaries. Folks from both industry and academia worldwide."

"What sort of specialties?"

"It's a really eclectic crew, almost like they're assembling a miniature version of Bell Labs. JAFFE has been hiring physicists, chemists, engineers, and some good management experts with a special emphasis on manufacturing productivity. Although he wasn't very specific, my friend indicated that JAFFE has managed to get at least two of the best chip manufacturing experts in Asia, and they don't even speak a word of English, let alone French. JAFFE has also just hired one of Chicago's best psychology professors as a consultant. His specialty is artificial intelligence."

McDarvid massaged his temples. "I'll have to think about this. There's more there than meets the eye, a lot more. But I promised Allyson I wouldn't be too late tonight. We might actually have a chance to eat together."

Jonnie reached for the envelope. "Well, I won't keep you too much longer. By the way, JAFFE sent me a copy of their annual report."

"Heidlinger won't be thrilled with your calling the client without his approval. He's convinced that only attorneys are smart enough to ask simple questions." McDarvid frowned as he reached behind the door for his coat. "I thought you found out all about their financial statements from your friends."

"I did. I never called JAFFE." Jonnie lifted the DHL air express envelope and laid it on McDarvid's desk. "Look at the address."

"JAFFE Internationale . . ." McDarvid stumbled over the street address, but the city was clear enough—Paris. "You said you didn't contact JAFFE."

"I didn't," responded Jonnie. "There's more. Read the cover letter."

The cover letter was succinct. McDarvid lingered over the key sentence in the second paragraph.

". . . in view of your interest in JAFFE Internationale, and your apparent concerns, enclosed are the most recent financial reports, as well as the corporate restructuring plan proposed and adopted last March . . ."

The two men exchanged glances.

"I never talked to anyone from JAFFE about this. Did you?" McDarvid shook his head.

"They just sent me the stuff. It arrived this afternoon. I'm not quite through with the analysis. Sometime tomorrow, I'd guess. Anyway, I thought you'd like to know."

"Right." McDarvid's voice sounded tired. "Any other surprises?"

"Well . . ." Jonnie grinned nervously. He looked down for a moment.

"Oh, shit," mumbled McDarvid.

Jonnie nodded. "I got a phone call a little while ago. A fellow wanted me to have coffee with him."

McDarvid shook his head slowly.

"He said his name was Murrill. He's with DOD and, I assume, DIA."

McDarvid groaned. "That's par for the day. I assume he didn't say what it was about."

Jonnie looked up sharply. "No. I don't think he was interested in the weather, though."

"No. I don't suppose so." McDarvid straightened as he pulled on his jacket. "It sounds like everyone in the world knows you were out there looking." He paused. "Scary, when you consider we don't even know what we're looking for."

"Jack?"

"Yes?"

"What do we do now?"

"You go and have coffee with the nice man. I'll try and find out who he is from some friends. You say his name is Merrill?"

"Murrill, with a *u*." Jonnie shrugged. "I already agreed to coffee. Maybe he can tell us something."

"He already has," observed McDarvid.

"Oh . . ."

"Right. He's told us that we're not totally crazy, that there *is* something strange going on." McDarvid put his hand on the briefcase. "So has JAFFE, and I'm not sure which is scarier."

"There is that," Jonnie said flatly.

"Yeah. Why is JAFFE spending time tracking what we're doing? Worse . . . maybe they're not, and they've got an intelligence network that just dragged us in."

"I don't know that I like that, either."

"Nothing we can do about either tonight." McDarvid shrugged. "And I did promise Allyson . . ."

"You're taking all this almost as if it were routine."

McDarvid smiled sadly. "It is to them, I'm sure. What else can a poor consultant do?"

Jonnie lifted his hands from the back of the chair, took a step toward the doorway, then turned. "It's been a long day . . . Good night, Jack."

"Good night, Jonnie. Pleasant dreams."

Jonnie picked up his briefcase. "You, too."

36

MCDARVID PICKED UP THE TELEPHONE three times in a row, setting it down twice before finally punching in the number he had been using all too often.

"You have reached a nonworking federal number."

McDarvid punched in the three digits.

"This is Jack McDarvid—"

"I'll see if he's available, Mr. McDarvid."

The line went dead as McDarvid waited.

"Yes, Jack. What's up now? Another policy paper? Or some new facts?"

"I thought you might be able to tell me, Eric. Yesterday my partner was asked to have a friendly chat with some fellows. Just a friendly chat, you understand, except they wanted to know why we were making inquiries."

"Hold on. I need a few more details."

McDarvid sighed. "All right. From the top. We were hired by JAFFE. You knew that. We keep running into brick walls. And people started tailing us. At least sometimes. So Jonnie decided to try another tack. He started by trying to find out more about JAFFE." He paused. "He started the inquiries last Wednesday. Today is Thursday, one week and one day later, and he's been requested to have coffee tomorrow morning. One of your off-site specials. Supposedly, the contact's name is Murrill. M-U-R-R-I-L-L. He says he's with DOD. Is there any way to find out if he's legitimate?"

McDarvid paused. "I'd also like to know what DIA is doing with a French multinational and environmental regs dealing with metals."

"Hmmmmm . . . I don't think he's one of ours. I'll get back to you shortly."

McDarvid turned back to the computer, forcing himself to concentrate on the summary of the status of the special review of yet another pesticide registered by United Agricare—for poor Steve Greene, who was still struggling with the effort to pick up Larry's pesticide practice.

". . . teratogenic effects illustrated by Rangely mouse study . . ."

He wondered how long before Eric would call back, if in fact his former boss would find out who and what special agent Murrill was all about. And in some ways, Murrill was less scary than JAFFE. Why was JAFFE keeping tabs on its contractors? Or running a private intelligence network?

Buzzzz . . .

He grabbed the intercom, nearly tipping over the swivel chair. "Yes."

"Find out anything yet, Jack?" Jonnie sounded preoccupied, and that was as close to worried as he ever sounded.

"No. I've got someone looking."

"Someone?"

"An old friend who might know. I'll let you know. All right?"

"Okay . . . I guess."

"I'll let you know," McDarvid repeated before setting the phone down.

Finally, he returned to explaining the likelihood of the special review resulting in a partial ban on the use of Kiltough, the United Agricare granular pesticide being investigated by DEP.

After a late lunch at his desk and another call from Jonnie, Eric actually called.

"He's not ours."

"You already knew that. Is he DIA?"

"Sort of. He's DIA, but on detail to the National Security Council."

"What does the White House have to do with this?"

"They didn't tell us."

"Any ideas?"

"None whatever. But check last Thursday's business section. And tomorrow's paper for . . . French developments. And, obviously, I know nothing, except that Murrill's for real. And . . . Jack . . ."

"Yes."

"I'm telling you this so you don't have to make any more inquiries."

"Understood. Thanks, Eric."

"My pleasure. This time."

McDarvid frowned. Eric didn't like the inquiries. That came across loud and clear. Probably a trade-off—but what? He reached for the intercom.

"Yes?" Jonnie's voice was cautious.

"Find the business section of last Thursday's *Post* and come on down."

"Last Thursday's business section—a week ago?"

"That's the one."

"All right, but what's the mystery?"

"We'll both have a better idea if you can locate it. I didn't get a straight answer."

"It may take a while."

McDarvid had finished the first draft of the special review paper by the time Jonnie dragged in with a tattered copy of the week-old business section.

"Managed to reclaim it from the recycling pile."

"Have you read it?"

"Not since last Thursday, if I even read it then. You do the honors, since you seem to know what you're looking for." Jonnie thrust the paper at McDarvid.

The story was buried on the bottom of F-2. McDarvid read it aloud.

*   *   *

Washington. Today, attorneys for the Justice Department
retracted their objections to the acquisition of Pherndahl-Elkins
by JAFFE International, a French multinational. According to
industry sources, JAFFE has recently acquired a number of
smaller companies involved in computer and space technology.
Pherndahl-Elkins, a Colorado-based manufacturer, specializes in
advanced microchip technology . . .

"They like to acquire high-tech companies." Jonnie's tone was
not quite sardonic.

"I learned something else," McDarvid added. "This was a
deal. The second half will appear in tomorrow's paper. And
Murrill's real. He is DIA, but he's on detail to the National
Security Council."

"What's he do there?"

"Beats me."

"How did you find this out?"

McDarvid repressed a sigh. "One of my former bosses. He also
suggested we stop investigating JAFFE. Very strongly."

"That doesn't exactly reassure me, Jack."

"It doesn't reassure me, either. I just hope we can figure out
what story he was referring to that's supposed to appear tomorrow morning."

"Un . . . huhhh . . ." Jonnie did not look at McDarvid.

McDarvid cleared his throat. "Jonnie, this ties rather neatly to
what you found out about JAFFE's hiring practices."

"Yeah, it does. Pherndahl-Elkins is a relatively small high-tech
company, working on the next generation chip manufacturing
technology. Right now, all sorts of chips can be designed that
can't be produced. Companies just can't etch enough lines
through the chip without the circuits crossing or the chip burning
out. Pherndahl-Elkins is developing techniques for manufacturing the next generation of very high density chips using new
technologies and materials." Jonnie suddenly grinned.

"Why do I suspect that these new technologies and materials
involve some of the same materials involved in the metals initiative?"

"You're just a quick study, I guess."

"Can we presume that Pherndahl sold out because they ran out of options to raise money."

Jonnie nodded. "It's not cheap trying to develop new high-technology manufacturing processes. Still, I'd bet there was a lot of opposition to the sale. Probably most of DOD and even a few people at Commerce objected to selling a high-tech firm like Pherndahl to a foreign company, even one based in a more or less friendly country."

"Like I said, this is some sort of deal. But we can't figure out what sort until we see the morning paper."

Jonnie yawned and looked at his watch. "What I don't understand is why an American firm didn't step in and buy Pherndahl. There are enough companies with more cash than they know what to do with. Getting Pherndahl would be a hell of an opportunity for someone."

"There's a simple answer there." McDarvid snorted. "American companies are long-term risk averse. They don't want to spend a lot of money on a project that may not pay off for years, if at all. Stockholders want to see profits now. They don't want to hear about buying a company that, at best, will only turn a small profit for years and isn't even good for a nice tax write-off. Even if doing so will contribute to the nation's technology base and their own long-term profitability."

"So the French will take over our high-tech industry?" asked Jonnie.

"You prefer the Japanese?"

"Does it make a difference? At least somebody is interested in building for the future."

McDarvid grimaced. "That's all I know for the moment. We can figure out the next step tomorrow—once we see what's in the paper." He stood up slowly and looked toward the briefcase on the credenza. "Late night for Allyson, and time to head out and rescue the baby-sitter from the kids."

"Oh . . . yeah . . . See you tomorrow, Jack."

McDarvid shook his head. What sort of trade-off had Eric hinted at, and why had he let on that much—just to stop further investigations?

No. Whatever happened tomorrow had to close a chapter. It was Eric's way of saying, it's over. Don't upset things by mucking around. But what was over, and what did it have to do with JAFFE?

He picked up the briefcase and walked toward the elevator.

37

THE MUSIC BARELY WHISPERED. McDarvid wanted to pull the pillow over his ears. Instead, he jabbed the alarm and lurched upright.

Five forty-five. The glowing numbers on the clock confirmed, as they did every morning, why he did not want to be up. Slowly, he eased himself through the darkness toward the closet, where the short pajamas came off and the underwear and sweat suit went on. As he sat back down on the edge of the bed to pull on socks and running shoes, Allyson pulled the pillow over her head.

He stood and headed downstairs. Taking the door by the kitchen, he stepped out into the December chill, pulling the sweatshirt hood over his ears as he walked toward the park, his pace faster than that of many joggers.

The paper would be on the doorstep by the time he finished his workout, not that he would have the chance to read it until after he had fixed breakfast and gotten the kids off to school and Allyson off to work.

Once he had covered the four blocks to the park and his feet touched the grass, he began the first of the premeasured sprints between the trees.

A lone dog skittered away into the gloom as McDarvid charged the old oak, practicing the few old kicks he remembered from training. Whacking and thudding at trees, doing broken field running—just the thing for cold mornings. But he only thought the words, not having the breath even to mumble them.

Despite his five-day-a-week devotion to his walk-run-modified workout-run-walk regime, age was creeping up on him. Not fat, but age. Unless the scales were lying and his trousers were stretching, neither totally beyond the realm of possibility.

He began another sprint along the edge of the park as a few oblivious commuters trudged toward the Metro stop, their faces averted from the idiot in the tattered Navy sweat suit, plunging from tree to tree, only halting to deliver poorly timed kicks to the unyielding trunks.

Despite the white stream of his breath, the sweat had begun to pour across his forehead, and he flicked back the sweatshirt's hood as he reached the monkey bars and began the pull-ups.

"Hate this . . ."

But he hated the thought of being fat and sloppy worse. So the pull-ups were followed by the inclined sit-ups. Then two more tree-hopping sprints to the far end of the park, where he slowed to a quick walk home. He had to walk then—running on hard surfaces left his back stiff for days. Grass was the only surface on which he ran, and only when the ground wasn't frozen solid.

The paper was waiting. He tucked it under his arm and walked around the front of the house to the side door by the kitchen. As he stepped inside, he glanced at the headlines: "Islamic Hard-liners Reassert Control in Somalia." Somehow, he doubted that even JAFFE was tied up in Somalia.

With the paper set aside on the buffet in the dining room, he put on the kettle for tea and hot chocolate and set up the coffee maker to deliver Allyson's two cups of decaffeinated coffee.

He emptied the dishwasher, knowing that the rattle of plates served more as an alarm for Allyson than the beautiful music station that was their compromise between her soft rock and his country music. Next he laid out the mugs and the plates and began setting up for the breakfasts to follow.

The sound of the kettle reminded him to turn down the gas before the water boiled out the spout and all over the stove. His and Elizabeth's bagels went into the toaster oven, and he laid out Allyson's bran.

"Breakfast is almost ready!"

"Dadddddd . . ."

"I will be there presently . . ."

"Here I am," announced his younger daughter.

McDarvid slipped the cereal bowl, the sliced bananas, and the hot chocolate before Kirsten. Then he started sectioning the grapefruit.

"David's yelling at his closet."

"He forgot to lay out his clothes again, I suppose." McDarvid poured his and Elizabeth's tea. Turning the kettle off, he retrieved the bagels.

After hearing the shower shut off, he poured Allyson's coffee and set it at the end of the long breakfast bar.

"Father . . ."

"It's in front of your stool."

"Thank you."

"I'm glad you're wearing the blue pants and top," said Kirsten. "The green stuff looks yukky."

"Father . . ."

"Kirsten, just eat your cereal." He looked up toward Allyson, in her heavy green robe, damp hair, and still-sleepy eyes. "Morning, sweetheart."

"Morning." She slipped onto the stool and grasped for the coffee.

He set the cereal bowl and milk pitcher in front of her, then turned to pour the still-boiling water into David's oatmeal. After that, he took three quick spoonfuls from his grapefruit, followed by a bite of bagel.

". . . no jeans . . . Kirsten, did you hide my good jeans? Where are my tennis shoes?" David slouched into the kitchen, barefoot, but with new jeans and a black sweatshirt proclaiming a musical group whose sounds reminded McDarvid of near-dead cats.

"Your shoes are where you left them. That usually means under your bed, under your desk, or in some corner in the family room. And do a better job in making your bed this morning. Yesterday, it was a mess." He mock-glared at Kirsten. "You, too, squirt."

"I'm not as sloppy as David."

"There is scarcely any difference between the two of you," announced Elizabeth.

Allyson winced and took another sip of coffee, then poured milk into her cereal.

"Can I have the milk, Mom?" David blared.

McDarvid, still standing behind the breakfast bar, finished his grapefruit, took another sip of tea, and removed Kirsten's cereal bowl. "You need to work on that hair before your mother puts it up. The deal was that you brush out the tangles first. Otherwise, it gets cut."

"Yes, Daddy."

Within minutes, the three children were upstairs, and McDarvid plopped onto the stool next to Allyson. "You didn't say much last night. Long day?"

"No. Just colds and flu going around. A lot with pretty high fevers, and that always gets parents worried." She took another sip of coffee.

McDarvid got up and retrieved the coffeepot, refilling her cup.

"You don't have to do that."

"I don't mind. You're not awake in the morning, anyway." He sat down.

Allyson rested her head against his shoulder for a moment, then reached down and squeezed his leg. "You're still worried a lot. You're tossing in your sleep again, all the time, and you haven't done that since you worked for the Agency."

"Sorry. Didn't mean to wake you up."

"I went back to sleep. I didn't remember anything after that; so you didn't keep me awake." Allyson methodically finished the small bowl of bran.

He took another swallow, emptying the last of his tea from the heavy mug.

"Is pot roast all right for dinner?" she asked.

"Fine. I shouldn't be late."

She touched his leg again, then set down her mug. "I'd better get up there and do Kirsten's hair."

"If you must . . ." His lips brushed her cheek, and he squeezed her shoulder gently. "Maybe this weekend?"

As she rose, Allyson smiled faintly, but whether the smile was mere fondness or a promise—that he couldn't tell, not even after all these years.

By the time everyone had piled out, either to school or to work, McDarvid had cleaned up the kitchen and shaved. He debated retrieving the paper, but, instead, stepped into the shower.

Finally, fully dressed, he took the paper into the small study. His eyes targeted the story about the early resignation of the

Admiral in charge of aircraft procurement. But the story was just another retelling of the typical Washington situation. The Admiral, apparently a good tactical commander, had gotten frustrated by the Washington fogbank of rumor and indirection and gone aground when he blamed the procurement mess on congressional legislative requirements. McDarvid shook his head wryly. It didn't matter whether the congressional requirements—procurement or environmental—were impossible. You didn't blame the imperial Congress, because the appropriations committees invariably cut your budget and the legislative committees added more requirements, and that just made the situation that much worse.

He scanned the rest of the paper, discovering that the only story that made sense was in the world news section on page 20.

FRENCH CONDUCT NUCLEAR TEST

. . . detonated a nuclear device in the South Pacific yesterday . . . the yield was undetermined . . . French sources refuse to speculate on the purpose of the test . . .

In a related development, Greenpeace reported that a Navy ship, identified tentatively as the destroyer *O'Falleron,* had been tracked in the area of the test for the past several days . . . neither the Pentagon nor the White House would offer comment . . .

McDarvid folded the story into his briefcase.

38

"I TAKE IT THAT IT WAS THE FRENCH NUCLEAR TEST STORY?" asked Jonnie, even before McDarvid could open his briefcase.

"Has to be."

"You want to speculate why? Before I go off to coffee with the spooks?"

McDarvid shrugged. "I can't figure out all the reasons, but the French don't tell anyone what goes on with their tests. The whole thing probably goes pretty high."

Jonnie nodded slowly. "Well, I got in early this morning. I had a chance to make a couple of calls. A buddy of mine at Commerce said there's a rumor that approval for the JAFFE deal came from high up, real high."

"The Secretary?"

Jonnie shook his head. "There are some folks who think that the White House made the call on this one."

McDarvid frowned. "About how long ago did JAFFE receive approval to buy Pherndahl?"

"No more than a couple of weeks ago, assuming the story hit the *Post* fairly soon after approval. Why?"

"Wasn't that about when what's-his-name at the Pentagon was in France? You know, the new Secretary?" mused McDarvid, pulling on his chin.

"I thought that was a couple of months ago. Besides, that was just the standard consult-with-the-allies tour taken by every new Secretary. I couldn't imagine that . . ."

"No. You're probably right about that. But if the JAFFE thing had a White House twist . . ."

"That might explain Murrill's interest?" Jonnie asked.

"I suppose so. But whatever's with that test must be really critical, if the White House types were willing to squash Justice."

"Why Justice? I thought Commerce had the objections."

"Justice always files the antitrust objections, no matter who raises them. Lawyers, again." McDarvid shrugged. "But why that ties to a French nuclear test, I don't know."

"The Russians monitor our tests," Jonnie observed, "and, under the agreement, we monitor theirs."

"Shhhhiit." The curse slipped from McDarvid's mouth. "No wonder they didn't like your inquiries."

Jonnie's forehead wrinkled.

McDarvid walked past him and closed the door. "It all fits. We can talk about the reasons later, but we have some test or equipment being conducted in conjunction with the French test, probably something that we don't want the Russians to know about. The French government politely called in a favor . . ."

"A favor?"

"They asked the White House to withdraw DOJ objections to the JAFFE acquisition of that chipmaker."

"And now Mr. Murrill wants to know why we're involved?"

"It looks that way." McDarvid looked at Jonnie and shrugged.

"What do I tell him?"

"The truth—that we were scoping out a new client and the potential problems."

"You sure he'll be satisfied with that?"

"No. But it's the truth."

"When has that counted?"

McDarvid shrugged again.

39

"FIRST, WE WERE GOING TO DEMAND MONITORING OF THE FENCE LINE, with some dust to get results. Now you're talking about scattering yellowcake dust in the field outside the plant. It just isn't a good idea." Veronica looked around the deserted park, then at the dark clouds that promised cold rain or sleet.

"Does that mean you're not going through with it? Once you get started, you'll be okay. You just need to work through it." Peter, hunched inside his rawhide jacket, stared directly at her.

"I'll be all right, because I'm not going to do it." The cold wind whipped through Veronica's hair, creating an auburn cloud about her face, as she stood beside the backless stone bench. "I joined the movement to protect the environment, not to spread radioactive dust in a field outside a nuclear processing facility. They've already released enough radiation. We don't need to spread any more. I mean, what if kids play in that field? That dust could give them cancer or kill them. That's carrying things too far."

"Don't be silly. This is a contaminated processing facility. You're not spreading radiation. You're stopping it. Don't you want to help close a death factory that's polluted the entire area with nuclear waste?''

"That's not the way." Veronica swept her hair back away from her face. "You'll destroy the movement, not the processing plant."

"No buts. Once the press finds out how much radiation is coming from that plant, public outrage will force the plant to close down. All we're doing is helping a fat and lazy media discover the radiation they would have found years ago if they had any guts."

"You still don't understand. It's one thing to call attention to evil—even violently. It's another to cause more pollution. It's wrong to poison the land and the water. I'm not going to be like the people I want to stop."

"It's that new guy you're sleeping with, isn't it? Black somebody." The bearded man turned directly toward the woman. "He works for the polluters, and he's turned you into one of them."

"Bullshit! Jonnie has nothing to do with this."

"I'm telling you. We're not polluting; we're putting an end to pollution. And you can't chicken out."

"You can do it without me. Tedor can plant the dust. After all, he's getting the yellowcake in the first place. Or you can do it yourself. If you think this is such a wonderful idea, why don't you go scatter the dust?"

"You are scared. If you were really so convinced this is wrong, you'd be talking to the police, not to me. You'd be telling them that a bunch of environmental zanies are going to dump radioactive dust outside a processing plant. Instead, you're telling me how I can dump the dust without your help."

"I agreed with the original idea. Putting a trace of dust along the fence wouldn't have hurt anyone. But you're asking for trouble if you start playing around with that stuff. That's your choice."

"I hope that's not a threat, babe." The man kicked a booted heel on the worn stone curbing by the leafless hedge.

She shook her head.

"Look, I can't make you scatter the powder. But once we do, you're into this right up to your gorgeous neck. Don't think you can play the self-righteous bitch and walk away from this with clean hands. You're as dirty as the rest of us."

"Fine. You think being dirty is the mark of a real environmentalist? I'll dump your damned dust. I'll dump it right in your fucking coffee. Maybe that'll get the factory shut down. I can see the headline now. 'Eco-Freak Dies from Radioactive Coffee—Thousands Converge to Shut Suspect Plant.'"

"Hey, babe, you can dump the stuff or not. I don't give a shit. But you better not put it in my coffee. It wouldn't stop me; it would just make me angry. And you sure as shit don't want me angry." Peter stepped back. "Like you said. It's your choice. Don't forget it."

Veronica turned, not watching the man in the dirty rawhide jacket, and not looking back even though she could feel his eyes on her as she walked toward the Ecology Now! office.

40

"MR. BLACK?" The man who rose from the corner table at the Gateaux et Pain was thin-faced, young, and balding. The dark hair that he did retain was cut short over the ears, not quite military-short, but close.

"Jonathon Black," acknowledged the consultant, settling into the bench seat of the booth opposite the other.

"Victor Murrill." The other man sat down, his back against the high cushion of the booth, reaching inside the breast pocket of his dark blue suit. The red-and-silver-striped tie was almost rep, but not quite. "You might want to look at these before we proceed." He extended a wallet-type folder of black leather.

Jonnie perused the credentials identifying one Victor E. Murrill as belonging to the Department of Defense. He noted the three-quarter-profile photo and three white stripes on the red background before handing the folder back. "Could be real; I wouldn't know."

Murrill gave Jonnie a skeptical look, replaced the wallet, and gestured toward a waiter. "Would you care for coffee?"

"Just coffee. Black."

"Two coffees," Murrill told the waiter in a cream and maroon jacket.

"What did you want to know?" asked Jonnie as the waiter withdrew after filling both cups.

"We were curious about the sudden interest in JAFFE." Murrill smiled over the cup he had raised and held in two hands.

"I would have thought there would have been a great deal of interest in JAFFE given the importance of the chip industry to U.S. high technology."

Murrill drank his coffee without responding.

Jonnie followed his example, refusing to be intimidated by silence into saying more.

Murrill set down his cup. "That's the intriguing thing. You might find it interesting to know that there were only three filings protesting the acquisition. All three were legal boilerplate." Murrill grinned. "At least, that's what the counsel's office told us."

"That does seem interesting," Jonnie admitted. "Could one assume that the objections were from the largest U.S. firms?"

Murrill shrugged. "They're in the record. You'd be right in two out of three cases. The third is pretty big also."

Jonnie took another sip of the coffee, which was too weak for the prices charged by the Gateaux et Pain. "So why were my small inquiries so interesting? As I told you on the telephone, we needed some background information on a new client."

"Why didn't you ask the client?"

Jonnie shook his head slowly. "Consultants are supposed to know everything, including their clients. For our rates, you just can't ask about a company's background. You're supposed to know it. Never mind that each of the Fortune 500 has a dozen subsidiaries and divisions that think the world revolves around them."

"I doubt that you would have had to go to Singapore to find out about JAFFE."

"You have been busy," observed Jonnie, taking another sip of the weak coffee and glancing around the room. Only a handful of the booths and tables were taken, although all would be full by lunchtime with those from the White House and those who hoped to meet, lunch with, or merely observe those reputed to be on the inside.

"We try to do our job," answered Murrill blandly.

Jonnie took another sip of the coffee, wishing Jack were the one at the table. McDarvid seemed more at home in reading through banalities. "So what did you want to tell me?"

"Tell you? You're just a consultant, and I'm just a government employee doing his job." Murrill took another sip from the cup, his dark eyes traveling the room. "What was so interesting is that your inquiry came after everything was supposedly settled."

Jonnie shrugged. "I told you. We weren't really even interested in the Pherndahl-Elkins acquisition. We got hired to do some regulatory work—that is what we do, you know—for JAFFE. We just started scoping out the job. That includes scoping out other impacts on the client. You don't want to recommend a solution that might save one client operation and screw another."

"Are all consultants that conscientious?"

"Hell, no. Just those that want to stay in business." Jonnie was surprised that the DIA man actually smiled.

"So you looked into the client and the regulatory situation. Why did it happen just as the acquisition issue was before Commerce and Justice?"

"That's when we got hired. The timing was theirs, not ours."

"You've made that clear, and that's what we'll report. Just coincidence. It sometimes happens in this business, but you never know . . ." The investigator shrugged again and drained the last coffee from the cup.

Again, Jonnie waited, determined not to finish the other's sentence for him. The silence dragged out.

"So your work is strictly regulatory . . ." ventured Murrill, glancing across the room, then back to Jonnie. His fingers toyed with the delicate cup.

"Pretty much, although we get into some financial analysis. The regulatory side is most of what we do."

"I would have expected that, somehow, having heard about Jack. It's too bad that we can't take more of an interest in environmental regulations, things like the metals initiative, but you know how it is. Unless the national security implications are clear, well, it's not our ballpark. Even then . . ." Murrill's eyes still did not quite meet Jonnie's. He turned to face the consultant with a smile. "In any case, it's been a pleasure to meet you, and I apologize for taking your time."

As Jonnie watched, Murrill nodded and slipped from the booth, leaving two dollar bills and two quarters on the off-white linen.

As Murrill crossed the room, the waiter placed the check on the table. The total for the two coffees was five dollars. Jonnie took care of his coffee and the tip.

41

"JACK?"

McDarvid looked up as Jonnie closed the door and plopped into the empty chair. He blinked, saved the document on the screen, and turned from the computer. "Yes?"

"Aren't you going to ask me how it went? Or tell me what you were thinking about that we were going to talk about?"

"Sorry . . . thinking about a lot of things." He gestured toward the screen. "Moreland Reclamation."

"Is that still alive?"

McDarvid grimaced. "Unfortunately, I appear to be a victim of my own success."

"Don't tell me they bought it?"

McDarvid grinned. "What other options did they have after the Inspector General's report?" The grin faded. "What did Murrill want?"

"Nothing."

"Nothing?" McDarvid pulled at his chin, then glanced over his shoulder out the window at the early December grayness. "Are you sure?"

Jonnie shrugged. "Sure sounded that way. Almost like a per-functory review. You know, why did you make inquiries about JAFFE? Oh, for regulatory and background purposes? Thank you very much, and have a happy life."

"Then what did he tell you?"

"How did you know?"

"They never do anything like that without a purpose, especially off-site. It had to be either a warning or a tip." McDarvid waited.

"You sound like you know that business."

"You pick up a lot on the Hill," McDarvid answered. "That's the way they operate there."

"He really wanted to slip it in, but I made it hard on him."

McDarvid nodded. "They prefer to have you guess and let them confirm it."

Jonnie paused fractionally, then continued. "He made this funny statement about it was too bad that they couldn't take more of an interest in environmental regulations, things like the metals initiative, but . . ." and Jonnie mimicked Murrill's shrug, "unless the national security implications were clear, well, it wasn't in their ballpark."

McDarvid slowly shook his head. "That's not good. Not at all good."

"I got that impression. You want to tell me why?"

"Two things. First, by the references to the newspaper stories, my contacts indicated that the Pherndahl-Elkins acquisition was part of a deal—or at least a deal forced by the French. We were clearly monitoring something associated with that nuclear test. According to *Aviation Leakly,* the *O'Falleron* is one of the Navy destroyers fitted with certain sophisticated monitoring gear. The ship shows up in the North Pacific when the Russians appear to be launching long-range tests—you've probably read about them. It could be coincidence, but just by linking the two, my . . . contacts indicated that it wasn't. Now, Murrill makes this pointed reference to the metals initiative as not being in the defense orbit. That's a clear sign that they're worried and that they can't do a damned thing about it."

"Which means that they think someone is mucking around with our regulatory rules?"

"Yeah. But it's awfully indirect. That's one reason why this whole thing bothers me a lot."

"It bothers you? I'm the one they called."

McDarvid smiled. "Don't worry. I'm sure they know we're both involved."

"That is so very reassuring." Jonnie looked over the older man's shoulder at the gray clouds in the December sky. "I don't like it when Defense people say they can't do anything . . ."

"We have another problem," McDarvid said.

"Yeah?"

"Devenant will be in next week, and Heidlinger wants us to brief him before the meeting."

"So what are we going to tell Devenant? That we've struck out on chlorohydrobenzilate, but that they won't find out for a couple of months, and that even the White House spooks don't want to act on the metals initiative?"

McDarvid shrugged. "A little more tactfully. We'll tell him that while we can't be certain on the pesticides, it appears as though all the key decisions—risk assessments, health effects, you know the list—were made before they hired us. That's unfortunately true. And it's going to be hard to change any of those decisions at this stage. We've circulated the policy paper and the supplemental analyses, and we've made sure they're part of the docket and the OMB record, and we'll keep trying. It may be that Heidlinger and his crew will have to file on one of several grounds . . ."

"Arbitrary and capricious again?" asked Jonnie sardonically.

"Hopefully, something more procedural—like the fact that the Agency failed to conduct the true risk-balancing required by FIFRA."

"Well, Heidlinger will get some legal work, and we won't get the sermon about remembering that this is a law firm, not a consulting firm."

"I don't think I'll tell Heidlinger about the chlorohydrobenzilate status until after we meet with Devenant."

"Is that wise?"

"If we tell him now, he'll take it for granted and start pushing for more legal emphasis on metals. Lawsuits won't work there. That's already clear."

"Will anything work?"

McDarvid turned toward the window and the clouds. "I don't know. I really don't know. We just have to try." He turned and slumped back into the chair, looking at Jonnie. "By the way, what did you get from the DARPA boys?" McDarvid's head ached, and he was coming down with a cold.

"Same as from Major Ruby at Space Comm. They like the papers and would be happy to have any more information we could supply. Yes, they're worried about the impact. No, they can't say exactly what they're doing." Jonnie took off his glasses and held them in his hand for a moment.

"What do they think about Japanese and German batteries for their satellites?"

"They aren't happy with anyone," Jonnie said slowly. "They have quality-control problems with the major U.S. supplier. They're leery of JAFFE, even if the plant is in Georgia, because they're French, and because the French are building their own space program. They like the Japanese quality control, but not the attitude, or the Japanese grab for world market share. The Germans? Well, the Germans are telling them how to specify the batteries."

McDarvid looked through his own notes, then glanced at the blank blue of his computer screen. "Will any of them talk to DEP?"

"Are you kidding? They're not sure they even know who in the Pentagon should handle it."

"If I didn't know better, I'd say I couldn't believe it." McDarvid stood up, walked behind his chair, and put his hands on the back, leaning forward.

"Jack?"

"Yes?"

"I've got a real dumb question. How does DEP get away with it?"

McDarvid laughed, a short harsh bark. "That took me almost the whole time I was there to figure out. It's so damned simple. They don't give the political appointees any choice."

"Run that one by me again."

McDarvid straightened up. "Take a chemical, any chemical. Every law but the pesticides act basically says that you have to protect human health and the environment. How do you figure out how to protect it from a chemical? First, you have to determine how much of something can hurt people. So you take the animal studies and calculate how much exposure to the chemical will kill the test animal. Then you extrapolate that back through models to get a dosage for people. Then you use the dosage and a projected level and duration of exposure to calculate an acceptable risk level. Right now, DEP says that a level of exposure that will result in more than a one-in-a-million chance of death is unacceptable."

"One in a million?"

"It varies from one in ten thousand to one in one hundred million. But even that figure is crazy."

"It is crazy—I mean if you exposed the whole population to something at that level, you'd get two hundred and fifty deaths over . . . what . . . thirty years? And nobody gets exposed like that."

McDarvid snorted. "Try to explain to people that cars kill forty thousand people a year. That's one point two million people over thirty years—a risk almost five thousand times greater than the unacceptable chemical risks. But even the one-in-a-million number is exaggerated. That's because they base the risk assessments on the most sensitive animal species, and then they extrapolate that to the most sensitive human beings, and then they assume that those people are exposed every moment of their lives for thirty to seventy years. I won't go into the other factors, but they're just as biased.

"Now, when the risk assessment comes up saying that a chemical will kill thirty percent of the work force, what does a political appointee do? If he questions the science, then he's a political hack. If he questions the cost for theoretically saving a few lives, then he's a heartless tool of the industrialists. But the agency— the department—is producing risk assessments that say that entire work forces will die, which is sort of strange when some of these chemicals have been used for forty years and no one has actually traced any statistically significant numbers of deaths, except from coal mines and asbestos. Or smoking and radon. Not from the workplace, despite all the rhetoric. Yes, maybe a handful of deaths here or there, but nothing on any scale. And that's even considering some plants that didn't even come close to meeting current standards."

"Jack, that can't—"

"It is. You can check the math yourself." McDarvid rummaged through the stuffed credenza, finally extracting a folder. "There."

Jonnie looked at the bulging stack of paper. "Thanks. I think."

"Anyway, what happens is that whatever low-level scientist or section chief sets the risk levels in effect determines whether the chemical is regulated or not."

Jonnie looked at the folder again.

"So." McDarvid shrugged, winced, and rubbed his forehead. "If you want to change something, it's a hell of a lot easier to work from the bottom. Except in this case, we're too damned late."

Jonnie stood up. "I'm due over at Commerce."

"I thought you didn't like late afternoon appointments."

"There's no point in leaving early. Veronica's out of town. They sent her to some little godforsaken place to investigate the success a strip-mining firm had in restoring wetlands they had previously destroyed." Jonnie shrugged. "Besides, this person doesn't like to meet in the light of day."

"Good luck with whatever it is."

"Thanks."

42

VERONICA PERCHED ON THE STOOL BY THE TELEPHONE. She wore the red flannel shirt that Jonnie had admired on their first picnic. Her eyes flickered for a moment toward the telephone, then toward the plate and the baklava with the honey dripping out.

Jonnie took a large bite from the pastry, trying not to get the flaky edges and walnuts all over everything. "Mmmmm . . ."

Veronica set her fork beside the plate as she finished her single bite. She looked at the baklava again. "Is there any food you don't like?"

He paused, wondering at the seriousness of her tone. "Some. I usually pass on turnip custard unless I'm really hungry."

"That's not funny."

"Really? You've never complained about my dessert preferences before."

"Oh, Jonnie . . ." Veronica shook her head. "Somehow, I don't feel like joking about food tonight."

"I could help you with some software."

A momentary smile flitted across her face. "You're impossible."

"No. Merely rather difficult."

She stood up and walked to the cabinet. There she pulled out the box of waxed paper and tore off a section, carefully replacing the paper before walking back to her stool, where she stood and began to wrap her baklava.

"You didn't like it?"

"It was . . . fine . . . I don't know. Maybe it was too rich for me tonight. Maybe it was the movie. I just don't feel hungry."

Jonnie frowned. What would the movie have to do with anything? They'd only gone to a rerelease of an old sixties movie he'd wanted to see for a while—*The Manchurian Candidate*. A brainwashed candidate for Vice President and a planned assassination of the presidential candidate—the film techniques had been good, but the plot? Hardly realistic. Jack's scenario of foreign interests using regulations as a weapon was more plausible. "The movie? I thought it would be a change-of-pace flick."

"I'm sorry." Veronica's voice didn't sound sorry.

Jonnie got the hint and finished his baklava. "Maybe I'd better be going." He carried the plate to the sink and rinsed it off, then opened the dishwasher door and slipped it onto the bottom rack.

He tried not to wince at the sound of the dishwasher door slamming. He hadn't meant to shut it *that* hard.

Veronica stood by her stool, almost as if she had not heard the noise.

Jonnie paused. "Are you all right?"

"I'm fine. I just have a few things to think about. I shouldn't have agreed to go, but it sounded like a nice spur-of-the-moment idea."

"I still don't like turnip custard."

Veronica grinned faintly. "Actually, I'm glad, but not tonight."

"Okay." He extracted his faded parka from the minuscule cupboard that passed for a hall closet and pulled it on.

"Jonnie?"

He turned, and her lips brushed his cheek as she gave him a hug.

"I'm sorry."

"I understand."

"No, you probably don't. But that's my problem, not yours." She squeezed him again and stepped away. "Good night."

"Good night," he repeated. At the moment, there was nothing else to say. So he didn't, instead stepping through the doorway into the darkness.

His steps clicked on the concrete, and his breath was white in the below-freezing air. His eyes passed over Veronica's battered Chevette and across the parking area. Perhaps one third of the spaces were filled—not surprisingly for so early in the evening.

Two tries and the engine caught, but the GTO shuddered in protest at the early winter chill, and the wind whistled through the no longer tight convertible top as Jonnie pulled out of the parking lot.

A quick glance in the rearview mirror showed nothing behind him as he turned onto the street—nothing except clouds of not exactly pristine GTO exhaust gases steaming in the December night.

Jonnie didn't want to be in the car. Veronica's apartment was a lot warmer, or had been, until the issue of food had come up.

What was bothering her?

He pushed the accelerator down. With any luck, he might actually get home before eleven, not that he really wanted to be there, either. And he'd be halfway home before the GTO's heater made much headway in warming the cold vinyl seats.

43

". . . APPRECIATE YOUR CONFIDENCE AND YOUR SUPPORT . . . continuing to marshal the full resources of the firm behind both these efforts . . . the weight of environmental law . . ." Behind the gold wire-rimmed glasses, Heidlinger, overflowing his semitailored charcoal pinstripe and overwhelming the red power tie that only emphasized his girth, droned on.

McDarvid had never thought he'd miss Larry at a client meeting, but Heidlinger was making it painfully clear why he did. Even the pastel watercolors of Washington—the Supreme Court building, the old Library of Congress building, and the Taft Carillon—seemed a shade yellow.

McDarvid glanced toward Pierre Devenant, again wearing a double-breasted, dark blue chalk stripe with wide lapels, with a pale pearl-rose tie that accentuated his tailored look.

Devenant's eyes met McDarvid's, then passed back to the senior partner. He cleared his throat, softly interrupting Heidlinger. "We at JAFFE do understand the considerable efforts you have made, and I personally appreciate the weekly reports from Messieurs McDarvid and Black."

Beside McDarvid, Jonnie shifted his weight ever so slightly.

"As they have indicated, the metals initiative has become more important than we had anticipated. We have circulated the policy paper widely within JAFFE, even to our headquarters, and parts of it have been translated and reprinted, with attribution, of course"—Devenant nodded toward the two consultants—"both within the company's journal and in several other publications. The reaction was most favorable, and that is one reason why we feel confident in continuing our work with Messieurs McDarvid and Black." Devenant flashed a smile at Heidlinger, who swallowed.

"Thank you," murmured McDarvid.

"Not to thank me, but your own excellent work."

McDarvid could see Jonnie struggling to keep a blank expression.

"We are wondering, however, what might be the next steps we could anticipate in your efforts."

"Well," McDarvid began quickly, in order to ensure that Heidlinger did not attempt to start in on the legal paperwork that paid so much and did so little, "the next steps are to follow up with each affected government agency. Basically, we'll take the key elements of the big paper, plus any specific facts we have or can develop from your people, and create a short one- or two-page summary. For example, take DOD. We know that the remnants of the space laser program—used to be called the Star Wars crew—have some specific concerns about the need to obtain rechargeable batteries from U.S.-based suppliers. Under the metals initiative nickel-cadmium batteries won't be manufactured in the U.S. So we point out in simple bottom-line terms that the metals initiative means they have to buy batteries for secret U.S. satellites from Japan or perhaps from Germany. There is also the issue of satellite construction and fabrication of other defense-related equipment." McDarvid paused. "Jonnie, here, is the one who tries to develop some specific numbers for each department or agency."

"All numbers are suspect," added Jonnie, "but we usually can relate them to each office's own budgets or costs."

Devenant nodded again. "I see. How long might this take?"

"That's hard to say. A couple of weeks for the individual papers—"

"At the same time," interrupted Heidlinger, "we need to begin tying the matter in these submissions into the overall legal strategy."

"I see," Devenant repeated. "You were saying about the individual papers, Mr. McDarvid?"

"After we run the papers by you, we see the key decision-makers. They've all seen, or at least received, the big policy paper. The individual papers are both a reminder and a targeted short impact statement for them, with recommended steps for them to take."

"And do they take these steps?" asked Devenant.

McDarvid laughed softly. "We hope they do. In the past, some have, and some haven't. That's why we try to reach as many as possible, showing how each has a direct interest and recommending a set of actions that they have the power to undertake. In some cases, it might just be a phone call. In others, they have real power to request a change or a review. Now, that's an oversimplification . . ."

"I understand . . . enough." Devenant moistened his lips. "And you hope . . . what?"

McDarvid shrugged. "We want to kill the whole NPRM—the proposed rule. That probably won't happen. DEP almost never withdraws a proposal. Sometimes, but not often. But if there's a lot of opposition, they often just quietly let it be known that nothing will happen and commission a study or say that they're waiting for further data."

"Even a significant delay would be helpful—"

"That's why . . ." began Heidlinger.

Devenant continued speaking, as if he had not even heard the senior attorney, "—and it appears as though you have already created some potential for delay."

"We hope so," McDarvid responded.

"That is good." Devenant stood. "I appreciate much the time you have spent and the work you have done. I wish I could remain longer, but my director will be arriving shortly on the Concorde and expects me to meet with him."

McDarvid and Jonnie both had risen; Heidlinger struggled from his chair.

"You are fortunate to have such conscientious associates, Monsieur Heidlinger." Devenant turned to the two men. "If you should need the slightest of information, please do not hesitate to let me know—even if it seems insignificant." Devenant's eyes flickered to Jonnie, then back to McDarvid. He half raised a hand. "Good day, good day." Devenant was gone with the last of his words.

McDarvid reached down and picked up the thin folder he had brought to the meeting, then turned toward Jonnie.

"Just a moment."

McDarvid turned to face Heidlinger. He did not sit down. Neither did Jonnie.

"You two are here for one reason, and that reason is to support the law firm. We are not a consulting firm. We are a law firm. We do legal work. Consulting is fine, but"—Heidlinger paused before completing the sentence that even Larry had used—"it doesn't help if it doesn't lead to legal work."

McDarvid nodded. "I understand. There should be a fair amount on the chlorohydrobenzilate issue. That's gone too far for the kind of work we do, and I'd be happy to draft a note to Devenant recommending stepping up the purely legal efforts. That ought to wait a day or two, though."

Heidlinger nodded. "What about the metals?"

"That's another question. It's too early to tell." McDarvid hoped he wasn't too transparent.

"You don't think much of our chances there?"

"Not unless things change. It's very . . . political."

"All right." Heidlinger waddled around the pedestal table. "So long as you remember this is a law firm."

As they walked from the conference room, Jonnie glanced at McDarvid. "He was pretty abrupt with Heidlinger."

"He never said a harsh word."

"That's what I mean. He never acknowledged a single thing he said."

McDarvid closed the door of his office. "I like this less and less."

"You and me both."

McDarvid took off his coat and hung it on the hanger behind the door. "Devenant knows what's going on. Most of it, anyway."

"I thought so, too. Especially when he suggested that we ask him for the minor information. Do you think Heidlinger understood that?"

"Yes and no. Lawyers get paid for rephrasing what the client tells them. In his book, he wouldn't have found it at all unusual." McDarvid looked out on the handful of overcoated men and women walking down Nineteenth Street, his back to Jonnie.

"Jack?"

"Yes?" McDarvid did not turn.

"Oh, never mind. What are you going to do now?"

McDarvid took a deep breath and turned. "Got to write up that letter suggesting it's time for the big legal push on chlorohydrobenzilate."

"At least, Heidlinger will be happy. It will let him start the junior associates writing their endless briefs."

"Wonderful," mumbled McDarvid as the younger man left. "Just wonderful. All of U.S. heavy industry and all the high-tech initiatives are being buried or bought, and we don't know who or why, and Heidlinger thinks about how many law briefs he can have the firm write."

44

"MR. BLACK? There's a Mr. Alvarez on the line for you. He won't say who he's with."

"Put him through, please." Jonnie slipped a folder from his briefcase and eased it into the only clear space on his desk, pulling the stack of papers out and laying them on top of the empty folder. "Hey, Snake! How's it going?"

"Don't ask, man. It's best you don't know."

"Lisa again, huh?" Jonnie asked sympathetically.

"I told you not to ask. That woman, she's so crazy about me it drives me crazy. Then she won't see me, which makes me crazier."

"Crazy isn't going to help the timetable."

"C'mon. Have I ever let you down? I'm calling with good news. I spent most of yesterday on the phone with one of Lao's techs in Texas. We worked out that bug in the communications protocol, the one that prevented the local server from acknowledging field inquiries. I spent last night pasting things together and this morning on testing. Everything's go."

"I just got the notice from Lao on the BIOS update. In fact I've got it right here." Jonnie's eyes dropped to the Lao Systems Technical Update Notice. "Was that the problem?"

"No. I read through the documentation, and the update apparently fixes a problem so obscure I haven't found it yet. This one we finally traced to some software parameters. Did you read through the entire tech notice?"

"Are you kidding? Half of it was in hex—not exactly my strong point. I just looked at the version number and the shipping date."

"Jonnie, Jonnie, how am I ever going to make a programmer out of you?" Snake paused. "Anyway, everything's go."

"Great. Looks like I'm going to owe you that case of beer, after all. Is there anything for me to look at now? I could come over in a couple of hours."

"Hours? You got to be kidding. Two weeks, maybe a little more, call it early January. I've spent so much time on this bug that I haven't finished the inquiry screens. But it's going to work, just the way you designed it."

"I've heard that before."

"Man, you haven't heard it from me. When I say so, it works."

"Good. I'll be glad when we can wrap it up."

"Then what are you going to do? We won't be spending any more money on subcontractors once the project's finished."

"Give me more credit than that. When has any consultant declared a project finished?"

"You should be doing this full-time."

Jonnie ignored Snake's pitch. "Besides, once this is on-line, there'll be plenty of work."

"It'll work, my friend. I promise. Everyone will love it. You just insert your key, turn the machine on, achieve crypto-ignition—"

"Snake! You know better."

"I told you to get a STU-III."

"Who's going to pay for it? Bill doesn't like consultants in general and me in particular. You think he's going to get me a secure telephone so I can spend even less time on-site?"

"Hang on," Snake announced. "I got another call."

Jonnie looked from the Lao notice to the computer screen, and then to his watch.

"Gotta go," Snake's voice resumed. "It's Lisa. She's crazy about me again and wants to see me."

"So go. Talk to you later."

45

"I READ YOUR POLICY PAPER, JACK. Tom insisted that I should." Renni Fowler, her shoulder-length mahogany-red hair swept away from her face with a pair of black combs, looked over the heavy desk at McDarvid.

Her office contained two couches, both upholstered in the blue leather of the House of Representatives, a pair of stuffed and battered wooden bookcases, the desk with a credenza and the A.A.'s chair behind it, and the two barely padded, blue leather armchairs. There might have been ten square feet of open floor space. Stacks of papers covered the desk, and a console rested on the credenza—a Macintosh computer.

McDarvid wondered how anyone could use an icon-driven machine. Then, his brother wondered how anyone could possibly settle for anything else.

McDarvid sat in one of the uncomfortable armchairs. "And?"

"It's very good. You make a clear case that environmental policy has hampered the space effort. The metals initiative looks particularly damaging." Her voice was calm, as it had always been on the few times he had met with her when he had been with EPA. "The Chairman would be happy, I'm sure, to make an inquiry at Environment. We can't do much with OSHA, you understand. We don't have any jurisdiction there."

McDarvid pursed his lips. "It's far more serious than that. I suspect the Chairman would find ample material and interest if he held a hearing."

The subcommittee counsel looked toward the single window, then back at McDarvid. "The schedule's filled already."

"I know you can't do anything in December," McDarvid admitted amiably. "But I checked with . . . I checked already. You've only got one hearing set for the entire month of January."

"I can't schedule hearings in January. No one will be back until after the twentieth, just before the State of the Union and the President's Budget."

"What's the problem?" McDarvid pushed again.

"The Chairman would be happy to send a letter over to the Secretary."

"What? Basically enclose our paper and ask for comment?"

"Yes. That's the normal procedure. Then, if there's no suitable response, there might be grounds for further inquiry."

"Renni, you know as well as I do that it will be two months before you get an answer. In the meantime, DEP will finish drafting the NPRM. The department response will say nothing, except that the department will consider all the factors submitted during the comment period."

"That's what they're supposed to do." Rennie smiled politely. "I would hope your old department would continue to follow the laws, Jack."

"I'm not asking them to do anything else, Renni. I am asking you to do more than draft a cover letter about a serious problem affecting U.S. heavy industry and high technology." McDarvid swallowed. "Let me put it another way. DEP has never issued a less restrictive final regulation than when they first proposed a rule. The only times rules have been changed is under a court order, and you can't get a court order until after the final rule is promulgated. So what you're telling me is that you'll be happy to look into the damage after it has occurred."

"Jack, I'm sure the department and the environmental groups who filed the petitions for emergency temporary standards have material almost as good as yours showing why tighter standards are vitally necessary."

"There's one difference, Renni."

"Oh?"

"Even their own material fails to show the need for tighter standards. Everything has a threshold value. Even water. Too little and you die. Too much and you drown. Just because cadmium causes kidney disease at high levels doesn't mean you ban it at any level. Arsenic is toxic at high levels, but the human body needs trace amounts to function properly. The same is true of iron."

"You've always been rather convincing, Jack. But the schedule doesn't allow a hearing in January. We will be happy to send an inquiry, however, and I'll even make an exception to the rule and send you a copy."

"No chance of a hearing?" McDarvid persisted.

"Not now."

"Thank you." He rose. "Mind if I keep in touch?" He did not ask about Michael Alroy, although he wondered how much the engineer/lobbyist/boyfriend influenced Renni.

"Certainly, but you know how we operate." She did not stand, but watched from behind the desk.

McDarvid closed the door.

Tom Lerwinsky looked up from the small desk in the alcove to the right of the empty secretary's desk. "How did it go?"

"Renni's agreed to send an inquiry from the subcommittee. I tried to persuade her to call a hearing, but she felt that was . . . premature." McDarvid shrugged. "I guess I need to be more persuasive."

"That paper seemed persuasive to me, Jack."

McDarvid forced a smile. "I thought so, but I'm not exactly unbiased. Rennie pointed out that the other side has some facts to back their case. Anyway, back to the drawing board." He nodded to the deputy counsel. "See you around." Then he paused. "Is Renni . . . I mean, I didn't want to say anything, but Mike Alroy . . . is he still in the picture?"

"You interested?" Tom's face showed disapproval.

"Lord, no. That wasn't what I meant at all. But this is an aerospace issue, and it might affect Mike's outfit. So I don't want to rock any boats."

"Oh . . . yeah, that might be a problem." Lerwinsky lowered his voice. "Yes. More than ever, but I didn't tell you."

McDarvid nodded. Was that why Renni was sticking to the safe formal track? Maybe Jonnie could check out whether Hesterton Engineering was involved with JAFFE's competitors. Then, again . . . "Thanks, Tom. I'll send you anything else we develop on this."

"No problem, Jack. Good luck."

"Thanks. Might need more than luck, though."

As McDarvid waited for the modernized elevator, he recalled when the building had been the FBI warehouse/annex. Now it housed floor after floor of subcommittee and support staff. He didn't know which use was worse.

46

MCDARVID KNOCKED ON THE DOOR and walked in without waiting. "You know anyone who has a large telephoto lens?"

"A telephoto lens?" Jonnie leaned back in the brown upholstered desk chair that matched neither the narrow desk nor the dark gray institutional carpet. The same carpet graced McDarvid's floor.

"Yeah. One that will fit my thirty-five millimeter. It's a Canon."

"You don't want to buy one, I take it?"

"Not really. This isn't exactly the time to go spending money we don't have. Except you're single."

"But I do have assorted obligations, albeit nothing in comparison to your encumbrances. Also student loans."

"I stand corrected."

"What do you want it for?"

"I want to take some pictures in the bright sunshine. In the light of day, at least." McDarvid smiled faintly as he noted the grayness of the afternoon through the narrow window behind his accomplice.

"You aren't taking up bird-watching?"

"That's another way of putting it."

"Do I really want to know?"

"No. But I'll show you the pictures if they turn out. Assuming I can get the lens." McDarvid wondered if he really wanted to go through with it. Did he really have any choice? Everywhere he turned, everyone was so polite, and so reluctant to do anything.

"My sister has one she might let me borrow."

"When?"

"My, you are in a hurry."

"The season's short."

"I'll give her a call as soon as I can."

"Thanks." McDarvid edged toward the doorway.

"I take it your meetings didn't go quite as planned."

"Not all that badly," he lied. "But it leaves a lot of work to do," he added more truthfully.

Jonnie raised his eyebrows.

"I need to write up some materials, suggest several dozen nasty questions, a background paper or two, and maybe a press release—that's for starters."

"Then the real work begins?"

McDarvid nodded. "Yeah."

47

FAR BENEATH HIS WINGS SHIMMERED THE PATCHY WHITE, broken only by highways and buildings. Winter, always the winter—the ever-present winter.

He glanced back at the instruments. The already-low fuel state was all too familiar. He rechecked the single small radar screen, then swallowed as the blip solidified at one o'clock—a red dot that no longer pulsed, but glowed bright red, then flared a handful of red sparks that darted toward him.

He jabbed the red button, then snapped the stick down and left with one hand, and the throttles through the detent with the other. The cockpit lurched as the missile separated.

The afterburners roared in his ears, and the green light showed his own lock-on, but the red sparks on the screen grew larger, larger . . .

McDarvid bolted upright, shaking, his forehead sweating cold droplets.

He took a deep breath, then another.

The same damned nightmare—except this time he had launched his own missiles. So damned real, just as though he had been back at the controls.

He shivered again, then slipped to his feet.

"Jack, are you all right?"

"Fine . . . I'm fine. Just having trouble sleeping . . . Back in a minute."

In the darkness, he walked down to the kitchen, his steps as soft as he could make them.

Why the Soviet cockpit? Was his subconscious telling him that the Russians weren't the real enemy? Or was it the uncertainty? The never knowing whether he'd be looking for yet another job, just like poor Ned Llewellyn? Or was it all the unconnected pieces involved with the metals initiative? Or just all the years of having to live by intuition, knowing you had to decide before you really knew what was going to happen?

He found the box of Popsicles in the freezer. All that were left were grape ones. After peeling down the paper, he bit off the tip, chewing the grape ice into slushy chips that cooled his raw throat. Several bites later, he closed the freezer door and walked toward the front of the house, stopping at the foot of the stairs.

The antique mantel clock chimed the half hour, but McDarvid didn't know which half hour, since he hadn't looked at the bedside clock radio.

Instead of going back upstairs, he stepped into the study. Looking out the side window, he took a bite of the grape ice. The streetlight sketched out the shadows of bare tree limbs on the nearly melted pile of snow by the driveway, on the flaking cold white concrete, and on the frozen lawn.

When he had finished the Popsicle, the last cold threads of liquid trickling down his throat, he dropped the stick and the damp paper into the wastebasket under his desk. With a last look at the shadows on the chill lawn, he stepped back into the hall, letting his bare feet carry him back upstairs and into the queen-sized Queen Anne bed.

Allyson's breathing was regular, unsnoring, and easy.

"The sleep of the guiltless," he murmured as he slipped under the covers, wondering why the nightmare recurred.

48

"VERONICA, I NEED TO TALK TO YOU." Peter's breath came in small frosty puffs that hovered above the grayness of the sidewalk.

"What are you doing here?" Veronica had just started up the steps of the Capitol Hill row house which housed the Ecology Now! operations.

"I want to talk with you. Isn't that what I just said?"

"I didn't think we had anything to talk about. Besides, talking here isn't the best idea."

"Why? Afraid that Mr. Clean will fire you for consorting with someone who's willing to take some real action for the environment?"

"Oh, Christ, you know better than that. You're the one who's got problems. Not me. If you want to talk, let's get a cup of coffee. I'm not about to stand out here and freeze. The place up the street should be open by now." Veronica quickly turned without looking to see if Peter followed.

She had a table and a small Styrofoam cup of steaming coffee by the time Peter appeared. He sat down without buying anything.

"So what do you want to talk to me about?" Veronica had her hands around the cup.

"I want to talk to you about rejoining the group."

"I told you once. I'm not going to take part in any crazy scheme to spread radiation." Her hushed tone did nothing to hide her anger.

"It's got to be that Black guy. You're never home, and you don't want to talk to your old friends. I never thought you were the kind of girl who would turn into a sappy-minded little lackey just because you finally got laid."

Veronica sighed. "You didn't listen the last time, and you're not listening now."

"Who's not listening? I told you that you've lost your nerve and your principles, and all you want to do is run away." Peter's voice rose.

"No. All I want to do is what's right."

"We're doing what's right."

"Bullshit. For the first time, we've finally got really strong grass-roots support. Even average consumers worry about the products they buy. More and more of them are recycling. The politicians are worrying about their environmental votes—"

"That's all little crap."

"Damn it. People are willing to make sacrifices for the environment. Little ones, but it's a start. The big danger is something crazy like this will alienate the public from the green movement."

"Public opinion. You've sold out to a pretty image, babe!"

She shook her head. "You're not listening. All you want to do is play the big macho protester. And I'm not getting tied up with your crazy scheme."

"You're going to listen to me for once, bitch." Peter grabbed Veronica's arm and pulled her back down.

Veronica clamped her lips together as she dropped into the hard chair.

"You listen to whoever you fuck? I'll fuck your brains out. Maybe then you'll come to your senses." Peter continued his painful grip on Veronica's arm. The counterman, having seen too many similar scenes and knowing the danger of getting involved, looked away.

"Fuck my brains out? You wouldn't know how."

"You . . ." Peter choked, and squeezed her arm harder.

"Now you've got two choices," Veronica hissed. "You can either let go of my arm, or you can see a plastic surgeon about getting your face repaired."

In Veronica's hand was a small, razor-edged Tekna knife she had pulled from her purse. The serrated blade was only inches from Peter's face.

Peter released the pressure on Veronica's arm without breaking contact.

"Okay, I'll go. But you just made it ten times worse. Instead of just dusting the fence line and a part of that field, I'm going to dust the creek and the water. Then, when people find out they're drinking radioactive water, they'll finally take some action. And your name, like it or not, is going to be written all over this one.

"Like I told you before," Peter said as he finally lifted his hand from Veronica's arm, "we're going to do whatever it takes to close that plant. And there's not a damn thing you can do to stop us, not without ruining that carefully planned future of yours.

"You see, babe," he added as he stood up, "you got yourself in too deep to walk away."

"You just went one step too far," Veronica said slowly, "and the only environmental groups that will have you will be the ones already in jail."

"Sure, babe."

She slowly replaced the knife, holding the coffee with the other hand, watching the man in the scratched leather jacket disappear.

49

"CAL, DO YOU HAVE A MINUTE?"

The balding ecologist looked up from the calendar. "You look worried. For that, and because you usually bring cheer around here, you can have as many minutes as you like. But you had better close the door. Otherwise, Ray will be in here at least twice in the next five minutes." His quick grin faded as he watched her face.

Veronica reached back and shut the door. Then she eased into the straight-backed chair across the desk from him.

"What's on your mind?" Griffen leaned back in the creased leather swivel, steepling his hands across his flat stomach.

"Do you remember Peter—Peter Andrewson? He used to be a friend of Ray's, I think."

Griffen's forehead creased; then he nodded slowly. "Didn't he have a motorcycle? He always wanted some sort of extreme action. Struck me as very unstable. I told Ray to ease him out— that happened about the time you became an intern, I think."

"He started his own group, and I went to the meetings for a while. Now he's decided to dump radioactive dust in the creek beside the Fayettetown processing plant as part of the big protest there next month. I told him it was a crazy idea . . ."

"That's insane," reflected the deep-voiced environmentalist. "The last thing the movement needs is a poisoned water supply. What do you want me to do?"

Veronica took a deep breath. "I kept going to the meetings longer than I should. Originally, he was just going to scatter a little yellowcake dust around the fence. But a couple of days ago, he came up with this latest idea. He won't listen. Now he says that he's somehow going to document that I had something to do with it. If I go to the police, they either won't believe me, or I'll be tarred with the same brush. Is there anything else I can do?"

"Hmmmm . . . that boy is definitely unbalanced. Can't have people doing things like that, you know. It's bad for us. It's one thing to lie in front of bulldozers or stop whalers who flaunt the international conventions. It's another to actually damage the environment."

Veronica waited.

"If you want, I *think* I can take care of this quietly, but I need some more information. If I do, your friend may end up in jail."

"In jail? He deserves that . . . I suppose."

Griffen nodded again. "Now . . . when is he . . ."

50

MCDARVID FINGERED THE CARD. Finally, he tapped out the number.

"Investigations."

"Detective Ngruma, please. This is Jack McDarvid."

"He's not in."

McDarvid left his name and number, then stood up and walked out of the office. He slipped into his overcoat in the elevator, buttoning it and pulling on his black gloves as he stepped out onto Nineteenth Street and headed toward K Street.

Several blocks later, he paused outside the Laura Ashley store, then pushed his way inside, out of the wind.

"Is there anything in particular you were looking for?"

McDarvid nodded. "Dresses."

"Ah . . . anything in particular?"

"Size twelve long, with drop waist, preferably in green."

"Here are the twelves."

McDarvid nodded again and studied the dresses, looking for the type that looked so good on Allyson.

"Hmmmm . . ." He pulled one out, then replaced it.

None of the others came close.

The next stop was Gantos.

The dress wasn't the green he envisioned, nor was it quite so simple, but the cut would still suit Allyson, and the pattern was soft enough that her complexion would draw from the colors, rather than be overshadowed.

He grinned as he paid for it and had it boxed, and the damp wind didn't even seem chill on the way back to the office.

Three messages were waiting. One was Detective Ngruma; the others were from Ned Llewellyn and Angela Siskin.

He tried Ngruma first.

"Yes, this is Jack McDarvid. I was just wondering if you . . . if there had been any developments in finding anything about Larry Partello's murderer?"

"Frankly, when you called, Mr. McDarvid, I was hoping you might have some information."

"Oh . . . I just hadn't heard anything . . ."

"There's not much to add. The M.E. identified the bullet as a nine-millimeter shell, but that could have come from anything from my own weapon to a MAC-10."

McDarvid promised to keep Ngruma informed if anything new turned up.

Then he tried Angela. She was out.

Ned Llewellyn was not.

"Thanks for calling back, Jack. It's not official yet, but the Secretary will be submitting his resignation after the State of the Union."

"Any ideas on who's being considered? What about Lew Engelbright?" McDarvid tried not to wince as he mentioned Engelbright's name.

"Lew? The President only made him Deputy to pay off Garth Reimers. It looks like a whole new team—probably Haylock Ellis."

"That means a new Counselor to the President." And that meant, McDarvid reflected, that the Chief of Staff and the head of the NSC had succeeded in getting Ellis—with his opposition to reductions in the Air Force arm of the strategic triad—away from the President's ear. Jonnie would find that interesting. "I take it things are slow in turning up?"

"Slow . . . that's a kind way of putting it, Jack."

"I told you about the Chlorine Institute and the Forest Products possibilities. Haven't heard anything else. Maybe after the first of the year." McDarvid tried to keep his voice cheerfully sympathetic. He'd been there before, and if the metals initiative didn't go right, he might be there again—unless he and Jonnie could find a way to become independent.

"Thanks. Mind if I keep in touch?"

"No. No problem."

51

RAY THOMAS PAUSED AT THE OPEN DOOR and peered inside. "Good night, Cal."

Griffen looked up from the stack of reading. "Good night, Ray."

"No receptions or meetings tonight?"

The other shook his head. "After I finish catching up on a few things, I'm headed home. Once in a while, I like to get some sleep."

"Pleasant dreams, then."

In time, a second figure appeared at the door. "Cal, I'm leaving. Is it all right if I lock up? You aren't expecting anyone, are you?"

Griffen smiled pleasantly. "No, Martha. Not tonight. I won't be too much longer, but go ahead and lock up. I did remember my keys."

"Don't stay too late," cautioned the dark-haired woman.

"I won't."

"That's what you always say."

"I'll try to do better this time."

With a headshake and a smile, she turned and made her way across the outer office to the front door.

The ecologist continued reading for a time after the front door had clicked shut. With a sigh, he pulled out several index cards covered in his own precise writing and studied them. Then he lifted the telephone.

"I'm sorry, but I'm not available at the moment. Please leave a message at the sound of the tone." The low, almost harsh, voice echoed in the receiver.

"Elizabeth, this is Cal. Our friend is getting out of hand. You can call me at home tonight or tomorrow night after eight. Thank you."

He set down the receiver and stood up, looking down at the reading he had yet to finish. Finally, he scooped it into a folder and set the folder on the corner of the desk while he put on his suit coat and his overcoat.

Then, folder in one hand, keys in the other, he walked toward the door.

52

"YOUR SERVE, TIGER." McDarvid tossed the Ping-Pong ball to David.

David caught it, dropped it on the table, and thwacked it across the net.

McDarvid, paddle in his right hand, awkwardly returned the serve to the far corner, but his son stabbed backhand, and the white ball arced up over the net and continued rising past the end of the table.

McDarvid caught the ball in his left hand and flicked it back to David.

Thwack.

McDarvid's return missed the corner of the table, and David bent down and reclaimed the ball.

Thwack.

McDarvid eased the ball just over the net.

David lunged and missed.

"That's it, Tiger."

"*Oooofff.* That wasn't fair, Dad."

"Fair?"

"All right. It was sneaky, though."

"You're right, but sneaky counts." McDarvid glanced at the stairs as he heard Allyson's steps coming down from the second floor.

"Jack?"

"I've got to go. See you two later."

"I never got a chance to play," Kirsten complained.

"Tomorrow," McDarvid promised as he turned and headed up the basement stairs.

Allyson wore matching sweatpants and jacket, both a slightly faded forest green. She was talking to a thin teenager. "Should be back before eleven. Number is on the pad next to the telephone."

McDarvid pulled on his ski jacket and picked up the bag with the racquets, balls, and the eye protectors.

"Any questions?"

"No, Dr. Newsome."

Allyson slipped into her parka. McDarvid held the door for her, and they walked to the car.

"I heard you playing Ping-Pong with David. I take it you won."

"It was twenty-one to fifteen, and I played right-handed."

"And when he starts to beat you, you'll play left-handed and keep winning?"

"He'll eventually beat me, and he'll know that he did it fair and square."

Allyson said nothing as McDarvid eased the car onto Forty-sixth.

"Who'll be there?" he asked.

"Probably most of the pediatrics group. Everyone liked the idea of a racquetball party instead of one of those Christmas parties where everyone stands around and eats and drinks."

"Best party idea I've heard of in a while."

"Jack?"

"Yes?"

"I know you're carrying around a lot right now, but ever since Larry's death, it's like all you do is talk consulting. I know I complained about not talking, but I've heard more about metals . . ."

"Sorry. I take it you're suggesting that I play racquetball and leave the consulting behind."

"Well, you've got about ten minutes before we get there." Allyson laughed softly.

"There's too much to say in ten minutes. Or too little." McDarvid paused. "Do you think we'll have any more snow this winter? Or are you up for an indecent proposal after the party?"

"Jack!" But there was a smile behind the protest.

He reached over and squeezed her thigh. For a moment, her cheek rested against his.

53

THE BLACK GTO PURRED AROUND THE CURVE AT SEVENTY. The traffic on the Inner Loop was relatively light—even though it was a bright, cloudless Saturday afternoon nearing Christmas. Jonnie signaled to pass the old purple hearse in front of him.

Would Veronica like to go to the January concert? Jonnie eyed the line of multicolored teddy bears performing the kick-step on the hearse's bumper sticker. "If she wants to go and I don't get tickets as soon as they go on sale, I'll have to visit my friendly neighborhood scalper."

While it was relatively easy to buy tickets to sold-out events around the world and the Washington scalpers accepted Visa, their prices demonstrated a certain high-spirited free market attitude. Jonnie shook his head at the memory of turning over an envelope containing five hundred-dollar bills to a young woman in an otherwise deserted Laurel office building the Saturday before a Redskins play-off game. Even Larry, who never objected to spending as much of the company's money as necessary to keep a client happy, gurgled slightly at the seven-hundred-dollar price tag when Jonnie handed over the two lower-deck forty-yard-line tickets Sunday morning, less than twenty-four hours after he had received a call at home from a desperate Partello.

Jonnie nodded at the bearded, ponytailed hearse driver as he passed him and entered the construction zone. Slowing slightly as the highway divided, he grinned as he passed the most honest construction-advisory sign he had ever seen. "Prepare for Sudden Aggravation," the notice warned. But there was no aggravation for the last twenty minutes of the drive.

Jonnie swung into the apartment complex's lot and parked next to an old Harley. He opened his oversized door, careful not to hit the bike.

The old Harley appeared to be a late 1940s Knucklehead. Like his own GTO, the Knucklehead, despite showing some scratches, a couple of dents, and even a few rust spots breaking through the dark red paint, was in basically good condition. With only minor restoration work, the bike would be considered a pricey classic.

He nodded and stepped away from the bike, thinking that something like the old Harley would be better for Veronica than her eco-conscious tinmobile. A Harley would get better mileage and be a hell of a lot more fun. A greasy-looking man in a leather jacket leaned against a leafless tree. He casually appraised Jonnie, then spat on the browning grass, saying nothing.

Was the greasy fellow the motorcycle's owner or did he belong to the battered Ford pickup with the country-music stickers? Jonnie decided on the country-music stickers. The Knucklehead had to belong to a yuppie lawyer. Few real bikers were lucky enough to own that kind of Harley.

Veronica opened the door quickly. "Come on in. I'm on the phone. Shut the door behind you."

Jonnie closed the door carefully. Instead of sitting down or going into the kitchen where Veronica stood with the telephone, he walked over toward the couch to take a closer look at Groucho to see if he could tell what brand of cigar the great man had preferred.

No luck. The cigar was merely a black torpedo, and Jonnie wandered toward the computer stand in the corner.

Veronica's voice carried from the small kitchen, and he stopped.

"Yes, I know, but I'm miles from where that happened. The newspapers make a big deal . . . Yes, I know. I will be careful . . . No, you don't have to worry about him. He was just someone who belongs to the same environmental group . . . Would you prefer someone safer—like a regulatory consultant? . . . I'm serious. That's who was at the door . . . He does have a beard, but it's well trimmed, and he doesn't drive—no, he works for a law firm. Now, that ought to be established enough . . . Yes, I will call more often."

Jonnie didn't hide the grin as Veronica stepped out of the kitchen. "Mother or sister?"

"Mother. She read the wire story about that law student who was assaulted off Dupont Circle. As if anyone in their right mind would wander down an alley at three A.M. Anyway, I couldn't just stop there, but I'm glad you got here on time. If you'd been late, I'd still be on the phone."

"Big phone bills?"

"Not that big. She usually calls me . . . unless she wants to make me feel guilty."

Jonnie laughed. "The old parental guilt trip. You'd think that it wouldn't work after so long—but it does."

"You're right. It does." Veronica shook her head, and her auburn hair tossed. "I'm almost ready. Hold on a moment while I check the Crockpot."

"Crockpot? I haven't seen one of those in years."

"I guess I'm just an old-fashioned girl." Veronica smiled. "We're going to have a stew after we get back from the movies. It'll be nice to have something hot later."

Jonnie watched as Veronica adjusted a dial on the contrivance that looked like a cross between a squat brown cookie jar and a pressure cooker.

"I'm ready." Veronica pulled out a quilted blue parka.

As they left the apartment, a gust of wind almost ripped the scratched and corroded aluminum storm door out of Jonnie's hand.

"It's really getting cold." Already holding Jonnie's arm, Veronica pressed even closer as they walked down the sidewalk to the car. "I just hope the stew turns out."

"You've never fed me a bad meal yet."

"It would be nice if you reciprocated once in a while, instead of just taking me to restaurants."

"Well . . . my cooking skills . . . you know . . ."

"Sure I know, but just think. It would give you a wonderful excuse to get me over to your apartment," Veronica purred in Jonnie's ear.

"On the other hand, I can be a really talented chef. Does microwave cooking count?"

"We'll count anything you like as long as you make it yourself. No prepared dinners from the gourmet grocery."

"How about if we make it together? I've always wanted cooking lessons."

"That's funny. I never noticed you needed lessons before."

"Can't hurt. Oh, want to see a really nifty old motorcycle?" Jonnie pointed at the dark red machine next to his car.

"Oh . . . That looks like . . . What . . . ?" Veronica turned, letting go of Jonnie's arm.

"Just checking up on you, babe."

Jonnie swiveled to see that the man who had been leaning against the tree stood less than ten feet away.

"I thought it might be a good idea to see what you were doing and who you were doing it with. I also wanted to remind you that dust-day is two weeks from next Saturday."

"Friend of yours?" Jonnie asked Veronica. He eyed the biker, who, up close, appeared rather larger and greasier than he had first realized. The man's long stringy black hair and ragged beard contrasted curiously with his watery blue eyes, pale fine-pored skin, and small, almost delicate features. The overall impression was that of a bookworm gone bad.

"Not even close," snapped Veronica. She addressed Peter. "What do you want?"

"Like I said, babe, I wanted to see what you were up to. So is this the prick you're screwing? Christ! I never thought you had much taste, but this?" Peter jabbed a finger toward Jonnie. "Couldn't you have at least picked a real man? So you like my bike? You some kinda fuckin' wannabe? I hate wannabes."

"Look, I don't know who you are or what your problem is, but why don't we just call it a day," Jonnie said, stepping between Peter and Veronica.

"You're my problem, wannabe. I don't like you. I don't like you screwing that woman. And I'm not getting the hell out of here." The biker moved even closer, his hands balled into fists held closely by his side.

"Fine," Jonnie said evenly. "You want to stay. Stay all night." He turned to Veronica. "Let's go."

"You're one dead prick." But Peter remained standing on the grass.

Jonnie opened the door, letting his eyes flick toward the greasy biker.

Veronica slipped into the front seat, but her eyes locked on Peter for an instant.

"You just remember . . . babe . . ."

Jonnie locked Veronica's door and stepped around the GTO. He opened the other door and slipped into the driver's seat, the keys going into the ignition even before he was seated.

"Heyyy!" The biker stumbled forward, then stopped with a bewildered look as the GTO momentarily lurched toward him.

"Have a nice evening," Jonnie called cheerfully as the GTO rumbled out of the parking lot.

Once onto the road, with no sign of a motorcycle in the rearview mirror, Jonnie glanced at a silent Veronica. "Now, would you like to tell me who this guy was and what's going on? And what is dust-day?" He slowed at the stop sign, again checking the mirror and seeing only a silver Chevy pickup.

"It's a long story." Veronica sighed.

Jonnie waited, but she said nothing more. They were on Route 29 south before Jonnie spoke again.

"Who was he?"

"You aren't going to give up?"

Jonnie glanced at the speedometer and eased off the accelerator.

"His name is Peter Andrewson. He and I used to belong to a

group, an environmental group. I decided they were too . . . Anyway, I joined because they promised to do more than just talk about environmental problems. Then Peter started getting ideas, really crazy ideas. So I quit. And he just wouldn't take no for an answer."

"What is dust-day?"

"I don't want to talk about it. It was one of his ideas, and I wouldn't have anything to do with it."

"He was spoiling for a fight."

"I'm glad you avoided that."

"You mean you didn't want me to display my skills with Okinawan karate?" Jonnie forced a grin.

"Not particularly. Usually unplanned violence just makes things worse."

"Planned violence makes things better?"

Veronica shrugged and shifted her weight on the vinyl seats. "His violence will get him in trouble before long."

This time Jonnie frowned. "Is that a general observation or a promise?"

"I don't want to talk about it anymore."

"Look." Jonnie took a deep breath. "This character shows up like a Wild West villain. He threatens you; then he threatens me, and you just want to act like it never happened. He doesn't look like the kind who's just going to up and disappear."

"He really doesn't have much choice," Veronica replied.

Jonnie applied the brakes abruptly to avoid the silver sports car that angled in front of them.

"Doesn't have much choice?"

"No. I'm not playing his game. Neither did you. He won't actually fight. Besides . . ." She closed her eyes and took a deep breath. "Can we just leave it at that? It's not your problem. It's mine. He wants me to keep playing his stupid games, and I won't."

"His games sound pretty rough."

"Jonnie, you're making more out of it than there is. Can we just enjoy the movies? I'd rather even talk about your dullest work than spend any more time on this. Peter's history. He just doesn't know it, and it will take a little time before . . . anyway . . . tell me what you know about the movie."

Jonnie nodded slowly. "All right. It's about this alcoholic poet who falls in love with . . ."

54

"DAMN!" MUTTERED MCDARVID as a spruce needle jabbed his finger.

"Father, profanity—"

"I know. Profanity is the last refuge of the inarticulate," he snapped at Elizabeth, perched on the edge of the couch. "These needles are sharp."

"That's because you got a dead tree. A live tree would have been more ecologically sound, and the needles wouldn't fall out all over the carpet. And they would have been softer."

McDarvid growled softly and eased another light into place.

"Daddy! Daddy! There's a package!" called Kirsten.

McDarvid climbed off the kitchen stool, carefully draping the Christmas lights on the armchair. He still had two strings to thread through the sticky branches of the Colorado blue spruce.

"Daddy, the deliveryman is coming up the walk!"

"I'm coming, Kirsten. I'm coming."

"You have to complete the lighting," announced Elizabeth from beside the carton of Christmas ornaments. "And you have to dislodge David from the television."

McDarvid had ignored the play-by-play from the family room. Football bored him, but not his son, who remained glued to any football telecast.

Brinnngggg . . .

McDarvid winced at the tinny doorbell that he kept thinking he should replace with chimes—or anything that didn't sound like the 1930s doorbell that it was. He opened the door.

"McDarvid residence?" asked the UPS deliveryman.

"That's us." McDarvid eased open the new storm door he had finally replaced the day before. A gust of cold air blew past him and into the entryway as he took the package. "Thank you."

He shut the door and looked at the label on the heavy package.

Allyson climbed up from the basement, the last small box of Christmas decorations in her arms. "What's that?"

"I'm not sure," McDarvid admitted. "It's from a client."

"Could it be work?"

McDarvid lifted the heavy oblong package, roughly eight inches high and a foot square. "I don't see how."

"Then open it," Allyson suggested.

"Open it, Daddy. Open it," Kirsten added more emphatically.

McDarvid carried the package into the kitchen, set it on the breakfast bar, and rummaged through a drawer to come up with scissors and a knife.

Inside the first heavy cardboard box was a second package wrapped in pale silver paper imprinted with stylized evergreen trees. A small envelope was lightly taped to the package. Precise black script proclaimed: "J. McDarvid and family."

"Maybe we should save it until Christmas."

"From a client?" asked Allyson. "Christmas is for family, not business."

"You're right." McDarvid removed the envelope, then extracted the card.

"What does it say?"

"Not much. Just 'Joyeux Noël' and his name."

"Can we see what's in the box?" asked Kirsten.

McDarvid pocketed the card, then slit the paper to reveal a thinner white cardboard box, with an imprint in the corner.

"That's D'Arques," Allyson volunteered from his shoulder.

"What's D'Arques, Mommy?" asked Kirsten.

"It's French crystal, almost as good as Orrefors."

"Go ahead, Daddy. Open it," prompted Kirsten.

McDarvid opened the box and parted the tissue and polystyrene beads. He lifted out a small package of colored crystalline Christmas candies wrapped within a plastic bag and set the package on the counter.

"Is that all?" asked Kirsten.

"Just hang on, squirt." McDarvid then lifted out the crystal candy dish and set it on the breakfast bar next to the candies.

"It's beautiful," murmured Allyson.

"It is pretty," admitted the littlest redhead.

"Might I see?" asked Elizabeth, finally drawn by the group in the kitchen from her station next to the largest box of Christmas ornaments.

"What is it?" demanded Kirsten. "The shape is funny."

McDarvid studied the crystal, a rough asymetric ovoid with an extrusion too small and delicate to be a handle emerging from the narrow end of the dish. The shape was vaguely familiar, but he couldn't have said why.

"It is . . . strange . . ." acknowledged Allyson.

"Might I see?" persisted Elizabeth.

"Oh, sure." McDarvid stepped aside.

Elizabeth looked at the dish for a long time. "What's this?" she finally asked, pointing to the emblem cut in the center of the dish.

"That? That's the emblem of the company. JAFFE. They're French."

"Why is it such a funny shape?" asked Kirsten.

"I don't know," McDarvid answered.

"There must be a logical reason." Elizabeth headed for the study.

"Elizabeth?"

"I will return."

McDarvid chuckled and shook his head, catching Allyson's eyes. In turn, she grinned.

"When can we have the candy?" asked Kirsten.

"Not yet." McDarvid looked around for somewhere to put the dish.

"I believe I have the solution," announced Elizabeth, lugging the open world atlas into the kitchen.

McDarvid raised his eyebrows and looked at Allyson. She shrugged.

"Yes, Elizabeth?"

The atlas came down on the counter next to the crystal. McDarvid grabbed for the dish to keep it from bouncing off the edge.

"Observe!" commanded the eleven-year-old.

"Observe what?" McDarvid asked.

"Corsica," Elizabeth announced matter-of-factly. "Anything that irregular could not have been geometric. You did say it came from France."

McDarvid followed his daughter's finger to the map of Corsica. Although the atlas's image was considerably smaller than the dish, the outlines of the island and the dish appeared identical.

"What an odd shape to make a dish," Allyson said quietly, "especially one so lovely."

McDarvid only swallowed, looking out through the kitchen window.

His older daughter picked up and closed the atlas.

McDarvid grabbed for the dish again, retrieving it and looking again for some place to put it out of harm's way.

"In the china cabinet," suggested Allyson.

"Can we resume our decorating, Father?" inquired Elizabeth.

"In a minute." McDarvid eased open the china cabinet and rearranged the wineglasses to make room for the crystal candy dish. Then he returned and grabbed the candies to put them inside the Corsica-shaped dish in the cabinet.

Allyson had carried the last box of decorations into the living room. "David, it's time to turn off the television."

"They're on the ten-yard line!"

"David," added McDarvid.

"But Dad!"

"Now! One, two . . ."

"All right, all right."

"It's about time," announced Elizabeth.

McDarvid closed the china cabinet and stepped into the living room, looking at the lights he had still not finished threading through the sharp needles of the blue spruce. The dead, cut, blue spruce.

55

"WE'LL MEET AT THE RENDEZVOUS POINT a week from Friday at seven A.M. A.M. stands for ante meridiem. In other words, morning."

"So you were an English scholar. We've all heard the crap about intellectuals being undervalued, about your hard-earned master's degree being worthless," complained the bull-necked young man with the shaved head. "Talk in plain English. What the fuck do you want?"

"All right, fuckhead. I want you to be there on fucking Friday morning. Is that fucking crude enough, Graeme?" Peter glared at Graeme, who stepped back, even though he bulked far larger than Peter. Peter turned, fixing his watery blue eyes on each of the others in turn before speaking. "That's to give us enough time to get ready before the police and the other protesters arrive. I want everything, and I mean everything, to be set before Saturday. You might want to leave Thursday afternoon so you have time to rest up before the morning. Figure on the trip down taking about five to six hours. I don't want anyone speeding. The last thing we need is for the cops to know that we're on our way. Another thing. We all travel separately, including you two." The speaker's hoarse voice growled at Mike and Liz.

The two lovers looked about the dingy room guiltily, but their arms remained entwined.

"Don't worry, Peter dear," Liz replied. The faint lines streaking back from the corners of her eyes were the only sign on her open, innocent face of how many years she had been civilly disobedient. "However, since we're going to such great lengths to help the environment, don't you think you could do something about the local environment? I mean, I don't mind that this couch is filthy or that you can't tell the stains on the rug from the pattern, but the air in here stinks. Couldn't you at least open a window?"

"I'm sorry my quarters aren't quite up to your standards." The hoarseness of the voice could not disguise the sneering sarcasm. "Maybe next time we'll meet at the Plaza. I'll reserve a suite—something suitable for plotting revolution. I'll even have room service bring up some champagne. Sommelier, what goes well with radiation, brut or rosé?"

Despite his tirade, Peter moved over to the nearest window and wrenched it all the way open. A gust of cold air threatened to lift the maps off the linoleum-topped table until Graeme dropped a huge hand on the papers.

Peter ignored the rustling. "Tuesday morning I'll get the dust from Tedor. I'm going to handle that myself."

Tedor nodded an acknowledgment from a cushion on the

floor, his extended drooping mustache almost touching his chest as his head bobbed.

"What about Veronica? Isn't she still a part of us?" Mike inquired, his long blond hair scarcely shorter than Liz's. Unlike Liz, his face displayed no lines.

"Veronica's still a part of us, all right." Peter gave his first grin of the afternoon, a not particularly flattering expression. "She has a very important role to play in our little operation. It's just that her mission requires that she stay away from us for a little bit. But I think when this is over, you'll be hearing quite a bit about Miss Lakas' role."

"Why do you keep everything such a fucking secret?"

Peter whirled. "Because you don't need to know. That's still the best way to operate."

"I thought that went out with Stalin."

"Just cut the wiseass stuff," growled Peter. "Let's get on with it. Any questions?"

"We know what we're supposed to do. You made that clear enough."

"Then I'll see you on Friday."

Liz stood, looking at Peter again. Finally, she nodded without speaking and jerked her head toward the door.

Mike followed her lead.

Tedor, looking like a slender walrus, bounced after them.

Peter did not move until the last of the group had departed, his eyes still following Liz until he closed the door. "Bitches, all of them."

56

MCDARVID SET THE TOOLBOX ON THE STAIRS, looking up at the new door chimes. The 1930s-style doorbell had rung one too many times. Probably he shouldn't have spent the time on installing the chimes, but . . . He shrugged. Sometimes it just took less time to do it yourself. While he wished he'd done it sooner—like a lot of things—there always seemed more things to do than time to do them.

He glanced into the study, looking at the year-end business section of the paper. Replacing the doorbell had definitely been more enjoyable than reading the summary of the year's key business developments—like the report of the closing of the last U.S. copper smelter or the speculation that all the new high-definition televisions would be produced in the third world, using an amalgam of U.S. and Japanese technology. The article on increased eco-terrorism in the redwood forests hadn't helped, either. He closed his eyes.

"Father?"

"Yes, Elizabeth." He opened his eyes again and looked out past the computer and over the bare bushes that bordered the walk to the driveway. On the shelf was the borrowed telephoto lens. He still hadn't had the nerve to use it—another disturbing, but probably necessary, thing yet to do.

"Would it trouble you if I used the computer?"

"For what?" McDarvid asked automatically.

"For a project," responded his dark-haired daughter, standing in the doorway from the hall.

"For just a little while," he answered. "Once I take my shower, I'll need it."

"For what?"

"For a project."

"Father!"

McDarvid grinned as he reached for the toolbox. "If you want to use it, you'd better get going."

"Thank you." Elizabeth did not open the folder she had carried into the study with her.

McDarvid stepped down the hallway toward the kitchen, where he could hear the television from the family room. "David?"

There was no answer.

"David?"

Still no answer.

"David!"

"Yes, Dad?"

"What are you watching?"

"Nothing."

"Fine. Turn it off."

"But . . ."

"You know the rules."

"I'm bored, and there's nothing to do."

"Have you cleaned your closet?"

"Dad . . ."

"I'm taking my shower. By the time I'm done, I expect you to have started."

"It's not fair. Elizabeth's closet is a bigger mess than mine."

McDarvid sighed again. David was right. He trundled back to the study door, toolbox still in hand. "Elizabeth?"

"Yes, Father."

"When I get out of the shower and get back here, you are to begin cleaning your closet."

"Father . . ."

"Elizabeth . . ."

"Yes, Father."

McDarvid carried the toolbox down to the basement storage room and set it on the metal shelf next to the circular saw he hadn't used since he had repaired the deck.

As he climbed back upstairs, he heard footsteps above him, and, after reaching the upstairs hall, he looked into Kirsten's room. The littlest redhead had begun to pull clothes and toys from her closet.

McDarvid grinned. "Little Miss Halo." Then he shook his head as he thought of televisions and smelters, of the metals initiative, and of the telephoto lens.

57

PETER FLICKED ON THE INTERIOR LIGHT and checked the map again. He flicked the light off. Another two miles before the turnoff to the state highway that eventually ran along the side of the facility boundary—not by the main gate. Outside the small blue Chevette, the sky continued to lighten into a predawn gray.

With his foot to the floor, he crept past a red Dodge Colt with the license plate I4C4U. "Fucking fortune-teller, probably. Wish I could have brought the Harley," Peter mumbled as his eyes flicked from the road, to the odometer, and to the rearview mirror. Except for the Colt, the highway was clear as he swung onto State Route 77.

"Just another couple of miles now. This is what it's about," Peter told himself as he shifted the underpowered Chevette back into fourth.

"Writers, artists, musicians—we're the people who should shape the world, not the brainless industrialists . . . Liz, Veronica . . . bitches who give in to any man who has looks and money, especially money. In the crunch, we'll see who carries through."

His eyes checked the odometer again.

"Well, they made the rules, the money boys did. All I can do is play by them. And we'll see how they like it when someone plays as dirty as they do." He smiled crookedly.

After taking his foot off the gas as the odometer clicked off the next mile, he began to look for the gap in the trees that held the dirt road he had scouted out back at Thanksgiving.

"There we go."

He frowned as he turned into the dirt road, noting the two hunters in blaze orange, standing by the pickup truck. One was looking at his watch. The other appeared to be checking a rifle.

Then he nodded. "Bastards! Waiting for the official sunrise to go out and zap some poor animal, calling it sport."

The Chevette lurched uphill along the rutted road for another half mile, passing another older truck with a second pair of hunters seated inside. Finally, up around a turn in the road, he pulled up behind a newer pale blue K car. An older brown Ford was parked in front of the Dodge. Farther uphill, there was a green pickup.

As he got out and stretched his legs, two other figures walked toward him. Less than a mile of winter-denuded woods running gently uphill separated the group from the steel fencing topped with six strands of barbed wire that marked the reprocessing plant's territory.

"You wanted us to be on time, and where were you? Where

were you? Especially after that long lecture at your place," demanded Graeme. The high-pitched whiny voice belied his hulking physical presence.

"Shut up, fuckhead. I said between six-thirty and seven. What time is it?"

"Six forty-five," responded a lower and cooler female voice.

"Now what?" asked the young man with the long blond hair, joining the group. "And where's Veronica?"

"I told you she'd play her part, and she will. Just you wait and see."

"I thought maybe you'd eloped," suggested Mike, now standing beside Liz.

"You can shut up, too."

Liz glanced uphill in the general direction of the reprocessing plant. "I suppose it's time to get on with it. What are we doing exactly, anyway?"

"There's been a little change in plans," snapped Peter. "We're going to take the dust and cover the creek and the area below where it leaves the processing plant grounds."

"I thought we were just going to dust along the fence line."

"We're going to do what I said."

Liz shrugged. "You think that will do anything? Anything more than you'd get with the regular protest?"

"The regular protest won't do shit. It's useless, and you know it."

"If protesting is such useless bullshit, then why don't blacks still ride at the back of buses and why aren't we still fighting in Vietnam?"

"Just stow it," growled Peter. "Now's not the time for arguments about protests. Besides, if protesting with signs is so effective, why are nuclear plants still poisoning us?"

"Peter's right," chimed in Graeme. "Protesting's not doing anything. That's why we need to take some real action."

"Graeme, shut up." Mike's voice was soft, almost exasperated.

"Right. Shut up and start moving." Peter turned back toward the blue hatchback. "There's enough dust here to peg every counter the media boys have right off the dial. That's what'll make some changes."

"Yes, let's go," added Tedor, his breath steaming from under the sweeping mustache.

A faint *cracckkk* echoed through the woods.

"What was that?"

"Hunters," suggested Liz. "You saw them when we came in."

"It's awfully late in the year for hunters," whined Graeme.

"Then why are they all over the place, fuckhead?" snapped Peter. "Come on. Help me get the dust out of the Chevette."

"I don't want to handle that shit," objected Graeme.

"We're each going to carry a pouch. I mean, for Christ's sake, you think I'm going to lug a hundred-pound bag of it for more than a half mile? That's why we put it in smaller bags. They're all in lead foil, anyway."

"I have some more in my trunk, too," offered Tedor. "One should plan for . . . contingencies." Tedor's breath came in white frosty puffs that hovered briefly above his drooping mustache.

"How much of the shit do we need to set off Geiger counters?" snorted Liz. "If we're going to do anything, let's get on with it. Then we can get out of here and still gather with everyone else tomorrow and demand that the plant be shut down."

"Why bother?" demanded Tedor. "The only reason we are here is because protests have led to protests, and still the factories poison the land. That is why we gathered to take some meaningful action." Grimacing, he added, "Besides, do you know how much trouble I went to in order to get the dust?"

"No. Every time I asked, you refused to tell me." Liz's voice was easy and somehow disapproving. "Besides, it's good cover to be there tomorrow."

"Well, you didn't need to know. But let me tell you—it was not easy." Tedor puffed again. "Why do we need cover?"

"Mike," Liz said in a louder voice. "Our packs are in the back there."

Peter lifted the Chevette's hatchback. "Come on, Graeme."

"What's he doing here?" Graeme whined as one of the hunters walked up the narrow road, rifle loosely cradled.

Peter halted as another hunter appeared standing in the trees. His rifle was not loosely cradled.

"Mr. Andrewson, Special Agent Barltrop. All of you are under arrest. You have the right . . ."

"Bastards! Fucking bastards!"

Two more hunters appeared, and two large black Broncos rumbled up the road.

"You can't do this," whined Graeme, his voice rising nearly into a screech. "We weren't doing anything. We weren't doing anything."

Peter looked from one hard face to another, from one rifle to another, as the special agents moved in.

58

JONNIE WANDERED DOWN THE HALLWAY, past the empty kitchen, wondering why he was even in the office on the day before New Year's Eve.

"Because," he mumbled to himself, "Jack isn't here, and Veronica went home to Columbus for a long holiday weekend."

He hung up his dark trench coat in the outside closet and continued into the larger closet that was his office. The unread *Washington Post,* still folded in half, he dropped on the only clear space on the desk. His suit coat went on the hanger behind the door.

He wondered why he couldn't see his breath—the office certainly seemed cold enough. Then he opened the panel on the office heating/air-conditioning unit and punched the heat stud.

"At least that's working." He turned back toward the kitchen.

When he returned to the office, he sat down, setting the steaming mug on the edge of the desk and looking at the dark computer screen. Then he shook his head and picked up the *Post.* Despite the relatively uncrowded Metro ride, he hadn't really looked beyond the headlines, wondering more about what Veronica was doing in that salt-of-the-earth town of Columbus.

On page 3, he noted the story on the resurgence in the development of lower sulfur western coal, and the complaints from the environmental groups about habitat damage. What else did they expect after hammering through a clean air bill that required utilities to spend millions either on scrubbers and other technology or on cleaner coal? Jonnie didn't even shake his head, not until he saw the story on the bottom of page 3.

> In conjunction with the protests at the Fayettetown nuclear processing plant, three individuals were arrested on criminal conspiracy charges. The three—Peter Andrewson, Graeme Deveau, and Tedor Jaenicke—are all from the Washington, D.C., area. In related events, federal agents also arrested and released a number of other protesters . . .

Jonnie took a too-large sip of the hot tea, burning his throat. Should he call Veronica? Was she even in Columbus? Dust-day indeed. He smiled grimly, wondering exactly what conspiracy the feds were charging Peter and his friends with.

There were no other references to the arrests or the protests in the *Post,* nor had there been anything on the news. Leaning back in the chair, Jonnie frowned.

Finally, he took a deep breath and returned to the financial section, observing in passing that the year's trade imbalance with Japan was projected to be higher than ever, despite another fall by the dollar.

After folding the paper and setting it aside—he'd put it in the newspaper recycling bin later—he turned the chair and flicked on the computer.

"Time to make an attempt at earning a living."

59

AS THE STORM DOOR SLAMMED BEHIND ELIZABETH, McDarvid took a deep breath and glanced at the clock. Even though he had gotten up fifteen minutes early in order to replace the cracked glass on the kitchen storm door, he was running late. Older houses kept coming apart faster than they could be fixed.

Still, he picked up the paper and began to read quickly, standing by the desk in the study. He let down the paper and watched as Elizabeth darted across Forty-sixth, then resumed reading.

The "Trade Association" business news announced that Lew Engelbright, the departing Deputy Secretary of the Treasury, had been named the new President of the Plastics Association. McDarvid grinned at the appropriateness of that match, then frowned. He hadn't heard lately from Ned Llewellyn. With a Deputy Secretary of the Treasury reduced to the Plastics Association, it was clear why poor Ned was having trouble.

McDarvid set aside the business section and picked up the Metro section, pausing at the scholastic notes. A name caught his eye.

> Keri Erison Saliers, a senior at Wilson High School, was awarded an Outreach Scholarship by the Lao Foundation. Keri is the daughter of Esther Saliers and the late Derik Saliers. She will attend Emory University. Melissa Anne Sommers, a senior at the Maret School . . .

McDarvid frowned. The Lao Foundation? Saliers? He walked into the study and pulled the DEP telephone book off the shelf, flipping quickly through the pages until he reached the alphabetical section. Esther Saliers was listed under one of the newer codes—H-7509-C in Crystal City. That would be Pesticides. He flipped back to the main directory until he found the name. The girl's mother was the director of the Health Effects Division.

Replacing the DEP directory on the shelf, he tightened his lips. The Lao Foundation? There had to be hundreds of foundations that gave scholarships, but something about a scholarship to the daughter of a bureaucrat in charge of setting health-effects levels bothered him—especially when he remembered the Lao notice and Roger's comments about the computer guy. He'd never mentioned Corellian by name, but Corellian's card in the Air Office, Roger's comments, the notice, and Lao Systems and the Lao Foundation seemed like too damned many coincidences.

Finally, he cut out the section and slipped it into the file under the blotter, the one that was his puzzle file, the bits and pieces that failed to fit anywhere.

Then he folded the paper under his arm and walked back to the kitchen. He was still late, and he had yet to shower and shave.

60

"AND I THOUGHT YOU WERE AN ENVIRONMENTAL EXTREMIST." Jonnie remembered to swallow the eggs he had been chewing before he spoke. "While you were gone, some guys were caught trying to dump radioactive dust into a stream outside that nuclear processing plant. How crazy can you get?"

"What? Let me see." Veronica's voice was calm as she reached across the small table to take the paper.

Jonnie shook his head. "It's not in this paper. It happened last week while you were . . . gone."

Veronica looked slowly at him, saying nothing.

"Veronica, that guy who nearly attacked us in the parking lot? Peter Andrewson, you said his name was. He said something about dust-day. Was he referring to the nuclear plant protest?"

Veronica sighed almost inaudibly as her eyes quickly flicked from the paper Jonnie had lowered and back to his face.

"The names were—here's the clipping. I saved it. I thought you might want to see it." Jonnie extended the ripped section of newsprint. His eyes did not meet hers.

"Tedor and Graeme are friends of Peter's."

"Veronica, what gives? Why are you mixed up with these people?"

Veronica pushed away the remains of her breakfast and looked at Jonnie. "A while ago I got involved with a group of fairly radical environmentalists. They were sort of a splinter from Ecology Now! They believed in taking what they called direct action against the worst polluters."

Jonnie continued mopping up egg yolk with toast.

"At first Peter was just going to demand monitoring on the plant fence line. That led to the idea of dusting the fence. Then Peter decided the group was going to spread the uranium oxide around and in the sediment of the creek running off the plant property. The idea was to try to convince the press that the radiation came from the plant. That was dust-day. I thought it was a crazy idea. I told Peter so and left the group. That made him angry. That was why he was here checking up on me, I think."

"You just left? Let them poison the water?"

"What was I supposed to do? Tell the police that I was involved?"

Jonnie waited for more.

"I did . . . let someone know . . . indirectly . . ." Veronica shrugged. "I can't say I'm surprised."

"It must have been someone special. Somebody knew a whole lot about this. You just don't throw conspiracy charges without a lot of background." Jonnie paused and folded the paper, his eyes still on Veronica. "And it was handled just right. The arrests and conspiracy charges kept them from actually spreading the dust. *That* would have made every news outlet in the country. Only a few people care about threats by radicals—there have been so many."

"Jonnie . . . I wasn't there. I went home to Columbus. And I haven't seen Peter since that day he was here. Thank God," she added.

"There's a lot you're not telling me. I just can't imagine you joining a group like that."

"You can't imagine me taking action to save the environment?"

Jonnie forced a brief grin. "Oh, I can imagine your taking action, all right. But not like that. It's too flaky. Everything you do is well thought out."

"Maybe I had a good reason to join."

"Like what?"

Veronica walked to the counter and returned with a half-full pot from the coffee maker. After filling both mugs and returning the pot, she sat down. "Do you know what the biggest danger to the environmental movement is?"

"My clients."

"Extremists, the kind who are willing to endanger or kill people to further their cause. For the first time, the environmental movement has gained really strong grass-roots support. Average consumers, the housewife in Moline, the attorney in Columbus, are considering the environmental impact of the products they buy. There's widespread recycling even where it's not required by law. And politicians know they'll be judged as much by their environmental record as their stand on taxes, foreign policy, or civil rights. People are willing to make sacrifices for the environment. Little ones, but it's a start. That's what's moving the politicos and businessmen. The big danger is that a handful of lunatics are going to do something really crazy and break the consensus. Anything that alienates the public from the green movement will do more long-run damage to the environment than a hundred Valdezes and Chernobyls."

"Something really crazy, like putting uranium in a stream?"

Veronica nodded slowly, her lips a tight line. "I knew Peter was dangerous when he was with Ecology Now! I thought that if I joined with him I could persuade him not to do anything drastic. It didn't work out that way. When I saw that I couldn't, I left. At least I tried to. Peter didn't want to let me go. I should have left earlier."

Jonnie reached over to Veronica and squeezed her free hand. "Well, Peter's . . . gone. You're no longer involved with illegal protests, and they'll be tagged for what they are. No real damage was done to the environmental movement. They'll be written off as minor flakes, and even by now nobody remembers their names."

"I know. I was lucky, but it's funny how things work out." Veronica set down the coffee cup and took Jonnie's hand in hers. "I still wonder. There were a couple of other people in the group, but they weren't mentioned. I wonder why not."

Jonnie got up and walked behind Veronica. He remembered her saying that Peter was already history. But he responded even as he began to massage her neck, "Who knows? Maybe they left, just like you did, and Peter and those two tried to do it all themselves."

Jonnie continued the massage.

Veronica leaned her head back and closed her eyes. "Maybe . . ." She shook her head, disrupting Jonnie's massage. "But you know something? Right now I just don't care." Veronica reached back, took Jonnie's head in her hands, and brought his lips to her own.

61

"EVER HEAR OF A COMPUTER COMPANY CALLED LAO SYSTEMS?" McDarvid asked. Outside his window, traffic clogged Nineteenth Street. January had already been a lousy month for snow, and early February didn't look any better.

"Sure. Why?"

"I've run across their name several times in odd places."

"They're a big company." Jonnie took off his glasses and began to rub his eyes. "Some of our clients have their equipment." Jonnie replaced his glasses and focused on McDarvid. "Why are you interested? You never cared about computers before. I had to twist your arm to get that one in your house."

"I still think they're overrated. Computers, I mean." McDarvid frowned for a moment. "Do you know much about Lao?"

"I've had to deal with them during some of my free-lance work. They used to be a really good company. Then they got big."

"They can't be too bad if they have that much business."

"I didn't say their quality was that bad. But, like all the others, the bigger they got, the less they paid attention to what made them successful. As for getting business, I've heard some odd . . ."

The buzz of McDarvid's intercom interrupted Jonnie.

"Mr. McDarvid? Mr. Ames regrets he is not able to make your five o'clock meeting today. He would like to reschedule for three-thirty tomorrow."

McDarvid took a quick look at his open appointment book. "Three-thirty's fine. Tell him I'll be there."

"Will do, Mr. McDarvid. I've already put it down on his calendar."

McDarvid replaced the receiver. How could someone who couldn't do anything by himself, not even dial the phone or keep a calendar, ever run a law firm? "It seems that George has decided to leave early."

"Leave early? It's barely started to flurry." Jonnie screwed up his face. "Besides, he's not even going home. If it's like any other night when he's afraid of the weather or has an early appointment the next morning, he's just going to whatever luxury hotel Cecelia can book him into."

McDarvid smiled. "Who are we to question the great and mighty?"

"What about you? Do you want to get out of here?" Jonnie motioned with his hand toward the window.

"No point. I'd be stuck in traffic. If it gets too bad, I'll leave the car, take the Metro, and walk half a mile. Besides, if I wait, the storm might blow over and traffic will have cleared out. Then I won't have to be a Metro sandwich." He grinned. "And, who knows, perhaps the plows and sand trucks will have had a chance to go through."

Jonnie raised his eyebrows. "You've lived here how long?"

"All right. If the city's snow removal services are up to their usual level of efficiency, the plows won't come until spring. After all, they're only calling for three to five inches."

"Only three to five inches?"

McDarvid snorted and looked out the window. Snow was just another issue that Washington was incapable of dealing with.

"Makes me glad I always take the subway," Jonnie continued. "Anyway, you asked about Lao Systems. I would not assume that they always use the most honest of methods to win all of their contracts."

"Who does?" McDarvid sometimes wished that Jonnie wouldn't be so damned elliptical and get to the point.

"Lao usually wins the first few contracts honestly. Their equipment's good enough. And they can lowball a bid as well as anyone. Once they get inside an organization, they make friends. Same as we do with our clients. Their techniques are somewhat more questionable." Jonnie took his glasses off and laid them on McDarvid's desk. "They make friends with the technical people, the ones who set the requirements for future purchases. For some contracts, setting the requirements is better than picking the vendor. I don't have any hard information, but it doesn't look like they even bother with the procurement folks."

Jonnie leaned back on the chair's rear legs until his head rested against the wall. McDarvid's office was too small to allow an accident from such practices. "Lao will often invite people down to their headquarters in Amarillo for 'technical seminars.' Those people are treated very well."

"Lao doesn't pay all their expenses?" McDarvid asked. "How do they get around the ethics rules?"

"Oh, they don't. Civil servants can't fly around the country at a contractor's expense. It's not like they're Congressmen. The seminars have enough substance to get the government to pay their way. But in the evenings those people who work out of basements and converted warehouses are treated to expensive food, booze, and bimbos."

"How do they manage that? Black magic?"

"It's not Lao's fault that the women who show up at the after-seminar receptions are eager to make friends with men from Washington."

"That could be tricky."

"Not really. All kinds of people attend those seminars. They're not restricted to government types. The lonely women could be from anywhere."

"Right." McDarvid's tone was sarcastic.

Jonnie put his hands behind his head to cushion it against the wall. He flinched as he heard the crunching of vehicles on the street below.

McDarvid stood and leaned over toward the window. "A Metrobus slid into a beer truck. That's it for the driving. I guess I'll hike home from the Metro later." He slumped back into the desk chair. "So what about Lao?"

"In addition to the party favors, I know that at least some people get cash payoffs. Maybe not a lot, but over a year it probably comes to at least several thousand dollars."

"Cash in an envelope? Isn't that a little crude?" McDarvid again thought of the notice from the Lao Foundation he had seen tacked up on a DEP bulletin board, the one advertising scholarships.

"Crude doesn't mean ineffective or unsafe. Cash is direct and untraceable. Besides, some of these people are pretty crude themselves. Their idea of a good lunch is a hot dog and a couple of beers. Sometimes they pass on the hot dog. And if you visit their office, don't use the men's room. They piss on the floors."

McDarvid stared at Jonnie. He had known some slobs in high positions and more than a few alcoholics. Even they knew how to use a toilet. The look on Jonnie's face indicated that he was not kidding, or not much.

"If things are that bad, why doesn't someone go to the I.G.?"

"Things aren't that simple." Jonnie rocked forward until all four chair legs were on the ground again. He picked his glasses up and began to polish the lenses with his gray silk tie. "If the situation is reported, assuming any action is taken at all, there will be an investigation. That's going to make some people unhappy. And unhappy people look for someone to blame. Like malcontents and junior associates who have asked embarrassing questions. Which sounds like a good description of the people who talk to me. If there were an investigation, their asses would be grass, or at least any future promotions would be, and who wants to be a GS-9 for life in the basement of Labor or Transportation? Besides, I wouldn't bet on them actually pinning Lao with specific charges. The Inspectors General are great for crucifying civil servants, even innocent ones, but not necessarily big contractors."

McDarvid shifted his weight in the desk chair as a siren blared from the street below.

"You remember the big fiasco with the new computer system for Social Security a few years back? That was a major scandal that cost taxpayers big bucks, but nothing ever came of it—even after a freshman Congressman supplied GAO with documents which showed what was going on. GAO eventually issued a few mealymouthed reports. And one GS-9 bookkeeper got canned." Jonnie gave an exaggerated shrug. "Even if Lao were found guilty, what makes you think that the next contractor would be any more honest?"

McDarvid looked out the window. The snow was thickening. Jonnie's voice broke his reverie.

"If you're really interested in Lao Systems, there is something else you ought to know." Jonnie's eyes glanced around the room as he bit his lower lip. "I had lunch a couple weeks ago with a friend over at Commerce. Anyway, the subject of Lao Systems came up. She was worried about them."

"Why?" McDarvid had stopped looking out his window and had started looking at his watch. Tonight was Allyson's late night. Mrs. Hughes had fixed dinner for the kids too many times lately.

"Over the last year, Commerce has been installing a global network and data base. The data base contains information about U.S. companies who want to do business overseas. It also has information about foreign firms looking for American partners and lists of products available for immediate export. That way someone in, say, Sweden who wanted to buy pine logs could just contact the trade officer at the nearest embassy or consulate and receive a list of American companies. To encourage foreign companies to use the system, it also has a similar list of foreign products available for export to the U.S."

"Lao Systems has the contract for the equipment?"

Jonnie nodded. "The system functions as a network as well as a data base. Because some of that stuff is very sensitive—semiconductor trade talks with the Japanese and grain sales to the Russians—the powers that be, and budget, decided to go with a secure system. Communications are encrypted, and all of the machines are fully TEMPESTed."

"TEMPESTed?" McDarvid's tired eyes focused on Jonnie.

"Computers, like all electronic equipment, have radio frequency emissions. With the right equipment, you can pick up those emissions and know everything—everything that's typed in, every message that's decoded. TEMPEST—that's the acronym—is a way of shielding the equipment. Even corporations use TEMPEST equipment to protect against industrial espionage." Jonnie stifled a yawn and rubbed his eyes again.

McDarvid drained the remains of a diet soda before tossing the can in the small plastic wastebasket for aluminum. "Commerce?" he prompted, looking toward his briefcase.

"Anyway, Lao is one of a handful of vertically integrated manufacturers of TEMPEST equipment. Most TEMPESTing is done after-market by third-party vendors. Lao builds TEMPEST equipment from the boards up on the factory floor. Board-level TEMPESTing is expensive, but a lot more convenient and lighter than putting lead enclosures around all the equipment. That helps Lao win some contracts. They even have their own TEMPEST tank."

"TEMPEST tank? They submerge the computers?"

"Not quite, not the way you mean. A TEMPEST tank is actually a testing room. Have you ever seen a special acoustic room, the kind with all the sound-absorbing panels?"

"I've seen pictures."

"Well, a TEMPEST tank is like that. Instead of being shielded from outside sound, it's protected against outside radiation. And instead of sound-absorbing panels, there are special directional antennas. If the equipment being tested works, the apparatus won't be able to gather any information."

"Lao's the only company that can test TEMPEST equipment?"

"No, several independents can do the testing, but Lao's one of a very small number of completely integrated companies that build and test their own TEMPEST systems. Even IBM doesn't build its own TEMPEST equipment. Lao's probably not the biggest TEMPEST company, but they are a major player."

"They sound qualified for the Commerce contract without any illicit activity."

"They're qualified, at least on paper. And I haven't heard of corruption problems at Commerce, not that that means much. The thing is that there have been a lot of problems with the system itself. More than usual. Software hasn't performed as designed, and there's an abundance of hardware problems. That's especially a pain in the third world where getting spare parts and replacement equipment is a bit time-consuming."

"That's a big project if they're putting stations in third-world countries."

"It's already a huge project, and it's not complete. When I said they were linking every trade attaché, I wasn't kidding. It's supposed to provide a big boost for U.S. exports and help the Commerce Department act a little more like MITI—the Japanese ministry of trade and industry. That got Congress to foot the bill even with all the budget cutbacks."

"So the system doesn't live up to expectations, and Commerce is unhappy. It sounds like a million and one government projects."

"A little more than that." Jonnie stroked his beard. "While the equipment was being checked, some pieces leaked. Despite Lao's testing and, more interesting, despite the government's testing and certification—they have their own tanks—the equipment leaked."

McDarvid shut his eyes for a few seconds and then glanced from Jonnie to his watch. He stood and looked out the window at Nineteenth Street. The snow was tapering off, and traffic was beginning to thin. Maybe he'd be able to drive home. He really hadn't been looking forward to the hike from the Friendship Heights station. "So it leaked."

"The problem is that the network stations weren't secure. Anyone properly equipped could receive all the information which went through those machines."

"What's the big problem? Who cares who's buying and selling pine logs?"

"All I know is that I talked to one worried lady. I've known her a lot of years, since we were at Georgetown. She doesn't worry without cause."

"This lady friend of yours seems to know a fair bit about some odd technical issues. Just what is it that she does at Commerce?"

Jonnie shrugged his shoulders. "I'm sure she's had a variety of jobs by now. She started there right after graduation. She even had a few foreign assignments."

"You'd rather not say."

Jonnie looked at McDarvid blandly.

"If Lao is such a big maker of secure computer equipment, they must sell it to a lot of other agencies."

"I would guess so."

"I wonder who else has a leaking Lao network."

"Good question," Jonnie replied. "I wish I could answer it."

"Too damned many speculations," mumbled McDarvid. "Next thing you know, you'll be implying that Lao is in cahoots with the Soviets or somebody."

Jonnie stood up. "Nothing I've said implies anything more than all-American corruption and incompetence."

McDarvid pursed his lips. The odd way Lao and the Lao Foundation kept cropping up didn't make sense. "Could they be working with the Russians or somebody?"

"Anything's possible, but I do remember reading that the

company's founder hated communists. He fled Red China. His wife was caught and executed. This was the guy who refused to locate his company with the other high-tech firms in Massachusetts because he said it reminded him too much of the country he left behind. The only thing Dr. Lao hated more than communists was Russians," Jonnie continued. "He said they were barbarians who should be kept in cages. However, he's been dead many years."

McDarvid shook his head and began drumming his fingers on the desktop. "Would it really be that important if a few Commerce Department computers in the third world weren't TEMPESTed quite right?"

"Oh, I never said that any equipment in the third world was unduly tempestuous. There were only a tiny handful of machines with that problem. One machine and a few cables in Tokyo, a computer and monitor in Leningrad, and a keyboard, monitor, and printer in Moscow had that particular defect."

"How convenient." McDarvid looked at his tired, bespectacled colleague and rubbed his forehead. "This is from your freelancing, I take it."

"It would be better if you didn't mention it. Call it deep background."

"All right." McDarvid paused. "I think I'd like to chat with some people at Lao Systems."

Jonnie looked over the top of his glasses at McDarvid, an expression McDarvid almost never saw from him. "I suppose you could go down to Texas. They have a decent Public Relations Department."

"JAFFE's plant's in Houston, not Amarillo."

"There's an alternative, if you just want to make some casual contacts. There's a federal network systems computer show at the Convention Center in two weeks. Lao will have a booth there. I've got a free pass. You're welcome to it if you like."

"I might just stop by for a few minutes." McDarvid walked to the window and looked out. "In the meantime, it's Allyson's late night, and I'd better get going."

62

JONNIE EASED THE GTO INTO THE INDUSTRIAL PARK'S LOT, then dodged around the icy spots, past the TV monitor, and opened the door next to the small metal Department of Commerce sign hanging on the painted brick wall.

He showed his photo ID to the woman behind the desk, who had already seen his face in the monitor before her. After she had nodded, he stepped past the desk to the interior door, placed his hand in the metal enclosure, and quickly tapped out the cipher lock's code. The releasing bolt's click was quickly followed by a solid thunk as the heavy door closed behind him.

"Oh . . . hi, Kathleen. I didn't expect to see you here. What brings you to Lower Nowhere?"

"That's the way it goes." Kathleen Matthews grinned. "You don't like the luxurious office space?"

Jonnie looked down the corridor toward the few offices crudely walled off in the converted warehouse. "Well . . . you usually stay downtown. If I knew you were going to be here, I would have worn one of those bow ties you like so much." Jonnie walked down the whitewashed hall to the small conference room.

"I don't like coming here any better than you, maybe less, but I wanted to do a little quality control before any more units go out to the field."

"More problems?"

Kathleen nodded, the shoulder-length jet-black hair bobbing against porcelain-white skin. "Apparently, we had a system-board failure in Karachi. Shipping a new board over is pretty easy, but it will take at least a week before someone who can do the installation can get there."

"Isn't anyone over there good with a screwdriver? Replacing the board isn't exactly high-tech. I mean, a few screws . . ." Jonnie opened the door to the tiny conference room and waited for the woman to enter.

"That's not the problem. You have to have someone who's

allowed access to that part of the embassy. You've done training; you know the level of mechanical skills of most of those folks." Kathleen's nose crinkled at the heavy odor of stale cigarette smoke. She moved a half-filled ashtray to the other end of the small scratched wooden table. "So . . . is version two of the query program ready yet?"

"Almost. Snake said he had something for me to look at today. That's why I came over. The new software will be completely menu-driven. That'll make it a lot easier for those technically gifted souls stationed in Outer Tuwoomba. It should also prevent their hitting the wrong key and accidentally nuking Disney World."

"I still can't believe you. You waltz in here for a few hours every now and then and act like you're the project manager. Not quite part-time consultants who make more than Cabinet Secretaries should at least have a little more respect for us drudges who have to work for a living."

"I don't make that much, not even close, except maybe on an hourly basis. And I have plenty of respect for civil servants." He grinned. "Didn't I promise to respect you in the morning?"

Kathleen made a face. "I'll have to ask—is it Veronica?—how well you carry through on that promise."

"Besides, I am the project manager, maybe not on paper, but it's my baby. It was my idea—at least the important refinements were. And anyway, Bill's not sober enough to be project manager."

"Tell me about it." She looked toward the closed door. "Meanwhile, if we don't start getting better equipment from Lao, this whole project's going to be derailed no matter how much money they . . . But there's no point in us both getting angry by talking through it again."

Jonnie tilted his head slightly and ran his hand over his beard. "Funny thing, Jack McDarvid, the guy I work with at the law firm, he was asking me about Lao Systems. Nothing specific, just wanted to see if I knew anything about the company."

"What did you tell him?"

"Not much. I hinted that a lot of Lao types were corrupt sons of bitches. I don't know if he picked it up, but I also suggested that they shouldn't be trusted in national security situations."

"Why was he asking about Lao?"

"I didn't ask, any more than he asked where I got my information."

"Does he know who you work for?" Kathleen looked concerned.

"No. He knows I do some outside work on info systems. I'm sure he knows that at least some of it's government-related, but we don't ask about each other's private affairs."

"I'll never get used to Washington. Where I grew up, everyone knew everyone else's business. This has to be the most impersonal damn place I have ever seen."

"That's the way this town is." Jonnie shrugged. "It'll be okay. I didn't disclose anything that's not already public. Besides, I know Jack well enough, and he's not going to do anything that would cause me trouble."

63

MCDARVID LOOKED AT THE CALENDAR, mentally calculating when he had talked to Renni and Tom in December. Nearly two months, and nothing had really happened. He'd talked to Renni in early January to ensure that the committee inquiry had, in fact, been sent, a conversation that had been all too formal.

With a sigh, he pulled the House of Representatives directory from his top desk drawer and flipped through to the committee section. Then he picked up the telephone and punched in the number.

"Subcommittee on Oversight."

"Jack McDarvid for Renni Fowler."

"She's in with the Chairman, Mr. McDarvid."

"Would you have her call me?"

"I'll give her the message that you called."

"Thank you."

McDarvid looked at the computer screen and the unfinished status report to Pierre Devenant. Then he turned to the "in" basket and a request from Bill Heidlinger for a memo summarizing the status of the new DEP restrictive-use rule-making for granular pesticides. He reached for the DEP semiannual regulatory agenda. He couldn't remember who in Pesticides was handling the issue. After finding the name in the agenda, he dialed another number.

"Office of Pesticide Programs."

"Jack McDarvid for Khereem Ydulla."

"I'm sorry. He's out of the office."

McDarvid left his name and number and shuffled to the next item—his own note to have Jonnie check the OSHA metals docket again.

He looked at the telephone, then stood up and headed for Jonnie's office.

Jonnie was in, studying a spreadsheet on his screen.

"I think your beard is getting grayer," McDarvid observed.

"Thanks lots. It must be because of the exciting work we're doing." Jonnie blanked the screen. "What's on your mind?"

"I think you ought to check out the metals docket at OSHA, if you wouldn't mind. It's all billable."

"What am I looking for?"

McDarvid shrugged. "I don't know. But we've concentrated on Environment. What if OSHA has some surprise buried in its docket?"

"Good point. Tomorrow soon enough?"

"Fine. The world won't collapse, but it would be nice to put in the update to Devenant."

"You hope it won't collapse."

McDarvid shook his head. "You're right. This one bothers me. And it keeps bothering me."

"It wouldn't be that you're worried about the total destruction of high-tech industry in the U.S.?"

"Heaven forbid. Then I wouldn't have to worry about computers."

"Wrong. You'd just have to worry about whether your kids learned German or Japanese."

"Don't sound so enthusiastic," grumbled the older consultant.

"You know . . . that's what's so encouraging," Jonnie mused.

"What?"

"If you were wrong, Jack, why did we get hired? If you were

wrong, why hasn't anyone bothered to tell us we're wrong? It's strange. Your friends don't tell you to stop. No one offers any proof against us. It's as though they're pointedly ignoring us." Jonnie paused. "Someone I respect told me a long time ago that when people in this town acted as though you'd committed a blunder, and just ignored you—that was the time to run, because you'd either told a truth that was unacceptable or you were about to lose your job."

"That's even more encouraging."

"Sorry."

"My guts still bother me." McDarvid paused. "Maybe . . . I don't know."

"Maybe, Jack, because we aren't thinking big enough," suggested Jonnie.

"Not big enough?"

"I've been thinking about something you keep pointing out. It started out with your incident at the airport."

McDarvid frowned. "Go on."

"Who really has an interest in standards that force U.S. industry offshore? That make us more and more vulnerable to third-world resource cutoffs? That give the rest of the world more and more control over our economy?"

"Jonnie, I don't believe in conspiracy theories. Besides, what evidence is there?"

"Evidence?" Jonnie shrugged. "There's not much. Larry's dead. That's a little odd when you consider he's the only one who's ever had much success in bringing common sense to environmental rules. Then, there's the business about the metals initiative, and how it could cripple the independence of the U.S. space effort. Meanwhile, that's one area where the Russians are having real money problems.

"As you pointed out, Jack, each rule shuts down a little more basic industry. You told me last year that there was only one factory that could build the castings for the main battle tank. A couple of weeks ago, there was a spiel on the old battleships, and one of the commentators said that there wasn't a steel mill left in the U.S. that could supply the plate for those ships. And the Middle East stuff—there was a piece in the paper about how no new oil refineries have been built in the U.S. in twenty years."

"And?" McDarvid prompted.

"Well . . . it might be cheaper for the Russians to make our weapons either impossible to build or so expensive that we have to build less."

"A lot of speculation, Jonnie."

"Probably. But the Russians really haven't been able to afford the arms race for a while. Did they just lie back and say, 'We give up'?"

McDarvid shook his head. "No. But there's no way you'd find homegrown U.S. environmentalists siding with the Russkies. Hell, they can't even agree with one another."

Jonnie laughed. "I never thought of that. What if they just helped our dear little capitalistic environmentalists to keep doing what they were already doing?"

McDarvid swallowed, then he grinned. "Nice theory. It would probably even work, but, somehow, I don't think the Russians could keep that sort of thing quiet, not the way . . ." McDarvid swallowed, then grinned. "Anyway, it's a nice theory." He half turned. "Let me know about OSHA."

"No problem."

Back in his office, McDarvid leaned back in the chair. Was Jonnie right? Or crazy? And what else could he do to get people interested in the issue?

The intercom buzzed.

"Yes?"

"Jack? Steve Greene. Bill said you were working on an update to the granular pesticides thing."

"I need to talk to a couple more people at Environment, Steve. With a little luck, I should have the whole thing tomorrow."

"Let me know. They're coming in next week."

"Understand. I'll do what I can."

McDarvid looked at the papers spread across the blotter, then at the computer screen, then at the buzzing phone.

"A Ms. Fowler for you."

"Put her through."

McDarvid cleared his throat before touching the button. "Renni?"

"You called. What can I do for you?"

"It's been a month since we talked, and I was curious about how we might be coming on a hearing on the metals initiative?"

"Jack, we still don't have a response from DEP." Renni Fowler's voice carried an exasperated tone, clear enough even over the telephone.

"Who did you send it to? Jerry Killorin?"

"We sent it to the Secretary. As usual. The department decides who drafts the response. You know the pattern, probably better than I do."

McDarvid did. The DEP correspondence center had already told him that Killorin's office had been assigned the response.

"Did you give them a deadline?" McDarvid glanced at his computer screen, bearing his latest status report to Devenant.

"No. We just asked for an answer as soon as practicable."

"No great urgency, I see."

"Jack, you're rather sarcastic about this, considering we're doing you a favor."

"Sorry, but I'm not sure that looking into the destruction of U.S. high technology is a favor to me. It is the committee's business."

"Jack . . ."

"Sorry. I am worried." McDarvid tried to sound contrite.

"You're always worried. So are we. We're worried about health, environment, and the research that supports environmental protection."

McDarvid repressed a sigh. "I stand corrected. How long before you do a follow-up or hold a hearing?"

"Jack, I told you before, and you know as well as I do, that this isn't what we hold hearings on. As for a follow-up, if we don't get some sort of response from DEP by the end of next week, say, I'd be happy to send a note over asking for some response to the committee."

"I'd appreciate that."

"No problem." Renni's voice was cool. "Anything else?"

"Not much. How's Hal?"

"Same as always. Working hard to please Hal Senior."

"The kids?"

"They're fine. I really have to go, Jack. Keep in touch."

McDarvid replaced the phone, shaking his head. Clearly, Renni had no intention of doing anything except sending a letter or two. And a letter or two wouldn't budge DEP a millimeter.

What else could he do? Was there any way he could push Jerry Killorin into responding? What did he know about Jerry? Really know?

McDarvid leaned back in the chair, thinking.

64

"JONNIE?" McDarvid leaned into the small office.

"What can I do you for?"

"Some creative financials."

"Aren't all financials creative?"

McDarvid shut the door. "These are more creative. I need a financial profile based on these numbers. Of an individual." McDarvid thrust three sheets of paper at his colleague.

Jonnie placed them on top of the stack of paper closest to the computer table that adjoined his desk. His desk was his filing system, consisting of stacks of paper of varying heights. "What are you up to?"

"No good, as usual. The Technology Committee can't be budged. At least, I can't figure out any way. But the more I look into it, Killorin is hiding something, and I'm going to give him another push."

Jonnie raised both eyebrows and took off his silver-rimmed glasses. "Just how are you presuming to administer such a push."

"Killorin never had money. He pays a shitload of alimony to his ex-wife, plus the house payment. He has a daughter in college. Even at a state school, it's not that cheap, and I think she goes to some private college. He drinks like a fish and spends all weekend at the track. And he has a small condo of his own. He can't borrow that kind of money. Yet his credit rating is all right."

"Do I want to know how you found that out?"

"I used the firm's service."

"So what do you want?"

"A nice tabular and graphic report that shows the minimum annual income necessary to support all of this. I think I've covered all the basics, like electricity and food, but if I haven't, make an estimate."

"Do I want to know what you're going to do with it?"

"Me? I'm just going to talk to somebody about it."

"That wouldn't be Killorin, would it?"

"Well . . . he's the first one."

"Jack . . . I sometimes wonder how anyone as devoted to public service and loving his family can come up with such nasty ideas. This fringes on blackmail."

"It's scarcely blackmail. In the first place, I'm not asking for anything. In the second place, Killorin is on someone's payroll, and he's not reporting the income."

"And how do you know that?"

"Simple enough. I just went and asked for his ethics form—his and several others. I said I was doing a study. He lists no other income except his job. Nothing except a small savings account earning two hundred a year at the most. Nothing else."

"Maybe he made the extra money at the track."

"Come on. Nobody, at least no civil servant, makes money at the track on a regular basis. Not unless they're tied into organized crime, and that's something that even Killorin wouldn't touch."

"Not true. There was somebody over at OPM who used some variety of exotic mathematical theory to turn a profit at the track on a regular basis."

McDarvid looked at him quizzically. "How did you find that out?"

"Because he taught me his system before he left government."

"You?" McDarvid shook his head.

Jonnie smiled slightly in return before continuing. "It was a while ago, before that place became so damn politicized. Now, instead of math whizzes, the place has become a refuge for low-grade political hacks. I heard there's even one crackpot whose big thing is to try and fire any SESers who have more than three documents turned back for spelling, grammar, or typos, even if they didn't write the document."

"Why doesn't that surprise me?"

Jonnie cleared his throat. "Anyway, about Killorin—he could have won the money at the track."

"He could have, but he didn't," McDarvid insisted. "Besides, even if he did win the money honestly, he'd still have to report it on his ethics forms, and it isn't there."

"What's this 'study' about? Assuming you intend to write it."

"Oh, I'll write it up. I asked for the forms of all the regulatory decision-makers at DEP and OSHA. I also requested their travel schedules for the past year."

"You have a nasty mind. I assume most of them are innocent."

"About half appear as pure as the driven snow. Including Killorin. But that's what bothers me. I know he's guilty. What I don't know is how guilty, or how many others are just like him."

"You realize that this is all hypothetical?" Jonnie lifted the three sheets of paper from where he had laid them.

"I suppose so. But Killorin is part of that group that can affect rules before any real scrutiny takes place."

"How will this help?"

McDarvid shrugged. "The ethics officer will send him a letter saying his form was released and that the reason for the request was a study. If he's innocent, well, I imagine not much will happen."

"Like I said, you have a nasty mind."

McDarvid shrugged again. "I'm running out of time and ideas. It's like punching a mattress. Unless you really zap people, they just write letters and smile and thank you for your time." He looked past Jonnie and out the window into the twilight. "The hell of it is that I still don't know who's doing this. All I know is that with every one of these regulations, we're losing a little more of our industrial base. And it's so gradual. It could be coincidence. Just sheer coincidence."

"You don't believe that."

"No. But I don't believe in grand conspiracies, either. Always thought the people who did were nuts. So maybe I'm just losing it."

"That's possible," answered Jonnie brightly. "But so many coincidences tend to be unlikely." He paused. "And you could be right *and* losing it."

"Thanks," McDarvid grumbled.

"But that brings up one other question."

"Oh? I need another question like a hole in the head."

"Maybe Larry's death was a coincidence."

"What?"

"Look at it this way. Everything else you've run into is very polite, very well organized. And almost completely nonviolent. You may get ignored, but not killed, at least not physically. And just as interesting is one other thing—you can only figure out the picture by relating very disparate facts and by understanding an entire range of regulations. How many people even deal with more than one environmental media? How many laws and regs are there?"

McDarvid nodded. "People—outside of government? I don't know. Might be a hundred people."

"And how many of those are also outside the greenie movement?"

"Oh . . ."

"Exactly. Lawyers and business people specialize. The high executives don't know the details, and the details have changed since they did. Government policymakers are all political, and they know nothing."

"Thanks. You just reinforced my paranoia."

"Well—who else looks at regs the way we do?"

"There's that outfit on Dupont Circle."

"They only work for Fortune 500 companies. Even if they know, who's about to let them rock the boat?"

"And you think Heidlinger will?"

"He doesn't know what you're doing—"

"—*we're* doing," corrected McDarvid.

"He only wants us to solve the client's problems."

The small office remained silent as clouds on the western horizon parted and the reddish light of the setting sun reflected onto the off-white walls.

"Christ," mumbled McDarvid. "Jesus fucking Christ." He stood up. "Can you get me something on that by tomorrow morning?"

"It shouldn't take long. Are you going to be here for a while?"

"No. It's Thursday, remember."

"Right. Then I'll have it for you first thing in the morning." Jonnie paused. "Speaking of nasty ideas, are you done with the telephoto lens? My sister asked about it yesterday. There's no hurry, but . . ."

"That's another thing I haven't gotten around to yet. Another week or so be a problem?"

"No. Just so I know. She mentioned that she'd need it by the end of March."

"I'll finish up and get it back." McDarvid opened the door and headed back toward his own large closet, wondering about telephoto lenses and creative financials and the integrity of men who employed either. He was still shaking his head, even after he had begun to pack up his briefcase.

65

MCDARVID TAPPED ON THE WALL NEXT TO THE OPEN DOOR. The nameplate on the wall read "Eleanor DiForio."

"Hello there."

"Jack! Come on in. I've just got a few minutes before I have to go off to a work group meeting."

McDarvid plopped into the white armchair. "Anything new?"

"Since we talked yesterday?"

McDarvid grinned at the heavyset woman with the cheerful voice and pleasant smile. "All right. How's Jerry?"

"He's still spending a lot of time on the metals initiative, but he's getting into figuring out the policy implications of the big study on pesticide contamination of groundwater."

"The one that was supposed to be finished two years ago, and wasn't?"

"The same one."

"So what's Jerry's concern? That there are trace contaminants hazardous to health, but that the current economics won't justify controls?"

"Pretty much. How did you know?"

McDarvid shook his head. "Sometimes I amaze myself."

Ellie laughed. "You haven't gotten any more modest since you left here. That's for certain."

"What can I say?" McDarvid gave Ellie an exaggerated shrug. "But it figures. Wasn't Jerry the one who worried about electric blankets giving Americans cancer?" McDarvid held up his hand. "I know. There's a possibility that extremely low frequency electric current may have a harmful effect on some unborn children. But not the one in a hundred Americans that Jerry cited."

"Jerry was partly right on that, Jack. We've got reports on more than a dozen children with a very rare brain tumor, and the only thing they had in common was that their mothers used an electric blanket while pregnant."

"Fine. A dozen children over how many years and how many million women? Everything is dangerous to someone. Jerry still doesn't understand that."

"You're down on Jerry this month, I take it."

"I'm probably down on everyone this month."

"Then tell me about Elizabeth while I pack this folder."

"I finally broke down and got a computer around Thanksgiving. She treats me like an interloper if I want to use it in the evenings. 'Really, Father, this is most inconvenient. My homework looks so much more professional on the computer. Even Mrs. Hoppes is pleased, and nothing pleases Mrs. Hoppes.'

"Then she smiles, and I think maybe I should buy one just for her use." McDarvid pursed his lips. "But she can be such a pain in the ass sometimes."

"Jack . . . sometimes I think you feel all women can be a pain in the ass." Ellie stood up, folder in hand.

McDarvid stood and stepped outside the small office. "They said Jerry should be back before long."

"He's headed down the hall now."

"So he is." McDarvid looked toward the center of the building, down the long straight corridor. "Better wait for him to get into his office."

"I've got to run, Jack."

"Thanks, Ellie."

McDarvid walked into the office bay adjacent to the one containing Killorin's office and up to the secretary.

"Yes?"

"Has the permanent replacement for Fran Berkey been named?" McDarvid knew the answer already.

"No."

"Thank you so very much." McDarvid nodded and turned to leave, following Jerry Killorin into the main reception/secretarial area. He hung back, waiting until Killorin was inside his office. Then he crossed the bay and stuck his head inside. "Hello, Jerry."

"Hello, Jack." Killorin's voice was neutral. He replaced the telephone handset, but continued holding the stack of papers, not bothering to set them down.

"Got a minute?"

"Just about that. There's never enough time."

McDarvid smiled but waited.

"What do you have in mind?" Killorin finally asked.

"Couple of things. First is the pesticides in groundwater study. Any idea when your shop will finish your input to Hank?"

Killorin frowned. "We just got the preliminary reports on the data from Pesticides. Zenobalia's still crunching the numbers. Then . . ." The division chief shrugged.

"Same old schedule—from the economists to the analysts" McDarvid nodded sympathetically. "What about the timetable for the metals initiative?"

"Jack . . . that one's about to go to Red Border. I really can't say much."

"When is it likely to go to OMB?"

"Who knows? That depends on what the other shops have to say." Killorin lifted the papers slightly, as if to signify he were running out of time.

McDarvid ignored the gesture, instead smiled brightly. "You know, Jerry, I've been working on another study. This one's about government employees. I don't recall when you came to Washington, but when we came fifteen years ago, we still had the chance to afford a house that wasn't halfway to Richmond, and it was possible to survive on a single income." McDarvid shook his head sadly. "That's all changed now. I mean, my wife's a doctor, and I don't do badly with the consulting, and we still live in the same house, and the kids still go to public schools, and I bought the cheapest car I could find. I just don't know how people can make it.

"Anyway, we've done an analysis of government salaries. Compared the salaries for various positions with the income needed for, say, housing, food, children's education, entertainment. Then we've made some adjustments using not just government officials' salaries, but their spouses' incomes and any other income they may have reported. For senior level people, we did that by using the ethics forms. We requested a number of them. Some were pretty interesting." McDarvid shrugged. "The results should be out one of these days."

"Who did you say you were doing this for?"

"I didn't. Until we make the results known to the right people, I wouldn't want to have the conclusions or the sponsor known." McDarvid smiled and straightened. "Anyhow, I've taken far too much of your time, but I do appreciate your comments on the groundwater thing. We'll have to see how the metals initiative comes out—assuming it does." He nodded, then turned, walking quickly toward the elevators.

He still needed to tell George Rendhaas about the as yet unwritten ethics study. He'd actually done a couple of tables. They showed that a number of civil servants were either getting impossibly deep in debt or not reporting all income.

George would spread the word, and a few others might get nervous.

McDarvid's stomach twisted, but he smiled as he neared the two women and the man standing by the elevator.

66

"VOLONINOV LEAVES YOU ALONE NOW?"

"He still wants whatever hard intelligence I may have picked up. He frowns if I have nothing interesting to say. But my budget and my people have not been touched." Kaprushkin looked at his wife.

The clear eyes and unlined face did nothing to betray her fifty years, nor did the few strands of gray in the black hair framing her angular face.

She wrapped her arm around his still-lean waist as they walked through the small park. "Your protector?" Her sardonic tone came with a smile. "How could anyone with the brains to understand your work have risen so high?"

"It is difficult to believe that anyone who could understand my little program could fail to understand its full extent." He laughed softly in the sunlight. "And since I'm still alive and with a new budget, more than I expected, no one has questioned my accounting."

"American parliamentarians are expensive," Irenia said with a slight chuckle.

"They would understand that. They would not appreciate not knowing one works for me." Kaprushkin shrugged. "Unfortunately, he is getting more expensive every year. I had to invent a new recruit to account for the Congressman's increased cost."

"It's better than letting your superiors know."

"There has not been a choice. Recruiting a congressional candidate over twenty years ago was not a problem, even when he won. But had I reported that victory, my control of him would have been taken. He is far too important for my program. If they had known then that I had bought a minor idealistic candidate, I would be a hero. If it were known now that I control a senior Congressman . . ."

Irenia tightened her hold on his waist.

"Let's not worry now. It is not often we have such a warm day so early in the year. We must enjoy this one." Kaprushkin placed his right hand in the rear pocket of his wife's tight jeans. Her giggling made him smile again. They continued through the park with its strollers, lovers, children, and parents. "When I was accepted at the academy all those years ago, the last thing anyone would have suspected was a true revolutionary. I would have been shot on sight. How could a country founded on revolution, guided by revolutionary principles, have been run for so long by such reactionaries?"

"Why don't you ask the Americans? They have the same problem."

The Colonel chuckled. "Our American friends? I wonder what would scare them more? Knowing how much we are shortsighted materialists like them, or finding out how they are like their feared communist enemies—noble revolutionaries gone bad?" Kaprushkin took his hand out of the pocket of his wife's black Levis and entwined his long arm around her waist. She leaned her head against his cheek as they walked.

"This new group—they are, in their own way, revolutionaries. They have made some serious changes," she observed.

"Many things appear to change," the gray-haired man conceded. "I suppose we had no choice. Empires are too expensive. But I think the Republics' leaders are just nationalist versions of Splotchhead. They see political freedom as just another economic lever. Let people mouth unapproved slogans, and they will work harder. Let them earn some worthless rubles from semiprivate enterprise, and the economy will be transformed. Meanwhile, one man has more power, the pollution increases, and most people still can't find a decent chicken or a roll of toilet paper."

"Still, they are important changes."

Kaprushkin snorted. "Like the capitalists, we will sow the seeds of our own self-destruction."

Irenia closed her eyes briefly but did not reply.

"I dreamed of Misha last night."

Irenia stopped walking but said nothing.

"I saw his body. I saw the growths. He was filled with pain." His arms left his wife.

"He is free now. He has no pain."

"How many children are filled with pain? How many fathers have nightmares of pain?"

"We can't stop the world's pain, not yet." Irenia placed her hands on his shoulders.

"We can't stop it all. Just some, just a little tiny bit. I must settle for that. There was no reason for Misha to die." Tears filled the corners of his eyes. "Why was so much pesticide used? Misha was drinking poison so some apparatchik could come closer to meeting his five-year plan."

When he continued, his voice was harder. "My protector, whoever he is, thinks that my plan will just weaken the capitalists' industrial and military structure. But it will also allow a few less fathers to have nightmares of pain. Russian children deserve the same health as the Americans. They don't understand that the green revolution is meant more for us than for them."

"Pyotr, they don't need to understand."

"I know." The gray-haired Colonel sighed. "I know."

"You feel so deeply. That's why I love you so much. But we made the hard decisions so many years ago. You cannot relive the past. Not over and over."

Kaprushkin nodded. He wrapped his arms around her body and held her close. Irenia returned the tight embrace.

Around them, in the park, no one looked at the familiar Colonel or his slender wife as the sunshine cascaded around them.

67

MCDARVID ADJUSTED THE SQUASHED THROW PILLOW that cushioned the old oak kitchen chair which served as his study desk chair. He peered absently through the flurries of wet flakes barely visible under the streetlight, ignoring the hum of the computer which beckoned for him to finish the revised Amalgamated Electric PCB update and recommended regulatory strategy.

He moistened his lips, not looking at the telephoto lens on the shelf. What if the I.G. issued the normal mealymouthed report on Killorin, something along the line of "apparent income discrepancy . . . recommend a more complete filing by employee"? That still wouldn't focus enough attention on the metals issue.

As for his old boss, the good Chairman of the Public Works Committee—there was no way Sam would touch something that obviously environmental, unless he was forced to.

McDarvid glanced at the pile of papers in the folder on the corner of the desk. Why didn't he recognize them? Was he already losing it? He picked up the folder, flipped open the cover, then grinned as he read the title page: "Princess Elizabeth and the Red Dragon." His daughter was clearly well along with her latest play. He closed the folder and replaced it on the corner of the desk, trying to position it exactly where Elizabeth had left it.

The morning's *Post* had included another article on high-technology multinationals relocating production facilities offshore—this time focusing on computer-controlled machine tools. Just one line mentioned environmental regulations, a cryptic reference to the impossibility of compliance with air toxics rules that made the executive quoted sound like a robber baron.

In the meantime, Devenant had called for an update, wanting to know about even delaying the final rule, and Heidlinger had sent a memo reminding him of the need for a *legal* strategy on the metals initiative.

The pieces were all there—the impact of the regulations, the subtle but direct influence on the standard through setting risk levels at impossibly conservative levels, Lao Systems and its Foundation, the unwillingness of the Congress to face reality . . .

He wondered what Jonnie really thought of the whole mess. Then again, beyond the day-to-day, what did he really know about Jonnie?

The younger consultant had a flair for financial analysis, had contacts worldwide, knew far too much about secure computer systems, and dated attractive young women. He was bright, and he loved terrible puns. And he had worked somewhere in OMB, but had avoided explaining much beyond the technical details. McDarvid shook his head angrily.

"You know more about Jonnie than anyone else in the firm. Now all you need to lose it all is to swallow Jonnie's half-assed suggestion that the Russkies control the U.S. environmental movement."

McDarvid's eyes strayed back to the telephoto lens. Still . . . what was he going to do if the pressure on Killorin didn't produce results? How could he get enough hard evidence, create enough pressure to break something loose?

He looked again at the telephoto lens.

"Jack?"

He reached over and turned off the computer.

"I'll be up in just a minute."

After turning off the study lights, he stood in the dimness for a time, watching the snow flurries, now fading into nothingness, leaving not even a thin white dusting on the browned grass of the lawn.

68

"MR. CORELLIAN? Esther Saliers is on the line."

"Oh . . . please put her through." Andrew Corellian flicked off the microphone on the speakerphone and grasped the handset.

"Esther, I was thinking about calling you, but somehow things have been rather rushed."

"I'm sorry to bother you, then. Am I interrupting anything? Would it be better if I called later?"

"No, no, not at all. I was just jotting down some notes for one of those reports I have to file with the head office now and then. They like to know what I'm doing to make them seem more responsible." The sandy-haired man glanced down at the yellow legal tablet and clipboard on his lap. The number 3 pencil had rolled against his belt. He reclaimed it, juggling the receiver between his shoulder and ear.

"Jotting? On paper? I can't believe you don't use your own products."

"Oh, I do. Lao makes sure that we all have the latest models. They even sent me for a week's training. But the truth is I prefer old-fashioned writing—don't tell anyone I said that. I still compose on paper and then transfer it to the machine. Editing is easier on the computer. Once the document is final, I just zap it down to headquarters. We have a WAN—a wide area network—that links all of our offices."

"That certainly beats the post office. Or government messenger service."

"That's for sure. Tell me—how does Keri like the idea of going to Emory?"

"She loves it. She went down there for a weekend and came back raving. I think she's really going to thrive down there. In a way, that brings me to my reason for calling. I'd like to invite you to lunch. In fact, I have a surprise for you."

"Really? What?"

"I can't tell you, or it wouldn't be a surprise. Actually, it's from Keri, not me. She was going to mail it, but we thought you should get it in person. So I'm sort of her stand-in."

"What are the chances she bakes French cheesecake?"

"Not good, I'm afraid. But I'll be glad to make one." There was a low laugh.

"I was kidding. I don't want to put you to any trouble."

"Baking is no trouble at all. I need something to take my mind off work when I get home. Keri—dear daughter as she is—is not exactly around that much. You know, the Hotel Saliers routine? That's what happens when they get to be high school seniors. And you can only think about pesticides for so long. When would you be free for lunch?"

"Let me check." The executive thumbed through the appointment book on the desk, again losing the pencil, which dropped onto the heavy carpet. "I have appointments tomorrow and Wednesday and a big meeting on Thursday. Next week I'm going to be on the road. How about this Friday?"

"Friday would be fine. Could we make it a little on the late side? I have a staff meeting in the morning, and they tend to drone on."

"How about one? Or is that too late?"

"One would be perfect. I'll see you then."

"I'll be there."

"Take care."

Corellian replaced the handset and looked down at the tablet. The first sheet had Esther's name on top and was followed by almost a full page of small light gray block letters. He tore the sheet off and slowly fed it into the wastebasket-sized paper shredder in the corner of his office.

The cheesecake had been good. That he had to admit.

69

MCDARVID LOOKED AT THE GLASS DOORS on the Ninth Street side of the Convention Center—stretching down the block. He tried a door at random.

Once inside, his eyes flickered over to the long lines in front of the registration signs spaced at not quite regular intervals. Having Jonnie's badge was definitely a good idea. He paused and removed the plastic oblong from his pocket, placed it in the clear-plastic holder, and affixed badge and holder as evenly as he could on the breast pocket of his older blue pinstripe. It was probably crooked. Certainly, had he been home, either Allyson or Elizabeth would have informed him of his lack of symmetry.

After walking under the banner proclaiming "Welcome to the FOSE Interconnectivity and Applications Exhibition," McDarvid looked around for several seconds, then, as he stepped on the escalator, glanced up to see a sign pointing toward the escalator on which he stood. On the next level, a line of tables awaited him, on which were stacked exhibition guides and assorted promotional materials.

McDarvid stepped through the wide doorway onto the main floor of the Convention Center, stopped, and took a deep breath before confronting the aisles and aisles of computer displays and banners.

He extracted the folded map of the exposition from his pocket, tracking down the list of exhibitors until he located "Lao Systems, Booth 1620."

Where was he? McDarvid glanced around, then back at the map. Despite his years of Navy flying, and his familiarity with assorted maps and charts, he still found the damned convention map confusing.

Finally, after checking the nearest exhibitor, Apple—that name he did recognize—and finding it on the convention map, he located Lao—seemingly as far into the center of the endless booths as possible. He began to stroll down the closest aisle, looking and listening as he walked.

". . . told the boss we needed a multiprocessor network server . . ."

". . . nothing more than a bunch of linked PCs . . ."

"If you need cross-platform connectivity . . ."

McDarvid forced a bored smile as he paused to study a display which featured a computer-controlled color copier. To think he was having enough trouble with one small computer in his study.

The Lao booth was staffed with five or six men and women in pale turquoise coats and dark blue ties surrounded by a dozen or so customers—or at least interested individuals—flocking around a demonstration.

McDarvid looked for something resembling the TEMPESTed equipment that Jonnie had mentioned, but only saw one small display, freestanding and unattended, which noted: "For zero emissions under all conditions, the Lao Systems SC-486."

He stepped up to the pedestal and picked up a brochure, trying to ignore the representative heading in his direction by continuing past the pedestal toward a circular container.

THE LAO FOUNDATION
Helping Provide the Best for the Best
Contributions are tax-deductible

Several plain cards printed in black upon thin but smooth white stock rested by the container. McDarvid picked up one and began to read, skimming the words quickly: "501 C(3) Foundation . . . dedicated to providing merit scholarships to outstanding students of middle-class backgrounds . . . allowing them a collegiate freedom of choice . . ."

He nodded as he recalled the same words from the poster at DEP. Elizabeth could certainly benefit from something like the Lao Foundation. Then he stopped, swallowed, and pocketed the card.

"Might I help you . . ."—the Lao employee smiled as he strained to read the badge—"Mr. Black? I see you're interested in TEMPEST equipment."

"Ah . . ." McDarvid stuttered. Mr. Black? Then he remembered that the badge carried Jonnie's name. "Actually, I was interested in the Lao Foundation. I'd seen an announcement or two, but never realized . . ."

"Yes, that's a relatively new endeavor. The Corporate Responsibility department helps with their fund-raising. It doesn't have much to do with marketing, but Mr. Corellian insists that we get a fair amount of publicity and even some contributions from the shows." The young man shrugged, then smiled. "I'm Allan DiTellio, organizational marketing. What sort of system are you looking for?"

"I'm not really sure," McDarvid admitted, trying to digest the confirmation of the link between Andy Corellian and the Lao Foundation.

"What platform are you using?"

"The secretaries use PCs," McDarvid said slowly. "Some of the attorneys have their own machines, generally the younger ones."

"Oh, you're with a law firm, then?"

McDarvid smiled faintly, hoping to get away from the man. "You said that the Lao Foundation was a new effort. What can you tell me about it?"

"Really not much more than the cards say. That's mostly handled by Corporate Responsibility out of the Washington office. Going for funding at the shows was Andy's idea. He insists it works, but we're not really equipped to answer detailed questions. That's why we insisted he leave the cards there." The young man nodded. "What applications are you running?"

"Standard stuff. I was just looking to get an idea of the possibilities for upgrading. We haven't determined our connectivity needs yet."

"I can understand that." DiTellio smiled broadly. "I'll tell you what. Let me have your pass there—it's made for a handy-dandy imprint—and I'll send you the full informational package designed for midsize firms."

"I don't know . . ."

"Oh, it's really no trouble at all. It really isn't. I mean, that's what we're here for—to make sure you get the information you need."

McDarvid surrendered the badge reluctantly, realizing belatedly that the follow-up information would go to Jonnie.

He glanced back at the SC-486, unattended and unnoticed, wondering why no one paid any attention to a product that Jonnie had assured him was one of the few unique products offered by Lao. He also wondered about the donation container for the Lao Foundation. He frowned as DiTellio returned the badge.

"It should just be a week or so, Mr. Black."

"No problem," answered the preoccupied McDarvid. "No problem." He wandered back down the aisle, trying to make sense of what had just happened.

70

"IS MR. BLACK IN? He's expecting me." The woman in gray smiled. The ash-gray dress, although modest, revealed a hint of well-shaped calf. The high-cut neckline scarcely concealed the elegant form underneath the soft fabric.

"May I please have your name?" The magnolias of Mississippi drenched the gentle voice of the young receptionist.

"Veronica Lakas."

"Let me see. Mr. Black—I know he's here somewhere."

Veronica added, "He's not an attorney."

"Not an attorney, ma'am? And I thought you were looking for a lawyer. Now you hang on a moment." The receptionist smiled and picked up a second photocopied personnel list. "Jonathon Black? Here he is. You sit down over there, and I'll ring him."

"Miss Lakas?"

Veronica turned her head at the unexpected male voice. The flow of auburn hair revealed a small freshwater-pearl earring. She looked at the graying man in the three-piece blue pinstripe polywool suit. Not an attorney. His clothes weren't excessively expensive, and he looked neither dim-witted nor conniving.

"I'm Jack McDarvid. I work with Jonnie. He's in a meeting, but should be out soon."

Veronica smiled, looked down for a second, and shook her head slightly. So much for catching Jonnie unaware.

"He's not answering his phone, ma'am. Should I page him?"

"No. I'll just wait a bit. Thank you."

"Would you prefer to wait in my office? It's not as spacious as this, but . . ." McDarvid waved his hand at the reception area professionally appointed in Upscale Lawyer Modern.

"Thank you. That would be lovely."

"Can I get you some coffee? Or tea or soda?"

"Oh, no, thank you. I'm fine." She followed him past several doors, all closed.

"Here we are."

Veronica sat down and looked at McDarvid over the neat, almost clean-topped desk. "Jonnie's mentioned you."

"He's also mentioned you." McDarvid smiled politely. "I understand you work for an environmental group."

"I do some policy work for Ecology Now! The issues probably aren't all that different from what you do. Except our perspective may be a bit different."

"Probably." McDarvid nodded. "Although I'm sure we share the same goals."

Veronica raised her eyebrows.

"A healthy environment."

"And a healthy economy?" Veronica grinned.

"We can't have a healthy environment without a good economy. Just look at East Europe, Mexico, Brazil, or any other third-world country."

"Now you sound like Jonnie."

McDarvid gave a half-smile. "We've worked together for a while."

"Well, this is a surprise." Jonnie stood in the open door.

"How did you know I was here? Let alone where I'd wait?" Veronica stood and turned toward the younger consultant.

Jonnie just grinned.

Veronica turned back as she stood. "It was a pleasure meeting you, Mr. McDarvid." She extended her hand across the desk.

"My pleasure." McDarvid stood, nodded, and returned the firm dry handshake. He remained standing as the couple left.

"Ready to go?" asked Jonnie.

"I've been ready since I got here," Veronica answered with an amused smile. "But I'd hoped for a little more surprise."

"I am surprised. But what can I say?" Jonnie stopped by the closet next to the reception area and pulled out his coat, slipping into it quickly.

After a moment, he extracted Veronica's powder-blue down coat. "This is good enough for the South Pole. Are you sure you'll be warm enough?"

"I like to be warm."

Jonnie grinned as the two stepped through the glass double doors and up to the elevators. "So . . . did Jack keep you entertained?" He pressed the "down" button.

"He offered me coffee."

"What do you think of him?"

"He's probably pretty bright. He's very pleasant."

"Everyone needs a good cover."

"I wondered about that. He seems so . . . bland. Not your type at all. I mean, to work with."

The elevator arrived. Two men in dark wool coats and carrying briefcases stood in the rear of the wood-paneled enclosure.

"No, he is genuinely nice. That's why it's such a great cover," Jonnie added as they entered the elevator.

Veronica looked at the two lawyers. Neither returned her look. She glanced at Jonnie. "You remember what I told you? About your being elliptical?"

"Jack's exactly what he seems to be, a generally mild, pleasant guy who loves his wife and is devoted to his kids. It's just that none of that has anything to do with anything else."

Jonnie stopped talking as the elevator door opened, waiting to resume the conversation until they were out of the building. Once on Nineteenth Street, he continued. "The good thing about Jack, or the scary thing, depending on your perspective, is that when he wants to accomplish something, he will. If something gets him started, there's no stopping him. He also has a feel for things— call it intuition—that you don't find often. Show him the starting line, give him a few hints on which way to go, and he has the smarts and skills and luck to reach the finish. He's also likely to destroy the course in the process, at least the parts that get in his way."

220 L. E. Modesitt, Jr./Bruce Scott Levinson

"So what's your perspective on him? Good or scary?"

"Useful." Jonnie shrugged. "I'm glad he's on my side or I'm on his."

"Are you sure that you two are on the same side?"

"Yeah. Most of the time."

They continued up Nineteenth Street toward the Dupont Circle Metro station. Jonnie ignored the plaintive music from two buskers as they stepped onto the long escalator into the station. After playing sardines all the way to Metro Center, changing to the blue line train, and playing sardines once more, they emerged from the Rosslyn Metro station.

"That's the drawback of taking the Metro," observed Jonnie. "You get a particular brand of air pollution."

"Sometimes, I think you don't like people as much as you say you do."

"I do like people," protested Jonnie. "But not in toxic doses."

"Hmmmm . . ." was all Veronica said.

They covered the remaining three blocks—footsteps lost in the noise of traffic and empty office buildings—to his apartment building.

"You're really going to prepare dinner? Yourself?" Veronica gave a slight shiver under the powder-blue down coat as she stepped into the lobby.

"Sure. Although I did take the liberty of preparing most of it in advance last night. It wasn't as hard as I thought. I just got the *Campbell Soup Cookbook* and followed the directions."

"You're kidding."

"No, I found out you can do some really amazing things with chicken noodle soup."

"If you really didn't want to cook, there were better ways of making your point."

"Give dinner a try. It may surprise you. You'll never believe it's all based on tinned soup."

"Why not?"

"Because it isn't."

She gave him an almost playful sock in the arm before entering the empty elevator.

Once inside the apartment, Jonnie took the down coat and hung it up before removing his own dark green Harris Tweed overcoat.

"I see you haven't redecorated."

"You don't like Early Basement?"

Veronica gave a slight chuckle as she sat in one of the two big green plaid chairs. Facing the chairs were two large speakers almost completely covered in black fabric on either side of a black metal stereo rack. The speakers rested on short three-legged black metal stands. On the far side of each speaker was a large crate filled with records. The walls were bare except for several unframed moody black-and-white pictures of Chesapeake Bay.

"I shouldn't complain, given what my place looks like."

"I like your place. It's comfortable. Of course, the extraordinary nature of the prime occupant doesn't hurt."

Veronica looked past Jonnie and focused on the picture of the Thomas Point lighthouse at dusk.

"Can I get you something to drink?" asked Jonnie. "Tea, coffee, soda, champagne, scotch, bourbon, gin, or—"

"What do you have in the way of water?"

"Sparkling or still?"

"Still."

"I have some very fine Green Spring water. I get it at the local co-op."

"You shop at a co-op?"

"Uh-huh. It's interesting."

"You don't trust the local water supply?"

"The local water is safe enough. It's not so much a lack of trust as the fact that I don't like all that water with my chlorine. Call it an aesthetic decision." Jonnie walked past the chipped veneer of the circular dining table and into the separate kitchen. He returned and handed her an off-green glass before disappearing back into the kitchen.

"Look around while I finish up in here," he called back.

Veronica got up and walked over to the low bookcase against the wall, where she began to read the titles. "You don't have many books," she observed after several minutes.

"No. I like to pass on books when I'm finished with them. Literature is like money. It should circulate. I usually only keep books I haven't read, intend to reread, or got as gifts."

"Let's see what you've got here. Charles McCarry, *The Last*

Supper, The Hammer of Darkness, a new copy of *Metamorphosis,* an old edition of *The Oxford Book of English Verse.* "

"That's one of my favorites—the most important book in the English language."

"You really believe that?" Veronica leafed through the thick volume.

As he returned to the living room, Jonnie nodded. "No other single volume contains a better, more complete distillation of the best of English-speaking culture. Do you like poetry?"

"Yes. I didn't think you would, though."

Jonnie smiled. "Why don't you leave that out?"

Veronica laid the squat book on top of the shelf and continued looking at the titles. "Now, here's something that doesn't surprise me. *Cynicisms.* Although I wouldn't have thought you needed a book to help you."

"You should read that. It's wickedly funny. It has a good section on lawyers, almost as good as the one on consultants and politicians."

She pulled out the book and thumbed through it, stopping at the section labeled "Environmentalists." Her eyes began to take in the short entries.

"Oooo . . ."

"What?"

" 'Clean water is getting scarcer. So are clean environmentalists.' "

"I didn't write it," protested Jonnie.

"How about this one? 'A true environmentalist protests building atomic power plants because their waste is hard to handle. They still allow coal-fired generators that have killed over a hundred thousand miners and most of the eastern forests. This is known as environmental purity.' "

"Well, I think there's an element of truth there." Jonnie's voice was cautious as he hovered over the stove.

"I like this one!"

"Yes?"

" 'An environmental attorney is a contradiction in terms.' "

"Anyone like that in your office?" asked Jonnie as he brought out a dish from the refrigerator.

"I'm not telling."

"But you're giggling."

"All right, it's a standing joke. Ray Thomas. He's a big red-bearded lawyer. He used to be a radical protester. Then he went to law school. Now he's telling all his old environmental friends that working within the system is the way to go. Except he always complains when we hold a reception for Congress."

"Don't know him," Jonnie admitted. "You need to put down the book."

"Why? It is funny. Well, not funny. Maybe witty, and . . . well . . . true . . ."

"Because," Jonnie announced, "dinner is served."

Veronica sat in the chair Jonnie held away from the table. A blue-edged Corelle salad plate sat between each place setting. Behind each knife was a frosted glass and an open bottle of Singha Gold beer. In the center of the table was a light beige mound on a bed of lettuce with rings of red onions off to the side of the plate.

"This doesn't look like it was made with noodle soup."

"The Campbell cookbook didn't have a good recipe for *larb,* so I substituted a Thai cookbook."

"Larb?"

"It's essentially cold spiced ground chicken. Give it a try. You said you enjoyed spicy Chinese food. So I thought you might like to try Thai."

"I do like Thai food," Veronica admitted. "On the few occasions I've had it." She began spooning the *larb* onto her plate. "Are you going to be having onions?"

"I will if you will."

Veronica took three of the reddish rings.

"This is good. And hot." Veronica reached for the cold beer and poured it quickly into the glass.

"I'm glad you like it. I tried to take it easy on the chilies since you're a novice."

"Where did you get the ingredients?" Veronica asked as she reached to take some more *larb* from the serving plate.

"Most of the stuff came from the local supermarket. The rest came from an Asian grocery store. There must be at least a half dozen within two miles of here. The toughest part was finding the native food colorings."

"Why did you use food coloring?" A tinge of suspicion edged her voice.

"So dinner would be Thai-dyed."

Veronica covered her face and emitted a pained sound.

Jonnie removed the empty dishes and disappeared into the kitchen. After several minutes of clankings and other less defined sounds, he returned carrying dinner plates and a steaming bowl of sliced beef and vegetables.

"Nue gra pao," he announced as he set down the plates and the bowl.

"Quoi?"

"Nue gra pao. Stir-fried beef with mint."

"I'm impressed."

"Thanks, but you may want to try it before committing yourself." Jonnie went back to the kitchen and quickly returned with a bowl of white rice and a glass container filled with black liquid.

"Fermented fish sauce," he explained as he set down the items and returned to his seat.

For a time, neither said anything.

After a sip from her tumbler, followed by plain rice, and a quick blotting of her forehead, Veronica said, "This is really good. I didn't think you could cook, at least like this."

"I have to confess that it was pretty easy. Nothing required elaborate preparation."

"You're a brave man."

"For admitting it was easy?"

"For serving your date a meal based on onions and garlic."

"I'm having what you are so we'll cancel each other. We won't notice a thing."

"There are some things I'm hoping to notice." Veronica's face crinkled into a smile.

Jonnie returned the grin. "Aside from corporeal nourishment, the purpose of food is to heighten the senses."

"I do believe you have succeeded," Veronica replied softly as Jonnie quickly cleared the table and returned with two cups, each containing glutinous rice covered with sweetened mung beans.

"It's delicious. Different, but delicious. I've never had anything like this. What is it?"

"Special dessert for a special lady. And a special friend."

"Thank you." Veronica closed her eyes for a second before finishing dessert.

"Would you like some music?" Jonnie asked after clearing the table for the last time and refilling the water glasses.

"Yes, I would."

"You choose." Jonnie motioned to the record crates.

"I don't believe this. Your amplifier or preamp, whatever it is, has tubes."

"Both the amp and preamp are tubed."

"No CD player, and tubes instead of transistors. I didn't realize how poorly you were paid."

"It's not a question of money. The equipment is very expensive. Tubes just provide a warm liquid sound that transistors can't produce."

"Another aesthetic decision?"

"All important decisions are when you think about them."

Veronica thumbed through the records. "This is not what I expected."

"It's an eclectic collection."

"I can see. I guess I expected mostly either heavy metal or top forty."

"What have you got there?"

Veronica began pulling up individual albums. "We've got some nice selections from the Chesky catalog, several Professor Johnson recordings, whoever he is. Any relation to Doc Johnson?" Veronica flashed a wicked grin.

"Guess you'll have to find out." Jonnie grinned back.

Veronica continued looking through the crate. "Now I'm really surprised. Norwegian jazz?"

Jonnie did not answer, watching as Veronica's fingers moved through the albums.

"Kate Wolf, Nick Drake, and, oh, you've got Bonnie Koloc albums. How did you ever even hear of her, let alone find the records?"

"You forget. I lived in Chicago for a while. The records I've been able to slowly accumulate. I think there's only one I'm missing. How did you ever hear of her?"

"I've been a fan of hers for . . . God, a long time. I wonder if she's even still alive."

Jonnie nodded. "She even had an album out not too long ago."

"Really? Despite all the heroin? I haven't heard of her in a long time."

"I guess she finally cleaned up her act. Here, let me put that on." Jonnie lifted the turntable dust cover, placed the disc on the platter, and screwed down the clamp before switching the player on, giving the record a quick swipe with a carbon fiber brush and releasing the needle.

The two bodies came together, slowing sinking to the soft thick carpeting as "You're Gonna Love Yourself in the Morning" played in the background. The bodies remained joined long after the record had finished.

71

MCDARVID LEANED INSIDE THE DOORWAY. "Hello, Jerry."

"Hi, Jack." Killorin's voice was flat.

"How are things with the metals initiative?"

"You know I can't talk about that. That's *ex parte.*"

McDarvid stepped inside the office, easing the door shut behind him. "Of course you can, Jerry. You just have to write it up."

Killorin looked up tiredly from the modular desk, leaned back in the chair, his paunch protruding over his thin brown belt and khaki trousers. "And I've got all sorts of time to write things like that up? We put your papers in the record. You have anything else to add, put it in writing, and we'll add it."

McDarvid nodded. "You're good about following procedures, Jerry. At least the ones that apply to rulemaking." He looked toward the picture of the girl in the graduation gown. "Pretty girl. Where's she go to school?"

"Mount Holyoke," admitted Killorin.

"She's bright, like her father." McDarvid shook his head. "Amazing how expensive schools like that have gotten. When I went to Amherst, I think the whole bill was maybe four grand a year. That went further then, but now it must be over twenty thousand."

"It's expensive, all right." Killorin swallowed. "What's on your mind, Jack? I've seen more of you in the past two weeks than in the past year."

"Well, you know how it is. Just depends on what issues I'm working. This metals thing is really fascinating. Goes so much deeper than ever shows up in the rule. I've really learned a lot following it." McDarvid shrugged. "It affects things like space, high technology, government procurements, even college tuition, in an odd way." He stepped back toward the door. "Since you're being very formal, though, I'll be submitting my stuff formally. Both to the docket and to the I.G." He held up the thick folder he carried. "Makes interesting reading."

"What does the Inspector General have to do with a proposed rule?" Killorin had eased himself forward in the battered gray swivel chair.

"Don't know that he does, but when ethics considerations involve those with a substantial input to a rule . . ." McDarvid shrugged. "I just couldn't be certain myself; so I thought the I.G. ought to look into it." He eased the door back open. "Appreciate the time, Jerry. Have a good day."

McDarvid nodded to Angelique as he passed her desk. "You have a good day, too."

"Thank you, Mr. McDarvid."

McDarvid walked the long corridor to the elevator, where he punched the button for the ground floor. He'd already provided the package to the Inspector General—and gotten a receipt.

Killorin was cool, very cool. So what could he do now?

72

"ALL OF A SUDDEN, it doesn't look so certain."

"Why not? Three months ago, you said it was a lock." Ray Thomas' voice grew sharper.

"Ray?" asked Killorin, his voice sounding thin in the receiver.
"Yeah . . ."

"You know Jack McDarvid?"

"I've run across his name somewhere recently. What was it?"
Thomas transferred the telephone receiver to his left shoulder,
opened the file that lay on his blotter, and flipped through the
sheets of paper. "Here it is. Something—you know, a propa-
ganda piece. I just glanced at the thing when it came in. It looks
like the same lobbyists' shit. He sent one to your office."

"I read it. That's one of the reasons why the metals thing might
come unglued."

"Junk," snorted the attorney.

"I wish it were, Ray. He's got some good points there. His
numbers are better than yours, or ours, and he knows how to get
people's attention. And he's a real bastard."

Thomas closed the file drawer, leaving the metals folder on the
desktop, then shifted the telephone back to his right ear. "You
don't make sense, Jerry. You say his stuff's good, and he's a
bastard."

"Ray, you're confusing character with ability." The sigh was
more than audible. "He's a bastard, and he may have me in deep
shit. He's polite and unassuming. He likes to tell you stories
about his kids, but when the time comes, he'll kick you in the
balls."

"Shit, Jerry." Thomas swallowed. "Can I do anything?"

"You can't do a friggin' thing about that smug son of a bitch.
Just stay out of his way."

"Why? He can't do anything to me."

"Don't say that. His numbers are good, and he knows how to
use them. They'll kill you. Take him serious, real serious." There
was a pause. "Don't . . . Never mind." There was a pause.
"Anyway, the short answer to your question is that it still looks
okay, but it's sure not a mortal lock."

Thomas frowned. "All right if I call you later?"

"Well . . . yeah, I guess I'll be . . . yeah. That's okay. But
remember McDarvid."

"Sure, Jerry. Sure."

73

MCDARVID SAT DOWN ON THE STONE BENCH and removed the standard lens from his camera, setting it in the top of the telephoto lens case. Then he took the 200mm lens from the case and attached it. The lens seemed to dwarf the camera.

He put the regular lens in the case, closed it, and eased the case into the right raincoat pocket. With a sigh he stood, checking the address on the piece of paper again—no more than a two-block walk. According to Tom, Renni usually had lunch out on Fridays. Sometimes on Mondays, but usually on Fridays. That figured, since most Fridays the committee had no hearings.

Number 345 was a modest three-story town house, perhaps thirty feet wide at the most, a Washington, D.C., imitation of a New York brownstone. McDarvid whistled as he walked past. The entire house had been gutted and refinished behind the original stonework. Not bad for a black engineer and lobbyist who had pulled himself out of the depths of Chicago. McDarvid shook his head. For sheer ability, Alroy had it, from the advanced MIT degrees to the reputed near-concert-level ability with his Steinway grand. He also clearly had charm, especially if cold, bitchy Renni Fowler warmed to him.

McDarvid checked his watch. Eleven-thirty. Could be as much as a thirty-to-forty-minute wait.

At the end of the block, he crossed the street and stopped. He tried focusing on the doorstep, but the trunk of a stately oak blocked a clear shot. He moved back toward the brownstone and tried again. This time a thinner and unidentified tree crossed the camera's field.

Moving back up the block on the other side of the street, he tried again. This time he got a clear image.

Overhead, the clouds thickened. McDarvid checked the settings on the camera again, then took a shot of the town house. And a second. After all, there were thirty-six exposures on the roll, and he doubted that he would get half that many at the right time, even with the autowinder.

Leaving the camera on the strap around his neck, he sat on a stone fence post one house closer to Alroy's and pulled out the notepad from his pocket. He began to list items:

ITEM: A dead and influential attorney known for his success in making the improbable occur

ITEM: A secret nuclear test in the Pacific

ITEM: A government favor to the French

ITEM: Environmental regulations targeted at high-tech industries

ITEM: Scholarships for the children of idealists setting environmental standards

ITEM: Not-perfectly-secure computers in key locations supplied by the same people who granted the scholarships

ITEM: At least two key low-level decision-makers receiving apparent financial aid

A well-dressed black woman walked past. Her eyes took in the camera and the notepad, and she immediately looked away.

McDarvid glanced up the block, but saw only a stroller and a younger woman pushing it. The wind ruffled through his hair, and his ears were getting cold.

A tall athletic figure appeared at the corner on the other end of the block. McDarvid stuffed the pad and felt-tip into the raincoat pocket and picked up the camera.

He managed five clear shots, the last of Alroy with his key in the lock.

While he waited, hoping Renni would show, he tore his list of items from the pad, folded the two sheets of paper, and put them in his pants pocket, not the raincoat pocket.

The faint tapping of heels alerted McDarvid, and he had the camera ready.

Renni looked neither right nor left, but walked quickly and determinedly toward the brownstone.

McDarvid's second shot caught a smile on her face. His last shot caught Mike Alroy's profile almost as if in a quick kiss with Renni's lips.

Good enough?

McDarvid's stomach twisted as he took another two shots of the brownstone. Then he put the lens cap in place and began to walk toward the Metro.

"Who do you work for?"

He stepped back at the question. Two middle-aged women in heavy dark cloth coats stood at the corner. "I beg your pardon?" he asked.

"He has to be from the press, Gladys. Look at that camera. That's a telephoto lens. Walter had one like that."

McDarvid shook his head. "I'm sorry. I don't work for anyone. Just . . . bird watching."

"Oh . . . what kind of birds, young man? I can tell you that about the only things you'll find around here are pigeons." The thinner woman was amused.

"This is so exciting . . ." interjected the other one. "I'll bet he works for someone like Scandal Tours. Digging up all the dirt."

"Excuse me, ladies." He stepped around the two women and continued walking toward the Capitol South Metro station.

"Maybe a private eye . . ."

"Bird watching indeed . . ."

McDarvid winced, thinking about how Eric regarded amateurs, thinking about how the pictures didn't quite prove anything—not by themselves. But, then, in Washington, there was seldom hard proof—until the hearings or the charges that were usually a professional obituary.

74

"MR. BLACK? There's a Mr. Adrian Pimm from Lao Systems here."

"What?"

"I said there's a Mr. Adrian . . ."

"Never mind. Tell him to wait a few minutes."

"If you would, please buzz me when you would like to see him."

"It'll be a couple of minutes."

Jonnie hung up the receiver and rubbed his forehead. It had not been a good day. He looked at the computer screen and mumbled, "I have three attorneys who all want me to work immediately on projects they don't have any budget for. I might be completely unemployed at any time. McDarvid's getting squirrelier every day, and Veronica barely wanted to talk to me last night, let alone get together. Now some lousy computer rep is knocking on my door. And it's only Wednesday." Jonnie rubbed his forehead again. He took a swig of cold strong tea from the beige stoneware no-spill coffee mug marked with the LBI logo. He hadn't even bothered to find out what LBI was before fast-talking the mug out of their representative at one computer show or another.

After shutting off his computer, he moved the stack of papers in the middle of his desk to the top of his overstuffed bookcase. He picked up the receiver again.

"Reception."

"This is Jonnie Black. Would you show Mr. Pimm to my office?"

"Certainly, Mr. Black."

Jonnie took a deep breath and used one hand to massage his neck, thinking about the book on massage that Veronica had mentioned. They could both use it lately.

A young earnest-looking man knocked on Jonnie's already open door. "Mr. Black? I'm Adrian Pimm from Lao Systems' Corporate Relations Department." He gave a brilliant white smile as he extended his business card.

Jonnie motioned to the chair in front of the desk. Christ, just what I needed, Jonnie thought, Wally Wonder Bread. He looks like he's about to offer me an incredible deal on a new Toyota. Well, I won't let him get my goat.

"Mr. Black, I do apologize for stopping by without an appointment. I was visiting someone in the building and thought I would stop by and see if you had a moment. Is this convenient for you?"

Jonnie nodded.

"Mr. DiTellio mentioned to me that you were interested in our company. That's why I thought I should drop by and answer any questions you had."

"Mr. DiTellio?"

"Yes, he's the gentleman you spoke with at the show last week."

"What show?"

"The FOSE Interconnectivity and Applications Exhibition. At the Convention Center."

"Oh . . . Yes. Sorry. There are so many different shows . . ."

"That's all right. I travel to so many of these exhibitions around the country that I'm lucky to remember what city I'm in, let alone which show." Pimm flashed another over-white-toothed grin. "You were interested in determining your connectivity needs."

"We're pretty happy with our Novell two point one five and ARCNET system over co-ax. Sure, it's a little old, and if we were going to start from scratch, we would probably go with unshielded twisted pair and maybe a different architecture, but what the hell . . . We can always upgrade to three point one three-eighty-six if we want. I've heard some good things about Banyan VINES, but I don't think we'd move to it."

Pimm looked at Jonnie curiously. "I can understand that. Did you get a chance to see our Windows display? We've made a major effort to put together a comprehensive package of Windows applications for our clients."

"I hate GUI. Computing for the postliterate."

"Well, we have found that firms which migrate to a graphical user interface environment experience significant increases in productivity."

"They would get even more productivity if they would teach their people how to read. Or even more to the point, how to think. Maybe then people would put some thought into what they were doing instead of just pushing the damn mouse around and assuming that because the output looks pretty that it has any value. I've found that people who work with icon-based systems are more interested in cute pictures than in critical reasoning or substance."

"Well . . . umm . . . we do offer and support a complete range of traditional DOS systems. Oh, I did bring some information you asked for."

"Really?"

"Yes, I have our complete information packet on the Lao Foundation. Since you were so curious about our charitable activities, I enclosed a copy of our 501 C(3) charter and our latest public interest statement showing how the funds are spent. I'm sure you'll find that the Foundation is a very worthy activity. There's also a set of corporate contribution forms."

"No doubt. Thanks. I'll look at this later." Jonnie took the large brown envelope Pimm had taken from his plastic attaché case, placed it in the upper left desk drawer, and began to stroke his beard.

"And since you were interested, I also have some information about our TEMPEST systems. As you might know, we are one of the few manufacturers that produce our own board-level TEMPEST equipment. Do you have any need for a secure environment?"

"Not that I know of."

"I see that you're not currently a Lao customer," he added, his eyes focusing on the IBM machine in the corner of the office. "Are you responsible for info systems procurement or support?"

"No. We have a Purchasing Department that worries about buying equipment. And we have a part-time techie on staff who provides assistance."

"So your interest in computers is personal? You have one at home?"

"No. I don't like computers. They're useful tools, sometimes even essential. Landfills are also essential, but I wouldn't want one in my backyard."

The Lao rep looked at Jonnie for a moment without saying a word. "Do you mind if I ask why you were interested in Lao Systems?"

"Just curious, that's all. I like to keep up with what's going on."

"Oh . . . well . . . you have my card with my local office number. If you have any questions, please don't hesitate to give me a call." Adrian Pimm snapped the gray plastic case shut and stood up.

"There is one favor I would like to ask." Jonnie gave his first smile of the afternoon.

"What?"

"Next time you hold one of your 'special receptions' in Amarillo, give me a call."

After a hard look, the Lao representative left without saying a word.

Jonnie shook his head and stared out the window for a moment before picking up the telephone handset.

"Jack, do you have a second?"

"What's up?"

"I was just wondering how your visit to the computer show went."

"Fine, I think. Do you want the pass back? I meant to return it."

Jonnie leaned as far back in his chair as the tilt mechanism would let him. "No, I don't need it. Did you ask lots of interesting questions?"

"What happened?"

"Nothing much, but a gentleman from Lao just stopped by to see if *I* had any questions."

"Oh, that's right. They think I'm you. Sorry."

"Jack, I've been to any number of these shows and asked all kinds of questions and never has anyone come to my office to see if they could be of any help. Just what did you say to them?"

"Not much. I asked a few questions about their equipment and asked if they had any information about the Lao Foundation. I'm not an expert on computers, but I couldn't have sounded that stupid."

"I don't think stupidity is what caught their attention. The fellow did leave me, or you, a packet of information about their Foundation. And another one on their TEMPEST equipment." Jonnie rocked forward in the chair.

"Oh. I'll stop by and pick it up."

"The corporate relations guy seemed interested in why *I* was interested in Lao. After talking to me, I think he left more confused than ever. I never asked why you were curious about Lao Systems. I don't mind talking with you about computer companies, and I don't mind your going to shows as me, but next time you do something like this, could you at least give me a little warning?"

"Sorry. I tried to say as little as possible. I'll come by in a little bit and pick up that stuff."

"Right. See you soon." Jonnie replaced the handset, stared out the window, and slowly sighed. Now what was McDarvid up to? And why wouldn't he say anything about his interest in Lao Systems?

Jonnie pulled the brown envelope out of the drawer. Jack at least owed him a look-see. Besides, he wasn't going to get any more work done for a while.

Idly, scanning the plain sheets that described the need for merit scholarships for the children of the "forgotten backbone of America," Jonnie leaned back in the chair again. He still needed a massage.

75

"YOU HAVE TO GET ME OUT OF THIS," stammered Killorin, pale-faced.

"Out of what? You've done nothing except follow your beliefs." The taller man looked out the window overlooking the river, but remained standing where he could take in both the nighttime view and his visitor.

"That's easy for you to say. You don't have the Inspector General breathing down your neck."

"No, I have you at my front door, whining about something that's not even a problem." The tall and still-athletic man snorted, glancing to the bookcase on his left. A miniature marble replica of the *David* rested on one end and another miniature of *Venus de Milo* on the other.

"Since when is the Inspector General no problem?"

"Why are you worried about that? You might get a reprimand. That's hardly something to worry about."

"Not after he's been briefed by that bastard McDarvid. Hell, McDarvid wrote the investigation for the I.G."

"McDarvid?"

"Jack McDarvid. He used to be the head of Policy Analysis.

He works for one of the law firms downtown, but he's not a lawyer."

"A lobbyist? You worry about a lobbyist? With the reputation they have?" The taller man stepped back until the back of his blue flannel blazer brushed the desk. Then he leaned against the heavy cherry replica.

"You don't understand. If anyone knows what questions to ask, it's McDarvid. He's been nosing around all over DEP and OSHA. Behind that broken-down old money front, he's a cold-blooded bastard."

"You're right. I don't understand. The Ethics Officer has released your ethics form, and the Inspector General has asked for an interview. You answer their questions. There's no documentary evidence to the contrary. They'll thank you. The Inspector General will write a letter indicating there was no evidence to support the claim, and everything will go on."

Killorin shook his head. "No. You don't understand. McDarvid *knows*. And if he does so does the I.G. That's why I'm here." His hands rested on the arms of the deep and soft-padded chair.

"So you lie a little." The man in the Brooks Brothers blazer laughed. "It won't be the first time."

"I tell you. He knows. And lying—that's the one thing that both the I.G. and the congressional committees can kill you for. That's how they got all the Ice Queen's people." Killorin's voice rose fractionally.

"Let's discuss this rationally. Haven't we always helped you out?"

Killorin flushed at the condescending tone. "Yeah. But this is worse." His feet shuffled as he looked up from the chair.

"First, what's the problem?"

"The damned ethics forms show I don't have that kind of money."

"Oh . . . I don't think so. Not if you consider it rationally."

"What about Denise?"

"Your daughter received a scholarship on her own."

"What about the alimony?"

"What alimony?"

"That's not how the committee will see it."

"How will they know?"

"McDarvid will tell them."

"He can't know."

"Well, he must be a good guesser. He dropped by the office last week. He said he wanted to chat, in that quiet polite way of his that means trouble. He talked about how funny Washington was, about how hard it was for him and his wife, and she's a doctor, to make ends meet—yet how some government employees seemed to live well, even with children in college."

"You, of course, looked agitated, and added to his suspicions." The older man's tone was sardonic.

"No. He didn't even look for a reaction. He just said that he had put together a theoretical financial profile showing the income necessary to do all that. Then he said that he had done a study based on a number of officials' forms, compared their incomes as reported on the ethics forms to what they were spending. Then he left." Killorin wiped his forehead. "I could deal with that. He was fishing. But a week later the Ethics Officer told me McDarvid had requested my forms."

"I fail to see the problem."

"Last Thursday, he stopped by again. This time it was worse. He almost flat out told me that I had taken a payoff for the metals initiative, that he had completed not only the study but a formal complaint to the I.G., and that the complaint would be lodged in the docket as well, because my actions had compromised the entire rule-making."

"He didn't say all that."

Killorin flushed. "Of course not. What he said was impartial and mealymouthed, but all the pieces were there. He even showed me the report. So I sat tight. Just like a good boy. The I.G. called Monday, but I didn't get back from Region Nine until today. That's less than forty-eight hours, and they never do that unless they're serious."

"You're reading too much into this . . . McDarvid's actions."

"Oh, come off it. McDarvid's figured it out, and he was letting me know that he knew I was being paid off."

"Money. So you received a few gifts from friends who have never asked you for anything. That's not precluded."

"It is now. The Ethics Act applied when I was a GS-13, but there was no way to check because I didn't have to file. As an office director, I have to file that form, and McDarvid's got mine. So it's either perjury or an apparent conflict of interest. I didn't put gifts on the form. And it's going to be hard to explain the amounts."

The older man shrugged. "You shouldn't worry. They caught Mike Deaver in the White House cookie jar, and he was acquitted."

"They convicted Ollie North, and he was doing what he believed." Killorin's voice trembled.

"You should be as successful as North. Besides, most of that was overturned on appeal. Bah . . . a token fine . . . community service . . . high fees for speeches, and he's still a hero to thousands."

"Damn it! It's my life. I don't have a half million to pay legal fees. Sure, I'll be a martyr to the cause, and famous—and broke as hell when I get out of Eglin. Now, what are you going to do about it?"

The older man straightened and walked around the desk, where he stood, staring out into the night. "First, you go and talk to the I.G. After all, nothing is likely to happen. This . . . McDarvid . . . knows he doesn't have hard evidence. That's why he pressured you."

"God damn it! You don't understand anything! It doesn't matter! Maybe you don't remember, but along with the creeps, when Ruckelshaus came in, he swept out a bunch of good people who had the misfortune to be in the wrong place. Some of them are still doing things like selling insurance. One engineer is a fucking diver for a marina! They're the lucky ones." Killorin lurched to his feet, heaving his thin frame and hardly slender belly from the overstuffed soft chair with both arms.

"Are you asking for more money?" The tall man straightened.

"More money, he offers. What will that do now? You're not the one that sits there under the lights with an eager-beaver investigator dying to find some real-live corruption. You said I shouldn't worry when this came up. Well, I'm worried, and you just stand behind that big desk and smile and ask if a little more money will help. 'Oh, yes, Mr. Killorin, here's a few thousand to help with the back alimony.' And will Andy Corellian show up next week to offer a postgraduate scholarship to Denise?"

"You're not making much sense tonight," observed the tall man.

"I know you guys. One minute I tell you a few grand won't cut it when I've got a daughter about to hit college. Three weeks later, your friend the computer guy shows up with a bona fide grant for Denise—the college of her choice."

The silver-haired man smiled. "Jerry, I may have mentioned your problems to a friend or two, but, believe me, the Lao Foundation is a bona fide 501 C(3) foundation. That's why I suggested your daughter's name to them. Whether they ever considered her was totally up to them and her record."

Killorin's right hand slid behind his back, under the sweater, as if massaging sore muscles. "You're not going to do one fucking thing, are you? You don't have to. Everything that's got a shred of paper is so legal and clean. They don't even know who you really work for, and no one would believe little Jerry Killorin, anyway. 'Jerry—he drinks too much. Sad about poor Jerry. He went right off the deep end.' But you know something else? They don't know I know you, either, Mr. Conservative Congressman."

His hand whipped from behind his body with the folded paper. "It's all here. Every last nickel, every damned request."

The taller man snorted again. "I suppose you drafted it up on the office computer so that everyone knows."

"And if I did?"

"You're in trouble, Jerry, but you really don't want the world to know. Who would give you the money to pay off your ex-wife? Or provide an extra few hundred when you overspend at the track? The Sierra Club? NRDC? Give me a break."

"You fucking bastard! Now I'll damn well make sure the whole world knows." Killorin lurched toward the silver-haired man.

The Congressman dodged the heavy man's rush.

Killorin grabbed the ornate and pointed letter opener from beside the desk pen set and turned. His breathing was heavy and irregular, and pushed the odor of stale alcohol toward the older man.

"Jerry, just get out of here."

"Bullshit! I'm not going under those lights. You get me off."

"I'll fix the I.G. investigation." The older man edged toward the bookcase. "Just don't say anything."

"Bastard!" Killorin lifted the paper knife. The blade glinted in the light from the desk lamp as he lunged again. "Sure you will. Like you fixed everything else."

The Congressman stepped back, but grasped the slim marble statuette from the bookcase as he twisted away from the slower-moving bureaucrat.

". . . force you . . ." Killorin's breath rasped as he jabbed the sharp pointed opener toward the tall man. He rushed again.

The Congressman dodged as he raised his arm, then brought the statuette down sharply.

The tall man stood for a moment, looking at the still-breathing figure twitching on the heavy carpet. The twitching stopped, but Killorin did not move. Shortly, the older man levered the unconscious man onto his back, noting the caved-in temple.

"Idiot."

He picked up the heavy chunk of marble that had snapped off when the statue's base had connected with Killorin's temple. He placed both pieces on the desk. "Damned idiot . . ." He shook his head again as he headed for the kitchen.

He returned with a plastic trash bag, edging the white plastic over the other's face. Then he went back to the kitchen.

When he returned a few minutes later, after packaging the statue pieces and making the other arrangements, Killorin was no longer breathing—either because of the blow to the temple or the plastic bag.

The Congressman shook his head. He still had a long night ahead. Too bad it wasn't Thursday, but Killorin's body would keep overnight—tucked away in the spare closet. And there wasn't much else he could do. Not now.

"Idiot . . ."

76

THE SILVER CONTINENTAL, although far from new, purred smoothly across the Route 50 bridge over Assawoman Bay and toward the dark shapes of the hibernating boardwalk structures. After two left turns and passing the White Marlin Club, the car pulled up to the Sommerset Street marina.

The silver-haired driver opened the door and got out, stretching his arms and broad shoulders. Then he closed the door and opened the one behind the driver's seat, extracting a small soft-sided gray suitcase.

"Evenin', Congressman," a voice called from the end of the pier.

"Good evening, Haley."

"You taking her out tonight?"

"I'm crazy, but not that crazy. It's been a long week. First I'll get some sleep. Then, in the morning . . ." The hawk-nosed man smiled and shrugged. "Then we'll see. I'm thinking of going out to the Canyon and bringing back some red ocean crabs, maybe even a few lobsters."

"You're crazy," agreed the gray-haired watchman who ambled toward the Continental. "That's a trip, even with your boat—just for crabs. Even if they are red crabs."

"It is a trip, but it has one advantage." The Congressman headed toward the pier, swinging the case.

"Oh?"

"There aren't any lobbyists out there, and no angry constituents."

"You've said that before. Guess you mean it." The watchman paused. "Can't leave the car here."

"I know. I have some heavy stuff, staples, cooler, special bait for the crabs, in the trunk. I'm going to get the dolly."

"I think I got one in the shed."

"Don't worry, Haley. I keep one on board. It comes in handy, like when I had that party last fall." The Congressman paused by the cruiser, looking at the builder's nameplate—Egg Harbor. He touched the side of the thirty-six-foot *Constituent Service,* then vaulted aboard.

After setting the suitcase down, he eased the gangway into place and opened the cabin.

"Better be getting back, Congressman."

"It's good to see you, Haley. I'll move the car as soon as I get the stuff out of the trunk."

"That's no problem, just so long as I know." The watchman shuffled back along the pier.

In time, the silver-haired man trundled a dolly back toward the Continental. The trunk opened soundlessly. Inside were two square House of Representatives file boxes, a cooler, and a large canvas bag more than half the width of the trunk.

He placed the heavier file box on the dolly. Then he reached for the bulky canvas.

After setting the waterproof canvas bag over the file box, he adjusted it. The ends still almost touched the concrete, and one side brushed the South Carolina license plate that read: "MC-8."

After easing the dolly backward, he pushed it slowly onto the pier.

"Need some help?" offered the guard.

"No. This is the heaviest part. One more trip, and I should be done. Then I'll get the car out of the way."

"No hurry. No hurry. Not this time of night."

The hawk-nosed man had to struggle to drag the sack across the gangway and onto the cruiser under the dim lights of the pier.

11

ANDREW CORELLIAN EASED INTO THE CHAIR across the desk from Esther Saliers. "So . . . what's my surprise?"

The grin was almost incongruous above the dark gray suit with thin red and purple stripes, the pale blue shirt, and the tie with matching stripes.

"Andrew! You haven't been here two minutes. And you were twelve minutes late to begin with. Didn't anyone ever teach you the art of polite conversation? I'm almost tempted not to give you the cake I made." A broad smile followed Esther's mock reproach.

"I can't help it. I like surprises." The grin faded, and the sandy-haired man's voice lowered. "I was kidding about the cake, though. I really didn't mean for you to go to all that work."

"Now you tell me." The division chief smiled shyly. "It is nice to have someone to bake for. With Derik gone, and Keri rushing around, I just don't have that much reason to do a lot of cooking. And if I cook"—she gestured toward her midsection—"I eat more than I can exercise off. It's hard. Puttering around in the kitchen was one of my few ways of relaxing, and Derik . . . well, he liked desserts."

"Sorry. I didn't mean . . ."

She waved his words away. "I'm glad you could come, even if the brown bag routine isn't up to the standard lobbyist's lunch."

Corellian held up a hand. "I'm not complaining. It's not often I get to have lunch and have a chance to learn something new." He paused. "You know, it is surprising that someone with your interests and abilities hasn't gotten more involved with an environmental group or something."

"Oh, a lot of people here do. Pete down the hall spends weekends replanting marsh grasses in Chesapeake Bay. But that's not what I'm interested in, not for relaxation. That's the nice thing about cooking. It gives me a chance to be creative and forget about work. I can only think about cancerous mice for so long without going crazy. And . . . oh, never mind. Here, since you asked for your surprise . . ." Esther reached under her desk and retrieved a large Hecht's shopping bag. "I hoped Keri would be able to come down to the office today, but she just couldn't make it. So . . . with you being out of town next week, I get to play delivery person."

The sandy-haired man took the bag and placed it on his lap, carefully extracting the heavy blue sweatshirt with the gold lettering. "Oh, this is the classy kind. I can really use this. I jog before work. I have a tattered warm-up shirt, but it's not nearly as classy as one from Emory."

"Keri was hoping you would like it. She brought it back from her weekend down there. We hoped that the extra large would be right. There's also a card that goes with the shirt." Esther produced a small sealed envelope.

Corellian took the envelope, then carefully folded the sweatshirt and replaced it in the plastic shopping bag, before setting the bag on the institutional gray carpet by his chair. "Thank you. For Keri. She's a thoughtful girl. I can't remember anyone giving me something just because I was the bearer of good news."

Esther looked down at the desk blotter for a moment, then raised her eyes. "I'd like to see if the three of us can have lunch together before she leaves. You think we could squeeze that into your busy schedule sometime in the next five months?"

"For such an offer, with two lovely ladies, how could I possibly refuse?" The grin faded—slightly. "I also brought something for you."

"Really? I didn't know that you could bake." Esther gave a sly smile.

"Not exactly. Actually, I'm returning the two studies you lent me. I now know more about chlorobenzohydrilate than I ever wanted to know." He set the two sheaves of paper on the desk.

"Chlorohydrobenzilate," corrected Esther automatically.

"Except how to pronounce it."

"Now you have an idea of what I have to put up with every day." Esther lifted her brown bag. "I do have to eat at some point, because I've got another meeting at two-thirty."

The executive retrieved his brown bag. "This time I actually fixed it."

"Really? Peanut butter and jelly?"

"Ham and cheese on rye, with hot mustard and lettuce."

Esther shook her head.

"I don't know how you do it," continued Corellian as he carefully folded the brown bag and laid out the sandwich. "My head was swimming before I was through the summary of the first study." He stopped, then looked at her. "Is this stuff as dangerous as it sounds to me?"

"You should be a little careful when you read those studies." The Pesticides official pursed her lips. "Especially the mouse studies. Some species, like the black three 'F' mice, are so sensitive. They're bred to get cancer. I mean, if you feed them cheese for a bedtime snack and overcrowd them in the slightest, half are going to have tumors by morning. The other thing you have to watch is the exposure levels. Too many studies tend to assume that there is no difference between a low exposure over a long period of time and a high exposure over a short time frame. Since either the mice are going to die or the researcher's funding will run out before too long, they tend to feed them pretty high doses."

"Well," mumbled the sandy-haired man as he finished a bite of sandwich, "I'm no scientist. But they kept mentioning that it was at least a probable human carcinogen at very low exposure levels."

"Any pesticide is dangerous," explained Esther. "It is a poison. But until genetic engineering or some other advance allows for the safe control of insects and other plant blights, we have to allow some chemicals."

"Are you going to do something about chloro . . ." Corellian motioned with both hands as if he were about to clap them.

"Chlorohydrobenzilate. The draft PD has already been issued, which offers a choice between highly restrictive uses or actual cancellation of the registration. We're still taking comments, but there's certainly enough evidence in the docket—well, I can't really say more right now. Our job is to summarize the latest scientific submissions and provide a short analysis for the Assistant Secretary."

The sandy-haired man took a large bite from his sandwich, then followed it with a careful swig from the bottle of natural soda.

Buzzzzz . . .

She grabbed the receiver reluctantly. "Health Effects, Saliers."

"Ms. Saliers? Mr. Metron's office called. Your two-thirty has been moved up to two. He has to meet with the Assistant Secretary at three."

"Fine. I'll be there." She replaced the receiver, shaking her head.

"Is there a problem?" asked the Lao executive.

"No. A meeting moved up a few minutes. Nothing serious." She lifted a forkful of salad from the plastic bowl, then paused. "Sometimes it seems that the meetings have meetings."

"I think that's true everywhere now." Corellian took another swig of the soda. "We were talking about safety. Now, I don't claim to know much about risk analysis or health standards. But I think I can read, and after reading through those studies,

I wouldn't want my kids to eat anything with that stuff on it. Is it really worth taking any sort of chance? Even a small one?"

Esther continued with her salad before responding. "You're probably right, in this case." She smiled wryly. "Although Keri's probably a little too old to be affected by trace quantities."

"Still . . ."

"There's one nice thing about FIFRA. We do have to balance risk, but it does allow us to be as stringent as necessary." She took another bite of salad.

Corellian finished the last of the sandwich, but waited for her to continue.

"People complain about government service, but the job does have some benefits more important than any bonus check." She sipped from her mug.

"I know what you mean. Although I could probably have made more if I had gone into sales, I like my job. As silly as it sounds, I really think I'm doing good, at least more good than by selling another computer."

"That's not silly at all. I just hope that when Keri's done with her education, she remembers there is more to life than buying BMWs."

"She will," affirmed the computer executive. "I read all her materials when reviewing the scholarship grant. Besides, if she weren't thoughtful, she never would have sent me this." Corellian raised the bag.

Esther looked at her watch. "I'm going to have to leave pretty soon."

"So soon? I didn't even get to say how much I agreed with those studies. At least, I think I did, if I read all the eight-syllable words right."

Esther shook her head. "I understand your feelings. But I wouldn't worry about where we're coming out on this one. That's all I can really say, and perhaps that's too much." She paused, and smiled again. "Give me a call when you get back. I'd like to arrange lunch for the three of us. I know Keri does want to thank you in person. And since we never got to the cheesecake, why don't you take it with you?"

Corellian grinned. "I'd say that I really shouldn't, but that wouldn't be the truth. So I'll just say thanks." He rose from the chair, bag in hand, and gathered up the plastic cake carrier Esther had laid on the desk. "And I will give you a call. I'm looking forward to meeting Keri in person."

"She'd like that. After all, it's not always that you get to meet the person who made your dreams come true."

"It's not like that at all," protested Corellian.

"Maybe not, but close enough."

Corellian shook his head slightly as he left.

78

THE SILVER-HAIRED CONGRESSMAN poured the cold beer into the mug of the woman on his right. "There you go, Anne. It goes nicely with the crab." He moved to the glass of the man beside her.

"I've never seen crab like this before." The voice came from one side of the table set for six. "What is it, Matt?"

"It's red ocean crab. They're sort of like Dungeness crabs. Some people consider them a delicacy, but I certainly won't be offended if you don't like them. I might eat yours, though, if you don't want any." Behind him, in the picture window, the lights of Washington glittered across the river.

"Where do you get them?" asked the white-haired woman to the left of the momentarily empty chair at the head of the table.

"You have to get them specially, Sarah. I caught these over the weekend. I thought you might like something different." The silver-haired man finished filling the mugs and sat down.

"You caught them? I'm impressed. Aren't you, George?" asked the white-haired woman. She turned to her husband, a tanned and graying man in a blue blazer.

George laughed. "Anything Matt does is done in style, even catching crabs."

"Where do you catch them?" asked the dark-haired Anne, raising a ringless left hand to her goblet.

"The only place I know is in the Baltimore Canyon." The silver-haired man sipped from his own goblet.

"That's a far ride, even in that high-powered boat of yours," commented the other man.

"It is. But there's no telephone on board, and no stack of correspondence to look at."

Both other men laughed. The white-haired woman and the gray-haired woman at the end of the table exchanged knowing glances.

"Does it take special equipment or special kinds of bait?" asked Anne, her eyes on the silver-haired man next to her.

"The equipment's a little different. Bait's bait. Raw meat does just fine." The silver-haired man nodded, thinking about the heavy canvas bag and its contents. At least, in the end, Jerry had been good for something in the environment.

"Those look like sharp claws."

"They are, but they're also quite tasty." He picked up the crackers. "You eat them just like a blue claw. Let me show you." Then he turned to the other two Congressmen and their wives. "Dig in. And don't worry about being sloppy. There's no neat way to enjoy crabs."

"Matt's dinners are so relaxing, and he's such a good cook. Especially for a single man."

79

THE ATTORNEY PICKED UP THE TELEPHONE, tapping in the numbers.

"Standards and Regs."

"This is Ray Thomas. Is Jerry in yet?"

"Ah . . . well . . . no . . . Mr. Thomas."

"I've been trying to reach him for almost a week. He doesn't answer his home number. Where is he?"

"Well . . . you'll have to talk to Angelique. Just a minute."

Thomas' fingers drummed on the desk.

"This is Angelique. May I help you?"

"Ray Thomas at Ecology Now! Is something wrong with Jerry? I'm a friend, and no one knows where he is."

"Oh?"

"Angelique, please cut the crap. Barbara—his ex-wife, if you don't know—hasn't heard from him in weeks. He hasn't been seen in his condo since last Tuesday. His . . . other friends don't know where he is."

"Mr. Killorin said you were his friend," Angelique offered tentatively.

Thomas sighed. "What does that mean?"

"We don't know, either. The police called here last Thursday. His car was towed away that morning from somewhere on Wilson Boulevard in Rosslyn. No one has seen him since he left work on Wednesday."

"That's over a week," Thomas repeated helplessly.

"I know. He didn't tell anyone he was going anywhere. It's like he just disappeared. He didn't have any travel plans. The message on his answering machine is the same as always. He even penciled in some appointments for the next day just before he left."

"Oh . . ." The comment was involuntary.

"I wish I could tell you more."

"That's all right. Thank you. I didn't mean to bother you." Thomas pursed his lips and swallowed. "But I was worried."

"If you find out anything . . . ?" asked the secretary.

"I'll certainly let you know. Can I check back later in the week?"

"That would be all right."

Thomas looked at the notes he had scribbled on the yellow pad.

"Peter arrested . . . Jerry missing . . . Metals? McDarvid?"

He looked around the office, shaking his head, before crumpling the yellow sheet and tossing it in the colored paper recycling basket by his desk.

Finally, he picked up the telephone once more.

80

MCDARVID LOOKED THROUGH THE ATTACHMENTS to his letter to the Ethics Committee. Heidlinger would be furious, but it couldn't be helped. He needed the law firm's letterhead on this one.

Attachment 1 was a chronological summary of the legislation authorizing the development and deployment of the earth observation satellites.

Attachment 2 was the highlighted language in the committee report accompanying the authorizing legislation: ". . . in the interests of geographically balanced procurement, at least one advanced inertial terrain scanning system shall be procured from a vendor located east of the Mississippi River and at least one from a vendor located west of the Mississippi."

Harmless enough, except Hesterton Engineering was the single competing vendor located in the West.

Attachment 3 was the summary of the NASA evaluation of the TRICOM and Hesterton systems, the evaluation which indicated TRICOM's superiority in price, delivery times, and satellite systems experience.

Attachment 4 was the Hesterton Engineering organization chart, listing Michael Alroy as the Washington, D.C., representative reporting directly to the President of Hesterton.

Attachment 5 was the subcommittee organization chart, listing Renni Fowler as the counsel and staff director.

Attachment 6 was the article from *The Legal Times* about the unsuccessful motion by Hartwicke, Fowler, and Prestigan on behalf of Hesterton Engineering contesting the original award of the inertial system to TRICOM.

Attachment 7 was a copy of Renni Fowler's ethics form.

Attachment 8 comprised Michael Alroy's federal lobbying reports for the past three years.

McDarvid read through the letter again, skimming the key points.

. . . clear and obvious conflict of interest . . . not reported according to the requirements of the committee and of the Ethics in Government Act . . . integrity of procurement process compromised . . . casts doubt upon the integrity of the subcommittee's actions with regard to all space efforts . . . failure to address obstacles to development of resources in space . . .

. . . request an investigation of the events chronicled in Attachment 1 . . . and public disclosure of the committee's findings . . .

McDarvid shook his head. It would have been so much easier if Renni had just agreed to hold one damned hearing on the metals initiative. He hoped the Ethics Committee would do something, but he wasn't counting on it. That was why he had the pictures he still didn't want to use. At least, the damned telephoto lens was back with Jonnie, presumably returned to his sister.

With a sigh, he sealed the envelope for the messenger.

81

"JACK MCDARVID FOR RENNI FOWLER." Holding the phone with his right hand, McDarvid used his left hand on the computer, saving the update for Steve Greene on the changes in the pesticide special review process.

"I'm sorry, Mr. McDarvid. She left word that she was not to be disturbed."

"Marianne? This is Marianne, isn't it?"

"Yes, sir."

"I've been trying to reach her for three days. She can't be that busy."

"Mr. McDarvid, sir . . . ?"

"Yes?"

"She actually said to tell you that no one could sink lower than you have, and that it would be a cold century in hell before she would ever talk to you again."

"Oh . . ."

"And I agree with her, Mr. McDarvid, sir."

Click.

McDarvid winced. He set the telephone back in place and stood up. Outside it was raining, the cold winter rain that made Washington so dreary.

"What am I supposed to do? There's something wrong, really wrong, and no one will do anything. Just send letters that no one reads?" He turned back to the desk and removed the unlabeled file folder that had covered the stack of heavy envelopes on the desk.

"She didn't really give me much choice."

Each of the envelopes contained the original complaint to the Ethics Committee, a plain white sheet outlining a few more salient facts, and the photos. The damned photos that were explicit enough at least for the tabloid types to look into the real substance of McDarvid's complaint.

Should he tell Jonnie? He shook his head. Having Jonnie know anything about it certainly wouldn't help the younger man.

His stomach tightened as he looked at the envelopes again. He'd used stamps; so they couldn't trace a postage meter number. They might ask him about the photos, but he'd have to ignore those questions and concentrate on talking about the actual complaint.

Larry was dead. Killorin was missing. According to Ellie, he'd disappeared with appointments on his calendar for the next day, and his car had been found in Rosslyn. Jerry wouldn't have driven the car out of the way, and he wasn't the type to run off. If he had been, he would have done it years before. So the poor bastard was probably dead. All the police-mentality types would say he was jumping to conclusions, but McDarvid knew. He just couldn't prove a damned thing.

Eric's hands were tied. So were the DIA's. Renni wouldn't do anything, and the Ethics Committee wasn't acting, although someone had certainly let Renni know. The metals initiative was headed onward. And U.S. industrial and technical capabilities were slowly being strangled, with the Japanese sitting on the sidelines smirking. JAFFE, who seemed to know more than

Devenant let on, had hired them for still undefined reasons, and then kept careful track of what they did. There was also the strange man in the gray suit. And then there was Lao Systems, which, for some reason, seemed to give scholarships to the children of the bureaucrats who set the critical risk assessments for environmental regulations.

McDarvid shook his head. That was just what he saw. God knew how much was still hidden. And if he didn't get it in the open before long, he might be following Larry and Jerry. Eric was right, though. McDarvid felt amateur, very amateur. The photos didn't help.

He looked at the envelopes again, and took a deep breath, before pulling his coat off its hook. He could get them in the box on Nineteenth before the two-thirty pickup.

82

"YOU'RE A BASTARD, McDarvid. A total bastard." Renni's voice was flat. "I wouldn't have called, but I wanted to let you know myself."

McDarvid raised his eyebrows as he cradled the telephone. "I appreciate the compliment, Renni, but I don't think I understand."

"Killorin's disappeared."

"What?"

"Don't sound so surprised. You knew he couldn't take the pressure. You set him up for this. So it's your turn."

"My turn?"

"Your subpoena should arrive this morning. I'm having Tom deliver it personally. Since you've charged the committee staff and DEP with a conflict of interest, I'd like you to explain everything."

McDarvid frowned. "If you insist."

"Why not? I'm losing everything. You might as well sweat some. Your wife must be a saint . . . or a masochist."

McDarvid looked up from the dead phone at the closed door of his office. Then he glanced out the window at the blurred pink marble facade across Nineteenth Street.

Testifying before Chairman Hancock wasn't going to be a picnic, not with Renni and Tom preparing the questions. Then he shook his head. There he was, acting like Jerry Killorin. But where was Killorin?

He jabbed the intercom button.

"Reception. This is Doris."

"Doris? This is Jack McDarvid. I'm expecting someone from the Science, Space, and Technology Committee. I need to see them."

"But if they're coming—"

"They may only want to drop off an envelope. I need to see them. Refuse the envelope. Insist that they deliver it personally."

"We can't do that—"

"It's a subpoena, and you certainly can. Check with Mr. Heidlinger or Mr. Ames if you doubt me."

"Yes, Mr. McDougal."

"McDarvid," he corrected, wondering how long it would be before George Ames would pay the receptionists enough to keep them at least until they could learn people's names.

"Excuse me, Mr. McDarvid."

He dialed Jonnie. No answer. Jonnie was out somewhere, but McDarvid didn't remember where. Then again, he was having trouble remembering his own name. The whole business was the regulatory equivalent of Vietnam. You didn't know who your friends were, who or where your enemies were, or even why you were fighting. Hell, he still wasn't sure there was a fight. Maybe . . . maybe, he was just losing it.

He took a deep breath, looked at the computer. He still had to finish the short follow-up paper he had promised to Steve Greene on the special review process. Steve still hadn't picked up all the distinctions involved in pesticide registration, cancellation, or restrictive uses. So McDarvid was still providing background memos after nearly six months.

"Status of Aldicarb," mumbled McDarvid as he looked at the keyboard, wishing he could leave, get out of the office—anything but wait for a subpoena. He wanted to talk to Tom, assuming the assistant counsel would say anything at all. Yet he didn't want to lounge around the reception area all morning.

He glanced at the rain outside, pelting down even more heavily, then back to the screen. Special reviews? Who cared?

Lurching to his feet, he walked to the window, where he studied the rain-splashed sidewalk five floors below, watching as a gust of wind turned an older woman's umbrella inside out, and finally looked back at the closed office door.

Jerry Killorin was scared to testify—that had been obvious. But he would never have run out. At least McDarvid didn't think so, but that raised a bigger question. Who would have done him in? As Eric had said so often, that wasn't the way the professionals worked.

McDarvid frowned. Killorin had never been that enthused about taking over Standards and Regs. Had it been the Ethics Act considerations? And who had been paying him off?

"McDarvid?" rasped Bill Heidlinger as he pushed his vested bulk through the open door. "What's this about a subpoena? Now what have you done?"

"Nothing out of the ordinary, Bill."

"With a subpoena coming?"

"I take it the receptionist called you."

"Of course she called me. I don't take subpoenas as lightly as you do."

"I scarcely take them lightly, but it's from the Science, Space, and Technology Committee."

"Oversight Subcommittee?"

McDarvid nodded.

"Would you like to explain?"

McDarvid shrugged. "I thought it was fairly simple. The JAFFE metals issue . . . the DEP push for reregulating well beyond the health thresholds? It didn't seem to make sense, and no one seemed to know where the idea started. Every time I talked to Jerry Killorin about it, he got nervous. Now . . . no one should get nervous about something like that. So I suggested that the Research Subcommittee ought to hold hearings."

Heidlinger looked blankly at the consultant. "Keep going. I still . . . Why the Science Committee?"

"Space." McDarvid stopped before shaking his head. "It goes like this. Every one of those metals is vital to the U.S. space effort. If the standards pushed by DEP go into effect, most U.S. producers will close or go offshore. Do you think DOD or NASA wants to rely on offshore suppliers for satellite communications power systems? Yet Environment never looked at that. So I suggested that the committee ask Killorin why. I hinted that Killorin might have some additional motivation."

"Did he?"

McDarvid shrugged. "I thought so, but I could never find anything hard, except for the fact that Killorin makes far more money than he reports on the ethics forms. So"—McDarvid swallowed—"I suggested that the DEP I.G. look into the coincidences. The I.G. asked Killorin to explain, and he disappeared."

"That still doesn't explain the subpoena."

"The committee still refused to act on the issue. So I did some more digging and discovered that there was a rather odd coincidence between Hesterton Engineering and the committee staff."

"Who represents Hesterton? Isn't that Hartwicke, Fowler, and Prestigan?"

McDarvid nodded.

"The more I hear, the less I like it. But you still haven't explained why you're getting a subpoena."

"I made a complaint to the House Ethics Committee, charging that the conflicts of interest created by several special relationships had prevented the necessary oversight and, in fact, resulted in more costly procurements in other cases."

"That's preposterous. Absolute cock and bull." Heidlinger swallowed. "People don't go running off to avoid testifying before the I.G. Especially on environmental matters."

"They did throw Rita LaVelle into jail, Bill. They destroyed a number of careers. Remember Deaver and Ollie North?"

"That might explain the DEP bureaucrat's disappearance."

McDarvid nodded. "That's right. That's why Killorin's disappearance, assuming he did in fact disappear, is so interesting. Jerry was scared about something, but what . . ." He shrugged. "I never could find out."

The senior partner shook his head. "I'm not sure I approve. But why is the committee mad enough to send you a subpoena? And why the Oversight Subcommittee? Did you charge Hancock himself with misfeasance?"

"No. I charged Renni Fowler with it."

"Ohhhh . . . Is she . . . ?"

"She's married to Hal Fowler, Jr.—not very happily from all accounts."

Heidlinger shook his head. "God, this is a mess. Why I ever let you two . . ."

"I don't have much choice, as you pointed out. All I have to do is tell the truth." *If I can ever figure out what it is,* McDarvid thought to himself.

83

TOM LERWINSKY HELD A STANDARD-SIZED BUSINESS ENVELOPE. "Mr. J. B. McDarvid?"

"If we're playing this formally—yes."

Tom extended the envelope. "This is a subpoena to appear before the Oversight and Investigations Subcommittee of the House Science, Space, and Technology Committee. You may be accompanied by counsel, if you so desire, and you may present any supporting materials pertinent to the subcommittee inquiry."

The receptionist kept her eyes on the switchboard.

McDarvid accepted the envelope.

"Sorry, Jack."

"Sorry you had to bring it." McDarvid paused. "I didn't mean to get you dragged into this."

"It's part of the job." Lerwinsky looked from the receptionist to McDarvid. "But you've already got people pretty upset. Richards' L.A. called yesterday about your inquiries."

"Bang-Bang Richards?" McDarvid frowned. "He's not on the committee."

Lerwinsky shrugged. "You got me. Quasie's staff is already drafting questions. Even Stayd isn't happy, and he's never happy with Environment."

"What about Renni?"

"You won't like her questions, either. Not that I blame her, Jack."

The two men stood for a moment longer.

"Any questions?" Lerwinsky asked.

"Why'd you deliver it?"

"Why not? As the country saying goes, 'You kill your own dog.'"

"Thanks . . . I think. I'll see you at the hearing."

"Probably not. Renni will be handling it."

84

"ERIC, WHAT IN THE HELL IS GOING ON?"

"You're going to have to be a little more precise, Jack. Everything or nothing could be occurring."

"You know exactly what I mean. You've been playing with us all along on this metals thing." McDarvid glanced at the closed door to his office, wondering who, if anyone, was listening.

"Jack, you're imagining things."

"I'm imagining things," McDarvid snorted. "My boss looks into the metals mess, and he's shot dead. The office director who masterminded the regulatory program is asked to talk to the I.G. When he can't get out of it, he disappears. And by the way, he also can't live the way he does on the income reported on his ethics form. Someone keeps shadowing me and my kids, and my telephone gives funny little rings with no one on the line." He took a deep breath. "Then we talk to the DARPA boys, and the Space Council, and the SDI office, and they all thank us for the information, agree that the issue is critical, and say that they're taking care of it, and please, Jack, don't raise the defense issues directly with Environment or OSHA. Oh, and how about the fellow from DIA who practically blares that they're worried about the metals issue and suggests oh so subtly that we could help?

"Yet I've practically got to goose everyone on the Science, Space, and Technology Committee to even look into the issue, and then they subpoena me to talk about my filing false ethics claims, and the subpoena doesn't even mention the issues. My old friend the assistant counsel essentially refuses to talk to me, even when he hands over the subpoena. The hearing's going to be a real picnic! Even the right-wingers are running from me. And no one at DEP even wants to admit where the screwball idea came from—except from the guy who disappeared." McDarvid paused. "Oh, and none of this counts the oh-so-legitimate computer foundation funded by the leaky TEMPEST equipment boys that gives scholarships to send bright middle-class kids to Ivy League schools. Did I mention that all of the parents just happen to work in setting risk assessments and critical assumptions that necessitate excessive environmental protection? Or that each one of those assessments makes high-tech equipment and weapons production more expensive or less possible in the U.S.?"

"I don't believe that you did, Jack. It is a rather . . . interesting . . ."

"Yeah, I know, Eric. Good old Jack has finally gone around the bend. He's lost it, but good."

"Jack, you're taking this too personally."

"It's taking me too personally. You still insist that the death and disappearance and all the strange things didn't happen?"

"I believe you. They happened. But some of it could easily be coincidence. As for the rest of it—we don't work like that. Neither do the other sides. It's far too messy that way."

"You haven't answered my question. What the hell is going on?"

"You know I can't tell you."

"Fine . . . just fine." McDarvid snorted.

"Jack?"

"Yeah?"

"We don't work that way."

"Thanks a lot."

"You're welcome, and be careful. Try not to muck things up like most amateurs."

"I notice you're not telling me I'm wrong."

"You wouldn't listen even if I said so, would you?"

"Probably not," McDarvid conceded. "But my guts tell me something's very wrong."

"Isn't it always?"

"Yeah," McDarvid admitted with a short laugh.

"Talk to you later."

McDarvid slowly set down the telephone. Try not to muck it up like most amateurs? How could he not muck it up? He shook his head slowly, wondering if he'd have nightmares again that night.

He had *something*. But what? With each regulation, more heavy industry and mining went offshore. A great conspiracy? Who was really benefiting?

He snorted again. He believed even less in the right-wing conspiracy theories. Hell, in Washington nobody could work together for more than a few months without backstabbing.

Coincidence? The problem was that he saw too many coincidences.

He picked up the telephone.

85

MCDARVID WAS REACHING FOR THE PHONE to see if Steve Greene was back in his office when the intercom buzzed.

"A Mr. Thomas for you."

"Thomas?"

"He said he was with Ecology Now!"

"Put him through." Veronica worked at Ecology Now! and he'd met Cal Griffen once, but Thomas? McDarvid touched the blinking line. "Hello."

"This is Ray Thomas from Ecology Now!" Silence followed the announcement.

"What can I do for you, Ray?"

"Well, I'm a friend of Jerry Killorin's. I was wondering if you might have any idea where he was. He mentioned that you'd been working on an issue that affected him."

McDarvid frowned, then decided to play it safe. "The last time I talked to Jerry was almost two weeks ago. We discussed the metals initiative briefly . . . Actually, we didn't discuss it at all. I brought it up, and he told me that the whole issue was *ex parte* and to submit anything else in writing."

"But do you know where he is?"

"I'd assume he was at Environment. In his office."

"Well, he's not. Do you know where he is?" Thomas' voice was rasping, almost grating.

"You seem to be hinting that Jerry's not where he should be."

"Hinting? Cut the crap, McDarvid. You know as well as I do that Jerry's disappeared, and I want to know where he is."

"I don't have the faintest idea where he is. Why would I know?" McDarvid paused, wondering if he should ask Thomas about the metals issue, deciding just as quickly not to mention it.

"Because he said that your work was going to cause him problems, and I'd like to know why."

"Look, Ray. I sent Ecology Now! a copy of the metals briefing papers we submitted. You know our position. Why would that have anything to do with Jerry's disappearing? He could have run off with a bimbo, been injured in an accident, suffered alcoholic amnesia—those things happen."

"Not this conveniently, they don't."

"Mr. Thomas," McDarvid said quietly, "you have called up, ostensibly to ask a question. Yet you seem to think that, because a man I scarcely know is not in his office, I am somehow to blame. I think you'll agree, if you think about it, that such an assumption is hardly warranted. I have told you what my connection is with Jerry, and you insist that there has to be more. Everything that I have done is in the official records, and I suggest that you review those before calling anyone else up and verbally assaulting them. Good day." He hung up the phone.

Great! Not only was he convinced that something had gone wrong with Jerry, but so was some idiot from Ecology Now! And Thomas was laying the blame at McDarvid's feet.

He reached for the telephone, but the intercom buzzed again.

"Mr. Thomas for you, Mr. McDarvid."

"Tell him I left for a meeting."

"Yes, sir."

McDarvid decided to walk around the corner to see Steve Greene, rather than call—or stay near his telephone.

Steve was in the kitchen, rather than his office.

"Got a minute?"

"Sure, Jack. This about the hearing?"

"Yeah." McDarvid followed Steve back to the attorney's office, marginally larger than McDarvid's, but with light oak furniture at least two cuts better than the consultant's.

Greene settled back into his chair. "You really don't need an attorney. You know the hearing process better than anyone in the firm."

"Heidlinger and Ames don't want me running around like a loose cannon." McDarvid smiled wryly. "Right now, I'm inclined to agree."

"I've read the subpoena. Who'd you piss off?"

"Renni Fowler—the subcommittee counsel. I . . . pushed a little hard."

Steve nodded. "That package you sent—George was furious." He shrugged. "What do you want me to do?"

"Just sit behind me and keep me from doing anything obviously stupid. Anything *else* obviously stupid."

"Do you have any more surprises?"

"Not that I know of." McDarvid reflected. "But the whole thing's so shadowy. I can almost sense the congressional angle. It's nagging at me, but I just can't focus on it."

"Why would Congress be tied up in something like this? Is this the business you mentioned about how environmental regs seem designed to choke off industry and high-tech development?"

"That's the problem. I know it, but there's no proof. Just results, and that's what bothers me. Statistically, the odds are against that high a string of coincidences, but whenever I try to explain it, people just look at me as if I'm crazy." McDarvid paused. "Maybe I am. Maybe I've lived in the political world too long. Anyway, before anything else happens, I need to get through the hearing, see if I can use it to get some publicity and pressure on the metals initiative. Then we'll take stock."

"You actually wanted this hearing?"

"I wanted *a* hearing. I didn't plan on being the prime witness."

86

"THAT WILL BE TWENTY-EIGHT FIFTY."

McDarvid reached for his checkbook. Nearly thirty dollars just to clean two suits. "How much would that have been if they had been two-piece suits?"

"Eighteen fifty," replied the bored young black woman behind the counter.

"Three-piece-suit owners have to be the last unprotected minority in the country," McDarvid grumbled to himself as he bent over the Formica counter.

"Nine twenty-five."

At the sound of the second clerk's voice, McDarvid glanced up as a gray polywool suit encased in plastic appeared on the rack beside him. A muscular arm removed the suit from the battered metal stand. McDarvid straightened, the check unfinished, the felt-tip pen still in his fingers. "Who are you?"

The muscular young man in jeans and a black turtleneck looked at McDarvid blankly.

McDarvid stepped between the other man and the doorway. "Who the hell are you, and why have you been following me?"

The Secret Service look-alike continued staring at McDarvid before turning his eyes toward the clerks. The two clerks exchanged glances.

"You were at the funeral," McDarvid prompted.

Despite his greater height and clear muscularity, the younger man backed away slightly from McDarvid.

"I asked you who you are." McDarvid's voice was low.

"Lucien Ferris. Now, who the hell are you?"

"Why were you at Larry Partello's funeral?" McDarvid asked.

"Mister . . . I asked who you are. I answered your question."

"Oh . . . sorry. Jack McDarvid. I work—I mean, I worked for Larry." McDarvid realized he had cornered the other man between the counter and the wall and stepped back.

Ferris shrugged. "I was at Larry's funeral because Larry Partello was my godfather."

"What were you doing at Woodies?" McDarvid's body remained tensed, ready, although he began to wonder how abrupt his questions must sound.

"When?"

"When you were looking at me, and my kids. After Larry's funeral."

"Buying underwear."

"Huh?"

"Buying underwear. Woodies had a sale on socks and underwear. I do buy new socks and underwear. I recognized you from the funeral and wondered who you were."

"And why were you over at my partner's apartment, looking for him? Wearing that suit?" McDarvid jabbed the pen at the gray suit.

Ferris' eyebrows raised.

"Potomac Place," McDarvid explained.

The younger man shook his head slowly. "It's none of your business, but . . . I was probably there to see my sister, and, if it was around Thanksgiving, I took her to our cousin's wedding. I only wear the suit for things like weddings and funerals. Now, what's this all about?"

"I worked for Larry," McDarvid repeated. "I kept seeing you and thought . . . I don't know. I'm sorry." He felt exhausted. "Why were you scanning everyone at the funeral?"

"I was looking for Mona. I wanted to thank her."

"Mona?"

"Mona Cyane. She was Larry's . . . girlfriend. I know Larry saw a lot of women, but Mona was different. Mona cared for him. In his last couple of years, I think Mona was the only person who really cared about Larry, not about his money or his business. I just wanted to thank her."

"Was she there?"

"Third row. Mona cared about Larry, but she sure didn't give a damn about anyone else, or what they thought. She's one fine lady."

"Probably better than Larry deserved," McDarvid mumbled, vaguely remembering a dark nymphlike woman in a subdued dress.

Ferris ignored the comment. "I'd like to thank you."

"Why? You enjoy kooks stopping you at the cleaner's?"

"I'm a tennis pro. I teach a couple of places, the Rock Creek Tennis Club, the new racquet club up on Connecticut . . . Larry always wanted me to be a lawyer or a doctor or something respectable. He offered to pay for everything. I never took him up. I was afraid of ending up the way he was, consumed by work, unable to hold on to his family, not able to lead a normal life. I always felt guilty about it. I've kept wondering if I made the right decision. Until now. Good-bye, Mr. McDarvid, and . . . have a happy life."

The tall man swung the cheap gray suit over his shoulder and marched out into the chill afternoon.

McDarvid looked dumbly down at the felt-tip pen in his fingers.

87

MCDARVID LOOKED SIDEWAYS AT STEVE GREENE as they stepped inside the horseshoe entrance to the Rayburn Building. He wasn't looking forward to testifying, especially not with Renni as the subcommittee counsel.

He put the briefcase on the conveyer belt and stepped through the detector himself, recovering the case on the other side and waiting for Steve. He nodded politely to the Capitol police officer. "Have a good day."

"You, too, sir."

The two men turned right and headed for the elevators, Greene half a step behind McDarvid. One flight of stairs he would have taken, but he wasn't in the mood for more. Not today.

Even as McDarvid stepped off the elevator, he could hear the mumble of voices from the hallway outside the committee room. He took a deep breath and rounded the corner.

"Holy shit," mumbled Greene.

"Yeah. I wonder what Renni told them."

Two closed-circuit camera control units were set up outside the hearing room—that he could tell from fifty feet away.

A tall red-bearded man walked toward the two of them. "Mr. McDarvid?" He was looking at Steve.

"I'm Jack McDarvid."

The man turned to McDarvid, standing as if to block his progress toward the hearing room. "Ray Thomas. I talked to you the other day."

"I'm due to testify in just a few minutes," McDarvid observed.

"What did you do to him?"

"To whom?" McDarvid asked.

"Jerry. Jerry Killorin." The bigger man raised a clenched fist. "Jerry said you got him in trouble, and then he disappeared."

McDarvid wrinkled his nose. The sharp, sour smell of whiskey—or something—wafted from the man's breath. "Whatever it was, Jerry did it to himself. I told you exactly what I did." He stepped around Thomas and started to walk toward the hearing room doors.

"Wait a minute!" Thomas' hand touched McDarvid's shoulder. "I'm talking to you!"

McDarvid stopped, lifted the other's hand off his shoulder. "You're trying my patience. I did a study which compared the income reported on ethics forms to the life-styles of federal officials. The results were interesting."

"What do you mean?"

"If Jerry got into trouble, it was his own doing. You might check with the Inspector General. Now, excuse me." McDarvid pulled away.

"There's Jack McDarvid," another voice murmured from the area by the television crews not five feet away.

"Jack, you need to—"

McDarvid forced a smile. It was going to be every bit as bad as he'd intended for poor Jerry Killorin.

"I'm not through talking with you!" Thomas' hand pawed at McDarvid's shoulder.

McDarvid was yanked around and tried to duck the clumsy swing from the bigger man, but his briefcase and Steve's closeness slowed his reactions as Thomas' fist grazed his forehead.

"Smartass . . . bastard . . ."

McDarvid dropped the briefcase, blocking Thomas' follow-up swing with his freed arm.

Thomas lunged and swung again.

McDarvid stepped inside the swing and brought his elbow across Thomas' throat, then slammed his knee into the man's groin.

"Call the police."

The red-haired and -bearded man lay curled on the white marble tiles, gagging and rasping.

"Are you all right?" asked Greene.

"Yeah, I think."

"Jesus . . . Christ."

"What happened?"

McDarvid took a deep breath as he turned to the Capitol police officer. "I don't know, Officer." He took another breath. "I was subpoenaed to testify. This man started to talk to me. Then, when I told him that he could get the information he wanted from the committee or the Inspector General, he kept grabbing at me. Then he started punching, or whatever. I tried to get away, but he grabbed my coat and wouldn't let go."

The bright lights of the television cameras washed over McDarvid, Steve Greene, the dark-haired young officer, and the whimpering redheaded man.

McDarvid could feel his legs shaking. He swallowed. "I'm a little . . . a little shaken up."

"But what happened to him?"

"He kept swinging." McDarvid gingerly felt his temple; a smear of blood streaked his fingers.

The cameras followed his actions.

"I . . . just tried to push him away."

"Some push" a soft voice carried from the back of the crowd.

McDarvid recognized the voice—Marianne's—and chilled, wondering whether Renni had put the man up to the attack. He took another deep breath. "I still have to appear." He turned to the officer, digging out a card and handing it to the man. "You have plenty of witnesses. I'll be in the committee room."

"But sir . . ."

The cameras followed him as he reclaimed his briefcase, still lying in the corridor, and walked up to the doorway of the hearing room, where another officer confronted him.

"It's full, sir."

McDarvid sighed. "I'm the witness. At least, I'm one of them. Jack McDarvid," he explained. "Do you want me to produce my subpoena?" He paused. "Mr. Greene is my attorney."

"No, sir. Sorry, sir."

McDarvid waited. "Do we get in? Or do I explain to the Chairman that his prize witness was denied at the door?"

The gray-haired veteran looked at McDarvid and Greene, then at the cameras pointed at McDarvid, and edged the door open. "None of you," he added, pointing at the man with the notebook.

Once inside the committee room, McDarvid took a deep breath.

"Jack, you ought to ask for another appearance. You're in no shape to testify." Greene's voice was barely above a whisper, but several people in the straight-backed chairs looked toward them.

"Steve, it took too damned much to get here. We cancel and I get all the flak—and no publicity. Nothing."

"Jack . . ."

"No." He shivered once, took another deep breath. He should have thought about it . . . but someone attack him? Especially after realizing he'd been too paranoid over Larry's godson? He'd never really threatened anyone, not physically. He took another deep breath.

The small room was packed, mainly with industry lobbyists, but also with a scattering of interns and junior staff. Finally, he began to walk toward the press table. Perhaps ten reporters lounged around a table that could have seated more than a dozen. Still, he could remember hearings where only one or two had showed up.

"Must be a slow news day," the consultant muttered to himself. As he neared the press table, he stopped and, balancing his briefcase, extracted the press packages he had prepared—summary sheet on the cover, his prepared statement that would never be read, and the attachments.

"Is that McDarvid?" The sotto voce question drifted down from the raised committee dais.

McDarvid quickly dropped the press packets into the center of the table, aware of Greene just behind his shoulder.

"Anything interesting, Jack?" asked a woman with short salt-and-pepper hair.

"Only if you believe that U.S. industry is important," he quipped, wishing he could remember who the woman worked for.

"That's not likely to make you very popular."

"What else is new?"

"Would the witness please come to the table? Is Mr. McDarvid here?"

McDarvid nodded to the reporter and walked the ten feet in front of the spectator chairs to the small square table with the microphone. A junior staffer waited, a young black-haired woman McDarvid had not met.

"Mr. McDarvid?"

McDarvid nodded. "I have thirty copies of my statement here." He handed her the folder. "Mr. Greene is my attorney."

McDarvid sat down, pulling the microphone directly before his chair. Steve laid his briefcase on the table and opened it, extracting a folder, then seated himself beside McDarvid.

The lights came on, and the red lights blinked on the television cameras.

"Mr. McDarvid? I understand that there was some unpleasantness involved with your arrival here. While we are most interested in your testimony, I would like to ask if you are comfortable in continuing, or if you would rather return at a later date."

McDarvid ignored Steve Greene. "Thank you, Mr. Chairman, for your concern, but, with the committee's permission, I would prefer to continue as scheduled."

"Very well."

The Chairman was clearly uninterested in the metals initiative. After insisting that McDarvid be sworn in, he began.

". . . remind the witness that you are under oath, and that anything which you say is admissible in a court of law . . .

"Do you have a statement? . . . in the interests of time, let the statement be included in the record as if read . . . we will begin with questions from the chair . . .

"Mr. McDarvid, you once worked at the Environmental

Protection Agency, before it was elevated to departmental status . . ."

"I served as the Director of the Office of Policy Analysis . . ."

". . . did not your submission to the Ethics Committee omit key facts?"

"Not to my knowledge, Mr. Chairman."

". . . would you not characterize that submission as a misrepresentation designed to punish staff for failing to recommend a hearing?"

"The submission was designed to prod the Congress into action, but, as the record shows, Mr. Chairman, that submission was factual." The consultant wanted to wipe his forehead, but did not.

". . . might I remind you that you are under oath . . ."

"Yes, Mr. Chairman . . ."

". . . what do you have to say . . ."

To the long list of ethics-related questions, McDarvid continued to answer truthfully, if briefly, watching Renni Fowler, sitting beside the Chairman. He recognized that the Chairman was not going to raise the metals issue. Renni's face told him that the last question had not been scripted, had been only a relic of courtesy that might be his only chance.

"Yes, Mr. Chairman. I do have a few things to add. First, my subpoena cited the metals issue, not an ethics question, which would be more properly under that committee's jurisdiction. Second, and more important, those issues which I freely admit that I raised to the Ethics Committee tie directly to the metals initiative in one particular. In both cases, the committee, although charged with the oversight of research and science, has failed in its duties. Failing to investigate the use of exposure models and risk assessments which choke off scientific research and U.S. technology and allowing staff to employ the committee's powers to secretly favor one contractor over another are an abuse of power. By failing to curb improper risk assessments, in effect, the committee has handed the future of U.S. high-technology industry over to Europe, Japan, and the multinational corporations.

"By failing to ensure the awarding of space procurements to the best-qualified contractors, the committee may also have turned our future in space over to others as well."

"Mr. McDarvid, the committee has limited time, and is not interested in speculations. Do you have any *factual* support for such wild allegations?"

"Yes, Mr. Chairman. I do."

Renni Fowler's mouth opened, then shut.

McDarvid could feel the closed-circuit cameras focusing on him.

"Item one is another government document. It is a NASA evaluation of the inertial systems provided by Hesterton Engineering and by TRICOM. There is a cover letter to the subcommittee counsel, Ms. Fowler, dated nearly two months before the committee report on the authorizing legislation. The evaluation states, and I quote, 'Although the Hesterton system appears equivalent to the TRICOM system, the quoted price is twenty percent higher. In addition, Hesterton has not ever delivered a system of this complexity, and in the case of their current NASA contract, is running three months behind schedule.'" McDarvid wiped his forehead from the glare of the lights, wondering if he would be allowed to continue. When the Chairman did not immediately jump in, he plunged ahead.

"Item two consists of a series of internal DEP memoranda on risk assessments critiquing an analysis of risk modeling which we had presented to the department. You can read the memoranda in detail, but the bottom line is that DEP admits that the guidelines and methodology employed are flawed and that the models which we suggested are technically far more accurate. Yet the authors recommend that the department retain the present methods, noting that the Congress would be displeased." McDarvid paused. "I do find it interesting, Mr. Chairman, that department staff would rather use incorrect, inaccurate, and damaging methods, rather than displease elected officials and their staff.

"Item three . . ."

McDarvid finished his listing of exhibits, all of which were included in summary form in the press packet, and turned them over to the committee staffer.

"Congressman Quasie? Do you have any questions for the witness?"

"I have a few, Mr. Chairman." The thin-faced natural-food Representative from Oregon adjusted the microphone before him.

McDarvid took a deep breath, waiting for the next barrage.

"Mr. McDarvid, your statement seems to indicate that health and environmental risks must be balanced against economic and technological progress. Wouldn't the risk assessment methodology you recommend reduce the margin of safety in protecting human health?

"Can you support the contention that a threshold level exists?

"Weren't the models you recommended developed by industry specialists and not impartial scientists?

"Do you honestly believe in the discounting approach to the value of human life and health?

"I have no further questions, Mr. Chairman."

McDarvid swallowed, hoping his answers were as accurate as he thought.

"Congressman Stayd?"

The Representative from Ohio nodded, then turned to McDarvid. "Mr. McDarvid, you seem to have engendered a great deal of emotion. According to the Capitol police, you were assaulted on your way into the hearing, and I understand you were subpoenaed to appear. Was the subpoena necessary?"

"No, Congressman. I was never asked."

"I see. Could you explain the importance of these risk assessments to the future of U.S. science and technology?

"Is it possible that your characterizations of the DEP reaction were excessive?

"What are the practical differences in health impacts between the two methodologies?

"Can you explain why the more conservative methodology should not be used?

"I have no further questions, Mr. Chairman."

McDarvid wiped his forehead, looking at the clock. Only eleven o'clock, and it seemed as though he had been under the lights for hours. And there were at least five other members waiting to question him. And that was only the first round. It was going to be a long, long day.

88

AS MCDARVID WALKED BACK UP THE SIDEWALK TO THE HOUSE, his breath steaming in the chill air, his muscles protesting from the extra sit-ups, he glanced at the front stoop.

The paper was sitting there, waiting like a time bomb. Forcing himself not to look at the headlines, he tucked it under his arm, then walked around to the side door by the kitchen. As he stepped inside, he finally glanced at the black and white of the *Post.* The story was below the fold at least—"Assault and Congressional Favors."

> Washington. A hard-punching environmental attorney, a conflict-of-interest charge that provoked a hearing, and a regulatory consultant exploded into a soap-opera-like drama on Capitol Hill . . .

McDarvid put down the *Post.* Dodging the cameras had been bad enough. Then, after the hearing had ended at three o'clock, he'd had to make a statement to the Capitol police about the attack. He'd gone straight home. That hadn't helped. He winced when he thought about Bill Heidlinger's call not twenty minutes after he'd walked in the front door. To have his name on the front page of every newspaper in the country was not exactly what he'd had in mind.

He set the paper on the buffet in the dining room, then stepped back into the kitchen, where he put on the kettle for tea and hot chocolate. He emptied the dishwasher, set out the mugs and the plates, and began preparing for all the breakfasts. The routine hadn't changed, hearing and newspapers or not.

"Breakfast is almost ready!"

"Not yet."

"I will be arriving presently."

"David's yelling at his dresser."

274

"Where . . ." began Elizabeth as she stepped into the kitchen.

"In front of your stool."

He looked up toward Allyson, in her heavy green robe and damp hair. There were circles under her eyes.

"Morning." She slumped onto the stool and grasped for the coffee.

He set the cereal bowl and milk pitcher in front of her. Retrieving an ice cube from the freezer, he dropped it into his own cup. Tea slopped on the counter. Tiredly, he reached for the sponge.

"Can I have the milk, Mom?" David asked sullenly.

McDarvid, still standing behind the breakfast bar, finished the orange slices, then took another sip of tea.

"Did he really jump you?" asked David.

"Yes," McDarvid answered tiredly.

"He really did?" blurted his son. "Really? Wait until I tell Jimmie."

"I told you that last night. It was very unsettling, and I really don't want to talk about it anymore."

"Poor Daddy," crooned Kirsten.

McDarvid winced, and Allyson grinned—briefly.

"Just eat your breakfast." McDarvid swallowed the second English muffin, nearly whole, then gulped the tea, nearly choking in an effort to keep the edges of the muffin from scraping his esophagus all the way down.

"You always tell us to chew our food thoroughly," admonished Elizabeth.

"All right, all right," he mumbled.

Allyson sipped her coffee and waited until the front door had slammed for the third and final time. "Are you ready to talk about it yet?"

"Don't know if I'll ever be ready to talk about it," he answered, seating himself on the stool next to hers.

Allyson waited.

"I never wanted to create this sort of mess. I just wanted to get to the bottom of things. But no one would say anything. No one would do anything. They all acted as if I were crazy. 'Sure, Jack, we'll send a nice letter.' " McDarvid got up, found a tea bag, and poured another cup of water from the kettle. Then he refilled Allyson's coffee.

" 'Right, Jack,' " he continued, " 'the Russians are using the environment to destroy U.S. industry.' But then, when I'd talk to Eric, he'd just chide me and tell me not to be an amateur, and that was scary."

"Because he didn't say you were crazy?" Allyson sipped her coffee.

"Right. Eric's never hesitated to tell me I'm nuts." McDarvid pulled the tea bag from his cup and dumped it into the trash. He shoveled three teaspoons of sugar into the cup. "Then Killorin disappears, and that's even scarier, because he's just gone. Poof!"

"Is it connected to what you're doing?"

"Hell, he could have run off with a woman or had amnesia. But I don't think so. His disappearance was just too convenient, and, in a way, it doesn't matter."

"Why not?"

"Jerry never ran from anything, just sat and took it. If this is enough for him to run . . . or if it's enough for him to get killed—what's the difference?"

Allyson nodded. "Why did that attorney go after you?"

"I don't know. Except that he mumbled something about Killorin. He'd called me a couple days ago. He's convinced that Killorin's disappearance is all my fault."

"Is it?"

"Probably. I just kept pushing the poor bastard." McDarvid paused. "But no one would do anything. No one would even look at the issue. Christ! They all think I'm either crazy or to blame."

"Is that anything new?" Allyson flushed, then added quickly, "Will they press charges?"

"Against me? I don't think so. He attacked me. There were enough witnesses to show I acted in self-defense."

"I meant against him."

"I really don't care. I just wish it hadn't happened."

Allyson sipped her coffee, and McDarvid caught the look in her eye.

"All right. I wish that part hadn't happened."

She set down the coffee cup and stood up, extending a hand.

McDarvid set his cup on the counter. Then he took her extended hand and reached for the other one. They held each other until the cuckoo clock blurted out the half hour.

89

JONNIE LOOKED AT THE COPY of *Inside the Environment* draped loosely on the stacked papers. The newsletter/scandal sheet lay folded back to the third-page story suggesting that the bizarre and irrelevant disclosures of one J. B. McDarvid, III, might stampede environmentally conscious Representatives into insisting that the metals initiative be withdrawn. An unnamed source stated, "McDarvid's respectable enough that a lot of people are running for cover."

Jonnie shook his head. Jack was thoroughly respectable—that was the problem. But why had Jack done it? Snapping off the computer, he stood up.

McDarvid's door was open.

Jonnie stepped inside and closed it.

McDarvid leaned back in his chair. "Hell of a way to make a living."

"Jack, we need to talk."

"About what?" McDarvid answered. "About how we start a business when the roof falls in here—which it has? Or about the strange and wonderful workings of the media?"

Jonnie took off the silver rimless glasses and laid them on the desk. McDarvid's desk was always clean. So were his bookcase and the credenza. "Let's start with you. What in the hell have you been doing? That I don't already know about? George Ames, our good fussy senior partner, has never bothered to notice my existence. Today, I'm hanging up my coat. He glares at me, sniffs, and walks away. Heidlinger turned around in the corridor and went back into his office.

"Last month, the Lao Systems rep comes barging in with all that crap about the Lao Foundation. You tell me that it all fits, but there's no way to prove it, and you really don't want to speculate until you know more."

McDarvid nodded slowly. "I've never liked speculating. My dad was a lawyer. Used to chop me up for making statements I couldn't prove. Maybe that's why I always try to prove everything—even when I know the answers."

"Jack, I've heard that before. You always get folksy and personal when someone asks you a question you don't want to answer."

"I don't know if I can come up with answers."

"Then what do you think? I'm not asking for facts proven in blood. I want to know why the law firm and half the environmental community are running scared of good old respectable Jack McDarvid."

McDarvid smiled. "Scared of poor old insecure . . ."

"Jack . . ." Jonnie's voice was low.

"All right. But there's no proof." McDarvid sat up straight. "It's simple enough, even if . . . Maybe it's not that simple." He paused. "I'm not really sure I believe it." There was another pause. "Let's start with the Lao Foundation. They give scholarships to bright kids who are almost uniformly the children of federal civil servants. I'd bet that almost all of the parents are involved in such jobs as risk assessments for regulations, setting critical dosages for toxics, all the sort of baseline assumptions that determine the regs."

Jonnie shrugged. "That's what Lao does with their procurement. They work on the people who set the specs, usually not as honestly."

"Fine. So the assumptions ensure that critical industrial processes can't economically continue in the U.S." McDarvid frowned. "Then we have Jerry Killorin living well beyond his means, and Jerry was one of those spec-setters before he got control of Standards and Regs. He had the procedural choke hold on the processing for regulations—before they did him in."

"He's *missing.*"

"I say the poor bastard's dead. They found his car in Rosslyn. No traces, no fingerprints except his and a garage attendant's, according to the *Post*. There won't be any."

"How do you know?" Jonnie asked slowly.

"I can't tell you how I know. That's just what my guts say. I mean, Jerry never had enough guts to run from an ex-wife who was bleeding him dry, or to stop drinking, or to stop gambling. He didn't run from that hearing. Something stopped him. Anyway, the other thing is JAFFE. They're moving into high tech, right in the areas where U.S. companies are being forced off-shore, and they hire us. And they know exactly who Larry is and we are and what Larry did and what we do. Larry's killed. Devenant insists on continuing. Us—not even lawyers. He just shuts out Heidlinger. And they keep tabs on what we're doing. They're playing for high stakes. Why? What do they know?"

Jonnie frowned. "I'm not sure where—"

"It's simple. Assume there is this crazy plot, the one I hate to even think about, to destroy U.S.-based high technology, especially space and weapons stuff. That's what you suggested, anyway. That creates incredible market opportunities. JAFFE is ready to take them, except the deal sours all of a sudden."

"Sours?"

"Yeah." McDarvid looked out the window. "The Europeans and the third-world countries start adopting U.S. environmental standards."

"Shit. Then . . ."

"Right," affirmed McDarvid, "there's a delay, but the U.S. standards threaten business worldwide. What do you do if you're a hard-bitten French multinational?"

"You go to the root of the problem," said Jonnie. "You really believed that about the Russians? All this rests on the assumption that someone is using environmental regulations as a weapon."

"It's worse than that. I'm saying that they're smart enough to act at the level of the underlying assumptions—the risk assessments, the critical dosages. For example, you'll notice that they always use animal studies, even if there are epidemiological studies available. Why? Because the human exposure history studies—just like we showed with cadmium—prove the real-life effects of chemicals are not nearly as catastrophic as the extrapolations from animal studies."

"That would mean somebody has been doing this for years."

"Longer, probably." McDarvid pulled himself out of the chair. "What could I really say? Without convincing you and the whole world that I had totally gone off the deep end?" He paused. "Maybe I have. Maybe I have."

Jonnie leaned forward and picked up his glasses. "I see all the pieces. There've even been articles on every point you mentioned."

"But no articles about conspiracies, right?" The older man turned toward the window and the light drizzle that cascaded down on Nineteenth Street.

"I've even seen a couple of small articles about environmental protests in the Soviet Union." Jonnie paused for a second. "They've gotten green groups trying to shut down industry—just like some U.S. environmentalists."

McDarvid shut his eyes. "Fine. They've grown enviro-nuts in Russia. But have you seen any articles about conspiracies to destroy U.S. industry?"

"Haven't seen any," Jonnie admitted.

"You won't. If it is a plot, no one will say anything, and if it's not"—McDarvid shrugged as he turned from the window—"then I'm as crazy as I seem."

"The facts are there," Jonnie admitted, thinking about McDarvid. Jack jumped to conclusions. But Jonnie had learned early that you never bet against Jack, no matter how screwy his reasoning. He stood up. "I guess I need to think this over."

"Be my guest. Be my guest."

As Jonnie stepped back into his office, he looked out the window, pursing his lips. McDarvid had still not told him what he had been doing—only why. Jonnie wondered what else he didn't know about the friendly but silently intense man he had worked with for nearly four years. Some of that was Washington, the side of the city that outsiders never saw, where people hid their personal lives because so much of their lives were public performances.

"JONNIE . . . JONNIE, WAKE UP." Veronica's voice was hushed but insistent.

Slowly, Jonnie eased himself upright.

"You kept kicking your legs and flailing."

Jonnie nodded. He continued to take deep, almost heaving breaths. "Did I say anything?"

"Nothing that I could hear, maybe grunting. You looked like you were trying to swim."

Swim? Jonnie shook his head groggily.

"Do you remember what it was about?"

Jonnie took another deep breath. "I think I was being questioned. There were men wearing what looked like army fatigues. But they didn't have any military insignia. Then someone started shooting—I don't know who. I don't think it was anyone in uniform. I picked up a dead man's pistol and ran." Jonnie swallowed, his breathing now regular.

"Did you fire back?"

"No, I don't think so. I just ran. I knew I had to get away." He shifted his weight and leaned toward her. "I'm sorry, I didn't mean to wake you up." His arm went around her naked shoulders.

Veronica snuggled closer as they leaned against the pillows propped up against the windowsill that served as a headboard. "It's all right. I really wasn't sleeping."

"You also had bad dreams?"

"Guess I couldn't relax. Stay close." Veronica rested her head on Jonnie's shoulder as he curled his arm around her neck. The auburn hair covered them both like a soft blanket. With her free hand, she drew the sheet up to their shoulders.

As she closed her eyes, Jonnie looked into the shadows in the far corner of the room. His eyes remained open long after Veronica's breathing had become soft and regular.

91

"JONNIE, ARE YOU GOING TO DRINK THE COFFEE or just stare at it?" Veronica asked.

"Sorry. I was thinking."

"You know that gives you a headache."

A smile flickered across Jonnie's face. His hands remained cupped around the cooling coffee.

"What are you worried about?"

Jonnie shrugged.

"I can tell. You didn't want anything for breakfast. I practically had to force the coffee on you, and now you're not talking. What's wrong?"

Jonnie looked down into the black liquid. Reflections danced on the surface as he gently shook the mug.

Veronica got up, walked behind Jonnie, and began massaging his neck.

"That feels good," he admitted, not looking up.

"Was it the dream last night?" she asked, fingers kneading into his tight shoulder muscles.

"No. Not the way you mean."

Veronica continued working on his shoulders and neck.

"It just got me thinking. Or wouldn't let me stop thinking. And you haven't been sleeping too well yourself."

"That comes with the territory. What have you been thinking about?"

"I think we need to talk." Jonnie abandoned the mug and began rubbing his forehead.

"Sure. Let's go into the living room. Leave the dishes." Veronica ran her fingers up his neck, then bent down. Her lips brushed his neck.

Jonnie shivered. After a moment, he stood and took the mug in both hands. Without looking at Veronica, he crossed the kitchen linoleum, the narrow entryway, and stepped into the living room. His eyes took in the picture of Groucho Marx, and a faint smile flickered on his lips. He settled himself on the sofa under Groucho.

Veronica sat next to him and put her arm around his shoulders.

"Veronica, who do you work for?"

"You know where I work."

"I know where you work, but I don't know who you work for."

"I work for Ecology Now!"

Jonnie turned toward Veronica and said nothing. He slowly

shook his head, thinking of J. Alfred Prufrock. "That's not what I meant. That is not it at all."

"You're strange sometimes." Veronica wrinkled her forehead. "Ecology Now! is just what it is—a group dedicated to improving the environment. That's what I believe in. If Cal is involved in anything besides the environment, it would be news to me."

"I wasn't necessarily talking about Ecology Now! Too many other things don't line up." Jonnie paused. "They're almost right, but not quite."

Veronica shifted her weight, withdrew the arm from Jonnie's shoulders, drew her knees up onto the sofa cushion, and put her arms around them.

"You live modestly, but you still spend more than a small public interest group could pay. Your dresses are the kind a junior executive wears." Jonnie swallowed before going on. "Your coat . . . even the amount of new tapes and books you buy. You said your folks don't support you financially."

"Is that all?"

Jonnie pulled at his beard. "Other stuff—some of it's hard to describe. No matter how well I may come to know you, there will always be a small intense part of you that's locked away, that I never see. It stands out by its absence . . . if that makes any sense."

Veronica nodded—a gesture of acknowledgment, not of agreement.

"Something strange is going on with environmental regulations. There are just too many standards and regs targeted at important industries that make no sense from a health and safety viewpoint. Jack and I have had a few laughs about conspiracies. I think he took that more seriously than I did, even though it was my suggestion. But Jack doesn't believe in conspiracies, and he's worried. So intense and so worried that it's scary."

"Isn't that just because of the job situation?"

"Maybe. But I don't think so. He's a former Navy pilot who worked on the Hill and at EPA. Just job security wouldn't tear him up that much."

"Maybe he's the one where things don't line up."

"Maybe, but that's not what we're talking about."

Veronica shrugged.

Jonnie sipped the cool coffee before setting the mug down.

"There was that business with Ray Thomas. And you never said a word about it."

"Ray just snapped. I can't believe he's a part of anything. He's too unstable. Too much like . . . Peter. You know, they used to be friends a long time ago. It's hard to believe." She shook her head slowly.

"That was the other thing. Peter." Jonnie swallowed. "That day in the parking lot. Afterward, when I pressed, you said something was going to happen to him. I think you said something like he was going to be history, that he wouldn't have any choice about it. Two weeks later he was in jail. You wanted him gone; you said he was a danger to the environmental movement. Well, he's gone, probably for a long time, one way or another. And it was handled in just the right way to keep it from becoming a public mess. That was just too convenient."

Veronica wrapped her arms around her knees more tightly. "So who do you think I work for?" asked Veronica. "You just about have me convicted."

"No . . . not convicted," Jonnie said slowly. "I didn't want to think about it. But last night after the nightmare, I just kept thinking."

"And?"

"There are two basic choices." Jonnie waited.

Outside in the parking lot, the rumble of an ill-mufflered truck was followed by a screech and a spray of gravel.

Jonnie turned and looked at Veronica.

"Two basic choices," he repeated.

"Us and them?"

In turn, Jonnie nodded without speaking.

"What makes you think that it would be us?"

"I guess that's what I hoped. That, and the business with Peter. You were involved, in a way that you aren't talking about, and something that could have been nasty turned out okay."

"Sometimes, things work out all right."

"It's not us, is it?"

Veronica looked at Jonnie sadly and shook her head.

Jonnie gave a deep sigh. "I guess this is the point where I'm supposed to ask why."

"Are you?"

"Supposed to ask?"

"Going to ask."

Jonnie sighed again. "Might as well."

"I suppose you think I'm a traitor."

"That's one obvious conclusion."

"Things aren't that simple. You can't divide the world into us and them. It's a lot more complicated."

"Actually, you're the one that said us and them," reminded Jonnie.

"That's what you were thinking. Either I work for us or I work for them. Did you think that I might do both?"

"You're a double agent?"

"You still don't understand. It doesn't matter who I work for. What matters is *what* I'm working for. That's for all of us. Everyone that breathes, regardless of nationality. I'm a loyal American. That may be hard for you to understand."

"You think that the Russians are interested in protecting American health? That they're just wonderful humanitarians competing for the Schweitzer Award?"

"No. I have few illusions about the Russians. Truth is—they're barbarians. The one time I met a couple of them, they made my skin crawl."

"So why do you work for them? Are you a communist?"

"Do I look like a communist?" Veronica laughed. "I'm not even close to being a Marxist . . . unless you mean a Groucho Marxist." Veronica angled a thumb at the picture over the couch. "That's why I put him up there. It was my own personal joke."

"So why?"

"Because fighting pollution is right regardless of who I do it for. Do you remember what Churchill said, that if Hitler invaded hell he would at least put in a good word for the devil in the House of Commons the next morning? The Russians are my devil." Veronica let go of her knees, put her feet back on the carpet, and half turned toward Jonnie.

"I've also heard that if you sup with the devil you should use a long spoon."

"I've taken steps to protect myself. I've given this a lot of thought and some research. I'm not doing anything wrong morally or legally."

"Not even legally?"

"If you want to be technical, I'm committing a minor violation of the foreign agents' registration act. If I were exposed, the worst that would happen is having to fill out a few forms, perhaps a fine. I have no secrets, and I don't work for the government. That gives me a pretty free rein to do as I please. I even pay all my taxes. Money, not a lot, is funneled to me through a temp agency for which I supposedly do some secretarial work. Withholding is taken, and I get a W-2 form."

"Still, you are working for the devil."

"If the CIA had asked me, I would have done the same for them."

"Soldier of fortune?" Jonnie immediately regretted the sarcastic words.

"Remember what you told me about you and Jack? That you were idealists? I also have ideals, ideals I won't sacrifice to anybody's ideology. Including yours."

Jonnie looked at Veronica and ran a hand through his hair. "You still haven't told me why the Russians would want to help the American ecology."

"I assume that they think they are undermining the U.S. military-industrial complex."

"Aren't they?"

"Probably. So what? If I can use the Russians to help me stop pollution, I will. I'll get more out of the deal than they will." She laughed softly. "Let me ask you—do you really think the Soviets are going to invade us? Their economy is in shambles, and the republics have disintegrated into ethnic fiefdoms. Do you really believe that they can conquer us or that they'd even seriously try?"

"Then why try and damage our economy? Why spend scarce resources on a program which won't be of benefit?"

"Because little boys are going to play their spy games to their dying breath. And unless major action is taken to halt global pollution, none of us will have that many breaths left. I just hope that someone is trying to undermine their economy the same way." Veronica looked away from Jonnie.

"You want to help people. You want children to breathe clean air and parents to work in safe places." Jonnie sighed softly. "But what you are doing is hurting people. Most of those standards you promote have little health benefit. But when factories close, people go hungry. Parents beat their children. Workers who have no other hope become alcoholics; they kill themselves."

Veronica began to gnaw on a knuckle. "I know. I think you're exaggerating the effects of the regs, but I know they cause some harm. I'd prefer another way, but I don't know one. I would also prefer that our oh-so-civilized society spend a tiny bit of our resources to help those people instead of leaving them to swing in the wind. Besides, we don't achieve everything we try to accomplish. We wouldn't achieve anything, though, unless we tried. If government and business had more of a social conscience, things would be all right."

"It doesn't bother you? What you're doing?"

"Of course it does. Why do you think I can't sleep? But I have to do something. Pickets and letters don't work. Not fast enough."

"You could get out of this."

"I could. I made it very clear that I would leave whenever I wanted to. I have no ideological commitment, and I can live without their money."

"You're going to keep doing this, aren't you?"

"Yes." Veronica met his eyes.

Jonnie took a deep breath, still reflecting on Peter, wondering if she would ever feel he had to go, just had to disappear. The room remained quiet. Finally, he asked, "How did you get involved in the first place?"

"It was at school after I had interned for Ecology Now! Some people claiming to represent a charitable trust came to see me. They explained that they knew I was committed to the environment and wanted to help me follow through. If I went to work for Ecology Now! after I graduated, they would supplement my income and provide advice on policy issues."

"Was this the Lao Foundation?"

Veronica cocked her head and looked at Jonnie curiously. "No, who are they?"

"Nothing. I was thinking of something else." Jonnie shook his head, thinking about the pieces that still didn't fit.

"I didn't believe them, and I let them know it. The truth is I figured they were either us or them. The whole thing was too weird. To this day I don't think Cal knows. He hates the Russians. Considers them very poor environmental role models. Anyway, a few months later I met with them. A month later I accepted their offer—after a lot of thought and a couple of discussions. I made my terms clear. They accepted. I also got more money than they originally offered. Helping the environment doesn't mean I can't make the bastards pay through the nose. So, do you still think I'm a traitor?"

Jonnie slowly shook his head and said nothing.

"Jonnie?"

The living room remained silent.

"Do you love me?"

Jonnie lowered his eyes and bit his lower lip. After a few seconds, he gave a slight nod.

"Jonnie?"

"Yes . . . I love you."

"Even being a traitor?"

"If you think of it that way and if that's part of the package."

Veronica shook her head and smiled. "No. I'm not a traitor . . . and you're not a traitor for loving me."

Jonnie took Veronica in his arms. Their mouths linked as their arms reached for each other. Slowly, they slid down against the old cushions.

Groucho leered approvingly.

92

THE HAWK-NOSED MAN PICKED UP THE TELEPHONE, punched in a number, and waited.

"Sloan."

"Sam . . . Matt Richards."

"Hold on a moment, would you?"

"Be happy to." Knowing that the Chairman of the Public Works Committee was either emptying the office or finishing another call, the Congressman waited. His eyes flicked over the

sheets in front of him as he scanned them one more time: the
report on the Science and Technology hearing; the news clip-
pings from the *Post;* the summary his staff had compiled on the
metals initiative; and the list of a dozen members and their direct
lines. The list was scrawled in his own writing. All but two of the
names were already crossed off.

"Yes, Matt. What can I do for you?"

"I noticed that one of your former staffers made some interesting news."

"Jack McDarvid. You didn't call to tell me that, Matt."

"No . . . not exactly, but what he said could make some things
rather difficult for me. Especially with those documents he presented and the wire stories."

"I'm not surprised. What things did you have in mind?"

"You're pushing for a big increase in the state sewage revolving fund authorization. I can only support so many—"

"What do you want?"

"Well, it seems to me that it might be timely for Environment
to withdraw the metals NPRM for further study. Obviously, I
wouldn't want to oppose needed environmental legislation, but
Defense does play a big part in the state economy."

"I get the picture. Now that the wires are playing the metals
initiative as anti-defense, anti-high technology—"

"It might be timely if the regulation went to the back burner
for further study," suggested the Congressman from South Carolina. "A number of us think that might be the best course."

"I'll think about it."

"That's all that I can ask," Richards agreed softly. "I do
appreciate it, Sam."

He punched in another number.

"Hello."

"George . . . Matt Richards. Could I drop by for a minute?"

"If it won't take too long."

"It won't take long at all."

The tall Congressman set down the receiver and stood, then
tapped the intercom. "Laurie? I'll be out for about fifteen minutes."

He left by the private door, the sounds of his heels echoing on
the marble floors of the Rayburn Building.

93

MCDARVID TAPPED ON THE SIDE OF THE DOOR, then peered in. "You asked for me to stop by, Bill?"

"I did, Jack." Heidlinger set down the file on one side of the broad teak table that served as his desk. "Why don't you close the door?"

McDarvid knew what was coming, but he eased the door shut, then took the wooden armchair across the table from the portly attorney in his striped shirt and bright red suspenders. The red in Heidlinger's tie matched the suspenders.

"Jack, you may recall that after Larry's death, we agreed to a six-month trial period for you and Jonathon Black, in order to see whether the firm could use your services as effectively as Larry had."

McDarvid nodded. "I thought that was a generous and fair offer, Bill, and I still do. We had never worked directly for anyone but Larry. To agree to such a lengthy trial was certainly fair."

Heidlinger cleared his throat. "The partners met yesterday to consider your future relationship with the firm. It was a long meeting."

McDarvid waited for the axe to fall.

Heidlinger glanced toward the teak bookcase at the side of the desk, then back to McDarvid before continuing. "First, let me say that everyone has been impressed with the quality of the work that you two have produced. Steve Greene also mentioned the timeliness of your pesticide materials. George Ames had a note from Carole Sturteval, and she was highly supportive of your creative approach in saving the Moreland Reclamation case."

"There's still a problem, or you wouldn't need to explain so thoroughly," McDarvid observed.

"You're also very perceptive," the senior partner continued, "perhaps too perceptive in understanding the linkages in this town. Did you know that Hal Fowler, Jr., has filed a restraining order against his wife? Hal Senior called me. He sent a copy of your ethics complaint for me to read. While one cannot argue with either your logic or your facts, Jack, the partners find the . . . bluntness . . . of your approach somewhat difficult to swallow. George, frankly, was almost apoplectic after reading the ethics letter."

"I take it that he was the one who found the approach too direct?"

Heidlinger nodded. "That leaves us in somewhat of a quandary. Thus far, several major clients seem satisfied with your work, and we would find it difficult to obtain a work product of equal quality anywhere else. At the same time, I suspect that the directness of your methods . . ."

"We basically followed the lead Larry laid out." McDarvid shifted his weight on the hard wooden chair.

"That's true, but Larry had a unique reputation, and he was well established as an attorney, of, shall we say, eccentric approach."

"And we're not attorneys or that well established."

"Not in the legal community," admitted the portly attorney. He cleared his throat. "So we need to come to a mutually beneficial arrangement."

McDarvid nodded. "What did you have in mind?"

"You are consultants. If you were established under your own letterhead . . ." Heidlinger let the words drop.

"That would provide more insulation. You could say, in effect, that's what our consultants said."

"Exactly."

McDarvid nodded again. From the firm's perspective it made sense, and he and Jonnie could simply have been dumped. "What sort of arrangement or transition did you have in mind?"

Heidlinger smiled faintly. "Obviously, you can't go out and lease space, get a letterhead, incorporate, and do all those things overnight. We would provide you with your present space and equipment—rent-free—for sixty days, but you would bill us for the services we request at your present internal rates. Once you are established in your own quarters, hopefully not too far away—there are several offices available on the sixth floor, I noticed—you would bill at whatever rate you consider fair, although I would suggest you use something close to the gross rate we currently charge clients for your services."

McDarvid straightened in the chair. "I can't speak for Jonnie, although I would suspect he would agree to such an arrangement. I presume that if he has any questions he can talk to you?"

"That would be fine."

"Given the circumstances, Bill, your offer is more than fair, and I certainly look forward to working with you and the others on the new basis."

Heidlinger stood.

So did McDarvid, leaning forward across the desk to shake the other's hand. "Appreciate it, Bill, and I'll tell Jonnie."

"Thank you, Jack. Despite your penchant for direct action, you do get results, and that is often necessary. I hope we can develop an even smoother working relationship as time goes on."

"So do I, Bill. So do I." McDarvid inclined his head, turned, and walked toward the door.

94

"A CALL FOR YOU, MR. MCDARVID. She didn't give her name."

McDarvid looked at the telephone on the desk. Should he answer it? Thinking it might be Allyson, he finally picked up the receiver. "Hello."

"Jack?" The feminine voice sounded puzzled.

"Yes? It's me."

"You sound . . . depressed. This is Ellie."

"Depressed? The always-exuberant Jack McDarvid depressed?"

"Want to tell me about it?" There was a pause. "Wait. Let me tell you. You were working the metals thing, right? Before Jerry cut and ran?"

"He didn't cut and run, Ellie. He's dead. I can't prove it, but I pushed the poor bastard until he cracked. He ran, and they did him in."

"Jack, that's crazy. You didn't have that much to do with it. Jerry was in big trouble on his own. The FBI or somebody just called the I.G. and provided some additional information on that inquiry you started. There were some very strange patterns in Jerry's personal accounts. Apparently, there are no checks for groceries, meals, or credit card records for dinners. All of his income—every last cent—went to mortgages, child support, and utilities. But that wasn't why I called."

"Very odd," McDarvid muttered to himself. It figured, but how did they get the actual proof? Eric again? "Yes?" he asked aloud.

"We just got the notice from the Secretary. It's already signed. It's going to the *Register* tonight. The metals NPRM has been withdrawn for further study of both the economic impacts and the risk assessment methodology. There's no timetable for future action. I thought you might like to know."

McDarvid swallowed. "Thanks, Ellie." He paused. "Is this public?"

"Not yet, but I'd hurry if I were you." She laughed softly.

"Thanks again."

"No problem. Don't stay away so long next time. Some of us do like to see your face, smiling or not. And take care of that daughter."

"I will."

McDarvid tapped out Jonnie's number, but there was no answer. He set down the phone while he dragged out the JAFFE file.

"JAFFE, Washington office." The voice held the faintest of accents.

"This is Jack McDarvid for Pierre. Is he in?"

"Yes, Monsieur McDarvid. He's in a meeting. But hold on. He told me to put you through whenever you called."

Very few clients rated him that important, McDarvid thought. He'd never been given the "he's on the phone or in a meeting" routine by the JAFFE office. If Devenant was there, he'd talk to McDarvid.

"Monsieur McDarvid. How might I help you today?"

McDarvid took a deep breath. "It's not final yet—"

"The metals rule?"

"Sorry. Let me explain. I just got word that the Secretary of the Department of Environmental Protection is withdrawing the metals NPRM for further study. This isn't one hundred percent certain, but pretty close."

"Withdrawing? Is that possible?" Devenant's voice was carefully neutral.

"It doesn't happen often. But it does happen. At the very least, it would be more than a year before this effort resumed. I'd guess it's dead for longer than that. Maybe permanently, at least in current political terms."

"If this is so, we would be most happy. How soon could this be confirmed?" Devenant's voice remained polite, if warm.

"There will probably be a *Federal Register* notice in three to five days. I can get a copy of the signed notice once it's been sent to the *Register.*"

"Again . . . should this turn out the way you report, I would like to meet with you and Monsieur Black once the notice is published."

"Whatever you feel is best," McDarvid temporized. Why wasn't Devenant more enthusiastic? He and Jonnie, or he and Jonnie and God knew who else, had pulled off a damned miracle, and Devenant was being very formal.

"After this is official, then, I shall contact you, and I look forward very much to meeting with you and Monsieur Black, perhaps over lunch. Until then . . ."

The consultant shook his head, then dialed another number, ready to hang up if a receptionist answered.

"Tom Lerwinsky."

"This is Jack McDarvid, Tom."

"I recognized your voice, you bastard." The obscenity was not totally jovial. "I suppose I owe you something, but you scare the hell out of me."

"I'm afraid I don't understand."

"It's not official yet, but all hell broke loose. First, Hal got some sort of a court order temporarily granting him custody of their kids. Then the Hammer called the Chairman, and the Chairman called Rennie into his office, and she came out and packed her desk. The guys in full committee called and told me that Mike Alroy was transferred to Houston." There was a pause. "Christ, Jack, all she did was refuse to hold a hearing for you. I know she's a brass bitch, but did you have to destroy her whole life?"

McDarvid held in a sigh. "I never meant it to turn out like that, Tom. All I wanted was to stop the damned metals rule. But nobody would listen."

"Somebody listened. Sloan called the Secretary and told him that he couldn't go shutting down high technology and aerospace and that even Sloane couldn't save him on that rule."

"Sam said that? But why?"

"I don't know. Rumor has it that Bang-Bang threatened to walk on the sewage grant revolving fund—and take everyone he could."

"Oh, shit." Bang-Bang Richards?

"Yeah . . . you'll be lucky if your former boss ever talks to you again."

"Anything else I screwed up?" asked McDarvid softly.

"What else do you want? Except Andy Corellian from LAO Systems showed up asking who the hell you were. And I told him about Bang-Bang's L.A. asking about you. Christ, Jack, you really threw a grenade in the fishpond, didn't you? Now what are you going to do?"

"Start my own consulting firm, I guess, for people who want grenades thrown."

"Oh."

"Yeah."

"I can't say I'm surprised, except that it didn't happen sooner. You play rough."

"I didn't think so, Tom. I just tried to do what was right."

"That's playing rough, real rough, in this town."

"I suppose so. Anyway, thanks for the scoop."

"No problem, I guess. Except I'm not sure being the counsel is going to be any picnic for a while."

"Good luck," offered McDarvid.

"I'll probably need it. Same to you."

The consultant looked out at the drizzle dropping down on Nineteenth Street, then picked up the phone again.

Jonnie was out, God knew where or doing what.

For a time he debated. Richards—it fit. Too damned well. He wondered how Richards had gotten to Killorin, but how didn't matter. The fact that the Congressman had walked on the metals rule was the clincher. Finally, he picked up the phone.

"You have reached a nonworking federal number."

He touched three digits subsequently.

"Hello."

"Jack McDarvid for Eric."

"Would you wait a moment, Mr. McDarvid?"

McDarvid leaned back in the chair, glancing at the veiled outlines of the building across Nineteenth Street, blurred by the continuing drizzle.

"Hello. Jack?"

"Yeah. It's your bungling amateur."

"I told you not to act like one."

"Thanks. How long have you known about Bang-Bang?"

"Known what?"

"Never mind. He's the only one that fits. Sloan doesn't, and Hancock doesn't, and it has to be a Republican, and a Representative, rather than a Senator."

"Jack, just because you don't like somebody's pro-environmental policies doesn't make them a Russian dupe—unwitting or otherwise. Look at your old boss Sloan. He's a hard-line environmentalist and absolutely loyal."

"I know that. I was talking about Richards."

"That's just a supposition."

"None of the others are bachelors, own boats, and have that much influence."

"What does that have to do with anything?"

"Do you want me to explain it all? Senators are too public, too heavily scrutinized, and most don't last more than two terms, and that's not long enough to be really effective as deep plants or dupes. Bachelors get to be eccentric and don't have to account for anything, and big boats give you a lot of freedom to pick up things and get rid of bodies."

"Your logic isn't quite sound—"

"Shit! I know it isn't, but the answer's right."

"Jack, even when you were here, we never doubted your ability to get the answers. But we have to be able to explain in detail. And we don't work that way. Look at the mess you created. Divorce and technology scandals; conspiracy arrests at uranium processing plants; an environmentalist attorney running crazy in the Rayburn Building; a missing bureaucrat—"

"Hold on. That idiot attacked me, and Killorin may be missing, but you and I know he's sure as shit dead."

"Without witnesses and without a body, that's a little hard to prove."

"That's right. You professionals leave no fingerprints, and you're not about to look for a Congressman's. So what are you going to do about Bang-Bang?"

"Jack, I just told you. No witnesses, no body, and no evidence. What would you suggest we do?"

McDarvid shook his head. "What about the uranium plant arrests? Can you tell me why the hell you're dumping that on me?"

"Oh, that's a matter of record. You could look it up in several places, but I'll save you the trouble. Names: Peter Andrewson, Tedor Jaenicke, and Graeme Deveau. They were part of a splinter group that left Ecology Now! They were the ones who tried to dump yellowcake in a stream outside the Fayettetown plant. Except someone tipped off someone." There was a pause. "Amateur or not, Jack, you get results. Your clients should be pleased."

"Thanks, but I didn't even know about your tip-off. As for the clients, they didn't sound especially pleased."

"Well . . . your style is hard on the nerves. If you're curious about Andrewson, try asking your partner. Oh, and one other thing, because I don't want you to keep acting like you're going to be shot. I checked into your boss's death. He really was just in the wrong place. Now, if you'll excuse me . . ."

"Thanks, Eric."

"No problem. Keep in touch. I'm sure I'll hear from you again."

McDarvid shivered as he recalled Eric's last sentence. He looked out the window again. He didn't really want to tell Jonnie, but the poor bastard had suffered enough from McDarvid's blunders.

Tiredly, he reached for the telephone again.

"Yes?"

"Jonnie? Could you come in?"

"Yep. You sound like hell. Be right there."

McDarvid closed his eyes.

He started in the chair as Jonnie closed the door.

"Jack?"

"Sorry." McDarvid paused. "Hell, I'm sorry for a lot right now."

"Jack, Heidlinger would have let us go, anyway. Even if we win this one somehow."

"We did," McDarvid announced. "A little while ago, someone from Environment called. I tried to reach you, but you weren't in."

"I went downstairs for a sandwich," Jonnie explained. "What happened? They decide on further comment? A little delay?"

"No. They killed it. Officially, they withdrew it. The Secretary already signed the notice."

"You're kidding."

"No. I just talked to Devenant. He wants to have lunch with us after that's official. He didn't seem too thrilled."

Jonnie shook his head slowly. "You don't deliver, and they complain, and you do, and they don't like it."

"They don't like the price, I suspect." McDarvid leaned back. "I talked to some friends. They indicated that I was a bungling amateur—"

"Jack, what did you do for the CIA?"

"Analysis . . . mostly." McDarvid looked at the blank computer screen, then back at Jonnie. "Anyway, they informed me that we were responsible for the arrests at the processing plant— the yellowcake mess and a guy named Peter Andrewson; Killorin's disappearance; the nutty environmental attorney who tried to nail me before the hearing; and the general disruption of the peace and tranquility of Washington. And they said that Larry was just in the wrong place." McDarvid paused, then looked straight at Jonnie. "Just out of curiosity, did you know anything about this guy Andrewson?"

"Not much. He used to be a friend of Veronica's. I met him once, briefly." Jonnie shrugged. "He seemed crazy."

McDarvid turned and looked toward the window.

"What else?" Jonnie swallowed almost as he asked the question.

"Oh, they confirmed my suspicion that Bang-Bang Richards is

probably a Russian agent of some sort and that he probably did in Killorin."

"They . . . what?"

"Not in so many words. It doesn't work that way. But what can you do? Like the man said—no body, no evidence, no fingerprints. That's what ties it all together."

"You just lost me."

"Simple. Why was the rule pulled?" McDarvid sat up in the chair and looked straight at Jonnie.

"I don't understand that."

"It makes perfect, screwy sense. We have one real issue. That's the metals initiative. All right, people attack me in the Capitol; a committee counsel's attempt to fry me backfires—again because of the metals initiative. Killorin, I think, went running for help—because of the metals initiative. Now, I don't know exactly what wires you tripped, but Eric led me to believe that you created problems with the eco-terrorists and foreign sources—all tied to metals. Then, there's the deal they tried to keep quiet about the JAFFE acquisition of Pherndahl-Elkins, again with a metals implication." McDarvid paused to moisten his lips.

"This was getting hot for someone—really hot, I think. How do you cool it off? Simple—remove the heat. Kill the metals initiative . . . at least for a couple of years. Bang-Bang dumped poor Jerry Killorin's body somewhere off the coast from his fancy boat, talked to a few people, pulled a few strings, and Sam the Hammer calls the Secretary and politely suggests that the NPRM be pulled."

"But why?"

"What exactly can we do now? We won. No more money from the client. No more evidence of screwball regulations—unless someone else hires us, and who else could provide the kind of detailed information we got from JAFFE?"

Jonnie sat silently for a moment.

"Well, what can we do?" asked McDarvid. "Write a book?"

"Jack . . . you missed a couple of things," Jonnie began slowly. "Maybe Devenant didn't want us to be so successful this quickly. Maybe he wanted more things revealed."

"Shit . . . I didn't think about that. But it fits. They want to stop all of those crazy regs, not because of the U.S., but because they don't want other countries copying them."

"Exactly," concurred Jonnie. "And whoever's behind Richards told him to pull the plug before it could get any further."

"But that confirms who and what Richards is," protested McDarvid.

"You don't think everyone in the CIA or wherever didn't already know?"

McDarvid sighed. "You're probably right. We're fucking amateurs, all right. They all know, and they play the game back and forth, and we just blew out all their tidy little agreements and understandings."

"You're assuming we're not part of those nice agreements. Do you think you could have gotten this far if your friends had really wanted to stop you?"

"I hadn't thought about that," McDarvid admitted.

"You—we—have a lot more freedom of action than they have. They couldn't get us or ask us to initiate anything for them, but if they liked where we were heading, they might decide to hang on for the ride." Jonnie paused and smiled wryly. "Not that it matters. We don't still have a steady income for it, no matter what."

"Sorry, Jonnie." McDarvid sighed again. "Didn't mean to drag you in this deep."

"What's done is done. Now what do we do?"

"I guess we set up shop and hope that we can find enough clients who need information or regulatory assistance." McDarvid looked out at the drizzle. "But I'm going home. It's been a long day."

"Good night, Jack." Jonnie opened the door.

"Good night."

95

"NO! I WON'T! NO . . ." The woman twisted in the sheets.

"Veronica?" Jonnie touched her shoulder even as he turned toward her in the darkened bedroom.

Outside, a siren wailed in the distance.

"No."

"Veronica, wake up!" He shook her shoulder harder.

"Whaa . . . what?"

"You were having a nightmare."

Veronica rolled over onto her back, pulling her arms out from under the flannel sheet and laying them alongside her otherwise uncovered body. Her breathing was still rapid.

"Are you all right?"

"I'll be fine."

"Are you sure?"

"I'll be fine."

Jonnie shook his head in the dimness, but did not protest, instead leaning over and lightly kissing her cheek. Then he took her hand and turned on his back, as close to her as he could, still gripping her fingers in his. "I'm here."

"I'm glad." She squeezed his fingers in return.

As he drifted back into sleep, he realized, abstractly, that Veronica's eyes were wide open and that she still looked at the ceiling.

He squeezed her fingers again and was rewarded with a gentle squeeze back.

96

"DEVENANT CALLED," McDarvid announced. "Apologized profusely, but wanted to know if it were at all possible for us to meet him for lunch today. I took the liberty of saying yes."

"You'd deprive me of my half-smoke and chili?"

"Guess you can get it at Dominique."

"French again," observed Jonnie.

"There aren't any Corsican restaurants in D.C.—not that I know of, anyway."

"Why did he push for today?" asked Jonnie.

"Something about a senior official being in town that he wanted us to meet," responded McDarvid. "He was more enthusiastic today."

"They didn't exactly seem pleased with your—our—methods."

"Skip the politeness, Jonnie. I tried to keep you out of it, but in the end, you're in this boat because you worked with me and because you're not a lawyer. I took us both out on a limb and sawed it off."

"You also stopped the metals initiative."

"Results don't always count. Paying the mortgage does."

"How do you figure it?" Jonnie fingered the beard that seemed almost a third gray.

"The new arrangement? Slow starvation. We'll do fine for three to five months, but you don't get the pickup work when you're not next door, and that will drop off. The next receptionist will forget who we are. Heidlinger will continue to use us, but only for the dirty work—the kind of hardball that I've proved to have an aptitude for, but not much stomach." McDarvid glanced down at his waist, where the trousers hung more loosely than in years.

"Doesn't sound like we have much in the way of options."

"Allyson asked if I would consider getting back into government." McDarvid looked at the closed door behind Jonnie's head, then at the clear blue later winter sky over Nineteenth Street.

"You don't sound exactly thrilled, Jack."

"I'm not. I only worked for fifteen years to get out of it. And my departures from . . . various places . . . were not exactly voluntary."

Jonnie shook his head slowly.

McDarvid wondered what the younger man might be thinking.

"You know," Jonnie said as he took off his glasses and held them, "I think that family-loving men who hate violence are more dangerous than all the professionals in the world." He grinned.

"Right," McDarvid snorted. "Now you'll be telling me that George Ames doesn't have the soul of a bookkeeper, but is an angel at heart." He stood up and walked toward the door, reaching around it for his coat. "Let's go."

"That's a long walk."

"Who said we're walking? The cab goes on the JAFFE bill."

"Meet you at the elevator."

McDarvid stopped at the front desk. Was it Mary Lou? "Mary Lou?"

"Bobbi Lou," corrected the round and painfully young face.

"Jack McDarvid. I'll be out for about two hours."

The new receptionist looked at the plastic board. She kept looking. McDarvid smiled. Finally, he reached over and pointed to his name.

"Thank you, Mr. McDarvid. It's so hard to learn everyone in the first week."

"Don't worry." He pushed open the glass doors, turning in time to see Jonnie repeating the same procedure with sweet Bobbi Lou.

"Well," McDarvid quipped as Jonnie joined him, "one thing doesn't change. No one still knows who we are."

"That from a man who complained about his face appearing all over nightly news?"

The elevator arrived, empty except for a UPS deliveryman and his dolly.

"Yeah, the people I don't want to know recognize me, and my own firm's receptionist doesn't."

"Not for long," Jonnie reminded him.

They rode the elevator down silently. Outside the building, the wind whipped papers along the gutters as the two men looked for a cab. Nineteenth Street was empty.

McDarvid shook his head and motioned in the direction of Dupont Circle—toward the power truck and barricades blocking the entire street. Low gray clouds scudded overhead, making the wind feel even colder.

"Go the other way," suggested Jonnie.

They walked down to the corner, still looking for a cab.

They arrived at Dominique five minutes early.

Devenant and a gray-haired and thinner man sat at a corner table. Both rose as the consultants approached.

"Monsieur McDarvid, Monsieur Black—this is Gerard de-Hihn. He is the Senior Vice President of JAFFE International."

McDarvid inclined his head. "Pleased to meet you, Monsieur deHihn."

Jonnie echoed the greeting.

"It is indeed my pleasure, my pleasure indeed." The older man's black eyes seemed to sparkle. "Please join us."

All four sat down.

Devenant motioned to a waiter, who served red wine to everyone but McDarvid.

McDarvid did not raise his eyebrows as he received a Perrier and lime. He had never shared a drink or meal with Devenant.

"If you would like to order . . ."

McDarvid nodded. Order, and then discuss the business of the day, such as exactly how much background work Devenant had done.

"The house salad and the veal . . ."

"Escargots, special soup, and the venison . . ."

"Salad and the veal special," McDarvid ordered.

Devenant sipped from his goblet while the waiter collected the menus. Then he cleared his throat softly. "I spoke to Monsieur Heidlinger yesterday about your success with the metals initiative. He was rather . . . noncommittal. He mentioned the need for rather extensive legal work to prepare the chlorohydrobenzilate record for challenge." The JAFFE executive smiled faintly, but his eyes remained unamused.

McDarvid shrugged. "That's the legal viewpoint. Sometimes it works." He really didn't care for the word games.

"And you, Monsieur Black? What do you think?"

"Lawyers like legal work," Jonnie responded simply. "The more detached, the better."

"Why do you work there?"

"Larry. Larry hired us because he said most lawyers were more interested in writing paper than in solving problems."

"Ah," noted Gerard deHihn. "But with Monsieur Partello gone . . ."

"Right," agreed McDarvid. "They're not exactly thrilled at working with us directly." He squeezed the lime into the sparkling water.

"That may present a problem . . . and an opportunity," observed Devenant. "Have you thought of starting your own business?"

McDarvid glanced at Jonnie. The younger man's face remained politely interested.

"It had crossed our minds," McDarvid admitted. "We still do work that lawyers sometimes need, but they prefer . . . a certain insulation. As an independent consulting firm, we might be able to provide that." He shrugged. "But it's not cheap to set up even a small firm. You need space, equipment, supplies."

Devenant and deHihn looked at each other.

"We do have the end suite, Gerard. It has its own entrance."

The older man nodded but said nothing.

"The details . . . we may have to work them out. We could supply two offices and a small space for a secretary, for perhaps a nominal fee. Occasional use of the conference room could be worked out. In return, would you consider a retainer arrangement? The retainer would be in addition to the space."

"For what sort of work?" asked Jonnie.

Devenant provided an exaggerated Gallic shrug. "For the same sort of work you have been doing. We are interested in many regulatory issues, perhaps even more in the years ahead, and we have no great love of using lawyers when they are not necessary. Too expensive, and"—he paused—"too . . . indirect."

"They are also always reacting," observed deHihn sourly.

"Would this make us . . . part of the family?" asked Jonnie.

McDarvid grinned briefly, thinking of the crystal candy dish resembling Corsica.

"You are amused, Monsieur McDarvid?" asked Devenant blandly.

"I just recall that beautiful crystal candy dish," McDarvid answered just as blandly. "It's just the sort that a grand aunt would send, except she wouldn't shape it like Corsica."

This time Devenant grinned, his eyes following his mouth. "One must be careful with you, Monsieur McDarvid. You seem so bland, so, I believe the term is, WASPish. Yet you are a dangerous man."

"Me?" McDarvid shook his head. "I'm just a man who loves his wife and children and country."

"That," observed deHihn, setting down his wineglass, "is precisely what makes you a very dangerous man. That is also why we would prefer to employ your services. Our interests coincide, and will doubtless do so for many years to come."

"You want to hire the policy papers and the talking? Or the other things I don't intend to do again?" McDarvid kept his voice level.

"Monsieur McDarvid, let us not kid one another." Devenant's voice remained amused. "You and Monsieur Black are, shall we say, reluctant idealists. You both will do what is necessary to preserve your families and the country you love. Nor should it be otherwise." He lifted his glass. "To your new business and to our continued friendship."

McDarvid looked at Jonnie, then lifted his glass.

After a moment, Jonnie lifted his glass.

They both smiled.

97

THE ROAR OF THE ENGINES whined even through the helmet. The pilot's eyes flicked through the heads-up display toward the attacker—that same red light that flashed on the screen.

"Bogey. Zero eight seven. Zero eight seven."

The pilot edged the throttles forward, his fingers straying toward the burner light-offs.

The red dot flared even brighter on the screen as a host of red sparks showered from it.

He jammed the stick forward, then into the turn, sucking his guts in at the gee force. The afterburners roared in his ears, but the red sparks on the screen grew larger, larger . . .

Crummmmmmppppp . . .

He was detached from the seat, hanging from the straps and swinging toward the green of the land below. No longer white . . . no longer winter. He took a breath.

Beneath him the ground rose, and the green became the uneven canopy of seemingly endless conifers, mile after mile of roadless wilderness.

"Shit t t t . . ."

He twisted in the straps, searching for open ground, searching as the trees speared toward him . . .

"Jack . . . Jack!"

McDarvid sat up in bed, shaking, his forehead coated in sweat.

Allyson had both arms wrapped around him even as he shook.

"Bad one?" she asked sleepily. She left one hand on his shoulder, squeezing gently.

The same damned nightmare . . . but not quite the same. Not quite.

"Yeah . . . I'll be all right." He took a deep breath and wiped his forehead. "Just been . . . a long year . . ."

He turned the pillow to the unsweaty side and lay back.

Allyson lay beside him, her hand on his even after her eyes closed and her mouth dropped open into a gentle snore. McDarvid looked at the ceiling for a long time, holding her hand. Thinking about Allyson, and the three others who slept guiltlessly in the rooms around him, he finally closed his eyes. At least the trees had been green, he reminded himself. Green.

GLOSSARY

ANPRM—Advance Notice of Proposed Rule-making. Notice published in the *Federal Register* that an agency is considering and seeking public comment on a specific regulatory proposal. This is the earliest step in the formal rule-making process.

ARARS—Applicable or Relevant and Appropriate Requirements. ARARS represent standards which can be used as an alternative to the existing standards represented in other EPA statutes, such as the Safe Drinking Water Act, in determining the extent to which contaminants must be removed from Superfund sites.

BADT—Best Available Demonstrated Technology. Legal term used in water and waste regulations requiring the use of the most advanced technology which is, in the opinion of the regulating agency, proven and available.

CFR—Code of Federal Regulations. The compilation of all federal regulations, reprinted on a phased basis annually, consisting of more than 250 individual volumes, with a total of more than 30,000 pages.

Clear Air Act—the major environmental legislation governing emissions and permissible concentration levels of major air pollutants. Under the act, EPA/DEP has a wide range of authority to compel whatever actions are necessary to bring metropolitan areas in compliance with ambient air-pollutant exposure standards.

DARPA—Defense Advanced Research Projects Agency. Division of DOD responsible for developing new technologies with defense applications.

DEP—Department of Environmental Protection. The government department responsible for enforcing all environmental regulations and legislation.

DIA—Defense Intelligence Agency.

Docket—the complete file kept on every proposed rule issued by a department. Theoretically, departments are required to answer questions and issues raised by docket submissions.

DOD—Department of Defense.

DOE—Department of Energy.

EPA—Environmental Protection Agency, from 1970 until it became a Cabinet department.

Ethics Act—Ethics in Government Act. The law which requires that federal officials in senior positions report all sources of income and which prohibits the receipt of all but the smallest of gifts from any source but long-standing friends and relatives. It effectively prohibits even accepting lunches from lobbyists.

FIFRA—Federal Insecticide, Fungicide and Rodenticide Act. Primary federal statute governing the permissibility and use of chemicals in agriculture. FIFRA also governs certain antimicrobial and antibacterial products.

I.G.—Inspector General. The head of the office within each federal agency and department charged with discovering and prosecuting wrongdoing, particularly abuse of contracting and procurement procedures.

NESHAPS—National Emissions Standards for Hazardous Air Pollutants. The standards required for emissions of pollutants defined as hazardous by EPA/DEP and the Congress. NESHAPS are set on a chemical-by-chemical basis.

NIOSH—National Institute for Occupational Safety and Health. Division of the Department of Health and Human Services responsible for conducting scientific research on issues pertaining to worker health.

NPRM—Notice of Proposed Rule-making. The first draft of a proposed rule published in the *Federal Register,* which seeks public comment on a specific regulatory proposal before a final rule is issued. This is the second step in the formal rule-making process.

NRDC—National Resources Defense Council. A major private environmental advocacy organization.

NSC—National Security Council. The White House office coordinating national security, defense, and defense-related foreign and domestic policy initiatives.

OMB—Office of Management and Budget. The Executive Branch organization responsible for federal budgeting. Under the Paperwork Reduction Act and Executive Order 12291, OMB, through the Office of Information and Regulatory Affairs (OIRA), is required to review and approve all proposed federal regulations before they are published in the *Federal Register.*

OPM—Office of Personnel Management. Federal agency responsible for overall Executive Branch personnel policies.

OPP—Office of Pesticide Programs. Office within EPA/DEP responsible for the development and implementation of pesticide rules.

OPPE—Office of Policy, Planning, and Evaluation. Office within EPA/DEP responsible for policy development. It contains the Office of Standards and Regulations and the Office of Policy Analysis. OPPE is not responsible for policy implementation.

OSHA—Occupational Safety and Health Administration. A division within the Department of Labor responsible for regulating workplace safety standards.

OSWER—Office of Solid Waste and Emergency Response. The EPA/DEP office responsible for regulating hazardous and solid wastes and for supervising the listing and cleanup of priority hazardous waste sites (Superfund sites).

PCBs—polychlorinated biphenyls. A highly carcinogenic class of chemicals once used widely, particularly in industrial and commercial electrical equipment.

P.D.—Position Document. A document issued by OPP indicating the positions and policies being considered by EPA/DEP in the regulation of a specific pesticide.

RCRA—Resource Conservation and Recovery Act. One of the major federal statutes governing the disposal of hazardous and nonhazardous waste.

Red Border—the final internal review of a proposed regulation by the EPA/DEP senior officials before it is sent to OMB for review prior to publication in the *Federal Register.*

Regs—short for regulations.

RPAR—Rebuttable Presumption Against Registration. Older term for Special Review, indicating that EPA/DEP has issued a presumption that a pesticide should not be registered (and is thus forbidden to be sold in the United States). Unless the manufacturer can rebut the presumption, the pesticide's use would be prohibited in the United States.

SDI—Strategic Defense Initiative. The DOD project to develop a defense against missile attack. More commonly known as Star Wars.

SES—Senior Executive Service. The most senior federal civil servants, constituting approximately the top five thousand employees of the federal civil service. Roughly 10 percent are political appointees and are termed "noncareer."

Standards and Regs—Office of Standards and Regulations. The office within EPA/DEP responsible for obtaining comments on and approval for proposed EPA/DEP rules by conducting the internal and external circulation and review of such rules.

STU-III—Secure Telephone Unit III. The latest generation of government-approved cryptographic (scrambler) telephones, available in desk and portable models.

Superfund—short term for CERCLA (Comprehensive Environmental Response, Compensation and Liability Act), the law which provides funding and guidelines for cleaning up abandoned hazardous waste sites.

TEMPEST—the study and control of spurious or compromising radio frequency emissions from electronic data processing equipment. TEMPEST standards are defined in National Communication Security Information Memorandum 5100A (NACISM 5100A).

Water Act—Clean Water Act. The primary federal statute protecting the water quality of streams, rivers, and lakes and restricting the discharge of pollutants into waters of the United States.

404 or Section 404—the section of the Clean Water Act requiring a special permit for any construction or usage of a land classified as a wetland. The permit is granted by the Army Corps of Engineers, but may be vetoed by EPA/DEP if the usage does not comply with the standing 404 criteria published by EPA/DEP.